The Silent Majority

Freedom in His Great Name

Carl L. McPherson

Preface

I wrote this book with the main characters being based off myself, my wife, and our daughter, (Substituted names: Jack, Megan, and Jordan).

After a few chapters, I found that Jack and Megan were going to be separated on different tasks during the book. I thought it would be a unique format for a book to have two parallel stories going on simultaneously.

You can read the odd chapters (1, 3, 5, 7, etc.) and get a complete story strictly from Jack's point of view. Or, you can read the even chapters (2, 4, 6, 8, etc.) and get a complete story from only Megan's point of view. Alternatively, you can read it straight through and bounce back and forth to see what happens through the eyes, thoughts, and feelings of both characters.

I found this style of writing entertaining when they shared the same space and time in conversation together. I could reveal the motivations and feelings of each of them in distinct ways in the same scene. It was a fun way to show conversations where the emotions, purposes, and objectives of two people could be so very different.

I hope you enjoy this book while I am working on volume II.

Acknowledgements

I want to thank my wife Tanya for encouraging me to turn my frustrations and anxieties into a productive format by writing this book. She has witnessed hundreds of hours with me in the home office typing, making notes and planning for this book. I could not ask for a better person to share my life with.

Kendra, my most amazing daughter. Her unashamed love for Christ and kind-hearted nature for those around her is an inspiration for everyone who knows her.

I want to thank Jon V; my best friend from my childhood who has seen the worst of me and is still willing to be associated with me. This is not an attack on his inability to choose better friends, but his ability to come along side someone and stand with them where they are. Jon V helped me from chapter one; giving encouragement while reading as I went forward. He offered suggestions on clarity, grammar and wording with a keen eye and is highly appreciated.

I want to thank Evelyn V for her encouragement and positive outlook. Her enthusiasm and kindness are contagious and makes me want to keep improving.

I want to thank my mother, Rose. What man would be worth his salt if he did not thank the person who has been in his corner his entire journey of life? She has snatched up every chapter as fast as I could write them and kept asking for more. She is encouraging not only to me but to everyone in life that she meets.

Frank Peretti's books opened my eyes as a young college student to the spiritual world, and battles that take place for the control or freedom of our souls. The unseen battles of angels and demons and the effect of prayer with eternal results sneak in for a visit here in my book.

Nothing in my life can ever repay the debt I owe Jesus Christ. My broken soul, lost, insecure and rage filled mind has been given hope and a purpose beyond the boundaries of my individual existence. I will never be able to earn the Grace and Hope given to me through Christ. Join me in accepting his gift of Life. If we never meet in this life, we will have eternity to share in the next

Chapter One (Jack)
Forced Underground

October 12

A small-scale fire in the forest several miles off had grown into a full-on blaze that was consuming vast swaths of the White Mountains in its fury to consume the dry fuel of the pine wilderness. The U.S. Forest Service resources had been pulled back to help keep control in the metropolitan areas. The fire was going to continue its natural progression until nature decided it was time to stop.

Riley, our tiny black and white Shih-Tzu, whimpered quietly at the front door of the small mountain home. She hoped to convince one of us to take her outside for a walk.

The smoke outside irritated our throats and with each day it became worse. It was unable to be ignored any longer. I can't imagine how painful it was to our dog at this point.

My hands were deep in the hot soapy water of the sink, washing dishes from dinner and before I could ask, Megan, my wife, walked over to the coat rack near the front door and snatched up the leash for the dog. She donned her mask by pulling back her hair with one hand, leaned forward with her chin into the gas mask first. Its soft rubber edges cupped around her face before her hair fell forward over the mask. She'd gotten impressively fast at putting on the mask these last couple days. She cinched up the straps over her head and then hooked Riley to the leash for the walk outside.

I glanced back to watch her carefully as she pulled back the curtains and checked outside. Megan checked the television on the wall that displayed the various cameras outside and around our home. She then shouldered the AR-15, opened the door, and slipped out and onto the front porch for the walk.

I waited a few moments to listen for any calls for help or gunfire and then I went back to washing the dishes in silence.

It didn't take but a few minutes before the two were back inside, a plume of smoke accompanying them before she closed the door. By now, I had the sink draining and was grabbing the towel to dry and put the dishes away.

"The smoke is getting terrible Honey, Riley is starting to sneeze constantly now, and her eyes look terrible," Megan explained with concern.

I took in a deep breath to offer back a concerned sigh, but the deep breath resulted in a rant of coughing from the fresh smoke in the cabin.

I nodded a few times in agreement as Megan began locking the front door and putting the 2x4 plank across the frame. She took off the gas mask and hung the AR-15 on the wall.

"Okay," I agreed, "We have everything we need well stocked in the bunker, so just a few things to grab and we can head down there and wait this fire out."

Megan looked relieved with a grin, "Remember when I thought the idea of a bunker was 'your idea' but I supported you anyway?"

I nodded with a careful smile.

Megan smirked with a chuckle, "Well, that was the third time you were right in our marriage."

We both shared in a long laugh on that one as we moved around the home picking up a few duffle bags and a couple backpacks that were the last of the things we kept up in the cabin with us.

We had the warning of the fire from the smoke at first and soon the ham radio gave us some specifics. We had been watching its progress and direction carefully while preparing to retreat to the bunker if needed.

Over the last year, we had cut back any dead pines, brush, and windfalls near the house. Any trees within 50 feet we cut down, even if they were alive, splitting them up into firewood for the winter. I wasn't too troubled that the fire would take the cabin, but the breathing was unbearable now and the bunker was set up with a full chemical/biological/nuclear air purifying system. There was no real reason to continue punishing ourselves by staying up in the cabin any longer.

The roof of our small home was metal, and I had soaked down the siding with a garden hose for a long while earlier in the day. There were no trees near enough to fall over against the house so I figured it would be just fine.

To call it a cabin is a bit of an exaggeration. It is a simple two-story "Tuff Shed" bought from Home Depot that was delivered and set in place on the concrete slab for a mere $25,000. Not bad for a two-bedroom home, but it is tiny for sure.

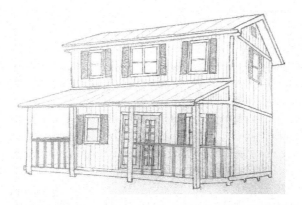

It is 16 feet from the front door to the back wall by the kitchen sink and twenty feet from the far left to the far-right side of the building. The ground floor is an unsophisticated layout with an open kitchen on the back wall and an enclosed bathroom in the far back right corner. The remaining space is a dining and living room and an old wood stove in the front right corner.

A simple stairway on the far-left wall led up to the second floor. The second floor has a simple hallway along the back wall with two small 10'x10' bedrooms with small closets.

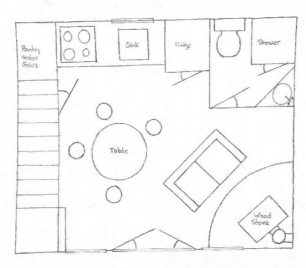

We purchased the land two years before and had just finished paying off the bank loan when the glue holding society together started to fail. On the initial land purchase, half of the loan was for drilling the deep well. Up here in the White Mountains of Arizona we had to go down 450 feet before we hit quality water that was sustainable. It was a hefty bill for sure, but we'd finally paid it off.

Our plan before things went sideways in the country was to get the land, camp on it as our get-away on the weekends while we saved up for the bunker and the cabin. Renting out the cabin through Airbnb was the idea but that never happened because of the fast descent of the country at the time.

It was just after we paid off the loan that California declared their entire state a sanctuary state, followed by Hawaii, Illinois, and Nevada to bring the total to 14 sanctuary states. It was then that we decided to put a push on moving the purchase and installation of the Atlas Bunker (™)1 from Texas in place, as well as the house. We figured the prices were going to shoot straight up and the company wouldn't be able to make them fast enough to keep up with demand.

I had never bought stocks low and sold high in the market. I had never been hired for a job just before they gave the historic big raises. I could count on one hand how many times I had stumbled into just the perfect thing at the perfect time. Moreover, this was one of the big ones.

With the collapse soon after of the economy and the entire banking system, those loans became moot. The bank we owed no longer existed. How many times does someone luck out like that?

The unrecoverable collapse came when the Federal government amended the 1st amendment to only cover the government media, the 2nd amendment had been removed completely, the one child limit was passed with free healthcare, free college education and finally the outlawing of coal and nuclear power plants. It was at that moment in time that we knew we had to make our move. There was no turning back and pretending that everything was going to work itself out any longer.

A long road of events led up to that point, which I recorded in my journal2 *(appendix for journal)* down in the bunker. It was at this point in the timeline that we knew the move north was no longer a retirement dream but an immediate necessity.

The Airbnb idea never came to fruition though. We had to install the wiring in the house ourselves, insulation in the walls, the pine plank walls inside, as well as the toilet, sink, shower, kitchen sink, wood stove and all the internal walls upstairs to make the bedrooms.

---

1 atlassurvivalshelters.com

2 See Appendix to read journal

It was a ridiculous time of getting everything we needed for the cabin.

Most of the employees at The Home Depot had already quit and the owners had retreated with their own families to fend for themselves.

I was able to connect to a Home-Depot (™) delivery trailer with our truck and load it up during the store being looted. We put pine board planking for the inside walls on the bottom of the trailer, on that we stacked coils of electrical wire, light switches, LED lights, outlets, outlet cover plates and junction boxes. Anywhere we could find space we stuffed nails, screws, hammers, hand saws and as many hand tools as we could find that would not need electricity, paint brushes and gallons of varnish.

I then selected anything that seemed important. As much as we could pull out of the store, I stacked high while Megan kept watch over me with the AR-15.

People were just looting, but strangely, it was polite looting. If someone snatched up something you were reaching for you just shrugged, wished them well and told them to keep safe. It felt a bit like after 9/11, when everyone was on the same team. You extended grace to the next guy because it was a wartime mentality where the little stuff no longer mattered. We overloaded the trailer, shoved the truck bed full of rolls of insulation and made our way back to the cabin.

Luckily, the refrigerator, toilet, sinks, shower, plumbing supplies, wood stove and the other big appliances had already been delivered.

It was a week after our last load of supplies for the house that the government criminalized the use of internal combustion engines. That's when the niceties of civilization crumbled and a survival instinct delegated kindness to each other to a low-level item of importance.

Since owning a vehicle was now illegal, we stacked up our supply of wood to construct a long pile about seven feet tall between two trees. Then we stacked another row of split firewood about ten feet away and made three walls of firewood. This allowed us to park the truck inside the little parking spot. Stacking wood in front of it to fill in the fourth wall made it look like rows of firewood stored and seasoned for burning in the winter.

Across the top of the firewood walls, we put planks and draped some tarps over the top. It looked just like every other neighbor's stockpile of prepared firewood for the winter, except ours hid our truck inside. Leaving the truck out in the open or just hidden from the road wouldn't have prevented it being discovered by satellites or government aircraft.

You see, the restrictions and rules that were being enforced did not cover the government. Those which subjugated from the top of the pyramid could still have security with guns, drive cars and ride in planes and all the other things of the old life. The new rules were only for the masses.

Before retreating down into the bunker, we finished stacking the last of the bags near the front door. I did one last sweep through the house to make sure I didn't overlook anything.

Checking upstairs, I made sure the windows were closed and then the bathroom window downstairs, the window behind the kitchen sink and the two front windows on either side of the front porch door. Things appeared to be in order. It was early fall; it wasn't getting below freezing temperatures yet. I didn't need to leave any fire going in the wood stove or drain the plumbing to prevent them from bursting.

The electricity for the house comes from our solar panels outside. The writing was on the wall to try to stay off the grid as much as possible. Everything in the home was LED lights and high efficiency appliances. The refrigerator itself was DC power and the wood stove was designed to cook on the top readily or to bake in a side oven. In the summer we could move the stove outside for cooking, so we did not have to bake the entire house to cook something.

We had thought it out as best we could, and it had served us well so far. The solar panels fed into the utility shed where the banks of batteries were along the wall under the switch gear and controls.

Hidden behind the wall of the shed, the power split to also go down under the shed and 30 feet below into the bunker.

The electricity for the water well was supplied by the battery bank. Thus far, we had learned how much power we could draw from the system and yet recharge it with the available sun.

I pulled my gas mask on as Megan donned hers. She shouldered the AR-15 while I checked the pistol on my thigh holster and then picked up my lever action .30-.30 from where it leaned against the wall.

Loading up with a backpack each and then a duffle bag we turned off the lights and went outside onto the front porch.

I was surprised how fast the fire had approached. An hour before I was outside hosing down the outside walls of the cabin and the concealed truck firewood walls. At that point the fire had just come into view on the opposite side of the valley at the ridge line to the north.

Since then, the fire had traveled down the ridge and was already at the bottom of the valley. I expected it would come up this side of the valley significantly faster than it did burning down the slope on the other side.

We were making a smart call; in 15 minutes the fire would be right up into the trees nearest the cabin.

I never thought about how loud a forest fire was before. The crackling and snapping were a staggering ruckus that caused us to shout to hear each other just a few paces apart.

"Go ahead baby," I offered to my wife as I pursued behind.

Riley, the astute little dog, was already at the fence door of the yard pacing to get out so she could get to the shed in the distance.

It wasn't a lengthy walk to get to the gate at the far end, we had to go through our garden and the fencing that kept out the wildlife.

It appeared like a creamy fog had settled over the area, but it swirled and churned as if it were alive in some way.

Without the gas masks, we would have been hacking and falling to the ground unable to breathe. I'd have to tell Megan later that I was right about a fourth thing since we got married. This made me chuckle quietly to myself in my gas mask as we moved along, through the yard and then over to the shed.

Megan reached the shed first, put her duffle down and raised the AR-15, eyes scanning around the yard, the driveway and out towards the small mountain road beyond.

She had adapted well and left the Disneyland (™) and amusement park life-style behind. Those lives were obviously well gone and never would return.

Now, it was survival. Her fiercely stubborn personality had always been a great ally when we agreed. She is focused, organized, and has a way of prioritizing whatever is the most important thing to do to get to what she needs. She is like having a wolverine on your team.

I dropped my duffle bag to the ground, fished the key out of my pocket and then unlocked the shed door. Riley bolted inside eagerly while she coughed and sneezed in an uncontrollable fit.

After I got inside, Megan filed in last and then I closed the door from the inside and bolted it.

The shed, from the outside, was a simple sheet metal sided shed with a metal roof. This was just a ruse.

It was a reinforced concrete room with six-inch-thick walls and a reinforced steel security door covered with what looked like simple thin sheet metal. We put no windows in the shed, that would have defeated the entire purpose of it being a safe room.

The air in the shed was much cleaner than out in the open, so we doffed the gas masks and Megan comforted Riley as I powered off the circuits to the house. All the power would go to the bunker and cameras now.

I didn't know how long we would be living below ground, so I wanted to give us the greatest potential available if we needed it.

The batteries were completely charged. It was the end of the day and they had more than enough sun to maximize their storage capacity today.

I'd designed the number of solar panels on the south facing side of the house roof, as well as several panels behind the house on the hillside to supply close to 300% more power than the batteries needed per day. I did this to account for cloudy days in the winter and the super rare occasion when a great forest fire could block out the sun completely for a few days. Little did I know that my "paranoia" would have paid off so well today.

Megan picked up Riley with her left arm as she bent down on one knee. She slid a concealed panel in the wall to the side, reached in with her right hand to pull up on a small lever within.

The floor eased upward slowly on the far-right side of the shed as a six-hundred-pound explosion-proof hydraulic door lifted. A fake floor covering had been concealing it when it was closed.

Megan pushed the lever back to lock it in place and moved the concealed panel in the wall back while waiting for the large door to stop rising.

"I will bring down the bags Honey, just take care of Riley and get things the way you want them okay?", I suggested to my wife.

She nodded simply and turned around to face the long steep stairway, making her descent. With Riley cradled in her left arm she grasped the handrail with her right hand while she went down.

The stairs went down 30 feet below the surface at a rather steep angle. Much like the steep stairs on a World War ll Navy ship, you had to turn around and hold onto the handrails to go down. Once she got down about three steps, Megan paused to flip on the switch on the side wall. The LED lights overhead in the tunnel lit up to illuminate the way.

I took a moment once she was out of sight to take in a deep breath, look upward at the ceiling and offer a quiet prayer to God in thanks. It was now illegal to pray in public; these private moments I had grown accustomed to were even more cherishing as they presented themselves.

Depression was a real threat these days.

Hope of a better future for yourself was a wispy specter to grasp now. Let alone the far-off idea that your children might have something other than misery and submissiveness under a tyrannical government.

Survival of the mind was as important as survival of the body; it was the refuge in God and in the Bible that kept me grounded.

The busy life of the city and constant activity in the frantic world that was once, had faded into solitude. Without the never-ending distractions, I found myself eagerly waiting for sunrise to grab my Bible and slip out into the forest for some time alone with the Creator of all the beauty around me.

There is no excuse for having neglected this in the past. Now, it was like a great gravitational pull that drew me in so strongly that I could not resist.

Finally, I felt like I was properly being the spiritual leader of my family. It was just me and Megan now, better late than never?

Another deep breath, a soft sigh and I started hauling the duffle bags and backpacks down the long stairway one bag at a time.

At the bottom of the stairs was a small decontamination room. A flexible hose and shower nozzle were coiled up on the wall so you could spray yourself down with water if you had biological, chemical, or nuclear fallout on yourself.

On the other side of the airtight explosion-proof door a refreshing 62°F awaited us. A constant temperature, be it the dead of winter under feet of snow, or in the blazing hot temperatures of the summer.

Riley was eager to greet me every time I came down with another bag. She acted excited with each descent at seeing me, as if for the first time.

The loyal love of a dog is a wonderful thing to keep in mind, helping me appreciate the important things.

On the last trip up, I pulled down on the lid as the hydraulic pistons let me gently pull it down. A solid click locked in place when it was fully in position. For good measure I twisted the steel levers on the underside that mechanically secured the door closed from below.

Megan had already taken the bags I had brought down and had them on the table inside. I flipped off the LED lights in the decontamination room and passed through the thick steel airtight doorway.

I turned and started latching the levers closed for the airtight seal as I talked with Megan, "I can't imagine more than a couple days and the fire will have passed by. The fire is going to burn up whatever fuel there is in a day at most and keep moving on. It's going to be smoldering black trees and black ground. The smoke is still going to be rough on the throat, but the actual danger of fire will be gone pretty quick."

Megan nodded as she started unzipping the bags on the table so that we could start putting things away, "Well, we have enough food and water for about five years, I think we'll be fine," she ended with a sideways smirk.

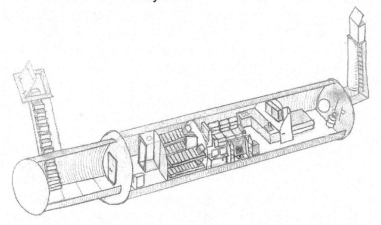

To explain how the bunker is laid out it's easiest to say it's a ten-foot diameter culvert with three feet of storage under the floor. You enter at one end of the conduit that is sealed by an air-tight reinforced steel door to step into a small area where there is a toilet and a shower. Much like a motor home design but the toilet is a waterless compost toilet.

Walking around the bathroom to the left, a small hallway leads a short distance to the bunk room where a bunk bed is built into the walls on each side, offering comfortable sleeping for four people. Each mattress can be lifted to reveal a nice space below for storage of personal items. The bunk room is separated by the area beyond by another door. This door is simply a standard household door and not another air-tight military grade blast door.

Beyond the bunk room door is the main living area. A small table with a restaurant booth seat is immediately on the left with a desk on the right. On the desk is where we keep the ham radio, CB radio, walkie talkies and the mounted LED monitors. The wall behind the desk is filled with displays for the various video cameras outside and around the property. On a shelf overhead we kept our other two ham radios with their extra batteries and various sized antennas.

Walking forward beyond the table and desk, is a couch on the left. Across from the couch on the right-side wall, is an LED television and a wall unit that is filled with board games, cards, movies, and the like.

Just beyond the couch along the left wall is a small L-shaped kitchen with a hotplate, sink and cupboards for cooking meals. On the right side of the kitchen is the last door that opens to the master bedroom.

The master bedroom is simplistic by house standards; just a queen bed immediately to the left, the right-side wall is filled with simple shelving packed with freeze-dried survival meal packs. The air purification equipment is along the back wall and to the left of the air equipment is another air-tight hatch that leads to the escape tunnel.

The escape tunnel is very simplistic. It is a standard 42" culvert going out horizontal 50 yards to where the slope of the hill outside comes down to the bottom of the valley. At the end of the escape tunnel it turns upward to a hatch above.

About 20 feet from the bottom of the valley floor, the hydraulic assisted six-hundred-pound steel door opens for an escape. I epoxied several large rocks and small stones to the lid to make it look just like the ground around it. Discovery would be almost impossible. Even if they did, it would take more than dynamite to ever get the door open.

Under the floor in the master bedroom is additional space but this space we had filled with more banks of marine grade batteries for the solar panels to store power into. The solar panels are linked to the batteries in the utility shed but they are also attached to a stationary bicycle that can be used to generate power if needed. It isn't an exciting option to have to pedal for lighting and power needs but with the LED and high-efficiency modern appliances it was easily a realistic option.

We spent the next half of an hour putting items from the duffle bags away. There is a great deal of storage places to put things. Down the center of the floor of the cylindrical bunker are hinged doors that lift to reveal a massive space under the floor. Twenty, thirty-gallon drums of pure drinking water went in a line down the center. These barrels are the emergency backup. The solar panels above power the high efficiency well for water to the storage tank on the surface and the pressure pump for the water. If the solar panels were destroyed or any component in the water system went out, we still had a solid year of water storage under the floor.

Also, under the floor we keep 50 plastic totes filled with supplies. In the inventory is toilet paper, canned food, jars of food supplied by our garden, soap/shampoo, clothes, ammunition, tools, books, sleeping bags, more bedding, pillows, medical supplies, and everything we could manage to horde. We could live for up to five years down here in the bunker.

If a nuclear attack was to happen there is a wide variation on how long you need to stay in a bunker.

Simply put, it is 2-30 days. It really depends on the fallout. If you are upwind of a nuclear blast and there is no fallout, you will be safe to leave your shelter immediately after the kinetic blast has passed. If you are downwind of a nuclear blast, you will be in your shelter for approximately 28 days. After 28 days, 99% of the radiation emitted by the fallout will have decayed and you can leave your shelter and try to resume life on the surface.

The lingering radiation hazard could represent a grave threat for as long as one to five years after the attack but the actual thermal and explosive effects of the bomb going off would not be a factor by the time you emerged from the shelter short term.

I confirmed from the battery display on the kitchen wall that the batteries under the master bedroom were also at full charge. I noted that the incoming power from the solar panels was only at 20% normal levels. I assumed, that this was due to the heavy amount of smoke outside blocking the sun.

Megan was at the desk when I turned around, checking the security monitors to see what we were picking up with the cameras outside. I came up behind her, leaned over her to kiss her gently on the top of the head, "Everything is going to be okay Love."

She nodded slowly but I knew that her mind was constantly on our daughter Jordan in Flagstaff.

Jordan started attending Northern Arizona University (NAU) a year previous when we were in our mad rush to finish off the cabin and move in. She was insistent on starting her own independent life and our plea to her to join us did not persuade her.

There was no angst or big fight, but she felt it was time for her to break off and lead her own life. A natural part of being a parent, but not easy this is for sure. With how society was crumbling, I feared martial law and riots would continue. It was no world I wanted my daughter to be in without me being there to protect her.

Then, add in that she is a Type I diabetic since the age of ten. Without her insulin she would die. Coupled with the now complete end of pharmaceutical supplies in pharmacies and everything being handed out scarcely through the government distribution centers it made it impossible to live without subjecting herself to living in the main cities they controlled.

It pained me to see her living under the conditions inside the city, but it was the only way long term that I could see her getting a consistent supply of insulin.

When the ban on combustion engines was a couple days away from going into effect, we made a trip to Flagstaff and met her outside the city. We didn't know how long it was going to be before we were able to see her again and she wanted us to take her new truck, her pride and joy, so that it would be safe, and hidden.

I couldn't blame Megan for worrying about Jordan, most of my day had her pressing on my mind as well.

I kept quiet as I stood behind and watched the monitors, letting Megan have some time to simply be still and think without me pestering her.

On the monitors, I took inventory of what information they shared with us. The first camera covered the road where I had hidden the camera inside a dead stump[3].

The fish-eye lens offered a wide view of the road in both directions, though a bit distorted on the sides. The rugged dirt road has some large rocks in it, and it was never upgraded to a gravel road, let alone an improved road or a paved road. It was just slightly better than a 2-track.

The road to the cabin went up and down several small hills, around a great many corners and over rugged unmaintained areas through scrubby pines. It was three miles back off the paved road and about five turns at intersections in the road. We could go weeks without seeing someone come down our road.

---

[3] 33°56'56.8"N 109°42'41.2"W

Before the collapse, we would go a couple days without seeing anyone and even then, it was an all-terrain vehicle or a jeep that was just out exploring. Since the collapse, it was now people on horseback or out scouting or hunting for food, but only once every few weeks.

The next cameras were mounted on the shed under the eaves to protect them from the sun and elements. These gave a full view around the shed and over the yard, garden and in front of the house.

The next batch of cameras are mounted looking over the hillside behind and the solar panels on the slope. Also, at the gable ends, two cameras I upgraded so that they could pivot and zoom. These were the two cameras with the best elevation advantage and were mounted out enough past the eaves to look all the way to the road and to the valley bottom on the other side.

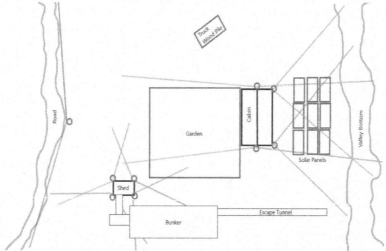

The last of the cameras were hidden in the house on the ground level, the upstairs hallway and in each bedroom upstairs. The power for the cameras of course came from the battery banks so we normally kept them all off to conserve power. We only turn them on periodically to check on conditions outside.

Things looked quiet right now. Most of the cameras offered nothing but a smokey swirl of gray and black. The leaping and rushing flames flashed on occasion as the smoke swirled upward in an up-draft.

Sparks fed into little tornadoes and shot the glowing embers skyward, high up out of view beyond the area the camera could view. Surely this was sending fresh hot sparks farther down wind to land on fuel ready to catch fire and keep the fire moving onward.

The only clear video feeds were those inside the house. It was still light enough outside for the cameras to be feeding normal video, not yet flipped over to the IR night-vision mode.

The fire was sweeping through the trees fast. The roaring blaze was burning up the dry tinder of the pine needles on the ground as well as the needles still on the trees. The shrubs and bushes were igniting into flames before the fire even reached them.

We watched as the fire came up into the trees nearest the house. Columns of fire shot straight to the sky as the fire consumed the fuel of tiny branches and needles. Sparks flew like snowflakes in a blizzard and rose on the heat currents, carried off in the wind.

It was soothing in a way to watch the fire and I tried to offer a bit of a distraction from what was obviously very destructive, "The heat from the fire will open up the pine cones on the ground and will release the seeds after the fire has passed by. In the spring we should have fields of tiny little spouts of new trees wanting to grow. In three years, it will be hard to walk through waist high trees thick as wheat in a field. Ten years from now it will be a real forest again, better than it was yesterday. It mostly depends on how long the fire stays in place and burns down through the trees into the roots or shrub roots into the soil. If it stays in place a long time it will do a lot more damage in the long term because what is below ground to offer nutrients to the new growth will be damaged and slow down the recovery. From what we know so far, this fire is burning fast and moving on. We should recover very well. Also, we already spaced out the trees by cutting firewood and selecting those that were close to each other to cut down, so we reduced the fuel for the fire. It won't stay and just keep burning in one place long," I droned on to my wife.

Megan didn't know I could see the smirk on her face in the reflection off the camera monitor as she responded, "Thank you professor," she said dryly and then turned and looked at me with a big smile.

I stuck out my tongue and playfully nudged her shoulder with my hand as I stepped away, "I'm going to check the periscope to make sure it's still in order."

Back in the master bedroom we had installed an old-school periscope. There were no electronics to it, just mirrors and the tube and lenses. If there had been a nuclear attack or an EMP, the electronics would be fried, and the cameras would be useless.

The periscope confirmed everything we saw on the camera monitors, but from a low perspective near the ground where the old rusty soup can was concealing the periscope head.

There wasn't anything we could do now except wait. There wouldn't be any marauding bands of Antifa pillaging with the fire so close, so we didn't need to worry about that for a while. Now, we would just be waiting out the fire and smoke until it was easier to breathe again on the surface.

Megan powered down most of the monitors to conserve power but kept on those she needed to watch for the progress of the fire up to the property's edge, through the trees and around the house. She called out updates as time went on. The rows of corn in the garden had burst into flames and some of the potatoes were burning but this was to be expected. We would surely lose all the corn, but the potato plants were ready to be harvested anyway and those were safe under the ground to be dug up later. The bell peppers, onions and most of the other vegetables had passed their picking season and we had already stored and canned them. Corn would be the only thing lost to the fire.

I spent time cleaning and organizing to keep my mind busy as Megan kept view on the cameras and made sure I was updated.

The fire neared about 50 feet of the house. The pine needles on the ground brought the fire up to about 20 feet from the house but that was a ground fire that was low and burned out within fifteen minutes.

The preparations and clearing around the house had saved the house from the fire, that, and the metal roof. The solar panels on the hillside went unharmed, the hillside was covered with fist sized rocks and only very sparse sprigs of vegetation so there wasn't any real fuel there for the fire to consume. The trees had been cleared away so that the sun could get to the panels from sunrise to sunset. For 100 feet around the solar panels there were no any trees at all.

The wood stacked around the pickup truck was lightly charred but did not catch fire. I had raked away the dry pine needles on the ground for 30 feet from the hidden truck. Some of the embers in the air landed in the trees and caught them on fire anyway. The branches were bare and burned up and embers fell onto the tarp. The heat of the fire had melted the tarp into dripping plastic drizzles onto the truck below.

Happily, the truck did not catch on fire or explode.

After three hours of bunker time, the fire safely moved beyond our land and continued to rage on, heading south. The sun had fully set by now and the air above would be thick with smoke for a couple days. It was time to get comfortable.

We prepared for bed, confirming our water supply still worked with a couple short showers and then retreated to the master bedroom for a good night's sleep.

Chapter Two (Megan)
We Leave the Sun Behind

October 12

The smoke from the forest fire outside had already made my throat raw and I was trying not to say anything. Every word felt like sandpaper in my throat. The smoke was blurring out most of the sun now. It had gotten worse over the last couple days as the thickness of the smoke continued to get denser while the fire moved towards our home.

Riley, our tiny black and white Shih-Tzu, whimpered quietly at the front door of the small mountain home in hopes of convincing one of us to take her outside for a walk.

My husband, Jack, was over at the sink washing dishes after dinner so I stopped sweeping the floor by the wood stove and made my way over to the front door to get the leash to take her outside.

I grabbed my gas mask and got it on, tightened the straps and then put my hand over the port on the filter and sucked in. The mask sucked in against my face to confirm a proper seal and then I took a few calm breaths.

I snatched up Riley's leash from the hook on the wall and hooked her up. A peek outside through the curtain confirmed things as they had been an hour before when I was out checking on the garden, all quiet, but smokey.

The LED screen that we had used as a television before the satellite internet was cut off, now had the feeds from our several security cameras around the home. I checked the screen to ensure there were going to be no surprises waiting for me in areas that I could not see from the front window. All looked clear.

I slipped the sling of the AR-15 over my head and across my chest positioning the rifle against my stomach, all set. I opened the door and Riley and I went out for a short walk around the yard.

The world has changed so much in the last couple years. Two years ago, and I would have been getting home about now from working as an accountant for a high-end luxury custom home builder. Jack would have had dinner ready and getting it on the table and our daughter would be chatting with friends on her phone after a day of working in childcare all day or working on one of her online classes through the university.

I would have had a few hours together as a family before Jack had to head off to work the midnight shift for the town's drinking water treatment plant and I could have helped Jordan work on her homework or done a bit of the medical transcription work over the internet that I had kept doing over the years.

Now though, none of that was the norm.

I couldn't call up a girlfriend now and meet her at a coffee shop to talk for a few hours and catch up. I couldn't take Riley or Hannah for a walk at the Riparian. Oh, Hannah, I sure missed that adorable Maltase/Shitz-Tzu mix that always wanted to sit in my lap and climb up and lick my face. She had given over to a liver disease about the time when everything started going wrong with the world. Now, it was Riley that filled that gap and stayed at my side through the day to distract me from spiraling down emotionally.

Riley was snorting and rubbing her nose against her front legs and shaking her head. The poor thing was doing her best to deal with this thickening smoke as best she could. I walked her over to the side of the dirt and rocky driveway so she could do her business as I looked around.

I could see the fire to the north at the top of the ridge line. Our property was at the top of a hill covered with pines and mesquite. The house was at the far northern edge of the property with several solar panels behind it on the slope that led down to a valley where a creek ran during rains. On the other side of the creek, the ground sloped up to the top of another ridge, covered with pines as well. The fire had reached the opposite ridge and the flames were clawing upward 100 feet above the ground with a terrifying crackle like a concert of drums in an auditorium.

The smoke from the fire rose like tornadoes in the heat of the flames and swirled and churned like ocean waves going upward as it sucked in the cool air in front of the fire and pulled it skyward with it.

Jack had been working on and off for the last several months for an hour or two every day clearing back brush, needles, dead pines and branches from around the house and property as best he could prepare for what he called "Nature's Cycle". He knew a forest fire would come at some point and he kept telling me that the forest needs a fire to give itself new life. He had gone on about pinecones opening and seeds releasing in the heat; something along those lines.

Jack had a way of going on with a conversation about five minutes longer than necessary. I think he feels connected, closer, when we are talking; and doesn't want to stop because having my attention calms him.

I suppose it makes sense to a point. It's the same reason I want to meet up with my girlfriends for coffee I suspect. Working the midnight shift at the water plant alone for years had probably made me the de facto human contact he was allotted.

Riley finished up her business, did a sniff of her deposit and then was ready to return inside. Dogs were weird.

I took a last look around the property and then we made our way back inside.

I closed the door behind me after entering, unhooked Riley's leash, hung the AR-15 on the wall hook and then took off my mask, "The smoke is getting really bad Honey, Riley is starting to sneeze constantly now and her eyes look terrible," I explained.

The churning cloud of smoke that came in with me from outside put Jack in a coughing fit for a little while. As he gathered his breath, I locked the front door and put the 2x4 plank across the brackets on each side of the door to make sure no one could kick in the door from the outside.

As I buttoned things up and made it secure again, I offered Jack a grin, "Remember when I thought the idea of a bunker was 'your idea' but I supported you anyway?"

He nodded with that grin that means he's not sure if he's in trouble or not.

I smirked with a chuckle, "Well, that was the third time you were right in our marriage."

We shared a long laugh at that one and I followed Jack's lead as he started to gather up our backpacks and duffle bags, we had prepared with the last of what we needed to move from the house down into the bunker.

It felt strange moving out of the cabin and into the bunker. On a few different levels it made me apprehensive. The first is I needed the sun. No, not just liked or preferred the sun, but actual biological need for the sun. I am certain in my DNA there is a strain of vegetation in there somewhere. Moving from Michigan to Arizona in 2010 had done wonders for my mental state. Every winter while in Michigan I had to go through 6 months without seeing the sun and it would put me into a funk so deep that poor Jack had to be married with a monster for half of the year.

The second was that this inexpensive little cabin had become our home. Jack and I had done a great amount of work in wiring it up for electricity, the solar panels, insulation in the walls and ceiling, plumbing, internal walls, the kitchen and inside walls making the bedrooms upstairs and the bathroom on the ground floor. Everywhere I looked as I shouldered my backpack was a memory of Jack and I working together fixing up something or making it better. The little home had already grown on me and it felt as if I was abandoning it now to save myself.

It never became the Airbnb hideaway we had hoped, but I'm so grateful that Jack had kept pushing us towards getting a place like this up in the mountains now.

Living in the city was perfect for me, but it was torture for Jack. I loved having a grocery store five minutes away, a movie theatre six minutes away and I loved having any option I wanted within 20 minutes. A doctor's visit, going to the mall, a coffee shop, Home Depot, Hobby Lobby, a park for a walk, an airport, anything I wanted was within arm's reach.

I could tell it was living in hell for Jack. He grew up five miles outside of a little town in northern Michigan that only had 450 people in it. It was within Antrim County where the 2020 election fraud was first spoken out against with direct evidence. His graduating class in 1987 was only sixteen people.

He had gone to college hoping to get a job in the Forestry Service or Fisheries or in the Parks Services but instead he ended up being funneled into working a job he didn't enjoy and always in a big city.

The sacrifices he made for me and Jordan I will never forget. His love for us, put him for decades into jobs he did not enjoy. He did it to assure we had a stable income and medical benefits. It was an expression of ultimate love for us.

As the national economy would rise and fall the city's drinking water jobs were always stable. They did not peak in pay raises when the economy was prosperous, but they did not leave you unemployed when things turned south either. The private water companies would offer a great deal more promises and money when the economy was high, and we could have had bursts of great living. However, it was when the economy turned downward that those companies laid off people and all those nice trucks, boats, and toys, they had been buying were then sold off to pay their high mortgages and to keep from going bankrupt.

It wasn't until Jordan had graduated from homeschooling, and I got anxious about being at home so much, that I started looking for work. I got a job with a luxury home company.

The job had been a Godsend. I started as just a receptionist at the front desk and within a few short weeks the company saw I was picking up on things very fast and working myself out of a job. That is when they wanted to make me a project manager for the multi-million-dollar homes they constructed. Before I could work into that position though, the company's accountant had to step down to focus her attention on doing the books for her husband's business and that left me to become the new accountant.

It was a funny time. They had no idea that I had a business degree when they hired me and were promoting me. But then, they never asked, and it didn't seem important to mention when I was hired as a receptionist.

It wasn't until I got this position and gained raises, that I equaled Jack's pay and swiftly passed his income in the next couple years.

It was a strange pill for Jack to be forced to swallow. I had been out of the workforce for 20 years while he was loyally working insane shifts at the water treatment plants, on the weekends, on the holidays and making sacrifices for pathetic pay. Then, when I decided to get a job, I passed his entire career's income within two years of work.

It made it easier that we were on the same team and were not competing, but I could tell it bit into his need to provide for his family and now he had been passed over in that regard.

Jack had stepped up around the house when I got the accounting job. It was obvious that with the increased income we would have many more options in life, and he supported me heartily. The cleaning of the house, meals, errands, and the like; he jumped in with both feet.

After hitting our debt real hard; we put our focus on purchasing some land and our small home just southwest of Springerville, Arizona.

After several months of riding the back trails and checking out United States Department of Agriculture water and soil reports and checking for just the right terrain for the installation of the bunker and ground content to allow digging in the rocky mountainous area we finally found the land just steps off the Apache Reservation near Greer, Arizona near Mount Baldy. Just 100 feet west of our driveway was the eastern edge of the Fort Apache Reservation.

Every couple of years or so we rented a little cabin up in Pinetop-Lakeside for a weekend that was owned by a schoolteacher down in Gilbert, Arizona. The idea of renting out a little cabin on the weeks and the weekends we were not there to pay the mortgage appeared smart and it inspired us to want to do the same. The area we selected was very close to a skiing area for winter customers and just being anywhere in the mountains was a selling point for people to rent because it was an easy 30 degrees cooler than down in the valley near Phoenix. You could only stay in the valley so long in the summer before you began to go mad from heat stroke and needed a break. The little cabins for rent on the weekends were popular and we knew it would be a smart investment. Also, Jack hoped we could retire there once he got another ten years or so in the State Retirement System working for the city.

To me, the best place for retirement would be near my grandchildren, wherever that might have become when Jordan married and had children. But we had to make some move because she wasn't dating anyone, and it could be another ten years before we had any grandchildren and the time for investing in a property and getting it paid off before then was at hand.

Jack was dead set against retirement. He didn't believe it was Biblical and felt it was morally lazy to fall into a life of strict leisure. He had other strong ideas about this involving social security. He felt it had gone from a safety net for the extreme old in the Country and become just another social payout. He explained that it raised taxes on everyone to pay for the retired to play golf for 20-30 years and live a life of luxury. Jack insisted it was morally bankrupt to force the vast majority of people to become indentured to the federal government, paying into a system they would never benefit from themselves. These were the sort of things that bothered him. I never gave it much thought myself.

Jack headed up the stairs to double check everything on the second floor as I checked the windows below and made sure they were locked. I powered off the camera monitor and unplugged it. In the kitchen I unplugged the microwave and DC powered refrigerator. All the food inside the refrigerator we had moved down into the bunker, so leaving it plugged in and keeping it cold inside was a waste. When Jack came back downstairs, I let him check the windows again anyway, he had a very OCD way of wanting to put his eyes on things to check off his mental checklist anyway and he would want to verify everything himself. It wasn't a lack of trust in me, but I think it was his way of feeling like there was some order in the world still.

Jack went for his gas mask and so I put mine on, slipped the sling of the AR-15 over my head and got ready to head outside again.

"Go ahead baby," he offered to me and was close behind me to close the front door once we both got outside onto the front porch.

I removed the 2x4 from the door braces and then unlocked it, opened it up and Riley shoot outside without her leash on, darting down between the garden paths towards the fence at the far side. She appeared to know exactly where we were going.

I opened the fence gate that protected the garden from the elk, deer and other animals eating our produce and Riley zipped across the distance to the shed in a hurry as she sneezed the whole way over.

Following the small dog, I dropped the duffle bags and then raised the AR to my shoulder to scan over the property looking for anything or anyone that might be coming at us.

The world was a very different place now. I never had really been interested in going out in the desert shooting when my husband wanted to. Things were different now though.

I had not needed to shoot anyone yet and I never wanted to, but I now knew I needed to know how and be willing to if the need arose. I had taken the conceal carry class with Jack back in 2012 but that was more of a date we went on together and a shared experience for me. Jack kept up on his permit and carried his pistol every day for years, but I never got my own gun to carry.

However, since we moved up to the cabin and the world had so drastically changed, I took it very seriously to learn how to shoot and to be safe about it. I picked up on it fast and was very skilled at being accurate with the AR-15. Its bullet was almost the same size as a .22 caliber, but it was a lot longer and the casing was a great deal larger to hold a bunch more gunpowder. But it had almost no 'kick' at all when you shot it, so it wasn't a gun that scared you when you pulled the trigger.

Only once had I been forced to aim the rifle at another person. It was several months before at The-Home-Depot when we were loading up supplies at the final collapse. Three guys had seen me at the truck and trailer with all the supplies and thought it was an easy grab. They all had guns themselves and thought they could bully and threaten me out of our ride back home and all our supplies.

A fast three shots put a bullet into the ground at the feet of each of them in less than one second changed their minds fast. The rounds went into the pavement just inches in front of their feet so fast that it let them know that if I had wanted, those bullets could have been in their heads or chests just as easily.

They left with a long string of curses and threats, but they left. My heart had raced like I had just spent 20 minutes on the stair stepper at the gym and it took a while to calm down. My hands felt shaky after that and hard to grip the rifle, like my muscles were made of Jell-O ™ for an hour after that. It was terrifying and I hoped I never had to do that again.

I kept watch as Jack unlocked the shed door and Riley darted inside to get out of the smoke.

I filed in after Jack, got the duffle bags inside and then lowered the rifle and flipped the safety back on while Jack closed and locked the door.

We took our gas masks off and then I knelt to pet Riley and comfort her. She was shaking and scared.

Jack worked on the electrical stuff in the shed with some switches over by the small bench where Jordan's truck battery was on the battery charger keeping it at full charge.

I picked up Riley to comfort her and then knelt and moved the hidden panel in the wall near the floor and pulled the lever inside. The floor behind me hissed up on the hydraulic rams and lifted the six-hundred-pound blast door to the bunker below. I waited for it to rise all the way up before I turned around to start climbing down while cradling Riley in one arm.

Jack offered to carry the bags down so that I could get Riley into the bunker and start putting things away as he brought them down to me, and that sounded like as good a plan as any.

I gave him a thankful smile and a nod and then moved Riley into my left arm and carefully began climbing down the steep stairway with the help of the handrail running down along the right side of the tunnel.

I flipped on the light switch after I was a few steps down and then went on down carefully to the decontamination room at the bottom. Riley was eager to scamper on through the airtight door once I got it open and she sped off into the bunker when I flipped on the light switch inside the thick metal door.

The cold 62°F temperature down here, well below the ground level, made me shiver. I was going to have to get a sweater on or my mood and attitude was going to start becoming abrasive.

When Jack descended with the first bag, I gave him a little kiss and then carried the bag inside the bunker as Riley greeted him with enthusiasm. She stayed at the bottom of the stairs to greet him each time with abundant eagerness.

Around the bathroom, through the bunk room and then to the main living quarters, I carried each bag and sat them on the dining room table and bench seat. Back and forth I took quick trips as they were brought down.

On the last load, I could hear Jack latch up the top hatch and then come on in and close the airtight door and latch it down as well.

Riley came bounding into the main quarters excited and filled with energy before Jack came along behind. He tried to comfort me by telling me it wouldn't be any more than a couple days down here in the bunker before we could move back topside. I sure hope the preparations and precautions we took worked; I'd hate to have the house burn down and be stuck down here in the bunker forever.

I offered back a nod and tried to smile and look reassured by his words before I started unzipping the bags to begin putting away the last things, "Well, we have enough food and water for about five years, I think we'll be fine," I offered, trying to seem optimistic.

I began stowing away boxes of food, produce we had from the garden, boxes of ammunition we had kept up in the house and the last items we had kept close before the final load down into the bunker. It was helpful to keep busy organizing and cleaning as I went, folding up each bag after it was empty and stowing it under one of the beds in the bunk room.

Jack was off stowing away some things as well and checking on the batteries and the charging from the solar panels.

It took a little while to get everything stashed in their proper places. I found myself sitting down at the desk watching the security monitors of what was going on outside. I felt isolated, confined, and held down as if the weight of 30 feet of dirt above me was going to press the air out of my lungs.

Jack could sense my stress and slipped behind me. He leaned down and kissed me on the top of my head and told me everything was going to be okay. How could he know that? Everything was not okay. The trees on our land were being burned down to charred black poles and the brush and vegetation was being consumed fully. Our daughter was in Flagstaff all alone. Did she have enough insulin? Did she still have a safe place to live? What job did the government make her do to earn her rations? Did she have any of her same friends? Were the people around her taken and put into the Federal Unification Camps? Was she in one of those camps now for refusing to keep her faith in God a secret now?

I nodded slowly to Jack, not because I believed him, but because I knew he needed to feel as if he was helping me.

Jack and I both just stared at the cameras on the monitor as he massaged my shoulders.

We couldn't see much on the cameras because of all the smoke but so far, all the cameras were still working, so the shielding and protecting of the wires Jack had taken the time to do must be working.

Jack started explaining to me how the forest uses fires like this to give itself new life. He explained how pine cones open in the fire and new seeds are spread on the ground and how the forest will come back in a few years even better than what it was last week, "Thank you professor," I offered him dryly. Oh, that felt snide, I didn't mean for it to sound so snotty, I turned and looked up at him and put on my best smile.

The turd stuck his tongue out at me and nudged my shoulder and then went off to check the periscope back in the master bedroom, the backup if the cameras ever went down.

Things looked in order outside and watching the monitor was just making me more stressed. I powered down the camera feeds to conserve power on the areas I didn't need to watch and kept only those that covered the garden, the house, solar panels, the areas where I was most concerned.

"It looks like the corn is going up in flames. The stalks were all dried out and they just went up like torches," I let Jack know while he was working elsewhere in the bunker organizing things.

He called back trying to keep a good mood, "Been a long time since I had any popcorn."

What a dork. Ah, but he was my dork and I loved him anyway.

I let him know that the house and the solar panels were doing just fine, and the fire wasn't burning up anything in those areas. I was worried a bit about Jordan's truck when the trees around it caught fire and the flaming needles fell on the tarp hiding it. The tarp lit up and molten plastic bits dropped down in burning globs, but they burned themselves out without starting a big blaze at the truck or the truck itself. That was a huge relief. That truck was the closest thing we still had of Jordan's here at the cabin. I felt her close when I looked over and saw the area, we had it hidden.

I had to get up from the chair after an hour to do stretches, lunges, and other exercises to keep from feeling so bottled up and suffocated.

It was so nice though to breathe purified clean air down in the bunker. I have to say, I wasn't going to ever second guess the wisdom of spending the money and the time and work putting it in now.

After a few hours, the fire had moved on past. Small fires were still here and there in the darkness that the cameras could see. Most of the danger was well past our land now and we had survived just fine, minus some corn and some bean plants.

I grabbed my sleeping shirt from the drawer under the bed, a fresh pair of underwear and a towel to clean up with a short shower.

I was thankful for the sound of the water and the curtain to keep me from view as I cried quietly in the shower. Sometimes I just had to release some of the stress. At times I don't even realize why I'm crying until it passes, and I realize how much better I feel.

It really freaked Jack out though, because he is always in a protector mode about me and Jordan. If either of us cried, he went into this military mode where he had to fix something or kill something to make things right for us. The dolt was adorable, but crying was a natural thing to do sometimes. There was no need troubling him with something he couldn't fix anyway.

Jack took a quick shower after me and then we turned to the bed and under the covers. He sat with his back against the headboard and my head on his chest as I leaned against him. His Bible was in his lap as he read aloud, and I turned the page for him when needed.

Prayers, that dramatically eased the stress, and then sleep took us.

Chapter Three (Jack)
A Meeting is Set

October 13

I woke up with Riley licking my face and standing on my chest. I opened my eyes and listened. The bunker was tranquil with only the sound of Megan breathing and the sound of my heart in my ears.

When we first moved up to the cabin to live a similar feeling took time to get accustomed to. The sound of a city always had the sounds of vehicles on the roads, car alarms in the distance, a fire truck racing to a call or the general hum of life that never stopped. Living within the flight patterns of the Phoenix International Airport and the Mesa Gateway Airport, the sounds of large passenger planes overhead weren't even noticed after a while living there.

When we moved to the cabin though, it was hard to get to sleep because something appeared wrong, too quiet.

In the bunker, it was another level of silence that made living in the cabin seem loud. Below, there is no sound of the wind in the trees, no birds, nothing.

I took in a long slow breath to wake myself up and get some energy in myself. The sound of my intake felt clamorous in my ears. I eased out from under the heavy quilt after putting Riley down on the floor and sat for a few moments taking a moment to appreciate the quiet and to offer up a prayer, thanking God for another day and his blessings, health, and safety.

I picked up the headlamp light from the headboard and put it on my head, flipped it on the dimmest setting and then started my day. I wanted to let Megan sleep as much as she could, but I knew my first foot scuff on the floor would wake her up.

Sure enough, I heard her move before I got into the kitchen. Riley's little feet clicked their nails on the wood floor in excitement as I led her to the airlock door so she could do her business out in the decontamination room.

The decontamination room smelled just slightly of smoke. That was to be expected though, the main bunker was airtight with air filters. This area outside the airlock would be stale with the air that came in when we climbed down from the shed.

The morning felt like a normal day; reading my Bible at the table and then putting on the coffee with a tiny breakfast for myself. Megan never liked breakfasts; her stomach never felt right in the morning.

After coffee was made, I brought her a cup in bed and then sat on the edge of the bed to chat with her.

"I want to get on the ham radio today and see what I can learn. I am still confused about their timing and frequencies for their portable towers," I explained.

Megan hadn't developed much interest in the radios, she trusted I could figure it out and learn what we needed to know while she put her energies elsewhere.

I spent the morning listening on the ham radio, trying to find anyone talking, scanning across the frequencies. This time felt like a huge waste with no results. From what I understood, the repeater towers for ham radio operators were taken over by the Federal Government when they adjusted the First Amendment to include only members of the media that supported the government. It no longer covered citizens within the country.

Now, it was illegal to use the ham radio system without going through one of the federally controlled towers. If you used them though, they would triangulate your position. Soon you would be visited, and your entire home gone through to see if you had any illegal items. A Bible, gun, or any items in the ever-growing list of terrorist paraphernalia would get you taken to a camp or killed on the spot.

What I understood so far was that the ham radio operators had constructed their own portable relay towers that they would install in secret. A backpack with interlocking short poles, assembled to create a quick antenna. They would power them up for 20 minutes with a charged motorcycle battery and then take them down quickly and move and get away from that area. They never put up the tower in the same place twice and the location always moved, as did the time of day it was put up. It felt impossible to find anyone to talk to on the ham radio because of these random times and frequencies.

I was persistent in putting in the effort to try to figure it out. My CB radio likewise was illegal, and it could only transmit at most up to four miles. A ham radio though could go up to 20-60 miles on its frequency and then hit a repeater tower and skip across repeater towers to go all the way around the world if they were all up and synced to run at the same times.

If I could identify how it worked, I could get information and talk to people back in Michigan where my wife's and my family are from and check in on them. We could coordinate with friends that lived in Idaho and others that lived in Colorado, Texas, and Alaska.

Right now, we didn't know who was even alive. We didn't know who was in the re-education camps or in the forced labor camps. Without information and confirmation, our minds worried that the worst had happened, and it felt worth the effort to try to get to the truth of it all.

Mostly, we wanted a way to get in touch with Jordan in Flagstaff. We would probably have to use intermediaries that would deliver a message to her and then bring back a message from her to be radioed back to us. It was the best we could think to keep informed about her and what she needed.

All of this would require contacting and getting the trust of the Rebellion.

At noon the government AM radio program came on each day. Today was no different and I took a break from contacting people on the radios to make lunch while we listened to the radio.

Welcome citizens of New America. Your safety and security remain our highest priority. On New American Radio we want to thank you for your assistance in making New America fair and equitable. Remember, the common good, before the individual good.

It is only with your help that we can hope to move forward in creating the country we know we can create.

Yesterday, in a late-night raid at Our Peoples Food Distribution Warehouse in Flagstaff a group of fascist terrorists attacked the facility, killed three of your fellow citizens and made off with a good amount of your food that was being stored there.

Mr. Ronald Franklin was killed while on guard duty, Ms. Tina Barron was killed trying to follow and report on where they were taking the stolen rations and Mr. Ryan Lambert was found in a dumpster behind the warehouse. Ryan was killed while trying to keep the building access key from the murderous hands of the deplorable terrorists.

We are troubled by this loss in each of their families and to their closest friends and our community.

Unfortunately, with this latest attack and loss of resources we are being forced to reduce rations to 80% of standard rations for one week. If information comes in about the location of the Terrorist and we can apprehend them, rations will be restored to full immediately.

Unfortunately, we must inform the public that if another attack by these terrorists happens, rations will be cut down to

50% of standard rations. It's imperative that citizens understand the importance of weeding these fascists out of our communities, for the safety of everyone.

Curfew every evening at sunset remains in effect.

In other news; Mr. and Mrs. Mark and Linda McDermont have been found concealing several cans of gasoline in their crawl space under their house. Not only was this perilous and put at risk the lives of their three children but this was a direct assault against several federal regulations. Mr. McDermont will have the opportunity to attend the nearest Federal Unification Camp. We trust he will learn how to better contribute to New America.

In our Community Shine Segment today, we would like to thank Ms. Renee Bascom for informing her community patrol officer that Mr. Ray Berkin has been hunting squirrels, hoarding, and smoking them in his backyard for food. This was a direct violation of code 12, section 15, and the inappropriate accumulation of assets at the expense of the community. This is his second infraction this month. Mr. Berkin will be relocated to a unification facility outside of the city. Ms. Bascom will be rewarded with a full portion of rations for her and those in her home this week.

Last, we would like to warn the Rebellion that we have informants within your ranks and will be moving in soon to apprehend several of your members by the end of the week.

Thank you for your attention citizens of New America. Together, we will build a brighter future for all.

I took a deep breath, as I could feel my face had turn a solid shade of red during the daily broadcast. I felt sick to my stomach like I do each time I tune in.

There was something other than the normal glaring lies and distortion. It was the three names used for those killed at the food distribution warehouse. As I thought over the other drivel and deceit, I reached over to the bookshelf behind the row of books to retrieve my hidden journal. I paged through it slowly as I scanned each page for those names.

Almost everything in the broadcast was a lie. Even the minuscule percentage that could be true, I'm certain were lies as well.

"Here, I found it," I blurted out. It was a scream in volume in the bunker and a great deal louder than I had intended for it to be.

Megan was sitting on the couch reading her Bible and writing in her journal when I shouted. She knocked her bottle of water off the arm of the couch from the surprise.

"Oh, I'm sorry Honey," I apologize as I turned around to explain what I found out.

She chuckled a little and leaned forward to pick up her bottle of water and then to listen.

I turned in the chair and flattened my journal out, tilting it a little forward on my legs to see it better in the light as I pointed to each part with my finger, "The radio report today mentioned three names of people that were killed defending the warehouse when it was hit and food was taken." I looked up, had eye contact, and then looked back down at the journal and continued.

"Four months ago, all three people were mentioned in the same daily broadcast. Here," I read from the journal directly, "June 4".

I skipped down a couple paragraphs after my Bible study notes, "Last night after the curfew, a Rebellion secret meeting was neutralized by federal security forces. Three in the meeting escaped, but after interrogation of those apprehended their identities are now known. Public enemy's number 1, 2 and 3 now are Ron Franklin, Ryan Lambert and Tina Barron."

I looked up with a befuddled and frustrated expression, "Four months ago these three were being hunted down as terrorists with orders to kill on sight. Somehow, last night they were guarding a food facility and were killed defending it?"

Megan Oh's softly, "Something smells fishy in Denmark Jack," she agreed with me.

The black market for most, was the only way to get enough food, medicine and supplies to stay alive. The government had set not only a one child limit per family with forced abortion and sterilization if becoming pregnant with a second child, but it also had a very strict law on how many calories each person could eat. However, you could get bonus credits and apply for more food if you turned your neighbor in for some crime.

Hiding gasoline under your house was very tame compared to what most others were forced to do just to be able to feed their children.

The story that really dug into my gut though was one neighbor turning in another just to get more food. It did not matter any longer if you worked 8-hour, 12-hour or 16-hour days, everyone got the same reward. Everyone got the same ration of electrical power for four hours every third day, 1500 calories per day, and guaranteed housing. The housing might be a cot in a high school gymnasium, but the government could claim they were keeping their word that way.

In theory, it was 100 percent employment. But production in the workforce had gone down to about 15% of what it once was. Work hard, or just show up and sleep all day and you get paid the same. There were no rich to envy, everyone was equally miserable. That is not entirely true, the leaders in the government were wealthy.

It was the perfect utopian society the socialists and communists had been fighting for since Woodrow Wilson. They had complete control over all branches of government as well as enough states to amend the constitution weekly if they felt like it.

The utopia was real. The utopia was perfect, for the few hundred people in the entire country that ran it.

I tried to piece things together from what I knew about how the government worked the broadcasts. Every word on the radio was carefully scripted to manipulate the people, "My best guess, if I am right on this, is that they were captured and killed. Their bodies were staged at the warehouse. But, why are they that short on food again? This way, they can blame The Silent Majority for everyone suffering without food. Also, they could claim a victory.

Megan considered the logic of it, "Could be one of several possibilities but we can't deny that four months ago those same people were being hunted down and now the government is declaring them some sort of heroes while at the same time making up a reason to cut everyone's food rations."

I nodded, thinking hard.

"It's too much of a coincidence," Megan offered, "that those same three people show up dead and rations are now cut. The shortage of food has to be real and they are just blaming it on The Silent Majority."

I turned around in the chair to face the desk again and started writing down everything from the radio broadcast I could remember. At the end I referred to the June 4th broadcast earlier in the journal and wrote in my guess as to the truth.

Megan started working on lunch while I continued writing in my Journal. Once I was able to write everything down, I then turned my attention to using the CB-Radio, listening to see if anyone was talking on any of the 40 channels. The antennas for the ham radio, the CB-radio and the walkie-talkie radios were mounted on a steel bracket attached to a pole, mounted to a large pine tree. The steel bracket was grounded to an iron rod I pounded deep into the ground. The wiring for all three antennas were put inside metal conduits and then buried all the way back to the bunker. I was glad now for putting the wires inside the conduit. Even so, I was surprised the fire had not melted the wires and ruined them. All the signals appeared to be fine still though, so that was a blessing.

Megan was almost finished getting lunch ready, when I finally came across two people talking on channel 22.

Man 1:	Roger that, all three of them were in the Flagstaff Chapter.
Man 2:	How do they think people won't remember?
Man 1:	Are you kidding? People are so distracted with just trying to get enough food to live. They're not going to remember three strangers' names from months ago.
Man 2:	I suppose you're right.
Man 1:	You going to be at the farm tonight?
Man 2:	Yeah, Rhonda is busy here at home tonight though.

I picked up the mic at the end of the cord, took in a breath and then spoke.

Jack:	Sorry guys, don't mean to interrupt.
Man 1:	Well then don't interrupt you moron.

I kept quiet, waited.
The two men on the radio had stopped talking now.
About three minutes later:

Man 2:	Okay stranger, what gives?
Jack:	My wife and I are safe at our place, but our daughter is in Flagstaff and has Type I diabetes. My wife is going out of her mind with worry that she might not be getting her insulin. The CB Radio won't reach but four miles or so and the ham radio is constantly changing times and frequencies, so we don't know how we get word to or from our daughter without walking 10 days through the brush.
Man 2:	Go to channel 38 and wait.

I looked over at Megan with an anxious look and then turned the knob on the CB-radio to channel 38 and then just waited. I could feel my heart pick up in speed and my throat felt tight.

After five minutes I felt worse, perhaps they told me to go to another channel so they could talk about me after I left.

At ten minutes I got up out of the chair and started pacing.

Megan called me over to eat lunch before it went completely cold, so I sat down with her at the table. We bowed our heads and gave thanks in prayer for the meal and prayed for the protection of our daughter.

Half-way through the meal our radio leapt to life again.

Man 2: Stranger, you there?

I nearly jumped out of the chair as I rushed over and slid into the chair at the desk to snatch up the microphone.

Jack: Affirmative, I'm here, go ahead.
Man 2: Do you know the old Hawley Lake
     Campground?
Jack: I do.
Man 2: Turn your radio channel now to the number of
     days you said it would take you to walk, in our
     last discussion.

I paused for a moment, remembering. I turned the radio to channel 10.

About ten seconds later:

Man 2: You there Stranger?
Jack: I am.
Man 2: On the East side, go 2 miles until you are at the
     eastern lake. Now, the last channel we were on,
     take the second digit and subtract it by the first
     digit. Turn your radio to that channel.

Hmm, okay. Channel 38, so that's 8 - 3 = 5
I turned the radio to channel 5.
Only about ten seconds after changing the channel:

Man 2: You their Stranger?
Jack: I am
Man 2: From that body of water, follow the creek bed
     east until it opens into a large field. We will have
     someone meet you in that field. We need to get

to know who you are to see if we can trust you or not.

Jack:	Understood, when?
Man 2:	Sunset tonight.
Jack:	I'll be there.
Man 2:	Be safe.

I put the mic down on the desk and let out a hiss of relief before looking over to Megan.

Megan didn't look all that pleased. Woops.

Megan started expressing herself fairly straight forward, "It could be a setup Jack. The way they jumped around on channels splitting up the information, could be just to make you feel like the government isn't going to know where the meeting is at. Alternatively, it could be the government themselves trying to lure you out. You mentioned using the CB, the ham radio, and the towers and without a permit that's very illegal. That makes you a criminal already just asking about it."

I nodded slowly, "Love, we're on the same team here. We have the same goals. It's going to be dangerous even if I took the 10 day walk to Flagstaff. This way we can set up a way to communicate, if it works out. If Jordan has a problem at any time, we can know within a day and identify what to do to help her. Without this, you're stuck never knowing how she's doing and if she's safe or not."

Megan looked anxious that there wasn't a simple way to just make things right and to be safe doing it.

I pulled from the bookshelf a cardboard tube that held my map and laid it out on the desk. Months before, I had printed out a mosaic of Google satellite screenshots and taped them all together to form an enormous map of the area that I rolled up and kept in a cardboard tube. I did the same thing for Topographic screenshots. I adjusted the overhead light so that it lit up properly and then studied what I knew about where they wanted to meet.

Megan came over to the desk as I measured out distances and traced routes with my finger. I finally came up with the meeting location and then started looking for a direct route to get me there before sunset.

It was only three miles away from our house, so our walkie-talkies would still work at their outer ranges, so that was good.

We planned together that I was going to head down into the valley to the north just below our house. I would follow that northeast taking the valley; then northward after a mile. This way, I could keep from silhouetting myself against the skyline and stay down low, out of view as much as I could. I'd be traveling in the day and in an area that had just had a forest fire, so there was going to be nowhere to hide on the route. The terrain itself was my only concealment.

The planned route was going to add a mile to my trip, but it was also easier walk. I would avoid climbing up the ridge on the other side of the valley and then down some steep hills and back up a few times. If I kept to the valley it would be far easier going.

If the hike would have been further away and more than I could easily remember, I likely would have hand drawn a route to include important landmarks along the way. I had the satellite and topographic screenshots saved, but I had no idea when I would ever get ink for my printer once we ran out.

It was clear that Megan was anxious, if I was going to be safe or not, but she knew simultaneously it was necessary.

We spent the next hour getting my backpack ready. We double-checked the radios and batteries and backup batteries, medical kits, ammunition, firearms, and knives. I added a few days of food just in case and other supplies until I had a solid thirty-pound pack to carry.

It might be stressful getting ready to go out like this, but it sure felt flattering to have Megan fawning over me so heavily, staying close, resting a hand on my shoulder. She didn't express her love for me normally my being like this. This was exactly what made me feel like skipping across the tops of the mountains. I hated to leave when now I was feeling so close to her. Was she just messing with my head?

I slipped my earpiece into my ear and then routed the thin wire under my collar and down into the two-way radio on my chest.

Also, on my chest, a desert tan tactical Molle armor plate vest. This put my wife's mind at ease when I left the house. The Kevlar plates inside protected my chest and back from every round less powerful than a .308 sniper rifle. It should stop a 9mm handgun, an AR-15, .22 cal, .380 auto, .45 cal, .357 magnum. Sure, some of those would probably knock me right on the ground and make me scream in pain for twenty minutes, but they wouldn't go through me.

Mounted on the chest gear were several pouches that held AR-15 magazines, as well as several that held .45 cal magazines for my Springfield 1911 .45 cal pistol. A combat knife sheathed horizontally across my belly; the handle accessible to my right hand. Directly under my knife I keep my

MX-99 necked flashlight. On the back left was my canteen of water and on my back, right was a large pouch stuffed full of medical supplies like bandages, BloodStop powder, sutures, and normal things you might need if cut or shot.

On my right leg I used a drop thigh holster. This put my pistol right at my hand when I was walking and not high up on my hip. The holster was made to hold two magazines on it as well. I had a great deal of magazines and ammo, something I had been stocking up on for years.

On my left hip, my large bag that held my gas mask and two extra filters jostled around where it was attached to my belt. It had a shoulder strap that went up over my head and across my right shoulder so that it was firmly held in place.

My boots were the same boots I had been buying year after year since my time as a contractor in Iraq back in 2007 and 2008. Your standard desert tan military boot with a zipper up the inside. Nothing more comfortable had I ever worn since and I kept coming back to it as the best boot ever made.

My backpack was stuffed full, a multitude of various sized pouches hooked to the Molle webbing on the outside as well. Against my back, inside a zipped-up pouch separate from the main area, was a camelback water bladder that fed the drinking tube.

In the pack, I had a plastic tarp folded and placed on the bottom, some para cord coiled up for making a shelter and a million other uses. Two MRE's inside on top of the tarp and a Ziploc bag full of elk jerky we had made a couple months back. Over that, a canvas sack with batteries for the radio and the flashlight, bandages, headlamp, cigarette lighter, ibuprofen, hand lotion, a small bar of soap in a small Ziploc bag, washcloth, and a few other random bits to keep all in one place. On top of it all was a carefully wrapped Bible.

There was a bit of space still available, but the rest of my items were in the pouches on the outside of the pack, easy to get access to. Another medical kit, another canteen, a pouch with six more AR-15 magazines, a pouch with my binoculars, a pouch with five more .45 cal magazines and last was a pouch with a Ziploc bag inside with my toothbrush, paste, deodorant and other pleasantries.

With everything double checked, Megan handed me the AR-15 and I checked it over. Years before I had bought it at a decent price but then I spent a profane amount of money over a long period as a hobby adding holographic sites, popup front and back hard sights, new foregrip, new trigger assembly, new pistol-grip, new butt stock, new charging handle, new take down pins. Now that I think about it, the barrel was probably the only thing from the original gun. I only used brass casing with green steel tip ammo in it. 5.56N was the only ammo that cycled properly through it. I bought 1,000 rounds of cheap Russian .223 and every other round would jam or not feed right. Brass casing .223 also was just slightly under power for the system and the carriage would not return all the way back to eject and pull in the next round consistently. It took a considerable amount of time to figure it all out. Those things happen when you start to modify and customize a weapon from the factory.

The Springfield 1911 I had been carrying daily, so I knew that it didn't need a check right now, I checked it about three times a day, so it was a part of me now.

I pulled on my desert tan tactical helmet, tested the flashlight mounted on the side and then fastened the strap up under my chin. Ready to go.

I knelt and gave Riley a little scratch on top of her ears and then after Megan picked up the dog. I gave Megan a real nice farewell kiss, and headed up the stairs to the entrance shack above.

The 4:00 pm sun blinded me when I opened the bunker access shed to go outside. Now our land was upwind of the fire and I could see clear blue sky overhead for the first time in a week.

My glasses started working hard to tint against the sun, but it would take a couple minutes before I didn't look like a mole peering around our property.

The fire had completely stripped the pines of their needles and their bark and were black like charcoal. The trees that didn't take more than 25% damage on their bark should grow back in the next year or two.

I adjusted the three-point strap of the AR-15 and then slung it down onto my chest before heading over to the metal bucket by the water tank to fill it up. I spent the next 30 minutes washing the ash and dust off the solar panels with buckets of water while being careful to look around and listen for any danger.

The birds had already started moving into the area. I'm sure they moved off as the smoke built up until they could find where it was safe to breath and go back to their business.

I checked in on the truck next and confirmed the tarp would need to be replaced. Inside the truck cab, I pulled a tarp out from behind the seat and worked for another 20 minutes stretching the tarp out over the top of the truck to hide it from the government satellites.

The house was the last thing I checked on, and it was just as we had left it. I got a washcloth from the kitchen and refilled the bucket with water. I then went around cleaning the globes and lenses of the various cameras installed on the property for about 30 minutes.

With only a few hours before sunset, I shouldered my pack, readied the AR-15 and checked the horizon to the north and east. It looked clear.

I offered a smile and a kiss to the nearest camera and then set off.

Chapter Four (Megan)
Left Alone

October 13

Riley's little puppy nails on the floor of the bunker woke me up and pulled me from my dream. We were on Laguna Beach in California. I was sitting on a towel with the sun in my face about two hours before sunset. A book was in my hands and resting on my legs as I looked up from my reading to see Jack and Jordan digging in the sand near the water's edge making a big hole that kept collapsing in on them. They kept laughing as their construction project kept failing. The more their plans were destroyed the more they laughed.

The seagulls squawked in the blue skies above while the sounds of cars on the traffic jammed road behind made the entire area feel busy. It was a sharp contrast between chaos behind and serenity and calm with the ocean in front.

An old delivery truck, louder than the other vehicles, rolled down the hill. The engine click-clicked louder and louder until it came to a stop directly behind me on the roadway. The engine clicking continued to get louder until I turned around to look at it and saw Riley running at me through the sand on the beach. That's when I woke up and realized I wasn't on the beach, but far below ground in a cold metal tube.

I sighed and rolled over.

I could hear Riley's little claws going further away and then the sound of Jack unlatching the six levers that sealed the airtight door at the other end of the bunker. It got quiet again and I drifted back off to sleep.

I was standing in the line for Space Mountain with Jordan at Disneyland. My feet were sore, and it was hot out but the heat felt soothing on my hair and the back of my neck. Jordan was talking about what ride we should go on next before we had to use our FastPass, somewhere in there she said she wanted to get something to eat.

We inched forward in the line in the sea of people pressing up close to each other. We snaked gradually closer and closer to the loading zone of the ride. Turning to the left around the string of guide chains, we saw a long line in front of us went 100 feet, then cut back again with a handrail that came back and passed where we were standing already. This snake of people zigzagged for a mile, or so it appeared.

The estimated wait time was two hours, this was so much fun.

Jack of course was back home in Arizona working the midnight shift on the weekend. Jack didn't like big crowds and liked California even less, so these trips that Jordan and I took to Disneyland a few times a year were something he gladly supported and encouraged. If we could only go out and have fun and adventures when he had a holiday off or a weekend, we would have been one dull family.

I heard a bird call out overhead and I looked to the sky to see a large raven flying overhead. It appeared a little smaller than the ravens we had seen at the Grand Canyon, but it still was large enough to dominate the smaller varieties of birds in the park. I squinted as I tried to shield the brilliance of the sun so I could watch the bird, when suddenly the ground shook beneath my feet and startled me.

I was awake before I realized that I was. The ground had not shaken beneath me, it was Jack sitting down on the edge of the bed. The sun was not blinding me, it was the small LED lamp on the headboard of the bed that had been flipped on.

Jack gave me a gentle morning kiss and a smile before he handed me a cup of coffee and then started talking about wanting to spend time on the ham radio. We spent some time sipping coffee and sitting on the bed before he brought in his Bible to talk about what he had been studying before I woke up. After I finished my cup of coffee, we prayed and then Jack moved to the desk to start his work, I got up to start my day.

I spent some time at the desk reading my Bible and then writing in my journal and praying and then I got up to exercise. I'm not sure why I felt I had to get changed into workout clothes. I think it was perhaps the changing of the clothes made it feel official and normal and not so much like I was still way underground in a cold metal tube.

I started my workout using the bike in the master bedroom. The rear wheel was hooked up with a belt to a pulley on an electrical motor. As I pedaled the bike the motor spun and sent electricity down into the electrical things under the floor and charged the batteries. It was an emergency backup that Jack had made and wasn't needed right now, but the exercise was needed right now, the power production was just a bonus.

Going for a run was out of the question but doing lunges from the back of the bedroom, through the main living area, through the bunk quarters and to the back-airlock door and then back again was an efficient substitute. It wasn't long until I had a generous sweat going and could feel the confining nature of the bunker falling away from my mood.

I pushed myself harder in the workout than I normally did as a distraction. I did push-ups until I collapsed on my face on the floor and sit-ups until I almost cried and had to roll over on my side to get up off the floor. The Leg lifts made my thighs burn with fire and my stomach spasmed and twitched from over exertion. At the end of it, I was a worthless mass of spent woman that could barely claw herself to the shower to clean up.

I wasn't sure what I was going to do with myself down here for days, already I felt like I was trapped and confined. I would need something to distract my mind and prevent it from thinking about how I couldn't go for a run, or warm myself under the sun.

I had dozens of books on a shelf in the bedroom, I guess I could start there.

Three hours passed like a blink of an eye. I got sucked into a book about an Amish community in Ohio and was a third of the way through the book before I realized it was noon. The government AM radio noon news program was tuned in by Jack, so I marked the books page corner by bending it over and then left the book on the bed as I moved over to join Jack in the main area.

Jack was moving to the kitchen to pull out some food for lunch, so I helped him by getting out what he needed as he worked.

We listened to the radio program as we prepared lunch to try to learn what we could of the outside world. It never made us feel better and always made us worry more each day. I guess that was one thing that was the same as the news before the collapse.

As the program progressed, Jack got increasingly irritated and put down what he was working on at the counter and I took over making lunch for him. Jack stepped to the side, pulled into the news completely. It wasn't long before he moved to the bookshelf and reached behind the row of books to his hidden journal and started flipping through its pages as he sat down at the desk.

The entire broadcast made the tension in the bunker increase as the frustration of living under a police state was so fully instituted now. I grabbed my Bible and moved over to the couch to start reading. It always calmed me when I was able to put things in perspective and not look at the stress of the moment. It was important to see the bigger picture of who I was and what my place was in this world and for what was waiting for me after.

The Old Testament was filled with accounts of the Jewish people under oppressive rulers and Kings and stories of how they would turn to God after great persecution. I found it comforting to know that in the timeline of it all, we were not alone now, others had gone through this as well.

Jack blurted out loud that he found something, and it startled me. My elbow bumped the bottle of water on the arm of the couch and knocked it to the floor. I dashed to pick it up as Jack apologized for surprising me. I chuckled at him as I picked up the bottle and then sat back up and placed the Bible on the couch next to me to listen to what he was so intent to talk to me about.

Jack pointed to his journal about the three names in the radio report and explained how months before the same three names were mentioned in the radio broadcast. He read from his notes that the three names were listed as terrorists. That didn't make sense, now they were defending a government food facility?

"Something smells fishy in Denmark Jack," I offered back to him in agreement.

Jack guessed that the three had finally been found and killed and that their bodies were staged at the warehouse. He figured the story made up about the shortage of food was to blame more ration cuts on The Silent Majority.

I considered the logic of it, "Could be one of several possibilities but we can't deny that four months ago those same people were being hunted down and now the government is declaring them some sort of heroes while at the same time making up a reason to cut everyone's food rations."

"It's too much of a coincidence," I offered, "that those same three people show up dead and rations are now cut. The shortage of food has to be real and they are just blaming it on The Silent Majority."

Jack's face was red with frustration and anxiety as he turned around and started updating his journal with notes on today's broadcast. He referred to the entries from months before and our theories on it all.

To distract myself, I picked up my Bible and closed it, put it on the shelf and finished making lunch for us.

Jack turned on the CB-Radio and started slowly moving through all the channels, listening for anyone that might be out there within the reach of the radio talking.

I took out two of the dehydrated meal packs from under the counter. I added water to the meal packets to hydrate them and activated the heat packets in them. I opened the other packets and started arranging the food on a couple plates. We could eat out of the packets, but it felt more like home if we could sit at the table like a real family with plates and utensils and not like beasts living out in the forest.

I was just starting to scoop the hot meals from the heating pouches to the plates, when Jack found a channel where two guys were talking.

Man 1:	Roger that. All three of them were in the Flagstaff Chapter.
Man 2:	How do they think people won't remember?
Man 1:	Are you kidding? People are so distracted with just trying to get enough food to live. They're not going to remember three strangers' names from months ago.
Man 2:	I suppose you're right.
Man 1:	You going to be at the farm tonight?
Man 2:	Yeah, Rhonda is busy here at home tonight though.

Jack picked up the microphone.

Jack:	Sorry guys, don't mean to interrupt.
Man 1:	Well then don't interrupt you moron.

Jack looked a bit frustrated but didn't respond.

I picked up the two plates and moved over to the table and sat them down. After a few minutes the men on the CB-Radio spoke again.

Man 2:	Okay stranger, what gives?
Jack:	My wife and I are safe at our place, but our daughter is in Flagstaff and has Type I diabetes. My wife is going out of her mind with worry that she might not be getting her insulin. The CB Radio won't reach but four miles or so and the ham radio is constantly changing times and frequencies, so we don't know how we get word to or from our daughter without walking 10 days through the brush.
Man 2:	Go to channel 38 and wait.

If there was a chance that these men knew anything, it would be an invaluable moment to see if we could find a way to contact Jordan.

Jack turned the dial on the radio to the channel they told him to, and he waited. After a couple minutes I started to eat my meal. It was surprising how a sealed meal pack that was five years old could taste so flavorful. Mine was a spicy spaghetti and meat sauce with applesauce in another packet, a chocolate chip cookie, and a cracker pack with some peanut butter. I used to chuckle at Jack when he would bring them camping or on a ride on his motorcycle but now it appeared a highlight of the week to pull one of these out of a box to enjoy.

I liked our time together when we had a meal. It felt isolated and lonely with him over at the radio waiting, so I ate slowly and waited for him. Still, I finished my plate before he came to the table to eat his. I called him over to eat before his food turned completely cold and we bowed our heads while he prayed for the meal.

Half-way through the meal our radio leapt to life again.

Man 2:   Stranger, you there?

Jack nearly jumped out of the chair as he rushed over and slid into the chair at the desk, snatching up the microphone.

Jack: Affirmative, I'm here, go ahead.
Man 2:   Do you know the old Hawley Lake
             Campground?
Jack: I do.
Man 2:   Turn your radio channel now to the number of
             days you said it would take you to walk, in our
             last discussion.

Jack waited a moment, thinking, then turned the radio to channel 10.

About ten seconds later:

Man 2:   You there Stranger?
Jack: I am.
Man 2:   Go two miles east to the eastern most body of
             water there. Now, the last channel we were on,
             take the second digit and subtract it by the first
             digit. Turn your radio to that channel.

Jack did the math in his head and then turned the radio channel.

After a few moments:

Man 2:	You there Stranger?
Jack:	I am
Man 2:	From that body of water, follow the creek bed east until it opens into a large field. We will have someone meet you in that field. We need to get to know who you are to see if we can trust you or not.
Jack:	Understood, when?
Man 2:	Sunset tonight.
Jack:	I'll be there.
Man 2:	Be safe.

Jack put the CB-Radio microphone down and sighed before he looked over to me.

I didn't like it in the slightest that he would be going out from the bunker on his own to meet some people. I knew it had to be done to get another step closer to getting in touch with Jordan but if something happened to him while he was out, I'm not sure what I would do. Yes, I would survive on my own. I could hunt like he taught me and I could maintain the garden and the homestead but the isolation and being without the man I wanted to spend the rest of my life with, that could be more than I could handle and I think it showed on my face by the way he looked at me.

I tried to explain it to him, "It could be a setup Jack. The way they jumped around on channels splitting up the information, could be just to make you feel like the government isn't going to know where the meeting is at. Alternatively, it could be the government themselves trying to lure you out. You mentioned using the CB, the ham radio and the towers and without a permit that's very illegal. That makes you a criminal already just asking about it."

Jack did his best to comfort me but mostly he just justified why the risk of his life was worth it, to ensure that Jordan was okay. Both of us would give our lives for her. I knew his commitment to our family and there would be no way to stop him. Also, I knew deep in my heart it was what needed to happen. It didn't make the pill any easier to swallow though.

Jack took out the map of the area and laid it on the communications table to look at where the meeting was going to be. I got up and joined him as he explained where the meeting was at and how he was going to get there. I helped him plan out the best route to be safe but the more real it became the more anxious I got.

We spent the next hour packing up his backpack and getting his gear ready to go. I felt like he was going to be gone for weeks and I found myself staying closer to him than normal, resting my hand on his arm or shoulder and just hovering over him when at all possible.

I helped him get dressed up, his armored vest, the radio, and handed him ammo magazines to put in their pouches. It took a while to get his food, medical supplies, and other gear all packed properly. I then handed him the AR-15. He put on his helmet and knelt to say goodbye to Riley.

I was almost crying at this point as my eyes teared up but I held it in as much as I could. I gave him a kiss to improve his anxiety in the decontamination room before he went up the stairs and up out of the big hatch at the top.

I felt alone already, even with Riley at my leg rubbing against me for me to pick her up. She could feel the tension as Jack left us in the bunker and knew things weren't right anymore.

Chapter Five (Jack)
Can Trust Be Earned?

October 13

When I reached the bottom of the valley, north of our cabin, I took a glance back. I was surprised how visible the cabin was now that the trees had been stripped. I hesitated a moment longer envisioning as I remembered the dirty water that will wash down the hills after a rain, thanks to the fire. The streams will fill with muck-fluid-ash then dump into the rivers, until there is a wave of twigs and ashy muck crackling and pushing through the valley floor. If the ash were able to stay in place for a while to help replenish the soil with nutrients it would be fantastic. If a rain came on the tail end of the fires it would really hinder the regrowth process and make the recovery last a great deal longer.

At the bottom of the valley, I tested our radios to ensure we could communicate. I flipped the switch to VOC (Voice Activated).

Jack: Testing, you hear me baby?
Megan: Yep, it sounds very clear.
Jack: Okay, I will check back every hour or if something comes up.
Megan: Okay, I'll be here.

I grinned at her response and moved at a steady pace in the valley heading eastward. I had an excellent field of view in every direction because the trees were now black poles reaching up out of the ground and not visually restrictive with branches and needles. I could see a great distance now, but that also meant that others could see me from far-off as well.

I fished my binoculars out of the pouch on the backpack and then slipped the pack back on and continued forward. I only went about 100 yards at a time before I found a stump or pile of boulders to crouch down behind. I spent about 1-2 minutes scanning the area in every direction, including behind me if anyone was following me.

The smell of the burned needles and charred underbrush was still shockingly strong. The breeze coming down the valley should have brought with it fresh air. Instead, the air coming at my face felt thick with ash and it made my eyes blink frequently. They felt heavy and swollen as they struggled to stay clear.

Thirty minutes later and one third of the way on my route, I spotted a black bear off to the east. It was down wind of me now and it failed to spot me. Strange, before the fire it would have been long gone and I would have never seen it through the pines. Now though, the heavy scent of the burning trees overwhelmed its nose. I looked down with a glance to my .45 caliber on my holster and then watched the bear a bit longer with the binoculars. We wouldn't have to deal with each other but it felt safer that I traded my 9mm pistol before we moved up to the mountains for this .45 cal.

One of my neighbors needed me to teach him how to make a water treatment system for his house. He wanted to treat his pool water to make it safe for his family. I was planning to move up into the mountains about that time. So, he traded his .45 caliber Springfield 1911 with three hundred rounds of ammunition for my Ruger SR9C with 500 rounds of ammunition and me setting up his family's drinking water system.

The 9mm would only have given the bear a searing point of pain upon impact, and done very little other than making it very upset. The .45 cal was powerful enough though to penetrate the skull. A direct hit to the skull was the only thing that was going to keep me from being mauled. Thankfully, we were not going to have to put that to the test today, the bear turned and lumbered off to the north.

I focused a bit closer on the area the bear was standing and noted a lump of black charred area on the ground. I felt a bit of a frown produce itself on my face as I deduced it was a bear cub that was burned to death in the fire.

It is a harsh world for not only bears these days. Now the luxury of safety and comfort had become elusive for even men.

I tucked the binoculars away and continued my route.

An hour later and I found myself entering pines that had missed being consumed by the fire. From my best estimate the path of the fire reached a mile north of our cabin, but did not burn the forest anywhere north of that point. If our home had been a mile north, the fire would have missed us. I offered a prayer thanking God we had not lost the house, Jordan's truck or been hurt ourselves.

I paused inside the pines where the branches offered an ample amount of shade from the late afternoon sun and keyed up the radio to contact Megan.

Jack:	Mama Bear, this is Hawk One, do you copy?
Megan:	Yes, I hear you.
Jack:	I will contact you again in one hour.
Megan:	Okay

Just a short little chat with Megan calmed me and focused my mind on the importance of this mission again. God had really given me the perfect wife. I think she's the only woman that would not have killed me in my sleep by now. However, I saw all my imperfections under a microscope. Hopefully no one else saw the same weakness I saw in myself. Did everyone else feel as inadequate in life as I did?

I had a feeling they did, unless they were narcissistic. Considering that, I think there are a great many people that see themselves as perfect. In this, I again found myself feeling isolated.

Why could I so easily get frustrated with other people, when I knew I had so many issues of my own that were not right? I am not sure that if I lived to be 500 years old, I would never be able to iron the wrinkles out of my life.

I stopped and sat on an old felled tree to rest, take a drink of water and to stop and pray for a while.

Without the distractions of living in the city, these times of just stopping whatever I was doing to take a moment and just pray, felt natural, the way it was supposed to be.

I chuckled a bit at remembering watching The Fiddler on The Roof with Chaim Topol playing Tevye. Like in the movie, I would stop mid project and look to the sky or the top of the trees and just talk to God as if he was right there in the place with me. Frank, and shockingly blunt conversations, sometimes complaints, and worry were brought out aloud and it was becoming more common in my day.

I had envied the life of Tevye in the movie and how close he was to God, but it wasn't until we moved up into the mountains that the dream became a reality.

I didn't know how long I had rested until I glanced down at my watch and saw it was a half hour later. Oh dear, I was going to have to pick up my pace to get into position before dark.

A half hour later, I crept up to the top of the hill to the west; with the valley below me I tried to radio again.

Jack:	Mama Bear, this is Hawk One, do you copy?
Megan:	I hear you.
Jack:	Okay, thank you baby. (a small pause), I love you.

Megan: I love you too Honey.

      I flipped the radio back to standby and then slowed back down for the last half an hour of stalking through the woods as I neared the large clearing.

      In the trees, the shadows were getting darker and the sounds of the birds were changing as some began to roost for the night and others were waking up for night hunting. The stillness of the forest always gripped me tight and mesmerized me.

      I had wanted to work in the parks service since I was young. I grew up in the country where a several mile walk cross-country through the woods, along creeks, and over hills to spend the day with my best friend Kevin was a perfectly normal day. There was no such thing as whining about being bored.

      There was no internet, no cell phones and I don't even think there was cable television. We had a small black and white television with rabbit ears and aluminum foil, and it was seldom used.

      It was those years spent camping in the woods with my friend, around a small campfire, sleeping in small tents and listening to the creatures in the forest at night, that created my love of being outside in the wild.

      I even went to college and got an associate degree in Natural Resources Technology so that I could get a job as a Forest Park Ranger or work in Fisheries or Wildlife Management, but I never landed a job like that. While in school I discovered it would only take a few classes in chemistry, hydraulics and some water associated classes and I could spend the same time in college and end up with another associate degree in Water Quality Technology. Why not, right?

      When I got out of college, I couldn't find a job and it was the United States Air Force that found me stepping forward and asking for an opportunity. I worked in their Civil Engineering Squadrons and as it turns out I started working under the water quality degree that I had. I stayed in that career for the next 30 years, for the most part.

      There were short stints on a dairy farm, a plumber, a Culligan (™) water softening installer, working on a pig farm, but those were temporary when life threw curve balls at us.

      Now, when all the rules of society had collapsed, now I had found myself right where I knew I would be the closest to God and it felt right.

      I stopped inside the tree line, at the southeastern most part of the clearing, and crouched down behind a tree. I stayed several feet back in the shadows of the forest and took out my binoculars. I slowly scanned the clearing and around its edge to where others might be hiding.

The field appeared empty during my first search. The grasses were brittle dry from the hot summer winds. The mountains up here in Northern Arizona acquire a feeble quantity of rain every year. Snow melting in the spring accounted for most of the water accumulation; adding up to more water available over all the rain in the spring, summer and fall combined.

A glint of light caught my attention off to the left at the edge of the field. I twisted around in the shadows of the trees to set my binoculars on that area more directly.

There, just over the height of the tall dead grasses of the field was the glint again. It looked like an ATV (All-Terrain Vehicle) mirror. I confirmed by following the mirror to the right and then saw the right-hand steering arm. The rest of the ATV was hidden beneath the height of the grass.

I folded the binoculars up and tucked them into their pouch as I started a crouched prowl inside the tree line to the left to get closer.

It was slower going now, crouched over and slinking along quiet, but I should still be able to get in to place by sunset.

It took 15 minutes to creep along quietly inside the trees until I could see the ATV clearly and get a better view of the situation.

The ATV was in an area where the grass had been mashed down flat over time and there was a bit of dried mud on the ground. When the spring melt brought rain from higher up in the hills toward the lake to the west, this area was under water for a few weeks. When water gathers, the elk, bear and other animals gather here and trample the ground and loosen it up.

The summer heat and dry fall turned the mud into hard crust with hoof prints as clear as the day they were first created.

The ATV was the most obvious thing I put my attention to; a desert tan paint job. On the back was a rack that held a supply tote strapped closed. On the front between the steering bars was a rack holding a bolt action rifle with a scope on it.

When my gaze fell upon the license plate of the ATV my heart nearly stopped for a moment. "G-13R5", it was a government owned vehicle.

I shrunk back into the shadows a little as this realization hit me. Moving back further changed my angle of what I could see. I spotted a boot at the end of a leg laying on the ground in front of the ATV. Someone was hurt.

I paused for a while as I looked from left to right, then behind me deeper into the trees and then forward across the open field, checking for any obvious trap.

It all appeared calm, so I moved forward out of the shadows of the trees in a crouch, up to the ATV and around it to get to the injured person.

Upon nearing the man, I dropped to one knee, still a few paces off, because he was dressed in a government patrol officer's uniform.

He lay on his back, eyes wide open and unblinking, looking at the sky. A deep wound from a knife was in his throat at his artery. His face had a grey ashen color to it that instinctively announced itself as very dead.

My eyes darted around in panic as I listened. If a federal patrol officer was killed, there would be nothing that would save me from getting blamed for it.

Far to the east, I could see a puff of dust and just barely the sound of a vehicle. A vehicle? Only the government could have vehicles with combustion engines. This was not good, not good at all.

That's when I heard the groaning of a young man in his late teens just inside the tall grass. I could see him lying there on his back with bandages around his stomach drenched in blood. He appeared to be in terrible pain as he moaned. He was dressed in jeans and a shirt and a green and black plaid hunting flannel. His face was struggling to grow a beard, but he was still too young for it to fill in properly.

The kid's eyes looked full of panic as he looked eastward to the sound of the approaching government vehicle. It appeared the kid killed the government officer, but that may be jumping to conclusions. Someone seeing me right where I was might be thinking the same about me.

I hurried to the young man's side and knelt as I reached for the wound.

He pushed my hands away in fear, the pain must be excruciating. I didn't know if it was a knife wound or a gunshot. I wanted to know what I was dealing with so I could determine if I could move him or not.

"Knife wound? Gunshot?" I questioned him fast.

"Does it matter? If we are here when the Feds get here, we're both dead."

I couldn't fault the kids' logic, "Fair enough, we need to get you out of here."

I looked over the grass to gauge the distance from the approaching vehicle to us, "One moment."

I darted over to the Fed and searched his body for anything useful and then checked the ATV as well.

It was no use taking the ATV, it surely would have a GPS tracker hidden on it some place.

In my quick search, I pilfered a zippo lighter, a 9mm pistol with three 10 round magazines, a handheld radio, a pack of gum, his .308 hunting rifle with its nice scope and in the box on the back of the ATV I pulled out a real nice medical kit.

Within a minute, I was back at the teens side and stuffing the items into my pack. I put my pack on again and shouldered the rifle and then carefully helped the kid to his feet so I could lead him into the shadows of the trees and away as fast as I could.

It was hard supporting his weight; his knees gave out several times while we moved away into the trees. Once we got into the trees, we could head off at a different angle to try and get out of view. If we had stayed in the grasses, our trail would be simple to follow, but now in the trees we could softly move over the bed of needles with little trace of our passing. If we could move along without breaking any branches or other vegetation or stepping on twigs and making fresh breaks, we just might get away.

After 100 yards, the truck came to a stop. We heard the doors shutting twice. At least two people got out of the truck to discover their dead man.

I stopped there to let the kid rest and catch his breath, and honestly to rest myself. It was no easy task to lug this kid up the hillside through the pines, taking most of his weight to help him walk.

A year before and I would not have been able to do it. It would have been hard enough to get up the hills on my back then. Moving out from behind the computer monitors at work, being active and outside working this past year, I had dropped any visible body fat and exchanged it for muscle. Granted, I didn't look like a bodybuilder now, but I could jog for four miles easily in the thin mountain air and do pushups for days. Of course, push-ups for days, is an exaggerated saying meant for humor. Nobody can do push-ups for days, right?

The Kid's body odor was enough to make my lunch try to come up. That wasn't unusual though since the collapse. Deodorant was something of a luxury that only the government employees seemed to be able to purchase with their credits.

I started up a conversation in a whisper and he responded quietly to me.

I asked, "You know this area?"

He responded, "Yeah, can you get me to my farm? It's a mile north from here?"

I pondered, "Is there concealment, trees that can hide us between here and there?"

The kid nodded, "What's your name Sir?"

I considered how the world had changed and didn't share with him my real name, "You can call me Kirby," it was the name I went by when I was involved with the motorcycle clubs in the east valley. It was my mother's maiden name and I used it because of my respect for my grandfather.

The expression on his face showed he knew it wasn't my real name, but then he nodded as if I passed some sort of new-world logic test.

"I'm John," he offered with a bit of a quizzical look as if testing me. John's hair had a reddish tinge to its light brown color and was thinning. He was only in his upper teens and my guess was that a lack of proper protein and nourishment was causing his hair to thin.

I grinned a little, knowing he picked a prevalent name for himself as well.

"Okay," I drilled him with more whispers, "What happened?" Then I helped him get up off the ground and began to shed his weight. We started working a lazy route northward. A few random directions I insisted on, when we came to places that had exposed bedrock. This allowed us to travel without leaving any prints and then continue.

As we moved along carefully, I took breaks to take a sip of water and share some with him. As we were making our way, he told me what happened.

He explained that he was sent to meet someone in the clearing at sunset, but he was spotted by the guy on the ATV and chased down. He feigned surrender, but when the government officer got off his ATV and approached to handcuff him, he attacked the Fed with his knife.

The two fought, both sustained injuries in the fight. John got stabbed in his side, but he figured he would be fine if he could get back to the farm and get sewn up. Of course, the Fed took the worst stab, in the side of his throat.

John's story matched what I could tell from the scene. There could be a bit of fudging of the truth to make himself sound better. I think anyone would try to portray themselves in the best light when retelling a story about something so traumatic. I also considered, he was with The Silent Majority and that I was the one he was sent to meet in the clearing. I had even more reason to help him out now than before. I could put my mind at ease that I wasn't missing the meeting in the clearing by going out of my way helping this kid now.

After half a mile I was confident the feds in the truck were no longer following us. They either gave up or were unable to identify where we had gone.

It was right about then that I thought I saw movement in the distance behind a large pile of boulders. I dropped to a knee after a few quick steps to get behind cover behind a large rock and brought my AR-15 to my shoulder. The holographic site didn't amplify what I was looking at, so I flipped up the 10x scope to line up with the site to get a better view of the area about fifty yards away.

I kept a bit of attention on John still. Though he was injured and laying on the ground now, I couldn't trust that there may be some sort of trick going on. The days of ever trusting another person or believing that mankind would bind together and help each other went out the window in the spring of 2020 with the Wuhan virus.

As I got sighted in on the outcropping of large boulders John spoke up with a hiss of a voice like a loud whisper, "Um... Kirby, it might be one of my guys on perimeter patrol."

I kept part of my mind on John as I looked down the scope and through the site. I took in a deep breath and called out, "I've got John here, he's been stabbed by a Fed in the stomach. I'm helping him get back to the farm. If you don't plan to harm him or I, step out into view."

A few moments passed, they felt like minutes, before a guy stepped out and came in to view on the left side of the boulders. He was holding a bolt action hunting rifle with a scope down at his side with his right hand. His left hand raised up in the air to show it was empty in a bit of a wave. The man wore jeans and cowboy boots and had on a dark green and black plaid flannel shirt. His hair was a mess of black long hair and had a meager attempt at containing it in a ponytail behind his head.

I made note that the green and black flannel was the same as John's shirt.

I took my cheekbone off the stock of my rifle and whispered down to John without taking my eyes off this stranger, "Quietly tell me this guy's name please."

John offered with a whisper, "Tony."

I called out in a loud voice again, "What's your name?"

They guy looked at me a bit strangely before answering, "Tony."

I nodded then, and lowered my gun.

A glance at John and he visibly relaxed. We were both on edge during the brandishing of weapons in the woods.

I motioned Tony to come on over, "I'm Kirby, sorry about that, you know how it is."

Tony nodded with a chuckle, "Oh do I ever, no hard feelings at all."

With Tony's help, both of us took an arm of John's and helped him get along back to the farm. It was much quicker with the help and we soon ate up the distance of the remaining half mile to the farmhouse.

As we came out of the pines and into another open field, it was easy to spot the weather-worn two-story farmhouse. Some of the siding had been blown loose in the winter winds and not been reattached or repaired. Some of the shingles on the roof had been ripped off to reveal the wood roofing below them.

There was a large metal water cistern near the house that looked like the best thing the farm had going for it. A full-sized barn was not far from the house and it looked in better condition and care than the home itself. There were no missing boards or signs of neglect like the family residence had.

John and Tony seemed more energized and eager now, grateful to be back on 'safe' ground it seemed to me.

Halfway across the clearing, the farmhouse door opened and a man in his seventies, in overalls came out with a shotgun. After the man, a woman about the same age as him in jeans and button-down floral shirt came out. The woman remained in the open doorway as the man with the shotgun slowly walked towards us. He didn't raise the gun and point it at us, nor did he seem threatening. These days, everyone outside the government areas carried a gun, so him just having it wasn't as unsettling as it may have been a year ago.

When we finally met up a short distance from the farmhouse the older man took my side in helping John and the two of them continued getting him to the farmhouse as I followed along behind.

The man with the shotgun introduced himself as Sal and thanked me for helping John get back to the farm, "What happened?"

John explained a short version of what happened as they got him in through the door and inside the living room of the house.

The lady in the doorway offered me a nod as she stepped inside. She motioned for me to come inside if I wanted.

I felt a little uneasy entering the home but did anyway because it was polite. I moved to the left to put my back against the wall. The AR-15 I let hang on its sling against my chest and I tucked my thumbs into the armpit areas of my armored vest to relax. I had a nasty amount of sweat from the work of getting John back to the farm. The lady was quick to introduce herself as Margaret and then go to fetch me a glass of water from the kitchen deeper in the house.

I couldn't see from my position because Sal's back was blocking my view, but they examined John for a bit and then got him up and escorted him down the hall.

Tony offered me a nod as they passed by, "We're gunna get him laid down in one of the bedrooms, thanks Kirby. Means a lot that you helped him get back to us."

The sun was setting now, and the inside of the house was getting darker as Margaret brought me a glass of water. I thanked her for it with a smile and drank it down in one long draw. I smiled as I handed it back to her, "Thank you Margaret, I appreciate it."

Margaret offered a nod, "So, you found John at a clearing about a mile south of here, did you?"

I nodded, "I did. I didn't expect to find a Federal Officer there though, nor the scene I came up on."

Margaret nodded with a frown, "Yeah, that's not going to be helpful for anyone. That truck rolling up on things and finding him is going to bring down search teams and heat in this area until they get some answers."

It left a pit in my stomach to know that she was right. The government was going to have to start paying more attention to this area and it was uncomfortably close to my home.

I asked her then, "Why would a Fed be out in the woods this far away from any main road?"

She shook her head with a little frown, "I'm not sure. Unless they have some reason to start snooping around. They usually stay to the cities to try and keep control over everyone. Something would have had to draw their attention to bring them out this way in the first place."

"I took a radio off the Fed and some other gear," I offered, "Perhaps I can learn more by listening to their radio as time goes on."

Margaret smiled at this, "Good, that's good. That should help us at least find out what they're up to."

It was about then that Sal and Tony came back into the living room from the hallway.

Sal sighed just a bit, "John's going to be okay, he's just going to need a few stitches. We have to keep him hydrated, resting, and not moving around."

"I can stitch him up if you want," I offered.

Margaret looked a little surprised and caught off guard by that, "No, it's okay, I can do that. We don't want to put you out. You've helped out a great deal already."

Sal moved over to the fireplace in the living room and started to arrange some wood in it to light a fire, "So, Kirby," he started while talking slowly, as if testing the conversation carefully as he went along, "If you met John at the clearing just before sunset, that means you might be the guy John was there to meet." He paused, "If you are the guy he was supposed to meet, you'd know what type of medicine his daughter needs."

I considered these might be the people I was supposed to meet with, the location, time I met John and how rare it was to see people out anymore. I responded honestly, "Insulin."

Sal smiled at that, "Nice, perfect. Then we've officially met."

I questioned cautiously, "Are you going to need to move or find a different place while the Feds start nosing about and searching the area?"

Tony leaned up against the door to the yard lazily. Him blocking the exit made me feel uneasy. It probably showed in the way I adjusted my face to try and not look annoyed by it.

Sal lit a match and started the fire, blowing on it gently during the conversation to get it properly lit, "We can move on to another location if the situation requires it. But, until they find out who killed their man, they're going to be real trouble for everyone around here for a while."

I nodded to the logic, "Well, I won't say anything, that's for sure. I've got no love for the Feds. Also, they're just as likely to blame me for it happening as anyone. I've got their radio, their med kit and the Fed's gun and ammo. I probably need to stash it away, so I don't get caught with it."

Sal nodded to my comment with a smile, "Smart, you do that for sure."

Tony just kept quiet at the front door. He still unsettled me staying there.

Margaret injected into the conversation, "I'm going to go sew up John. You men figure out what we're doing next." She then moved on down the hallway and out of view.

Sal continued on, he had the fire going strong now, he stood up and leaned against the mantle, "Well Kirby, it's not as easy as walking in and introducing yourself and us handing over the secrets of the nationwide ham radio communications. You understand we have to build some level of trust with you first, right?"

I nodded to that, fully understanding the need for exactly what he was proposing.

Sal added, "You have to look at it from our point of view. We set up a meeting with someone and then the Fed showed up to arrest our guy. Out in the middle of nowhere. What are the chances of that? It makes us seriously question you, you understand?"

I nodded again, "I can't blame you at all. That makes sense."

Sal took in a deep breath as if about to lay out an idea that had some weight to it, "There is an old reservation power plant northeast of here about 35 miles cross-country that the Feds took over. It's the Springerville Generating Station. Like a forty-five-minute drive back when we had cars, but it's a long hike now to make it there. When the coal plants were outlawed, the Reservation refused to close and the Feds moved in to force the compliance. It wasn't pretty," he explained.

I nodded once as I listened, "I heard rumors but no specifics."

Sal went on, "The men that worked there were slaughtered, and that left a great many sons and daughters, wives and mothers back on the Reservation in a fury. They can't race in there seeking revenge or they'll be gunned down as well. It was the financial center of the area and now they're left high and dry living off the promises of the Federal Government. It is well-known that they are putting all their resources into the big cities to keep control there. The Reservation has been left to starve and fend for themselves."

I could feel a pit in my stomach growing as the story went on.

Sal added, "We're not going to plan any stupid revenge attack on the plant, but we need to know what's going on there right now. We want you to recon the facility. Get near it, get pictures with a camera we have and get numbers of Feds on the site. Perhaps how and where they patrol the area, the types and locations of their defenses."

I nodded, "I should be able to do that. Yeah." I answered back, "I can do it."

Sal looked happy with my answer, "Good," he nodded with a smile, "good."

Sal looked over to Tony, "Can you get the camera for him please?"

Tony nodded and left his position at the door, heading down the hallway.

Not being blocked in now, things felt a whole lot better and I waited for Tony to return.

Sal added another piece of wood to the fireplace just before. Tony came back with a small case and handed it to me, "Here you go."

"Thanks," I offered back and took the case, tucking it into a pocket on the leg of my pants.

I then looked to Sal, "I'd like to head there now. Any specific directions or things I should know?"

Sal nodded as he stepped closer, "I can give you a week to get there and back with the pictures." He paused, "You think you can manage that?"

I did the math in my head. Thirty-five miles cross-country on flat prairie land was still a ten hour walk one way. That didn't account for trying to stay in the woods and only traveling at night when the woods gave way to the open highland desert about a third of the way there.

I would need to go back home and supply for a longer time away with food and water. I could head out first thing in the morning.

I needed to double check my maps, but I had studied them quite a bit over the last several months. I was certain that after about four hours steady walk through the woods the trees would stop as the land dropped off into the highland deserts. Then it was open land with ditches and rain runoff gullies as the only thing to hide yourself when going over land.

It should only take me four hours to reach the highland desert and then I'd be exposed during the daylight. I would want to hit that location at or just after dark so that I could go right into the open with the cover of darkness hiding me. From sunset to sunrise was 11 hours, so I should be able to get all the way there before sunrise on that first day. I'd need to hide somewhere during the day and then come out again at night. Sneaking around the area would take forever, slow going, stopping, looking, and listening and then moving again. That work was tedious and took a bunch of time. That might take the entire night all on its own. Then hide the next morning and sleep through the day and the next night would travel all the way back.

With the math and plan worked out in my head I nodded to Sal, "I can make it happen," and I held out my gloved right hand to shake on it and make it official.

Sal and I shook on the arrangement.

I asked as I prepared to leave, "you sure John is going to be okay?"

Sal nodded yes and his face showed appreciation that I asked about him and was concerned, "The kid is young and he's tough, he will pull through."

I gave Sal a curt nod and then turned and headed out the door into the darkness of the farmyard.

It was too far away to get Megan on the radio. I would have to get back about a third of the way before I could let her know I was okay. It had been over the one-hour check-in call. I was worried about her concern.

I looked around as I walked across the farmyard. Two story farm house behind me, barn ahead and to the left about 50 yards. The doors of the barn were closed and the gabble doors high on the peaks were also closed. A dim light showed from the cracks between the vertical boards, but it was dim.

It was already dark as I walked across the gravel driveway. Near the barn was an old tractor with tall grass grown up under and around it from lack of use. On the back side of the barn, I could hear the soft murmurs of chickens inside a roosting shed. The shed and chicken yard was fenced in with chicken wire and over the top as well to keep out the hawks and owls. I figured if things went well, perhaps I could buy or earn a few chickens off from them to add to our homestead.

I didn't want to lurk around and appear as if I was scoping out the place. They were probably watching me as I left. I took the exact route towards the trees we had emerged from together, so I didn't give them any hint on where I lived.

It got significantly darker once I got inside the tree line. I had to slow down to dodge pine tree limbs and bare twigs on the branches that tried to find their way to my eyes with every step.

I wanted to make sure I wasn't followed back home so after half way back to where I met John, and the killed Fed was at, I turned west. My plan was to follow the terrain, gradually work south across the creek bed and then head south after I was sure I wasn't being followed.

It was slower traveling in the dark and I found myself stopping more often than before, listening, and looking around. It was mostly listening that was being the most helpful right now. The creatures in the woods woke up for their night hunting. They had an entirely different set of noises from the way things were in the daylight.

I walked 30 minutes after turning west, stopping three times along the way to listen to see if I was being followed. I then turned south down the ridge line until I reached the creek bed at the bottom. The creek bed was dry now. Normal for this time of year, and the rocks I had to cross were loose. I took out my flashlight and flipped on the red LED option so I could have just enough light to see my footing as I crossed. The trees in this area escaped the fire so they made great concealment for me again. Slipping into the pines, I slowly worked my way up the opposite slope.

It was another 30 minutes of following the terrain south before I picked a higher rise and climbed to the top to get a radio call back home.

The night sky was black, so deep and dark I had to pause. Even so many months later of living in the mountains, it still took my breath away not to have the light pollution of the greater Phoenix area muddling up the night sky and dulling the stars.

Here, the stars were vibrant and alive. It was times like this, that I felt all those years living in the city were like with a pillowcase over my head, and thinking that was normal.

Jack: Mama Bear, this is Hawk One, do you copy?
Megan: Where have you been!?!
Jack: Sorry Mama Bear, got out of range of the radios.
            I will be home in one hour to fill you in.
Megan: Okay, be careful.
Jack: Roger that, Hawk One Out.

Okay, that made me feel a lot better that she didn't have to worry any more. Being down in that bunker without knowing what was going on would have been a killer for me to deal with if it was her out away from home.

The remainder of my return to the homestead was without any shocking discoveries and issues. I was going to be nice and sore though. Certainly, I was going to sleep solid through the night with as much climbing up and down these ridge lines as I was doing.

The concealment of the trees dropped off about half-way home where the fire had passed through. I picked up the pace at that point and tried to stay in the valleys. I did not want to silhouette myself against the night sky.

Finally, back on our property, I keyed up the radio again.

Jack: Mama Bear, this is Hawk One, do you copy?
Megan: I hear you, you almost home?

Jack:	Affirmative Mama Bear, you should see me in less than a minute. I don't want to say what direction to watch because people are listening to the radio and I don't want anyone to know what direction I went to get home.
Megan:	Okay, makes sense.
Megan:	Oh, I see you now, see you soon love.

I did a walk around our property to check on things and take a look at and around the house. I then made my way into the shed, down the hatch and into the bunker where Riley was skittering about my ankles with joy and Megan was there to greet me with a big hug. Wow, this apocalyptic life sure has its perks.

Chapter Six (Megan)
Assessing the Damage

October 13

I picked up Riley as the tears started to come down my face and held her close to me as we went back into the bunker. I sealed the heavy air-tight door closed again.

I hurried to get to the monitors and flip them on so I could see outside and watched as Jack turned and looked at the camera, smiled at me and blew me a kiss. That's when I lost it and just started sobbing.

I watched Jack move off checking things around the house through tear filled eyes. Poor little Riley kept trying to lick my face and comfort me, confused about it all. I offered her frequent smiles and tried to sound calm and happy, but I think she knew it was all fake.

It looked like the air was clean enough to breathe without the gas masks so I figured I could go up and take care of some things for a few hours before sunset came. It would help to keep my mind off things.

Once Jack was off and out of view of the cameras I got up and started to take care of the dishes from our meal. Cleaning was something I did when I was stressed. Things these days were kept spotless.

Jack's voice came over the radio at the communications table:

Jack: Testing, you hear me baby?

I rushed over from the sink and snatched up the radio and pushed the button.

Megan: Yep, sounds very clear.
Jack: Okay, I will check back in every hour or if something comes up.

It felt like a lifeboat in the middle of the ocean to hear his voice.

Megan: Okay, I'll be here.

I put the radio back down on the desk and made sure the wire plugging into the side. I was concerned it may have pulled loose when I snatched it up. The wire ran into the wall and then up and out of the bunker to where Jack had installed an external antenna high up in a tree. Without the antenna, I'd never be able to contact anyone with the radios here below-ground.

It didn't take long to finish cleaning up after the meal, putting things away, and stowing the garbage. Riley was getting anxious for another restroom break by the time I had things all managed in the bunker, so I decided I would get prepared to head up to the surface for a look around before it got too dark outside.

I didn't need to get all geared up as much as Jack. I didn't plan on venturing far from the homestead, so I wouldn't need to bring much water or food, which were much of the weight and space needed for a distant excursion.

I did pack a small backpack of medical supplies just in case. I filled the water bladder in the pack to keep hydrated and I brought a pair of binoculars, extra ammo for the .357 magnum revolver, and the 12-gauge shotgun I would keep over my shoulder on its strap.

I disconnected the radio from the external antenna and clipped it on my belt and then moved towards the exit.

Riley got more anxious the closer I came to be prepared. As I started walking through the bunk room, she was in full play mode, hopping around and darting back and forth.

When I broke the seal on the air-tight door it surprised me how preserved that smell of the forest fire still lingered in the decontamination room. I flipped the light switch to the LED lights inside the bunker and it went pitch black before I turned on the switch for the decontamination room.

Riley hopped over the door threshold and out of the bunker before I closed the door and latched it tight again.

It was a little steep of a climb for Riley to head up the stairs on her own. She was just a tiny little lapdog of eight pounds, she had her limitations. I snatched her up in my left arm and held onto the handrail with my right and moved on up the steep stairway to the hatch at the top.

Jack had closed the lid down tight from the top, but the extra levers below had been left open so that he could get back in. The concealed lever in the wall on the top was the only thing keeping someone from opening the hatch from above. I pondered if I should have turned the extra locking cams closed once Jack had left. I am pretty sure I wouldn't forget that again.

I pulled the lever that released the heavy hatch and it started to hiss upward on its hydraulic arms until it was fully upright. I raised Riley up, set her on the shed floor and then climbed out myself.

I took a deep breath and could still smell the effects of the fire, but the smoke was gone now, and it was easy enough to breathe without the gas mask.

I pushed the bunker trap door down against the force of the hydraulic arms slowly. It took several seconds of leaning on the top of the door to get it to ease down into the shed floor and disappear, become part of the normal wood floor again.

I opened the metal panel to the left of the solar charge control equipment to reveal a camera monitor and pressed the power button to turn it on. Under the monitor, I pressed the buttons that cycled through the different camera feeds until I was sure there was no ambush outside waiting for me and then I shut off the monitor, closed the panel, and went outside with Riley.

Riley was cautious at first, testing the ground with her paws carefully as the bits of pine needles and dry ash from the fire had settled down. She started to venture out a bit more bravely as time went on, though with infrequent bits of caution when she found a spot that was still hot to the touch.

I emerged from the shed with the shotgun at the ready. It didn't have slugs in it, but 00-buck, so my range was going to be reduced to about 50 yards. It could mess someone up at 100 yards well, at half that range I was very confident it would deal with any threat the most effectively.

Everything was quiet and tranquil. The birds hadn't come back yet, so there was an eerie silence that was unsettling.

After a short walk around the property with the shotgun at the ready, I shouldered the gun and went to check out Jordan's truck.

There were some melted plastic tarp blobs on the truck that would probably leave permanent marks on the paint job, but for the most part the truck survived nicely. The battery of course was still in the shed on the charger, ready to be put into the truck in an emergency if we were forced to get it out of hiding and use it.

I pulled the scraps of tarp together into a big ball and put it in the bed of the truck.

Riley seemed to have found a small vole in the garden as she yipped at it and hopped back and lunged forward playing with it as it stuck it's nose up out from its tunnel in the ground. I couldn't help but smile at the little dog, she brought such joy to us every day.

The house was my next thing to check on and Riley decided to join me on this one, abandoning her little rodent companion to dash inside after I opened the door.

The house held the smell of the forest fire strong, so I took the time to move through the house and open all the windows and let it air out. It was going to have that smell of a campfire for weeks to come, I think. That charcoal smell would be the new normal until some rain or new vegetation came to start covering things up again.

Up in the house now, I flipped on the CB-Radio and turned it to Channel 17. Our neighbors, Todd, and Jill McVeenson, lived one mile, down the entrance road at the intersection of the next crossroad. Todd and Jill were a little older than us and had been living up here in the mountains for years before we moved into the area. They were more established, with a metal pole barn, some horses, a chicken coop, some goats, and some rabbits. They had a nice German Shepherd that Jack was in love with that he would sneak treats to whenever we went to visit them.

I tried to talk to Jill every couple of weeks on the radio, just to chat about life. Jack and I tried to walk down to visit them every couple of weeks.

Jack had been negotiating with Todd to get a few chickens and a few rabbits, but they hadn't figured out the exact details to agree on yet. The fire started up and both our families started concentrating all out time on trying to get last minute preparations for the fire sweeping through our lands.

I squeezed the microphone to push in the button on the side and called out over the radio for Jill, "Farmer Jane, this is Mama Bear, do you copy?

I waited a while, and then a while longer. I started to get a strange feeling. It was taking a bit long.

I tried again, "Farmer Jane, this is Mama Bear, do you copy?"

Silence

I waited a few minutes and tried again, twice. They could be busy cleaning up after the fire and repairing things that got damaged and may not be near the radio. It wasn't anything to get alarmed about yet.

I left the windows to the house open and then I turned my attention to the garden to try to salvage and take inventory of what survived the fire.

I confirmed the corn was a complete loss. It was nearly harvest time for the corn, so the stalks had already turned brown and brittle before the fire came. We probably should have just yanked off the ears of corn before the fire came through. Again, hindsight taught us another lesson not to forget the next time.

The potatoes could probably be dug up. In a couple weeks they were going to be harvested anyway. We had already had several pickings of the green beans and peppers. Those were already canned and stored away, so the loss of those plants to the fire was not a disappointment. Several of the onions had already been dug up as they grew large enough to pull up and take. A few remained of the onions withered and cooked from the heat of the fire. I could go down the row just pulling those out and putting them in buckets.

There was a copious amount of work to do in the garden that would keep me busy for a couple days, a solid day if Jack was here to help me.

I tried the radio to call Jill again but still got no response. It wasn't unheard of to go several attempts before I was able to get her on the radio, but with each attempt a small pit grew in my stomach that didn't feel right. The fire sweeping through our property and then heading towards them made me nervous. I just wanted to hear her voice and know that she and Todd were okay.

I'd try back again at sunset before I went down into the bunker for the night. Maybe again after that, from the radio down in the bunker as well.

As I left the cabin and closed the door behind me, I turned to head for the side of the house where we have our shovels, rakes, hoes, and things hanging on hooks on the side of the house. It is where we keep the buckets, the wheelbarrow and various things stored as well.

Jack was planning on building a sloped roof off the side of the house to shelter the tools and the equipment. Someday, the plan was to wall in the sides to make a sort of carriage house or small garage to keep the equipment safe from the rain and weather. He hadn't been able to find the supplies of wood yet to make that happen.

As I rounded the corner and stepped off the front porch, Jack called me on the radio.

Jack's voice came across clear from the radio clipped on my hip.

Jack: Mama Bear, this is Hawk One, do you copy?

I fumbled quickly to get the radio off my belt and lift it up and squeeze the button to talk.

Megan: Yes, I hear you.

Jack appeared tired, perhaps stressed.

Jack: I will contact you again in one hour.

He sounded distant, distracted, and very focused.

Megan: Okay

I tried to keep my voice sounding uplifting and supportive.

I clipped the radio back on my belt with a smile and got back to work. I decided it would be easier to use the wheelbarrow to collect the onions, so I got it and a hoe and made my way to the garden. I started pulling up the onions and filling the wheelbarrow as I went.

About half-way through the row of onions I was interrupted by another call on the radio.

Jack's voice called me again.

Jack: Mama Bear, this is Hawk One, do you copy?

I was quick to get the radio this time and called back.

Megan: I hear you.

Jack's voice seemed more relieved now. I could tell that getting closer to home made him feel better.

Jack: Okay, thank you baby. (a small pause), I love
                you.

What a sap, so I responded

Megan: I love you too Honey.

I clipped the radio back on my belt and stood there a moment to take a break and sip water out of the camelback tube. Riley was back playing with her vole and enjoying her new friend.

I only had a half hour before sunset, and it seemed I could finish digging up all the onions in about that same time if I kept hard at it and didn't get distracted.

As I returned to flipping the onions up out of the ground with the hoe and collecting them up for the wheelbarrow, I couldn't help but let my mind drift to when I first met Jack.

I met Jack at church, when I was in Junior Highschool, when he came to Sault Ste. Marie to attend Lake Superior State College (the next year they would become a University). Our new pastor had come from Jack's hometown just a couple years before to lead our church.

Jack had been raised several years in the Wesleyan church by our new pastor in that tiny little town he was raised in. Coming to college in a bigger city was quite daunting to him. The fact that he knew the pastor of our church, it was a place he could go when stressed out or worried. He could grab onto a lifeline if things got too much for him through the school year.

He of course, attended the college aged Bible studies and classes, and I was stuck in the younger classes. I knew early on that I was going to marry this guy. So much so, that during that first year, I came right up to his mother when she was visiting on the weekend and told her I was going to marry her son. It was bold, audacious, but it was clear and there was no doubt in my mind.

Jack didn't jump on that train with me right away. We dated in a strange sort of way for a few months. He was only seventeen at the time and I was quite a bit younger than him. The relationship was quite innocent by today's standards. We would sit close on the couch to watch a television show or hold hands on a couples-skate roller skating at a youth group outing. Mostly, it was just sharing time together.

Jack had been on/off dating a girl through his entire junior-high and high school from his hometown for five years and he was still shell shocked and messed up about that falling apart. He hadn't planned on going to college until that relationship blew up, so his senior year was putting all his effort into getting perfect grades in school, suddenly caring about his classes to prove he could make it in college to the admissions boards. Even so, LSSU admitted him under a probationary period to prove that he could handle college classes. He was a meager C-Student until he focused his efforts and became an A-Student his senior year.

He made the grades in college when he started in the fall, but he really had to put a great amount of work in to getting the grades. The foundation of many of the classes that the other college students took for granted, Jack was learning for the first time.

The other students had spent years building up the basic foundations of math, writing, and knowledge by studying hard through high school to prepare themselves for college.

Jack had let these years of high school education slip by while daydreaming about his high school girlfriend, basketball, baseball, camping and working on the various farms to make money. Jack had to put in hours every night to study, work on extra reading, and projects to hammer into his head what the other students seemed to understand and master readily.

It was smart for the college to put Jack on probation. Not many students could have flipped the switch the way he did his senior year and kept up the effort to dig out of the educational hole he was in when he started his freshman year of college.

Our innocent little relationship didn't last long that first year though. His college friends, the guys, really laid into him hard calling him a cradle robber and teasing him without mercy. He was already rather young starting out in college at seventeen, and being behind in all the classes while his friends skated by with little effort.

The pressure from them was more than he could deal with, and while we were both away with the youth group at a church event in Grand Rapids, he dropped it on me that he just wanted to be friends.

I was young at the time and didn't take it very well. It was pretty much a crushing blow that made me furious with him. I knew I was going to marry him, that we would be happy together for the rest of our lives. Why was he being so stupid and messing it all up?

It took a couple years, as he went through his sophomore year and Junior year, dating another college girl. She was about a year older than him, this of course made me feel my plans with him were never going to happen. I didn't know how we were going to get back together.

Jack appeared to have moved on and fell head over heels for this new girl, and that just fanned the flames of my anger. How could he so readily get over what we had and move on to someone new? Did he ever really care about me? I had some issues over the situation for a long time.

I didn't much care for school myself. I was there to see friends and could not care less about the actual schooling that was supposed to be going on.

I was a normal high school girl with drama with my friends. We lived for the dances on Friday nights, meeting at Taco Bell, and just hanging out. We didn't have a big mall to gather at. Sault Ste. Marie was stretched out along some main roads for miles and the big city concept of a mall never made it that far north to the Canadian border.

All my friends were from church, or once removed from church; friends of those that I knew from church.

I went on a few dates, but nothing seemed to stick. Until; Jack woke up and came back to me like I knew was going to happen someday.

At the beginning of his senior year at the university, she left him. "Left him", is a rather polite way of saying she dumped him without a word, dropped off everything he ever gave her to his parents' home and vanished from his life, never to be seen again. He was shattered by that. He didn't know 'why' or what he had done wrong.

Still, Jack has moved on and found love with me. Everything has worked out for the best. It just took some time and drama to get him back to me.

I know that she is still an empty hole in his life; not knowing what went wrong with that entire relationship. I am confident though, that he is glad it turned out the way it has. But I know it's like a nagging question that will never be answered that annoys him still.

He was a real mess his Senior year, in a daze most of the time. It was like a shell-shocked soldier back from a war. He appeared a bit hollow; like he really wasn't inside when you looked in his eyes. I guess I probably looked the same way when he broke up with me in Grand Rapids a few years before. I was probably a bit more of a Pitbull in my response though. He was more of a wispy ghost, floating around lost.

We never started dating his senior year, but we at least started being able to be in the same room again more civilly.

I was in the high school group now as a junior and he was a senior in the college group so most of the gatherings at church we were not in the same room. We would pass on occasion and as more time went on, I could feel less of a desire to stab him in the eye with a long narrow knife than I did before. Seriously, I had some real anger issues with him for a couple years there.

After he graduated from LSSU, he went back down to the lower peninsula of Michigan to find work. He spent all summer sending out resumes and trying to get job interviews while he worked at the State Park as a park ranger for a summer job.

He wasn't finding any luck getting a job in his forestry and wildlife degree, and when the winter came, he found himself working in a factory organizing their inventory and working into a job as a warehouse manager.

I suppose it could have turned into a rather steady and dependable job if he would have stuck with it, but the economy at the time was hard going for everyone. People that had been with the factory for thirty years were being 'let go' and that scared him. If he was ever to get a family, he needed to be sure he had a job that was dependable.

It wasn't much after that, that he went off and joined the United States Air Force. It was mid-January when he flew down to San Antonio, Texas for basic training.

Six-months or so after basic training, he started writing me letters. This was before email or cell phones, so about every other week I'd get a letter from him and I'd write him back. It was basic, and it wasn't like he was asking to restart our relationship.

In fact, the dweeb kept asking about one of my best friends and asking how she was doing in each letter. I wasn't sure how thick Jack's head was, but he was proving to be dense in coming around to our destiny together.

For over four years, as I went into college to work on my business degree, we kept writing and sharing our experiences with each other. He even made some cassette tapes from music he bought on CD's in Germany while stationed there. He would record his voice like he was a radio station DJ between songs. It was quite refreshing to see him enjoying life again, and not being so depressed.

I still was not dating anyone. I didn't see any real point in it, Jack would wake up one day and figure it out and we would be together, I knew it.

In the summer, after Jack had put in four years with the Air Force, he got out and moved back to Michigan. Jack invited me down to spend time with him. We went together with his parents to watch the fireworks on the 4th of July.

It took him long enough, but finally we got to cuddle and hold hands in the back seat of his parent's car on the ride home. I was starting to doubt if the dweeb was ever going to figure it out.

He had only been home for a couple weeks when a town down in the southern part of lower Michigan wanted to hire him for a job in a city drinking water treatment plant. A day later, he was moving into an apartment and starting his new life about five hours south of where I lived in the Soo.

Man, he sure wasn't making any of this easy.

We started hanging out more often, after he began working for the town. He got a motorcycle, and would drive up on the weekends to visit, sleeping at my parents' house while I was with my roommate renting a little house elsewhere in the city.

I knew he was finally figuring it out when he rode that motorcycle five hours north to visit on a Friday night and then drive back five hours on a Sunday afternoon. It was about time.

When the winter turned too cold and the snow and ice claimed its grip on the roads, he still came up in his little red Chevy pickup truck. He tried teaching me how to drive the stick-shift but that didn't work out very well. My roommate learned fast; but I got frustrated with it jerking and chugging as I tried to work my feet and hands all simultaneously. I finally just gave up on it.

It was that October that he came up north for a friend's wedding. After we took off together to spend the day on Mackinac Island. Half-way down to St. Ignace on the highway I had to come out and just ask him plainly, "Are we dating? People keep asking me."

It was rather awkward honestly. We had been hanging out and spending time with each other. He was driving up every week to see me. I think we were dating, but I don't think it ever clicked in his brain that he was dating me.

He grinned when I asked him, considered for a moment, and nodded, "Yeah, I think we are."

About 20 seconds later, he reached his hand over, "Well, since we are dating, we should probably hold hands."

It was hilarious the way he said it, and we spent the entire day laughing, standing close, and cuddling on the island. It was before selfies were a thing. It was even before digital cameras. If we had those things, it would have been an incredible barrage of posts on Facebook if such a thing existed at the time.

It was after that, when I would come visit him on occasion at his apartment. It was a real stupid thing to do because of the temptation for sex. Though the kissing got intense, we were both committed enough not to let it get too crazy. Still though, looking back at it, I wouldn't make that same choice again. It was just asking for trouble.

The next spring, he proposed to me while I was at work with the bank as a mortgage processor. It was a madhouse after that because we set the wedding for October. Only six months to prepare for a wedding is insane.

October 11, 1997 we were married. We don't have any real traumatic stories like many do about splitting up, infidelity or near divorce issues. Divorce was known from day one never to be an option. It wasn't even thought about as a distant option in some far-off place. It wasn't an option at all and never would be. With that firmly put in our heads, it changed every argument or disagreement into something we were working through together. There was no emergency get-out-of-jail-free card, everything life threw at us was a challenge for us to work together, as a team.

Sure, there were some arguments and frustration in the first years where he could be a serious jerk. Those were short-lived and quickly passed. Looking back, well over 20 years together, I can say we never even came close to leaving each other. It just wasn't an option that even came into our heads.

I got interrupted from my walk down memory lane when I reached the end of the row of onions and put the last of them in the heaped-up wheelbarrow.

It took some doing to keep the wheelbarrow from tipping over as I turned it around and eased it back through the garden to the front porch. I set it down with a sigh and stood up to ease the pain in my back. I planned on waiting until tomorrow to spread them on the porch and wash them off with the hose. For now, I needed to close the windows in the house, lock things all back up again and get down in the bunker for the night.

Riley kept closer to me as darkness started to claim the mountain. She did her business out in the yard as I locked up the front door of the cabin and then made my way to the shed.

We slipped into the shed, locked things up the right way and then made our way down inside and back to the normal bunker life below.

I plugged in the radio to the external antenna and then gave Riley a little rawhide chew stick while I got my things together for a shower.

Keeping busy up top in the garden, and on the projects on the homestead worked well in keeping my mind off from what Jack was doing. Now, as I stepped into the shower and pulled the curtain shut, the worry for him flooded back as fast as the water flowing out of the shower head.

I jumped to my default, prayer. While the hot water came over me, I started to wash away the dirt of the garden and the sweat from the hard work above. I kept in a constant conversation with God aloud in the shower.

I had heard Jack months before and thought he was talking to someone in the trees. It surprised me a bit to find him alone when I came near. He was talking to God as if he was right there in front of him and they were conversing back and forth. That stuck with me and I found my prayers were less closed eyed now and more talking to a dear friend that was right there next to me.

It had become a new family joke. Several times we would think the other was talking to the other and ask what they said, only to get a response that they were talking to God.

The default worked as it always did. The more I talked with God the more I relaxed and was able to cope with the situation.

The shower was amazing. Being able to have a hot shower down here in this cold bunker was incredible. Jack had his heart set on getting a bunker for many years before it happened, and I have to say he went about it the right way. There were shortcuts that were cheaper we could have done. There were buried semi-truck type metal boxes but those were not as safe and had problems with caving in sides from the ground pressure. There were many ideas of cheap bunkers under $10,000 but each of them had major concerns of safety. Spending a bit more and getting his bunker from Atlas Bunkers out of Texas was a very smart move. It came fully finished with electric wires, plumbing, walls installed, bunk beds, even the leather couch and table and bench seat and fully finished kitchen and the bed in the master bedroom. The only thing we had to add were our supplies, water barrels, bedding and the solar panel batteries and camera options. The basic core shelter was laid in place by the company and there was no second guessing if something was going to go wrong down the road. It was the difference between buying a new car and buying a homemade vehicle a guy made from scrap metal in the barn.

Riley was fully involved with chewing her rawhide stick in the living quarters when I came out of the shower and made my way back to the opposite end of the bunker wrapped in a towel.

When I passed the communications desk, I checked the radio to ensure it was charged and plugged in and then continued back to get into some pajamas.

I unloaded the shotgun and glanced up at the clock and saw that it was ten minutes after the hour. Jack should have radioed back and checked in by now. On a normal day it would just be causing moderate concern, but going out and meeting people after dark with all the drama behind setting up the meeting, this was down-right nerve wracking.

I didn't want to call him on the radio. If I called him and the sound of me calling him revealed his position while he was hiding, that would be supremely bad, so I waited.

Poor Riley had to pay the price for my anxiety. I filled up the sink with warm water and grabbed the soap. Poor little Riley got a bath in the sink to keep my mind off from waiting for the radio call.

The poor little pup; it was cold down here in the bunker and after the bath she was soaked. No amount of shaking and running around trying to rub against the furniture to dry off was working. I wrapped her tight in a fresh towel, held her close to me and got in the bed under the covers to warm her up properly. It was the only way to get her to stop shaking.

This was a pleasant diversion for about half an hour. However, after that, the anxiety started to find its way back while I waited.

Riley was content to be left under the blankets, in the warmth we had created there, and she stayed as I got up out of the bed. I pulled my journal from the bookshelf and took a seat at the communications desk to write down my thoughts of the day and the things that I had done. I also started to make a checklist of the things we needed to do around the homestead.

- Wash onion, dry, bag, and put in the decontamination room.
- Have Jack make wood shelves in the decontamination room for pantry storage.
- Jack to make a sloped roof/shed at side of house for tools/equipment.
- Harvest potatoes
- Jack to make coop for chickens. Finish deal with Todd to get chickens.
- Jack to make a hutch for rabbits. Finish deal with Todd to get rabbits.
- Find pine seedlings from the north to transplant them around the house to jumpstart growing trees near the house.
- Visit Todd and Jill if they do not answer CB-Radio soon.

I finished this last entry, closed my journal, and tried the CB-Radio again on channel 17.

Megan: Farmer Jane, this is Mama Bear, do you read?

Silence

Three more times I tried and then I sat back with a frown. This wasn't an encouraging thing. It was well after dark now and they should be back in the house for certain by this time in the evening. I decided to try once more in the morning, if they didn't respond, I was going down there first thing in the morning to see what was going on.

Looking over at the radio, it appeared to look back at me and mock me. It had a conversation from Jack waiting for me but was just holding back to torture me. Stupid radio.

I left the journal open on the table so that I could talk to Jack about the checklist when he got back. Also, so I could remember to talk to him about the McVeenson's.

I found myself pacing from one end of the bunker to the other. A year or two earlier and it would have been me "getting in my steps" with my iWatch, trying to get into shape. Now, it was because my mind was racing in circles worrying about Jack.

On one of my countless laps back and forth, I was in the bedroom when I heard Jack's voice come across the radio. I ran across the bunker at a sprint to snatch up the radio.

Jack: Mama Bear, this is Hawk One, do you copy?

I slid to a stop in front of the table and snatched up the microphone.

Megan: Where have you Been!?!

Jack's voice seemed stressed.

Jack: Sorry Mama Bear, got out of range of the radios. I will be home in one hour to fill you in.

I knew my voice had come across with the emotional snap from my tension, so I tried to sound more loving this time.

Megan: Okay, be careful.
Jack: Roger that, Hawk One Out.

I put the radio down, and flopped into the chair, exhausted. Not so much from the walking workout, but from the mental fatigue. Riley managed to get out from under the blankets on the bed, hopped down to the floor, and skittered her way across the floor to my leg. She stood up on her hind legs and leaned against my knee to get picked up. I snatched her up and cuddled her as I laughed. The emotional roller coaster today was incredible.

Looking at the clock to note when to expect Jack's next radio call, I got up and started gathering our laundry together. I began hand washing them in the kitchen sink and hanging them on a rope to dry in the decontamination room. I turned on an mp3 player that was plugged into the bunker speakers to listen to some worship music. I found I calmed down fast when getting my mind on God and less on the situation.

I was coming in from the decontamination room after hanging up the last of the clothes when the radio woke up again.

Jack's voice filled the bunker on the speaker.

Jack: Mama Bear, this is Hawk One, do you copy?

I raced through the bunk room, to the table with the electronics and grabbed the microphone.

Megan: I hear you, you almost home?
Jack tried to comfort me with encouraging news.

Jack: Affirmative Mama Bear, you should see me in less than a minute. I don't want to say what direction to watch because people are listening to the radio and I don't want anyone to know what direction I went to get home.
Megan: Okay, that makes sense.

That's when I spotted him on one of the camera monitors.

Megan: Oh, I see you now, see you soon love.

I was watching the monitors and spotted Jack on one of them. He had turned on his headlamp on a dim red setting and I caught a brief red glimmer in the distance.

Moving from the communications desk with Riley, both of us were anxious from hearing Jack's voice on the radio. We waited in the decontamination room for him to come in.

It felt like several minutes for Jack to get from the open hatch above, to the bottom next to me. I'm sure it was just seconds, but it sure didn't seem that fast.

I latched onto Jack when he got down next to me in a huge hug and didn't let him go for a long time. He smelled of dirt, wood smoke and sweat, but I didn't care, he was home, he was safe.

Chapter Seven (Jack)
Love, Spies and Drones

October 13

I picked up Riley after Megan allowed the hug to break off, and let the dog lick me, getting the salty sweat off my face. Megan led the way into the bunker and closed the door, levering the locking cams on the airtight door while I played with Riley and chuckled at the little wiggling dog.

I was about to head deeper into the bunker with the dog when Megan took a quick step in front of me, blocking my way, "I don't think so babe. You strip down right here and get those nasty clothes off and take a shower before you come in any farther."

I bit the inside of my cheek to keep from saying anything and forced a smile and a nod. It was important that Megan had some control over something in this world; and her home. Even if her new home was a bunker, it was a place she needed to have some rules, where life could be managed. I didn't fault her in the slightest. We had been together long enough that I knew it wasn't about controlling me, but just trying to get a grip on a life that was spinning in chaos. I did not need to add to the chaos, I needed to be willing to help create calm and predictability. It wasn't a bad unspoken agreement we had. Calm in the chaos of the world also benefited me. Who wants to come home to a place of chaos? No, it was best this way for everyone.

Megan took Riley from me and stood where the hall started going deeper into the bunker, to chat with me as I washed up. I leaned my AR-15 against the wall, unbuckled my belt with my pistol and pouches and hung that on a hook on the wall above the rifle. Taking off my helmet, and armored vest, I began shedding a significant amount of weight. The exhaustion of the trip was starting to hit me hard.

Megan stood there about 30 seconds while I was shedding the gear before the debriefing started.

"Okay," she began, "You left here and started walking to the north. What happened next?"

I offered her a grin as I hung the weapons belt up on the hook on the wall, "I went along the route we had planned without any issues. When I got near the clearing where the meeting was supposed to take place, I saw a Federal Scouting ATV at the far western edge near the trees, where a dry creek bed came in from the lake."

Megan's eyes widened at the mention of the federal vehicle. I knew I couldn't keep any of the details from her to protect her from anxiety. She also, was going to be out of the bunker at times and needed to be aware of all the threats that were in the area.

I continued, "There was a federal officer killed in the tall grass and then I found a teenage boy in the grass that had been stabbed. It looked like the two had been in a fight. The kid wouldn't let me tend to his stab wound so I took what I could off the federal officer," I offered as I pointed to my backpack on the floor," There was a 9mm pistol with three magazines, a handheld radio, a .308 sniper rifle with a nice scope and that medical kit pack."

Megan put Riley down and went to the pack, and began pulling those out, "I'll clean the pistol and make sure it works and is dependable, if you want to check the rifle later. We don't have a .308 like this so it's probably better than your Remington .270."

I nodded to Megan, "That's what I was thinking. I don't have a lot of ammo for it. With what is in it, and the extra ammo I got off the guy, we only have 30 rounds. It's a gun you don't rapid shoot and run through a lot of ammo, so 30 rounds could last a long while."

Megan pulled out the gear as I continued explaining what happened, "I helped the kid get into the trees as the sound of a truck approaching from the east was getting closer. It turns out, he was my contact for The Silent Majority and the ham radio meeting I was there to meet in the first place."

Megan unzipped the nice medical pack that I had picked up and stopped a moment to offer, "They could have been going to scout the area and set up an ambush to get you guys. Perhaps they heard the CB-Radio talk and figured out the meeting location."

I nodded to that with a frown, "I thought we were being pretty careful about setting up that meeting, jumping around the frequencies, but I guess the feds could have an auto scanning radio that just locks on to any transmitting frequency in the CB-Radio range and wouldn't have been tricked at all." I frowned at that, frustrated that we would always be behind the feds on tech, quality of gear, and assets.

I went on with the story, "I told him my name was Kirby, he said his was John. We got away from the ATV area and back near a farmhouse to the north where a guy named Tony came out and helped me get John to the farmhouse they have up there. They have a barn, a couple sheds and a main farmhouse, and water tank up there. At the farmhouse, there was an old fella named Sal and a woman I think was his wife, named Margaret."

I hesitated at this point because I knew what was coming next was going to upset Megan. She picked up on it instantly and gave me a look that said to stop delaying and get to it.

I sat down on the toilet, unzipped my boots, pulled them off, and started taking off my socks, pants, shirt, underwear and getting into the shower as I explained, "Sal has me doing a task for them so that I prove I am not with the Feds, by doing recon on a place and giving a report back to them. The old Apache coal power generation plant in Springerville is like thirty-seven miles cross country from here to the northeast and it's the target."

"37 miles?" Megan blurted out in protest.

I moved into the shower, "I know", I returned, "It's a long hike for sure and it's going to take several days to get there, do the job, get back with a report to Sal, and then get back here to you."

I could hear the tense tone in Megan's voice as the warm water of the shower came over my head, face, and down my body, "You can't be serious."

I spit some water off my face as I tried to talk under the deluge of water, while I was grabbing for the shampoo, "It's this, or we don't get a way to contact Jordan."

Megan didn't respond.

I went on, "I'll travel only during the dark and use the terrain to keep out of site. I'll cover up in the day, conceal my position, and just sleep and hide during the day. They gave me a digital camera to take pictures of the power plant when I get there. I'll try and move into a position during the night so that when it turns day, I can get pictures. Then I will just wait until it turns dark again, to sneak back out of the area and start working my way back."

My plan appeared to put Megan a bit more at ease, as I grabbed the bar of soap to wash up.

Megan fished around in my pack a bit more, "Ah, I have the camera. I'm going to go check on something." She got up and walked into the bunker, leaving me alone in the shower.

Hmm, what was she up to now?

I finished my shower, dried off and then roamed up through the bunker with a towel around my waist. I came through the bunk room and into the main living area where Megan was sitting at the communications table with the laptop opened and the camera on the table to its left.

Megan turned as I neared and smiled, "I'm running a file recovery program on their memory chip in the camera. It looks like there are several pictures that were deleted. They didn't hard wipe it."

About then, the program started bringing up several thumbnails of the pictures that had been deleted from the memory chip. It started reconstructing the photos back to their original state. A progress bar at the bottom, estimated the time needed to finish was 15 minutes.

I bent over just a bit to reach across Megan and point at the progress bar. I waited until she looked up to me. I met her eyes with a grin and a wink and then a glance back to the bedroom.

"For heaven's sake Jack," she refuted with a raised voice, "Is that all you think about?"

I nodded to her, "Yes, yes, it is."

I stepped back as she got up from the chair and kissed me, "Well, if I must."

The fifteen minutes sped up time like two teenagers in their parents' car on a date. We were tangled in a sweaty mess in the bed when the laptop let out a loud "Ding" sound. It had completed the reconstruction of the photos.

Grabbing what clothes were at hand, we dressed and then raced to the laptop while laughing. I kept trying to tickle Megan as we went, but she kept turning and slapping me because of how much she hated to be tickled. As we neared the laptop she slowed, and I got in a tickle at her ribs, she pivoted and laid a full force fist right into my face.

There was a flash of bright light, then the searing pain from her fist as I shook off the pain.

"I told you!" She reminded me of her rule, that I was never to tickle her.

"Fair enough," I relented, as the left side of my face began to redden.

We turned together to look at the laptop, I dropped into the chair to bring up the first picture, and then to flip through them one at a time. Megan stood behind me and rested her hands on my shoulders in a light massage.

My face burned with the punch still and I grimaced, I felt the inside of my left cheek where it had been forcefully smashed into my teeth.

The first picture was of the farmhouse in the living room. It was a picture of Sal, Tony and John sitting around a coffee table on the furniture playing cards with poker chips. It was obviously taken by Margaret.

The second picture was of a water pump partly disassembled. It was probably a picture done when repairing the pump. Before taking it apart any further, they wanted a proper picture of how it looked when it was put together the correct way.

The third picture was a bit dark and there was a great amount of straw or hay and a large beam like in a barn. It seemed a bit out of focus and there wasn't much to see in it.

The next picture though was a bit shocking and took both of us by surprise. It was Tony with a woman I had not seen in the barn in an obvious bit of homemade pornography. Megan reached over me to fast-forward to the next picture.

"Wait," I blurted out and grabbed her wrist to stop her.

In the background, something had caught my attention and I felt my heart accelerate fast. Not because of the lewd picture of the couple doing something that appeared physically impossible, but the tan colored ATV in the background.

"The ATV," I explained, then let go of Megan's wrist to reach for the mouse. I selected that portion of the photo and zoomed in, adjusted the lighting, resolution, and sharpened the editing of the photo.

G-13R5, it was a little fuzzy and grainy from the magnification of the photo, but it was the same plate number that was on the Feds ATV at the clearing.

I put my fingertip on the license plate and turned to look up at Megan, "That's the same ATV the fed had at the clearing."

"But how," Megan asked, "could they have a picture of the ATV in their barn before you saw the ATV in the clearing with John?"

We both knew the answer to that, even as she was saying it. Talking it out, appeared to help us put the bigger picture into play for each other.

I moved my hand back to the mouse, "Okay, so the plot thickens," I said with a bit of dry humor in my voice, "The ATV was a plant, and not a real fed scout vehicle. Or..."

Megan more clearly voiced it, "It was a Fed vehicle at one time, but these people got it, then used it to set up a scene to make you think a Fed agent was killed. They wanted you to think you might get blamed for it, if you were caught in the area, and used it to pressure you, and force you to trust them."

I clicked for the next picture and that didn't make things any better. Inside the barn, the next picture was at a slightly different angle of the two lovers, and in the picture was a tan colored Federal pickup truck.

I started to guess at the pieces aloud, "Okay, this woman with Tony, my guess she was driving the pickup truck when I came upon John and the ATV. It was to pressure us away from the area, to get John to safety." I paused with a sneer, "I bet John wasn't even hurt. They refused to let me tend to his wound and he wouldn't even let me help him at the ATV when I found him."

Megan nodded to that line of thinking, "If she was in the truck, she would probably wait until you guys were away. Those at the farm would radio to her when they saw you enter with John and Tony and then she would load the ATV up in the truck. She could then move away and wait until they radioed, that it was clear for her to come back, to the barn after you were gone."

I hummed, "Well then, who's the dead body?"

Megan shook her head, "A neighbor they didn't like, or a member of their own group that betrayed them? Maybe even a real Fed officer?"

I sighed a bit at all the twists and possibilities.

I flipped through more pictures a bit faster. The next ten or so were of Tony and what I assumed now was his wife. I guessed that John was their son from what I recalled of John's facial features, they seemed like a fit of Tony and this woman's faces convincingly.

Once getting past the homemade porn, there were some pictures with various members of the group posing with guns.

About the thirty-fifth picture though caused both Megan and I to jump back from the laptop and gasp. I slid back in the chair, Megan sidestepped and stepped back, "No way!" we both blurted out.

The laptop had a picture of our house. It was taken before the forest fire, and it was a picture where I was putting in one of the windows of the house, and Megan was putting up fencing around the garden. The area over the bunker was already smoothed and weathered with sprouts of vegetation in the garden already starting to come up. If this was the first, they had taken pictures, spying on us, then they wouldn't know about the bunker beneath. At least there was that going for us.

I scooched up further with the chair to the table, highlighted all the pictures with the mouse, and copied/pasted them onto the hard drive of the laptop. I wanted to ensure we had our own copies.

As I scrolled slowly through the other pictures of our neighbors, terrain taken from climbing up trees on the tops of hilltops, Megan pondered out loud, "If they have a picture of our place, and of us, then they know where we live now. I mean, you sneaking back home careful for them not to know where you live, they do anyway."

I responded with a nod, "We should assume they do. They may have not kept the pictures or have forgotten. But we should assume they kept copies of all these pictures from the camera on another computer. Once they met me, they went back to check all the pictures they had of the neighbors to see who I was."

Megan began to pace slowly behind me, as Riley jumped up on the dining table bench to sit and watch us. Megan offered additional ideas as she paced, "Tomorrow, I'm going down to Todd and Jill's to check in on them. They haven't been responding to any of my radio calls today."

I turned around a bit in the chair to look at her, "Do you want me to put off this recon job a day, and go down with you?"

Megan shook her head, "No, we need to get this done as soon as possible, so we can get in touch with Jordan. I'm sure they probably just had their radio wire melted in the fire or something simple."

Nodding to her, I turned back to the laptop and moved through the pictures. I made some sub-folders on the laptop for Neighbors, Terrain, The Silent Majority, and sorted the pictures into the different categories. It was helpful to keep some of the pictures. Some of the neighbors I didn't even know or had never seen. The pictures were rather informative and helpful. Also, when I did a 'right-click' on the photo the info for them had the GPS coordinates where the pictures were taken. With our map, we were able to narrow down each neighbor within a 1/4-mile range and put faces to each home and get a far better idea of who was around us.

Megan turned her attention to making a late dinner, "I assume you didn't eat while you were out?"

I nodded and glanced over my left shoulder to where she was in the kitchen area, "Just a little snack, I was too anxious to consider eating."

Megan nodded, "I'll make something really quick. You're probably going to sleep like the dead tonight, and you have a bunch of exhausting days coming up. I'll pack up some MRE's and other supplies for you tonight, so you don't have so much to prepare in the morning before you go."

I had to take a few moments just to watch her and appreciate her. I had to be one of the luckiest men in the world. She was hard-headed, and had her ideas, sure. However, she was everything I needed in a friend and in a wife. She was one of the least selfish people I had ever met. I guess that offset how I was. I worked hard not to be selfish, but my mind was always working on ways to make things better around the homestead and in the world. Recently, it wasn't so much the world. I had spent thirty plus years working to educate myself and engage those around me in political conversation, in hopes of heading off the gradual decline into socialism and communism I saw the country going. That had been a fruitless effort for most of my life. After everything fell apart and we fled to the mountains, it appeared every day was focused on day to day existence and trying to make us safer. It felt selfish. After decades of always being worried about the country, now I had given up on everyone else. The country had given up on God, centered their lives around their own pleasure, twisted perversions, and that had led them naturally down a path of destruction. To isolate myself mentally, I had now withdrawn into a circle where only Megan, Jordan and myself mattered. The rest of the world had stopped being a concern in the slightest. They literally, could and had gone to hell, and they were no longer important to me.

I knew it was a shameful way to think, and I could feel God whispering to me and trying to get my attention on how I could still contribute to shining his light in this dark world. It was going to have to be hidden though whatever I was to do. To own a Bible, to pray openly or even to mention God was a terrorist act and punishable by death.

Megan and I had grown closer to God in our studies and prayers, but Megan was far more social than I and it made me ache to know she may never see a church service with singing and worshiping God ever again.

Megan cleared her throat, "Jack... hello? You there?"

Apparently, I had just been staring at her and lost in thought, she was now repeating something to me that I had not heard.

I blinked a bit and came out of my trance, "Um, sorry, what's that love?"

Megan chuckled, "Wow, you were somewhere else, completely."

I grinned just a smidge, "Sorry about that."

Megan turned from the counter, with a sandwich on a plate and a glass of water, she carrying to the dining table, "Here you go."

Megan took over examining the pictures and organizing them while I took a seat at the table for my meal.

Megan considered aloud as she sorted the pictures, "You might want to bring your drone with you."

I swallowed the bite I was working on before responding, "That's a fantastic idea. Let's make sure the cellphone is recharged and the drone battery is fully charged. I'll bring along the folding solar panel for recharging while I'm out if needed."

Megan nodded to that, as she got up and went to retrieve the drone, cellphone, and started hooking things up on the communications table to recharge batteries, "You're sure the cellphone can't be tracked right?"

I nodded, "I'll have the cellular option turned off and only have Wi-Fi turned on. That's the signal the drone uses."

Megan sighed softly, "I wonder if the phones make you think the cellular is turned off, but it's really not. I hate the idea of them being able to find you if you turn your phone on to use the drone."

I finished up my sandwich and carried it over to the kitchen counter to clean it and put it away, "I can run the drone on its own controller, record the video, and photos on the data chip in the drone but I can't see what the drone is seeing. I might not be facing right, or have the camera looking in the right position to take pictures. I really have to use the phone to make sure I'm getting the information I need recorded correctly."

Megan pursed her lips in frustration, "I know... I just don't like it."

I put the plate back in the cupboard and came to stand behind Megan. I rested my hands on her shoulders as she finished up the last of the photos. Megan then did a hard clean and wipe on the data chip. This time so that the pictures could never be recovered again, "I'll be super careful. I am going to bring that ghillie suit that I made from the netting, and the dyed cloth strips, and use that to hide during the day, and sleep in the day. I'll only move at night, and I'll stay away from any farms or people all the way there and back."

Megan nodded a bit, as she finished the data chip, pulled it from the laptop and then powered down the computer. She closed its lid and then put the chip back into the camera.

Megan stood up from the desk, and looked around, "You go ahead and get to bed and get some sleep. I'm going to stay up and start packing for you and getting things ready for you."

I gave her a long kiss, a tight hug for a while, and then made my way back to the bedroom section of the bunker. Stripping back down, I fell into a deep sleep filled with unsettling dreams through the night.

Chapter Eight (Megan)
Interrogation, Pictures, and Planning

October 13

Jack had spent 18 months in Iraq working as a private contractor during the war and I thought I missed him horribly back then. Today, he was only gone for a few hours and it felt so much worse. I closed the bunker door tight. When I saw Jack turn to head past me, "I don't think so babe. You strip down right here, get those nasty clothes off, and take a shower before you come in any farther."

I could see Jack's eyes focus on me, his mind churning for what to say, but he then nodded with a forced smile. I took Riley from him, and he began to put his gear against the wall, take off his nasty clothes.

Okay, enough time, I had to know, "Okay, you left here and started walking to the north. What happened next?"

Jack explained how he followed the route we had laid out with the maps and how he came upon a clearing where they were supposed to meet and saw a Federal ATV there. I could feel my heart beating harder and I think he could see the stress building as the story continued.

Jack explained that he came across a Federal Officer who had been killed, and a teenage boy who was stabbed but still alive. This story did not sound encouraging at all so far. I prayed silently, that it would get more encouraging.

Jack said he got a sniper rifle, pistol, radio, and a medical kit off the guy and the ATV, and then helped the kid get away from that area as a truck was approaching from the east. Well, obviously, he got away safe or he wouldn't be here telling me this story, "I'll clean the pistol and make sure it works and is dependable if you want to check the rifle later. We don't have a .308 like this so it's probably better than your .270 for taking out."

He explained he only had 30 rounds for the new rifle, but it should be enough for his trip. I guess that made sense. You didn't spray down cover fire with a sniper rifle that much.

I knelt and started pulling out the gear from his pack as he explained a bit about the teenage boy. I looked up as I unzipped the medical pack, "They could have been going to scout the area and set up an ambush to get you guys. Perhaps heard the CB-Radio talk and figured out the meeting location."

Jack seemed as frustrated about the whole encounter, as I was hearing about it. He said he told the boy his name was Kirby, and the boy called himself John. Jack said he helped the kid get away, through the woods, to the north a nice long hike, to a farm. Along the way near the farm they came across a guy named Tony, who was from the farm and who helped him get John back to the farmhouse. An older guy named Sal and a woman named Margaret were there to meet them.

Jack sat down on the toilet to start removing his boots and paused a bit. The pause concerned me. Jack tended to worry about how I would take bad news and these pauses caused me to worry even more, because I knew what was coming next wasn't going to be pleasant.

Jack explained that it was indeed people from The Silent Majority, but that to earn their trust they were going to have Jack do a job for them. The job was to go on a several days hike, 37 miles away, to spy on a federal power plant they stole from the Apache tribe. He was to take pictures and then come back and report on what he learned to the group."

Jack got up, moved into the shower, and turned on the water, "You can't be serious," I blurted out. I wanted to launch into a great list of concerns, but Jack interrupted me.

"It's this," he explained, "or we don't get a way to contact Jordan.

Dang him, I didn't like it, but he was right.

Jack tried to calm me by explaining that he would only travel at night and hide in the daylight. At least he was thinking ahead of how to be the safest about it and how to get back home to me alive. He wasn't just haphazardly going to hike up there and get killed. I knew he would be as safe as he could, but it was even more safe if he just stayed here with me at home.

I found the camera in the pack and pulled it out, "Ah, I have the camera. I'm going to go check on something." I wanted to pull the data chip out of it and see if I could find any old pictures or information on it to help us.

While Jack was in the shower, I moved to the communications desk and sat down. I opened the laptop, turned it on and while it booted up, I found the data chip port on the camera and popped out the chip.

I had just put the chip into the laptop and was loading up a file recovery program when Jack came into the room from the bunk area. He must have taken a speed shower to finish up and get out here to me so quick, wrapped with a towel around his waist he came padding bare foot towards me with wet legs.

As Jack got closer, I turned and tried to offer him a smile, "I'm running a file recovery program on their memory chip in the camera. It looks like there are several pictures that were deleted to make more space. They didn't hard wipe it."

Jack was looking at the laptop with interest and as I turned back around, I could see some tiny little thumbnails coming up on the screen in the preliminary process of recovering the pictures that had been deleted.

Jack startled me just a bit as he leaned down over me and pointed at the progress bar and held his hand there. I looked up to him and he grinned at me, winked, me and then looked back to the bedroom.

"For heaven's sake", he had to be the most consistent and predictable man on the planet, "Is that all you think about?"

He nodded with a grin, "Yes, yes, it is," and then he stepped back as I got up from the chair.

I met his lips with a kiss reserved for the most private of moments, "Well, if I must."

We played in the bedroom until the laptop buzzed that it had completed its job. I grabbed my underwear and shirt and left the rest of things there on the floor to race Jack to the laptop. We were laughing like teens as he grabbed at me, trying to hold me so he could get in front and win.

When I got close to the table and slowed, he grabbed my ribs in his hands and tickled me. Without even thinking I turned, my right fist came spinning around to slam forcefully into the left side of his face with a CLAP of noise. His eyes briefly went distant before they focused again.

"I told you!", I warned him, my mind still in panic survival mode. Getting tickled was something that just completely unleashed a monster in me that would take over, like an instinct.

"Fair enough," he muttered with a painful grin, as the left side of his face began to turn red.

Phew, okay, he'd learned his lesson. He took the chair to examine the laptop, as I moved behind him and gently put my hands on his shoulders for a light massage. I felt a little bad for having clocked him so hard in the face. He knew better. It wasn't a conscious decision when someone tickled me and he knew it. I decided not to feel bad about it anymore.

Jack brought up the pictures one at a time, slowly flipping through them and pointing out the people in the pictures when they came up as Sal, Tony, John. A few boring pictures of a water pump and then a fuzzy picture taken inside a barn. The next picture was of Tony and a woman naked in the barn. I reached over quickly to forward to the next picture.

"Wait," Jack blurted out and grabbed my wrist.

Jack had seen something in the picture that must be important.

"The ATV," he pointed after letting go of my wrist. He selected a portion of the picture with the mouse and zoomed in, adjusted the lighting, and some other editing effects of the picture.

Jack zoomed in on the license plate of the ATV and then looked back at me, "That's the same ATV the Feds had at the clearing."

"But how," I asked, "could they have a picture of the ATV in their barn before you saw the ATV in the clearing with John?"

Something most certainly was very wrong with what had happened today. If that ATV was owned by The Silent Majority farmstead people. That means it was all some sort of a ruse.

Jack clarified aloud what we were both thinking, "Okay, so the plot thickens," he said with a bit of dry humor in his voice, "So the ATV was a plant and not a real Fed scout vehicle... Or..."

I jumped in to add, "It was a federal vehicle at one time. These people got it, then used it to set up a scene. They wanted you to think a Federal agent was killed, and you might get blamed for it if you were caught in the area. This way they could pressure you and force you to trust them."

Jack looked back to the laptop, scrolled to the next picture. It showed a tan colored federal pickup truck. He mulled over slightly, "Hmmm, Okay, this woman with Tony, my guess, she was driving the pickup truck when I came upon John and the ATV. It was to pressure us away from the area to get John to safety." He paused with a sneer, "I bet John wasn't even hurt." He continued," He wouldn't let me help him at the ATV when I found him, and they refused to let me tend to his wound at the farm."

That appeared reasonable, and logical so I offered, "If she was in the truck, she would probably wait until you guys were off. Those at the farm would radio to her when they saw you enter with John and Tony. She would load the ATV up into the truck, move away to wait until they radioed that it was clear, then return to the farm."

Jack considered the idea, "Well then, who's the dead body?"

I shook my head as I wasn't fully convinced on any certainties, "A neighbor they didn't like, or a member of their own group that betrayed them? Alternatively, perhaps he was even a real Federal Officer."

Jack sighed a bit at all the twists and possibilities.

Jack slowly looked through additional pictures and past the homemade porn. There were pictures of their group posing with guns around the farm and then a picture came up that made me gasp and step back in concern, "No Way!"

The laptop had a picture of our house. It was taken before the forest fire, and it was a picture where Jack was putting in one of the windows of the house, and I was putting up fencing around the garden. The area over the bunker was already smoothed, weathered, and sprouts of vegetation in the garden were already starting to come up. If this was the first time, they had taken pictures, spying on us, then they wouldn't know about the bunker beneath. At least there was that going for us.

Jack started copying the pictures off the data chip and putting them into folders and subfolders, organizing them so that we had copies of everything for ourselves.

As the copying began to transfer the files, he moved through the remaining pictures slowly. The others showed some of our neighbors, and the terrain taken from high vantage points. I observed and I commented, "If they have a picture of our place, and of us, then they know where we live now. I mean, you sneaking back home careful for them not to know where you live... they do anyway."

Jack nodded with a grim expression on his face, "We should assume they do. They may have not kept the pictures or have forgotten these of us. But we should assume they kept copies of all these pictures on another computer. Once they met me, they went back to check all the pictures they have of the neighbors to see who I was."

This was getting complicated and far more dangerous. I had grown to find some comfort in being far away from everyone. It was a security blanket that made me feel safer. Nonetheless, now these people knew where we lived, and we knew they were exploiting us. They were people I wasn't trusting already. I began pacing, not really thinking about the pacing but just out of anxious nerves, "Tomorrow I'm going down to Todd and Jill's to check in on them. They haven't been responding to any of my radio calls." I needed to change the subject somehow, I needed to find something that appeared like normal life.

Jack turned a bit in the chair, to look over at me, "Do you want me to put off this recon job a day and go down with you?"

Oh no, certainly not, I responded as such, "No, we need to get this done as soon as possible so we can get in touch with

Jordan. I'm sure they probably just had their radio wire melted in the fire, or something simple."

Jack gave in to my insistence and went back to organizing and learning what he could of the pictures, "I assume you didn't eat while you were out?" I asked while I moved to make him some food in the kitchen.

Jack nodded and glanced over his left shoulder to where I was, "Just a little snack, I was too anxious to consider eating."

Seemed the same as I would be, "I'll make something up quick. You're probably going to sleep like the dead tonight, and you have a bunch of exhausting days coming up. I'll pack up some MRE's, and other supplies for you tonight, so you don't have so much to prepare in the morning before you go."

I pulled out some bread, meat, and cheese and made up a quick sandwich, chatting with Jack as I did, "I'm going to take Riley with me for a walk when we go down to the McVeenson's. See if we can get their CB radio back up and running. I'll bring down about 10 feet of CB cable so they can just move their antenna closer to their house outside their window if that was the problem." I just kept on talking because he was looking at me. He must be listening, right? I went on, "They might need a bit of help around their house anyway for a few hours. With a few horses, their dog, goats, chickens, rabbits and all their other stuff, they have their hands full even on days that didn't include a forest fire."

I looked over again to Jack, I expected some sort of agreement or comment by now, nothing. He was just staring at me, "Jack... hello? You there?"

He blinked and came out of his trance with a grin, "Um, sorry, what's that love?"

I chuckled at the goofball, "Wow, you were like somewhere else, completely."

He grinned at me a little, "Sorry about that."

I picked up the plate with the sandwich, got him a glass of water, and brought it over to the little dining table with the bench seats and sat it down for him, "Here you go."

When Jack got up and moved to the dining table to eat while I took the spot at the communications desk and started checking out the pictures myself, "You might want to bring your drone with you."

Jack finished his bite and nodded with a big smile, "That's a fantastic idea. Let's make sure the cellphone is recharged, the drone battery is fully charged, and I'll bring along the folding solar panel."

I wanted to get things ready for him. Sitting and talking had achieved all it was going to do, now I needed to get things started. I got up and went to the cupboard under the bookshelves and got out the drone, the cellphone, and started unzipping the small drone case. I pulled out the batteries got everything plugged in, to ensure they were fully charged by morning.

I still didn't trust cellphones, "You're sure the cellphone can't be tracked right?"

He nodded, "I'll have the cellular option turned off, and only have Wi-Fi turned on. That's the signal the drone uses."

I sighed softly, "I just wonder if the phones only make you think the cellular is turned off. I hate the idea of them being able to find you if you turn your phone on to use the drone."

Jack finished up his sandwich and carried it over to the kitchen counter, to clean it and put it away, "I can run the drone on its own controller, record the video and photos on the data chip in the drone, but I can't see what the drone is seeing. I might not be facing right, or have the camera looking in the right position to take pictures. I really have to use the phone to make sure I'm getting the information I need recorded correctly."

I still didn't like it, "I know... I just don't like it."

Jack put his plate and glass back in the cupboard and came over to rest his hands on my shoulders as he stood behind me. I was working on wiping the files off the data chip with a program that would prevent them from ever being recovered again, as he tried to reassure me, "I'll be super careful. I am going to bring that ghillie suit that I made from the netting and the dyed cloth strips, use that to hide and sleep during the day. I'll only move at night and I'll stay away from any farms or people all the way there and back."

I pulled the data chip out of the laptop, nodded a little before turning the laptop off, and closing the lid. I put the chip back into the camera and then stood up to face Jack and look around the bunker, "You go ahead and get to bed and get some sleep, I'm going to stay up and start packing for you and getting things ready."

Jack gave me a sweet kiss, a tight hug, and then went on back to get ready for bed and to get some sleep.

Chapter Nine (Jack)
Apache Rider

October 14

I slept so hard through the night that I don't remember when Megan joined me in the bed. I woke up feeling refreshed and ready for the day but couldn't force myself to get out of bed right away. I slid over to cuddle up to Megan, put my arm over her and held her close to me as I nuzzled up behind her.

I smelled her hair on the pillow next to me and felt her chest rise and fall with each breath. I wanted to stay close to her, to hold her like this all day, but as the minutes slipped by and she kept sleeping, I could feel the need for the bathroom becoming more urgent. With a soft sigh, I eased away from her to try to let her keep sleeping. I eased out of the blankets carefully and out of the bed.

Riley was quick to jump out of the bed with me and eagerly await being let out into the decontamination room to relieve herself.

The two of us kept as quiet as we could while we moved through the bunker and away from the bedroom. I opened the sealed bunker door to let Riley out. I left the door open as I used the toilet, washed up, and brushed my teeth.

I could probably leave the gas tight door open, the blast door up at the surface was locked tight. But it was a good habit to keep the door closed, so I secured it after Riley hopped over the threshold to join me again.

When I moved back through the bunk room, I noted Megan had collected up all my gear on one of the bunks, so it was ready. The new .308 sniper rifle and the 9mm pistol were both freshly cleaned and smelled of FrogLube (tm). I would still need to sight in the rifle to ensure it was going to be on target when I needed it to be.

My larger pack was filled with the gear I was going to need but I had to double check it. It wasn't that I didn't trust her, my OCD insisted I double and triple check anything like this myself.

I decided to leave the 9mm in the bunker and just keep my .45 with me on the trip. I put the 9mm on the bunk above and then started going through what she had prepared for me.

Unzipping the main pouch of the pack, I dug everything out and started to make a mental inventory of where everything was as I put them all back inside. An army green wool blanket stuffed down flat on the very bottom, six MREs, a pound of elk jerky, my small travel Bible in a sealed Ziploc bag, a large Ziploc with a couple fresh pair of underwear and socks, a toothbrush and paste. Then I set in my drone and the tri-fold backpacking solar panel.

On the top of all, I stuffed the homemade ghillie suit down and then pulled the drawstrings tight to cinch it up.

Going through the outside pouches and pockets, I made sure I knew where everything was so I could get to them when I needed them. Canteen of water and a filtration straw, medical kit, Garmin GPS, compass, folded up map, backup pair of glasses, binoculars, flashlight, multi-tool, small tool kit, lighter, wet-wipes/toilet paper and a few other small items that might be needed on the journey.

Riley began to pace around, begging for breakfast as I closed the last of the pouches on the pack. I set it back on the far-right side of the bunk, to pick up on the way out later. Glancing back to Riley, I saw Megan step out from the bedroom in the back of the bunker dressed in her nightshirt and wearing a pair of socks to keep her warm against the cool bunker floor. My eyes met her, and we exchanged quiet morning smiles as she shuffled closer to me on her way to the bathroom at the far end of the bunker behind me. As she passed me, I wrapped her up in my arms for a hug while very softly whispering to her, "I'm going to be okay baby. I won't do anything to risk not being able to come home to you."

She nodded against my shoulder in the hug, "I know," her voice was soft and warm on my neck, "I know."

After we broke away from the hug, she moved back towards the bathroom while I went to the kitchen to start making some coffee and a simple breakfast. Megan never ate breakfast, it upset her stomach to eat in the morning. I pulled out a saucepan and started boiling some water to make some oatmeal, taking out the butter and some brown sugar. I wished I had a tablespoon of maple syrup, but we hadn't seen maple syrup for several months.

I was stirring the oatmeal in the pan when Megan slipped up behind me and wrapped her arms up under my arms and held me close from behind as I worked at the stove, "Perhaps we should start going to meet our neighbors and touch base with them. Not sharing too much information about us, but just the basics like first names and making sure we have some way to come help them or join up with them if we need to; like a community or neighborhood watch thing."

I nodded to that, as I turned off the burner and moved to pour the oatmeal into the bowl, and she stepped back away to let me move freely, "Probably a smart idea. But before you do, check out the pictures and locations we got off that camera data chip, so you know the people you are looking for. Stay at a distance, examine them for a while before going near their homes. People may have killed them and/or taken over their homes, so we want to make sure we watch the place and ensure it all looks relaxed and normal before revealing ourselves to them at all."

Megan nodded to that as she moved towards the bedroom, "Might be best to wait until we can go together for that then. You could stay back with the sniper rifle hidden and I can go ahead alone. Less alarming for me to come up alone, and safer for me as well if you are back watching over me with that sniper rifle."

I smiled over to her as she then slipped out of view into the bedroom. The quiet of the bunker made it easy to keep a conversation going without raising your voice, "Let's plan on doing that after I get back then. We should have what we need to contact Jordan on the radio, then we can concentrate on this idea of gathering the neighbors together, at least communicating and being able to call on each other for help would be a smart way to get started."

Megan's voice came through the open doorway of the bedroom as I filled the pan with hot water and a little bit of dish soap to soak in the sink, "Sounds like a plan. I'll ask Todd and Jill today if they know of any of the neighbors and what they are like. I won't tell them anything about our pictures of course, nothing about The Silent Majority."

I turned, with the hot bowl of oatmeal and a spoon, to walk to the small table and take a seat, "I still need to see about trading with them for some rabbits and chickens." I bowed my head then and prayed as Megan was talking. I was too lacking in multi-tasking though and failed to hear anything she was saying, "I'm sorry baby, I was praying, what was that?"

She readily repeated what she had said without annoyance in her tone, "I'll take Riley down with me, but on a leash. I still don't trust her to run off and get eaten by coyotes."

I slipped off the seat at the table and moved to the bookshelf to get my Bible, then returned to the table to read while I had my breakfast, "Take the AR-15 with you please, and the new 9mm pistol as well."

Megan agreed to taking the weapons with her, "You are going to be outside of radio range pretty much by noon, won't you?"

I nodded and finished the bite of oatmeal before responding, "Yeah, only like a five-mile range on the hand-held."

The conversation trailed off at this point as I studied my Bible and Megan started getting dressed and ready for her day. We spent about an hour after my breakfast and Bible study to take out the maps, satellite pics on the laptop, and plan my route to the power plant. We laid out how long certain routes would take, distances to water sources, where to bed down and hide in general areas for the daytime. As we went along and planned more, Megan began to get more calm, feeling that it wasn't as terrifying now that facts were here to replace her fears.

The morning routine continued past the mundane acts until I found myself pulling on my boots and zipping up the inside zipper, standing up to fasten on my weapons belt, leg holster for the .45 pistol, and then pulling my plate carrier up over my head and down over my chest. I put the full canteen of water into its pouch on my right side and made sure my magazines for my .45 were in their pouches and the rounds for the .308 were also accounted for. I had Megan get the laser bore siter out of the cupboard, under the bookshelves, to bring with me to sight in the sniper rifle before I got far from the house. With Megan's help, I hoisted the backpack up and got my arms into the straps, pulled the belt around me, and buckled it securely in place. Everything seemed balanced and ready to go, and it was only 0800 hrs.

Goodbyes were always tough these days. Just leaving each other's sight felt like a risk we didn't want to take anymore. The calm of a "normal" day of leaving, going to work and coming back home being a certain leisurely experience, was no longer to be taken for granted.

Megan and Riley escorted me to the bottom of the stairs in the decontamination room, we both gnarled up our noses at the stink of Riley's poo at the other end of the small room. We shared a little chuckle, a quick kiss, and then I leaned forward and eased my way up one step at a time to gradually emerge from the heavy blast door in the shed above, to head out for a long and dangerous adventure.

I took one last look down the lit stairway tube, to the room below to give Megan and Riley a little wave. I blew them a kiss, and pulled the blast door down, and latched it into place.

I didn't go outside right away, instead I went over to the wall with the cabinet doors, opened them to reveal the two monitors, and powered them on, so that I could view all the security cameras outside. I wanted to make sure everything was clear before I went outside.

I keyed up my radio, the mic attached on my left shoulder, "Mama Bear, you copy?"

Megan's voice came back to me about 30 seconds later, "Sorry, yes, I'm here."

I Offered, "Can you check the monitors as well while I'm looking, another set of eyes to make sure the way is safe?"

She came back, "Yeah, absolutely."

I took my time looking at each camera around the property, looking for shapes out of the ordinary, movements that could reveal a person hiding or sneaking about. I gave it ten minutes of watching through all the cameras before I keyed up the mic again, "I can't see anything to worry about. All looks clear to you?"

Megan's voice came back to me, "It looks good baby, you be careful okay?"

"Roger that," I responded, "Be back soon."

I powered down the monitors, to conserve battery power, and then closed the cabinet doors, opened the shed door, and stepped outside.

The smell of the forest fire was still hanging in the air, but it wasn't choking strong any longer. The charred wood smell would probably stay for months, or until we got several rains. Here in the mountains of Arizona, a few rains could be a couple months, depending on the season of the year.

I took my pack off, leaned the sniper rifle up against the shed, and spent the next half hour going around the house. I checked on the solar panels, the well, pump and water storage tank to ensure nothing had been tampered with. Everything was in full working order still.

My mind at ease, I shouldered my pack, and took up the rifle before keying the mic again, "Mama Bear, this is Hawk One. All looks good. I'm going to head off a distance before I tune this thing in, you stay safe too baby."

Megan's voice came back, "Okay, I'll be praying for you."

I nodded solemnly, "Me also baby, back soon."

I had taken my bipod off my .270 bolt action Remington model 700 and put it on the new .308 sniper rifle. I also put the leather shoulder strap on the new rifle for carrying it on my back when I thought it was safe enough to do that.

The first part of my trip was going to repeat the same route I took to meet up with The Silent Majority in the field where they staged the ATV. From there though, my route branched off north and eastward away from the field, and away from the farm, to head up towards Springerville.

I moved off at a quick pace, adjusted the strap around my right leg that held my .45 1911 in place so it wouldn't flop around loosely, and then tightened the straps over my shoulders from the backpack. I took a brief sip from the camelback straw out of the backpack to clear the line and fill it with fresh cool water, so it was ready when I needed it.

The first mile from the bunker was without any issues. The forest fire had left its lasting mark over the land, and it would be some time before it recovered very well. There were a couple mysterious patches of green randomly about that made no sense; small patches that had escaped the fire. Maybe when I had more time, I'd investigate them more, for now though, I expected a full four nights hard hike to get to where I needed to be. It was still eerily quiet, with a lack of birds and the sound of the wind through the pines was different, without branches and needles on the black charred poles that had been the trees a week earlier.

A mile out from the bunker, I found myself in a long valley between two sloping hills and decided it was a proper place to site in the new sniper rifle. It felt relieving to shed the weight of the pack. I unstrapped it, leaned it against a charred tree, and then knelt to pull out the small zippered pack that held the laser bore siter. It was a simple device that emitted a laser at the end of a metal rod. The rod slipped into the end of the barrel, you tightened it down so that the laser shot straight out from the barrel. Then, it was just a matter of lining up the laser on the target and adjusting your scope or iron sights to move left or right, up or down until the scope lined up perfectly with the laser dot on the target. It saved an incredible amount of frustration, walking back/forth to and from a target all afternoon to get it set.

I laid down on the ground on my stomach, with the sniper rifle, extended the bipod legs, adjusted their small rubber tipped legs to the proper height, made sure there was no ammo in the rifle, then slid the laser siter into the end of the barrel and adjusting and tightening it down. It was a simple five-minute job, as I popped the covers off each end of the scope, rested my cheek on the butt stock of the rifle and took the position I would be using when shooting the rifle.

I selected a tree about 200 yards out, that had a stump of a branch about ten feet up from the ground that had not been burned off completely. The laser didn't show up on the small burned stumpy and I didn't know where it was going. I carefully moved the gun around until the red dot of the laser finally showed up on the tree itself. I moved it gradually up the tree and then out onto the stumpy burned branch, so it was in place. It was then, that I looked through the scope and noted it was considerably off.

Peeking back and forth several times, I had to adjust the horizontal on the scope a foot to the right and the vertical about six inches down. I removed my cheek from the stock of the rifle, repositioned about a dozen times to ensure my sight picture was going to be consistent every time. I had to know that the scope maintained an exact and repetitive alignment with the red laser dot, to ensure it was going to be perfect.

One last step; I removed the laser bore siter from the end of the barrel, put it away in its case, zipped it up and put it back into my pack. I then laid down on the ground and loaded the rifle with the large sniper rounds. I had three 10 round magazines for the rifle, so I slipped one of them into the bottom of the stock, tapped it solidly to make sure it was in place and then tugged down on it to make sure it was in fully and latched. I racked in the first round with the bolt and then placed my cheek on the stock as before, lined up the shot with the scope.

I carefully lined up the scope to the burned stumpy branch, took in a calm breath, let it out slowly as I moved my index finger over the trigger. I slipped my finger back off it until just the very tip of my first finger joint was on the trigger, careful to pull gently back on the trigger, exactly back towards me and not to the side.

The rifle barked and bucked solidly against my shoulder and surprised me a bit. I had never shot the rifle before, so I wasn't sure when the trigger was going to break. Perfect, not knowing when the rifle is going to go off on the pull is the best way to be accurate. I wasn't anticipating, tensing up, or pre-flinching on the shot.

The rifle did a small hop up and then settled back down an instant later upon the bipod; right back to the position it was in just moments before, ready for the next shot. I didn't use the bolt to rack in the next shot though, I just looked through the scope to check the shot.

Perfect, the burned branch stump off the side of the tree was missing, shattered right off the tree with fresh wood flesh exposed where the branch was before.

I remembered before the laser bore siter, when I'd spend a couple hours frustrated, trying just to hit a cardboard box at range. I had to get a bullet to hit, and finally start sighting in the scope. Sometimes, having the correct tool for the job, made all the difference in the world. One shot, perfect, and I was ready to get back on the trail.

If Megan had been up in the house, I would have called her on the radio, to let her know I had made the shot, and everything was set. But down in the bunker, she wouldn't have heard the shot at all. I hefted up my pack, strapped it on, and got back on my route without calling her.

As I started to move down the valley towards the target tree, I pulled the bolt back and it ejected the spent brass casing of the round I shot. I tried to catch it in the air, thought it would look cool. Thankfully nobody was around, as it flipped up and tumbled through the air. My attempted catch failed and it landed on the ground. I slid the bolt forward, chambered in the next round, and locked the bolt down in place before picking up the spent casing off the ground. Well, it looked cool when they did it in the movies. I chuckled to myself as I continued.

After a half an hour, I got out of the fire damage and moved into the trees that had not been taken by the fire. It felt great to be in the shade of the trees again, the cooler temperature, the sound of the wind above in the tops, and the return of the sound of birds. I was heading mostly due north, on the west side of a ridge of steep hills. The sun was just now reaching down into the valley from the mornings eastern approach.

It was just after fall harvest, so the days were not as hot, and the nights were rather chilly. The fall rains normally come soon, and I expected them to make a presence any day now. The second half of October normally brought in temperatures around the mid-seventies in the heat of the day, and mid to low forties at night. That worked for me, a heavy hoody and a hat while hiking through the night would work great to keep at a comfortable temperature. Sleeping in the day, in the mid-seventies would be fantastic. Couldn't ask for better temperatures. Unless it started raining, then 40's would be miserable at night if I got wet. My poncho would have to save the day if that happened.

I started moving a bit slower as the day wore on. I moved my binoculars into the pouch I carried by my canteen and put the canteen in the backpack. If I needed a sip of water, I just used the camelback straw coming down over my right shoulder. Every five minutes or a couple hundred yards, I would start looking for a place to kneel behind a tree or a bunch of boulders. I would then scan around with the binoculars, to see if I was being followed, look ahead, around for any houses, movement (people or animals), or anything out of the ordinary that I should be concerned about.

Just before the sun was highest in the sky, I stopped for one of my searches. I knelt to check the map and my route. There was a small lake that I was planning to top off my water from, just a short distance down into the next valley. I wanted to check out carefully before moving into the open. I wanted to make it fast, get in, get the water, and get back into the trees quickly.

I peered down through the trees without the binoculars first, to see if any motion would catch my eye, looking in all directions before I got tunnel vision using the binoculars. Down at the small lake or honestly large pond, I could see a horse at the water's edge drinking and a man kneeling while filling up something with water. The area around the water was a few hundred meters of open grass, dirt, and rock. There wasn't much to conceal myself behind so I had to decide if I would go out of my way, around a little further, or to just skip the water and wait until the next option on the planned route.

I double-checked and determined my camelback bladder was about half empty and my two canteens of water were still filled. I could probably go two days without running out of water, so I had a day and a half of water remaining. I decided to play it safe, scoot around to the south, and keep moving along. It was a disappointment that my first chance at water was canceled. The rare places for water were expected to have the greatest chance of encountering other people. If the same situation happened later when I was lower on water reserves, I'd have to just lay in hiding and wait for a chance after it looked clear, likely after dark to refill my water. This first watering hole though was a no-go.

I picked up the sniper rifle, slipped back the way I had arrived; off the top of the ridge line. I crept back some distance, then headed eastward around and through the trees, away from the clearing of the lake. I crept on in the shadows, back on my route to the next watering hole.

An hour later, I was back on my planned route. I was being more careful now. Someone, out on a horse, may be taking the same planned route I am making to the next water source. Someone from the next waterhole, might be coming back towards me on the same route as well. I did my best to stay off any obvious trails that had been worn by horses or hikers. I took care to stay a generous distance off trails, prowling parallel to them in the thicker patches. Someone on horseback would want to stay a little more in the open or on the trails more properly, they would not want to get smacked by branches and constantly, weaving in and out of trees and make frustratingly slow progress. They would have to dismount, lead the horse by the reins if they wanted to get off the trail. I hoped that would give me the advantage of hearing the horse cracking through the dried pine branches and brittle undergrowth before they got close enough to spot me.

Luck was on my side though, or God was keeping watch on my mission. Late in the afternoon about an hour before sunset, I came to an overlook on a ridge. I had planned to stop and wait there until nightfall. To the east, a lake about two miles long east to west and a quarter mile from north to south, was visible down in the valley below.

I settled down in a thicket of trees with some shrubs that would hide me well, took off my pack and pulled out one of the MREs off the bottom of the pack. I refilled my camelback pouch with water from one of the canteens and drank what remained of that canteen. I also used that water for my meal and for heating up the food pack in the MRE.

It felt so nice to have a cool breeze across my sweaty back after I removed my pack. I had to work to get dried off though before the sun set. A wet shirt could get incredibly uncomfortable when the temperatures were just a handful of degrees above freezing. Right now, it was a nice 65°F, probably about 60°F here in the shade of the pines I was in. After sunset though, the temperature dropped like a stone. It would probably be 50°F by midnight and 40°F by sunrise. It was going to be exhausting the way I had the route planned. After sunset, I needed to refill my canteen down in the valley at the lake and then press on through the dark. I was going to be fully spent by sunrise in the morning, but it's what I needed to do in order to get on the sleeping schedule so that I was traveling at night and sleeping in the day.

While my MRE was bubbling in the chemical heater pouch inside the cardboard box it came in, I leaned it up against a tree, took out my old daily devotional from 2019 and my Bible to get in some reading and prayer while I waited.

The small pocket-sized devotional book broke down a couple pages for each day, so that you had some scripture to read, a story, and a way to focus on what you read from the scripture to help you apply it into your own life. Sometimes, just reading the Bible, you felt like you were swimming in an ocean being blown to the side randomly. The devotionals had a way of grounding you, and letting you feel less buffeted by the waves of life.

Today's devotional was written by Whitney Hopler at Crosswalk.com and it was old. It was copied into the book from an article she wrote back on August 29 of 2013. The title for the day was "How Your Ordinary Life Can Make an Extraordinary Impact on the World."

So many devotionals feel disconnected from reality these days. Devotionals tell you how to apply your love for God at work, or in the world. They were written in a time where all those normal things in life no longer applied. There was no job, or work. There was no church, and there were no social interactions and influences like before. Everything seemed so broken that things written in even the near past appeared worlds away now.

I took in a calm deep breath, closed my eyes a moment to pray for peace, a clear mind to learn what God wanted me to learn through this, and to give me guidance in how to apply his Will in my life. I then opened my eyes to the smell of clear and clean wind through the pine trees and the sounds of nature around me. It was as perfect as life got. I turned my eyes down to the book and read the first paragraph.

"There are so many problems in our fallen world that it's easy to feel as if one person's efforts can't do much to fix them. But God calls every believer to help solve the world's problems, and one ordinary person's life can actually make an extraordinary impact on the world." 4

I almost snorted in reaction to the very first sentence. "Many problems in our fallen world?" It was almost humorous the naivety of the author to have written this less than a decade ago, and how it applied to the world we now all found ourselves in. Still, I had to remind myself that if I went back a couple hundred years there was the chaos of growing enough crops to feed your family through the winter months and bringing in a poor harvest. There were raids of enemy clans, armies of neighboring kingdoms, slavery, disease and petulance and many other problems in the fallen world. My world of chaos right now is different, but no less stressful than those in history. I contemplated how easy it was to focus like a sniper down a scope on the minuscule details at the end and to forget the larger picture around you. When I am in the middle of a forest fire, I see only the danger and damage to me and the area right around me. I don't see the raging fire on the other side of the

---

4 https://www.crosswalk.com/faith/spiritual-life/how-your-ordinary-life-can-make-an-extraordinary-impact-on-the-world.html

ridge line, or the families that did not have a bunker to escape to and may have died in the fire.

Just the first paragraph and I was already finding my mind aligning with that of God's. Stepping back from it being all about me and thinking of others.

As I took my time to slowly read down through the devotional, I found red flags in my life I knew I did not line up properly with. The devotional went into ways to impact the world with God's love and some of them were things I failed poorly at implementing in my own life.

The first was to shift my focus from heroism to love. This smacked me across the face right at the start of the devotional. This was my largest issue. I always felt I needed to fix what was wrong, to do something, to act. Yes, I needed to act, but that didn't mean I needed to get in the face of someone and argue or point out the problems with the world. It might indicate that I needed to simply bring love to people who need love. It was something I kept having to reset my attention on and to make it a purposeful intent in my life. I needed to pause, listen, put myself in their position and then not be judgmental, and to show love.

It wasn't a horribly difficult thing to do with someone where the subject was a simple disagreement. The things of life these days appeared so bipolar and divisive that there was no longer any grey area between "sides".

I wanted to try to find ways to show the love of God and it felt like I was making an excuse, wimpping out and betraying the truth. It was uncomfortable, but I worked to try to find a path through the muddled thoughts in my head.

I flipped the pages of the devotional to the back where I could take notes and started to make a simple chart of the ideas as they came into my head.

I lined out some boxes in a chart to structure my thoughts and it took a long while just to make the title across the top. It had entered my mind several times over the years how Satan ruled through lies, deception, half-truths and manipulations and fear. It appeared so obvious when you took a serious look at the Democrat party that every angle that Satan would take in a situation the democrats lined up perfectly. Anything against God was promoted, anything pushed towards enslaving the people in lies and hatred was pushed forward as wholesome. Anything that was good and wholesome was said to be evil and wrong. Truly, the end times were at hand. "Woe unto them that call evil good, and good evil; that put darkness for light, and light for darkness; that put bitter for sweet, and sweet for bitter!"5

  There was a social barrier, you were a conspiracy theorist, mocked, and hunted down if you voiced the obvious fact that the democrat party had become the party of Satan. It felt as if I was condemning myself just by making this comparison in my chart I was making right now.

Democrats / Lies / Satan	Conservatives / Truth / God
Government controlled health care - Long lines (death waiting) - government paid for abortions - Letting senior citizens die if they are too expensive.	Private/competitive health insurance companies - health care based on customer needs - Government not paying for killing children - All life is precious, even the elderly.
Open boarders, free flow of sex trafficking, free flow of murderers, free flow of rapists, free flow of drugs.	Secure boarders, stopping sex trafficking of children. Keeping murders, rapists, and drugs out of country.
Illegal aliens and anyone on the planet voting in US elections.	Only citizens and those paying taxes and living with the results of the vote/elections should vote.
Making illegal any means of defense of the population from a tyrannical government.	Upholding the 2nd amendment and the citizens being able to stand up against a tyrannical government.
Setting free from prison murderers, rapists, drug dealers and letting them vote to ensure democrats stay in power.	Maintaining a system of punishment for those that break the laws, murder, rape, etc.

5 Isaiah 5:20 (KJV)

Remove funding for local police departments, replace with the militant arm of the democrat party (Antifa, BLM).	Maintain law and order and peaceful communities. Keep a system that holds all equal under the law to keep a civil society.
Promote lawlessness, chaos, disorder.	Promote peace, justice, and a system where people are not in fear of anarchy and violence on their streets.
Promote billionaire influence to keep riots and chaos by paying immediate release from jail those that are the militant wing of the party.	Keep those in jail that are murdering, raping, burning down cities and rioting and attacking the police until they can have a legit day in court on their innocence/guilt.
The U.S. History should be changed, taught to change facts to promote hatred for all things that make the country loved by the citizens.	Keep and teach the truth of the country's history, the good along with the bad. To show what has been overcome over time and how great an influence has been within the country and across the world.
Promotion of the citizens need to rely on the government for daily needs: Housing, food, healthcare. To increase taxes and take more from the efforts of those that produce to distribute through programs to those that will continue to elect them into power due to their need to keep housed, fed, and cared for.	Promotion of citizens to be independent, free to live where and how you want, freedom to earn a living to improve your life and your family life through creative and determined use of your labor to increase your station in life and raise yourself economically to improve your food/healthcare/housing.

Pushes government only schools, no homeschooling, charter schools or any choices outside of anti-America hate indoctrination.	Free choice of parents to decide where/how their children get an education. Allowing children to get an education outside of indoctrination camps of the government.

I opened the heated pack of spaghetti and meatballs, spooned it out slowly, while enjoying the crackers, peanut butter, and other treats in the pack as I continued my charts.

Before I realized it, I had spent well over an hour working on my chart and organizing my thoughts. I had only just started the devotional and now the darkness in the pines was going to require me to pull out a flashlight to continue. Out of time, I had to get back underway and would need to finish my studies later.

Chapter Ten (Megan)
The Big Move

October 14

Jack move back into the bedroom and I stared at the open doorway for a while longer. It felt as if I looked away from where he was would mean he would vanish, and I'd never see him again.

If I wanted to do everything to ensure he would return to me safely, I had to get busy and do my part.

I started collecting everything I could think he may need onto the small dining room table, running through a mental checklist as I laid them out.

I started stretching out electrical cords to the things that needed batteries charged. Drone, drone controller, iPhone (™), flashlight, Garmin (™) GPS, folding solar panel, rechargeable backup battery, extra rechargeable batteries for the flashlight and GPS and other items that needed batteries.

I collected all the items, trying to keep quiet so that Jack could get some sleep was tricky. Laser bore sighter, 2-way handheld radio, camera from The Silent Majority farmyard were added to the table. I then started placing other items on one of the bunk beds with his backpack.

Most of the gear was gathered from his hike earlier. I had to unpacked everything, lay them out to ensure we were not overlooking anything. I picked out his favorite MRE's, an army green wool blanket, his homemade ghillie suit, 2 canteens, his camelback (™) pouch, Med kit, a folding pocket knife, a large Bowie knife, toilet paper, wet wipes, underwear, socks, his Bible, and a small journal/notebook. I then came to the 9mm pistol he got from the fake Federal Officer at the ATV.

I wanted to clean the 9mm pistol, so I decided to go and pack him a Ziploc bag filled with elk jerky first. I didn't want to get my hands dirty with the gun cleaning before I fixed his food.

Glancing over to the small table, I could not help but grin at all the little colored lights with the batteries charging. It looked like a Christmas tree laid out across the table with all the green, orange, and red LED indicator colors.

To save Jack time in the morning; I started preparing his pack with the wool blanket on the bottom, the MREs next and then the other items slowly layered above as they showed they were fully charged with their batteries. A few of the items I knew he would want in pouches on his armored vest and pouches on his belt. I figured he would probably unpack everything I was doing to double check. Mostly though, it was important for him to know exactly where everything was so that he could get to them in a hurry or in the dark when he couldn't see.

There were still several things charging on the table, so I turned my attention to the new pistol and sat down at the communications table. I moved the laptop off to the side, leaning it against the wall to make as much space as I could.

Jack has a special toolbox for cleaning the guns, so I got that out and unrolled the long rubber mat across the desktop to keep from scratching the desk and to keep things organized. I popped the magazine out of the pistol and then pulled the slide back. The 9mm round in the chamber flipped out and landed on the rubber mat, I set it to the side. I removed all the ammo from the magazine and put all the loose rounds to the side.

The slide on the top of the pistol held the barrel and the return spring. It had to come off and it took quite some time to identify the release, to slide it off.

Every manufacturer seemed to have a different way to remove its slide, and this was a new one that I had never seen before. Trial and error, and some patience, and I finally found that the slide had to be locked back in its open position, then near the front there was a toggle that needed turned. This released the pressure on the slide and unlocked it, let me slide off the top rail, and separate it from the base.

I spent about thirty minutes cleaning the gun with the small brushes and swabs from the supplies, lubricating all the little parts just a tiny bit with the FrogLube (™). Jack had shown me that using too much would make the surface oozing with the liquid and it would be like a magnet for dust and dirt. It was worse to use too much of the cleaner. It was best, to have just a thin coat across the parts to keep it from rusting from moisture.

After getting it, all put back together, I put just a single 9mm round into the magazine, put it into the gun and pulled back the slide. With only one round in the magazine, it would test the spring in the magazine. It would have the least amount of pressure on the spring. If one round would feed properly into the magazine, then more ammo in the magazines was sure to work as well.

Thankfully, the round fed into the pistol just fine, so I put the safety on and then ejected the round and magazine. It was impossible to clean inside the magazine where the spring was. At least, I didn't know how to get in there and make sure it was all perfect inside where I couldn't see.

I filled up the magazine with ammo, slid the magazine into the pistol, then set it aside on the bunk bed with the other items. We didn't have much 9mm ammo anymore. Jack had traded his beloved Ruger SR9c and all his 9mm ammo before we moved up into the mountains permanently. He made a deal with a neighbor to help him with a water filtration system. Jack also gave the man his 9mm pistol in exchange for a much larger Springfield 1911 .45 caliber pistol and a generous amount of ammo with it.

So, we didn't have any real amount of 9mm ammo saved up right now. For now, we had the magazine in the pistol and the two extra magazines that he found with it. 30 rounds would have to do for now.

A few of the larger batteries needed more time to charge, so I pulled out my Bible and sat down to pray and then read for a while. There was nothing better to put my mind at ease; to know that the God that created everything, the God that was here before time itself, was here with me in this very moment.

The record of events written in the Bible encouraged me. It showed me how God was involved in, and actively a part of all the events that took place. Many times, God would step in and take a part in what transpired. But also, many times it would be generations of families before things turned around and 'got better'. On the other hand, God was always in control.

If our life was difficult, if we went through great trials and persecution, we were in good company. Even if we passed on before we saw the world around us improve, it was okay. I lived in this world, but this was not my home. Even my deep love for my husband and daughter, the center of my faith was not in them. It was firmly set in my relationship in Christ. That could never be removed by a collapsing country and society around me. That was all superficial and temporary. It was important to remind myself of the larger picture, to keep from getting depressed about the here and now.

I wrote down my thoughts in my journal, then ended my time with prayer. The stress was gone, God was in control. God as good.

I unplugged all the fully charged batteries and items and put them with the gear ready to go. I put the wires away, washed my hands again in the kitchen, and then spent a little time cleaning up in the bathroom. Trying to be a bed Ninja, I crawled carefully into bed with Jack, snuggling up close to him under the blankets, to drift off slowly to sleep.

******

I don't remember any dreams I have. I wasn't like Jack, who could recall long stories about his night's dreams, but I felt refreshed and it felt great to have had a deep long sleep through the night.

It was the small sounds of Jack and Riley out in the main area of the bunker that pulled me out of my sleep. An aching stretch of muscles protested as I reached up over my head and pushed down with my legs. I twisted my back left and right, it felt fantastic.

Easing my legs down over the edge of the bed, I pulled my warm socks up before stepping onto the cold floor. The blankets received my attention next. I never used to be consistent at making the bed in the morning, but in the bunker, it was easier to remember to do it. Life was slower now; the little things didn't slip into the gaps of chaos as much as they once had.

I felt a smile on my face as I stepped out into the main room and saw Jack and Riley together.

Moving forward to head for the bathroom at the far end of the bunker, Jack met my eyes with a kind smile. He offered, trying to comfort me, "I'm going to be okay baby. I won't do anything to risk not being able to come home to you," as he moved to me, wrapped his arms around me in a tight hug.

I nodded against his shoulder in the hug, "I know," I repeated quietly as I rested the side of my face on his shoulder, "I know."

I slipped out of the hug and made my way back to the bathroom. Passing the bunkbed, I saw the 9mm pistol placed off to the side like he wasn't going to take it with him. The pack had been gone through. After 25 years together, it was fun to predict what he would do.

I spent a short bit of time in the bathroom, brushed my teeth, took care of my hair, and then made my way back into the main room. Jack was over in the kitchen area. It smelled like he was making oatmeal.

I slipped up behind him as Riley was playfully walking around my feet. Wrapping my arms up under his arms and pressed myself tight against his back, I offered "Perhaps we should start going to meet our neighbors and touch base with them. Not share too much information about ourselves, but just the basics like first names and making sure we have some way to come help them or join up with them if we need to, like a community or neighborhood watch thing."

Jack nodded at my suggestion as he turned off the burner and moved to pour the oatmeal into the bowl. I stepped back to let him work on his breakfast as he replied, "Probably a smart idea. But before you do, check out the pictures and locations we got off that camera data chip, so you know the people you are looking for. Stay at a distance, examine them for a while before going near their homes. People may have killed them or taken over their homes. We want to ensure we watch the places, are certain it all looks relaxed and normal, before revealing ourselves to them at all."

I nodded at that logic. It appeared smart, and I took a couple steps toward the bedroom as I thought it out a bit more, "Might be best to wait until we can go together for that. You could stay back with the sniper rifle hidden, and I can go ahead alone. Less alarming for me to come up alone, and safer for me as well if you are back watching over me with that rifle."

Jack smiled to me as I slipped out of view into the bedroom.

Jack raised his voice just a bit so I could keep hearing him in the bedroom, "Let's plan on doing that after I get back then. We should have what we need to contact Jordan on the radio, and then we can concentrate on this idea of gathering the neighbors together, and at least communicating and being able to call on each other for help."

I could hear Jack filling something with water in the sink, "Sounds like a plan. I'll ask Todd and Jill today, if they know of any of the neighbors and what they are like. I won't tell them anything about our pictures of course, nothing about The Silent Majority."

Jack moved to the table with his oatmeal and a spoon to take a seat and have his breakfast, "I still need to look about trading with them for some rabbits and chickens." He bowed his head then and prayed as I was talking. I didn't realize at first that he was praying. When he raised his head, he asked me to repeat myself.

I repeated what I had said, "I'll take Riley down with me, but on a leash. I still don't trust her not to run off and get eaten by coyotes."

Jack slipped off the seat and moved to the bookshelf to get his Bible, then returned to read while he had his breakfast, "Take the AR-15 with you please, and the new 9mm pistol."

I nodded in agreement, "You are going to be outside of radio range pretty much by noon, won't you?"

He nodded and finished the bite of oatmeal before responding, "Yeah, only like a five-mile range on the hand-held."

The conversation trailed off at this point as he studied his Bible, so I moved off to change my clothes for the day.

We spent about an hour taking out the maps and satellite pics on the laptop to plan Jack's route to the power plant. We laid out how long certain routes would take, distances to water sources, where to bed down and hide in the daytime. As we went along and planned more, I could feel myself becoming calmer, feeling that it wasn't as terrifying now that facts were here to replace my concerns.

The normal morning to-do's we worked through together, seemed normal, until Jack started pulling his armored vest over his head and into place. He began putting on his gear belt, his guns, and ammo. I helped him lift his pack onto his shoulders, and made sure the straps were not twisted.

Riley and I escorted Jack to the bottom of the stairs in the decontamination room. Jack and I gnarled up our noses at the stink of Riley's poo in the small room. We shared a little chuckle with a quick kiss at the end.

Jack then leaned forward, and eased his way up one step at a time to emerge out of the heavy blast door in the shed above to head out for a long and dangerous adventure.

Jack turned around when he got to the top and looked down at us. He gave us a little wave, and blew me a kiss. I returned the gesture, then he pushed the heavy blast door down and latched it into place.

I was alone now, just me and Riley. It was probably going to be a week or so before I had my husband back again.

I took a few moments just to stand there and be in the moment of quiet. When I felt the moment slip away, I went through the airtight door. I left the door open as I went through to flip on the computer monitors to watch the cameras outside.

As the monitors were warming up Jack's voice came across the radio:

Jack: Mama Bear, you copy?

I snatched up the radio and squeezed on the button.

Megan: Sorry, yes, I'm here.

He came back.

Jack: Can you check the monitors, while I'm looking? I could use another set of eyes to ensure the way is safe.

The monitors were just beginning to sync with the cameras at that moment.

Megan: Yes, absolutely.

I pulled the chair around and got comfortable, checking each camera in turn. I used the mouse to select the area on the monitor view with the camera outside. I could pan them left and right and to zoom in if needed. I could see quite a bit more now, so many trees had been burned down.
I couldn't see anything to really worry about. I didn't see any movement in the open areas. It looked clear and safe all the way out to where the forest fire had left tees unburned.
After a while, Jack's voice startled me over the radio in the quiet of the bunker:

Jack: I can't see anything to worry about. All looks clear to you?

I keyed the mic back up

Megan: It looks good baby; you be careful okay?
Jack: Roger that, be back soon.

I put the microphone back down, and picked Riley up to hold in my lap while I spied around with the cameras. I saw Jack come out of the shack above the bunker, take off his pack, lean it and the sniper rifle up against the wall. He then started going around the house, solar panels, the water tank, and other things in the yard checking things.
After a half hour or so, Jack started coming back towards the shack to get his pack and the rifle.

Jack: Mama Bear, this is Hawk One. Everything looks good. I'm going to head off a good distance before I tune this thing in.

He raised the rifle to the camera to show me what he was cryptically talking about.

Jack: You stay safe too baby.

I went back to him over the radio:

Megan: Okay, I'll be praying for you.

Jack: Me also baby, back soon.

     I watched him head off in the area we had laid out for his route. I kept track of him on the cameras until I couldn't see him any longer.

     Letting out a soft sigh, I then turned off the monitors and carried Riley on my way back to the bedroom to get dressed. I had to get ready for the day and head down to Todd and Jill's house.

     I pulled on a pair of black jeans, put on a plain black bra, and then pulled a black tank top over my head.

     I made a quick pack of gear to take with me and piled it all on the bunk. I put the 9mm pistol in a holster to carry on my hip and put the AR-15 on the bunk as well. I put a respirator on the bunk. Not the full-face gas mask because the irritation of the smoke wasn't strong enough to hurt my eyes any longer, but could get irritable to my throat if I was out several hours.

     Also, on the bed, I put a quick-make meal from our storage and a canteen of water. I filled the camelback (™) with water from the kitchen for the pack and made sure I put in a simple medical kit. A hatchet went into the pack and then I got together a lightweight scarf and a jacket to put on until it started to warm up mid-day.

     The last thing I brought to the bunk was the plate carrier vest Jack got me. I made sure the ammo pouches were filled with the magazines for the AR-15 and the two 9mm magazines that were for the pistol I now had.

     Bushing my teeth was the last of my prep, then putting my hair back in a ponytail. I put on my jacket, then pulled my plate carrier over my head, and wrapped my scarf around my neck. I pulled on a simple knit cap and gathered the gear up. Pack on, pistol in my holster, AR-15 and I was ready to get going.

     Out in the decontamination room, I cleaned up Riley's mess, then put her harness on and her leash. I carried her up the steep steps, up out of the bunker and into the shed.

     After latching the bunker hatch down, I checked the panel of monitors in the cupboard to ensure no one was around the area. Once confirmed, I stepped out with Riley, and closed the door behind me. A firm yank on the handle and I made sure it was locked tight.

     The small bag of poo from Riley I tossed into a nearby garbage can by the shed. Ready to go, we started casually moving down the driveway to the simple rugged 2-track road. At the road, we paused so I could look around and listen to everything around us. It was so strange with all the pines immediately near us having been charred to black poles.

I shouldered the strap of the AR-15 so that I was carrying it under my right arm, with the strap up and over my head and resting across my left shoulder.

Riley was thankful to be out for a walk, she moved on ahead while I held the leash. I gave her a great deal of lead from the retracting leash to let her go ahead and have lots of freedom. She dashed around, left, and right, along the route, and sniffed at everything as she got out her energy.

It was a mile hike down the rugged road to get to the McVeenson's homestead so I just strolled along at a comfortable pace. I kept looking into the distance as far as I could, to try and keep from letting anyone sneak up on me. There was no real cover for me to hide, now that the trees were barren and burned. If I was to have any advantage, it was in being able to see any threat in the distance before they noticed me. All the same, if they were not moving, or were looking towards me, I would be seen first. I was at a distinct disadvantage heading down the road, but there wasn't anything I could do to change those odds right now.

After a half mile, I surprised myself when I heard myself softly singing. I hadn't realized that I was singing until it suddenly occurred to me that I was hearing someone singing. I chuckled, shrugged, and kept on singing the Friends (™) theme song.

The lyrics stuck in my throat as I came over the last rise. The land below opened to let me see the McVeenson's home. Their house was visible now, down lower on the hillside ahead. The roof was gone, two of the walls were missing, and it was a charred mass of burned wood and smoldering whips of smoke twisting up from their home.

The sheet metal sided barn and outbuildings looked to have made it through the forest fire fine, but they also had lost all their pine trees in the blaze.

I took a quick glance around to make sure it was safe, then grabbed the AR-15 with both hands so that I could get to a fast jog down the roadway without the rifle bouncing around uncontrollably off my hip.

Riley wasn't sure why we were now moving so fast. She did her best not to get underfoot as my boots crunched on the loose gravel and sharp rocks of the Arizona mountain trail. It didn't take long to get the last bit to their home, and we slowed to a fast walk. I raised the rifle to my shoulder and kept a careful eye on anything in the area that might be a threat.

Chapter Eleven (Jack)
Scout Team Charlie

October 14 evening - October 15 morning

I packed away my Bible, my devotional, stowed away my food garbage into a Ziplock bag, and stowed it all back in my pack, so that upon leaving everything would look just the way it had when I arrived.

Before I got up to move from my hidden spot in the trees, I scanned the area down at the long lake, and the other areas around me to ensure it was clear.

It took ten minutes to be confident, but it looked clear. I got up slow, stretched the cramps out of my stiff legs and back, then donned my backpack again. I picked up the sniper rifle from against the tree and eased my way slope of trees down the hill towards the lake.

I felt the fatigue of the hike hitting me now. The hour of rest and eating really wanted to wrap its arms around me and force me to sleep. I pushed on through the aches and pain anyway.

When I reached the bottom of the hill, where the pines stopped, I stopped again to kneel beside a large tree and scope out the area with my binoculars again.

I spotted on the south side of the lake, three elk down at the water's edge drinking. One of them held a huge rack of antlers. On the north side of the lake, I spotted movement and it took a while to guess what it was in the dark. The binoculars gather some light from the moon to help me see but it was still blinding dark now. My best guess was they were a couple coyotes prowling the water's edge for a drink and to hunt what might come to the water.

My largest concern were things like bears, mountain lions, or to a greater extent people. On those counts, it looked safe to proceed.

I picked up my pace, faster than how I had been traveling. I wanted to get across this large open area and back to the tree line that awaited me. I was going to be out in the open for three miles.

In the distance, an elk bleated into the night sky, an eerie and unsettling sound if you weren't accustomed to it. A quick look over to the southern edge, I could see the male elk with the huge rack look around, sniff the air, and return a challenge loudly across the open lake and field. A quick look back to the north side and I couldn't find the coyotes any longer, they'd rushed off somewhere I couldn't see.

I tucked the binoculars away and broke from the edge of the trees at a fast walk. Best to cover as much distance as I could while out in the open.

I failed to catch a sniper's bullet in the side of my head, nor mauled by a charging bear, or sprain an ankle while crossing my way to about the midpoint of the lake. I stopped and knelt to look again and listen before I pulled out my empty canteen and filled it with water. Later, I would hook up the rubber hose, I carried to have it pass from the canteen, through the hose and then through my water filtering straw. In this way I could refill my camelback with fresh filtered and safe water.

With the canteen of lake water filled, I capped it, tucked it away, and got up to head east again.

Glancing at my watch, I confirmed it was a little before midnight, right on schedule. I still picked up my pace, because it felt so vulnerable to be out in the open field like this. It would take an hour or so before I would reach the safety of the trees and get into the hills again.

Half an hour later, I heard a horse neighing back behind me to the west. I dropped to my knees and pulled out my binoculars to look back. It sounded a great way off.

A half mile back behind me, I saw a horse with a rider on it bucking and trying to protect itself. I didn't know if it was a coyote, rattlesnake, or another threat, but I'm glad the horse gave away the position of the rider. I couldn't be certain it was the same guy I saw the day before at the water hole. Regardless, I had to consider it the same person, perhaps even someone that was stalking me. Better to be safe than sorry.

I stood back up and moved into a jog to cover the remaining half mile to the trees as fast as I could. I was losing a great deal of my ability to listen and look around me as I went. I figured the greatest threat to me was the rider behind me, and not a possible bit of wildlife lurking ahead.

By the time I reached the edge of the trees, I had copious sweat going and could feel my back drenched under my shirt. Sweat ran down my face, and I had to occasionally nudge my glasses back up my nose with a free hand. I was panting heavily when I broke into the trees, then turned sharply to the south to off the main trail for a distance before I dropped to my knees, shed my backpack, and took out my .45 cal 1911. I kept behind a larger pine tree to get my breathing under control, while listening and watching the main trail as best I could.

It wasn't hard now to pick out the shape of the man atop a horse as it was nearing. I was glad I had broken into a jog when I did, or he would have caught me out in the open before I had been able to reach the tree line. In the dark, I couldn't tell if it was the same guy with the horse I had seen before, but I was still assuming him a threat. I flipped the safety off on the 1911 and just held it at the read, pointed down at the ground in my crouched position. I waited, watched.

The man looked to have a long dark hair and a heavy jacket on. He appeared to be traveling light, without a cluster of packs or bags on his saddle.

If he was going to pass by without stopping, all would be safe. I didn't want to have to engage this guy. A silent prayer went up to God without me even really thinking about it, just hoping that the rider would keep moving on past. The last thing I wanted to do was to have to shoot someone. I didn't even know if he was a threat.

The rider kept to the path through the trees, continued heading up the slope of the land beyond me, and continued to move away.

Phew! I could feel the arteries on the sides of my neck thumping and my hands slightly shaking. I holstered my 1911 into the leg holster until it clicked into place, then took a moment to wipe my forehead of sweat, lick the sweat off my lips and take in a few deep breaths.

While keeping in hiding off the trail; I pulled my ghillie suit out. It was rather confusing doing this in the dark, I dared not turn on my flashlight. I made the ghillie suit from some netting, strips of burlap cloth dyed with different shades of greens and browns to match the upland mountains here in Arizona. Some of the burlap I did not put any coloring on so that the light-colored tans had a nice mix across it as well. It was just a base, the idea was that once you had it over you and adjusted to cover your body, you were crouched in a shrub or under trees or out in the a field, you slowly pulled bits of grass and parts off shrubs and tuck them into the gaps and holes in the netting. You would then take on the exact mix of colors and textures of where you were hiding at that moment.

In the dark, it was a real task to try and find the up from the down, left from the right on the suit. It probably took me three minutes to get the backpack on myself again, then the suit up and over everything; twisting and pulling it to fit properly over my body and down my legs to my feet.

Finally, satisfied that I was properly covered by the suit, I crouched down to get my sniper rifle from where I had leaned it. I took one last look around before getting back on my way.

My blood suddenly felt cold. The hair stood up on the back of my neck, and it felt like a five-pound brick was resting on my chest. Something was wrong. I didn't hear anything nor see anything, out of the ordinary, but there was something that petrified me in the moment.

I eased down onto my knees with the rifle, tucked the rifle under me, and laid down on my stomach in the pine needles beside the tree.

Just a few seconds later, I heard a hushed voice to the east on the trail, "... affirmative FOB 1, Scout Charlie is approaching now."

There were a few seconds next of complete silence where I was sure the sound of my heart could be heard for several feet.

I spotted the smallest glimpse of a green light for a moment as I peered out from under the ghillie suit. For a second, I thought I could see a man's face around his eyes before a quiet whisper of a voice spoke from that same area, "... negative FOB 1, no contact yet. We will press farther west towards the lake."

I had to stop breathing completely now, as the movement of three dark shapes in the shadows of the pines stood up on the trail and began to stalk forward on the trail to the west.

They looked 100% military, night vision goggles mounted on helmets, plate carrier vests, webbing, and gear much like my own, rifles as well.

I held my breath as they formed a line behind each other, and they moved along the trail. If I had been a second longer before hiding myself, or even not put on the ghillie suit, I am certain they would have seen me.

That spooky feeling and chill that ran through me had saved my life, I am certain. The sniper rifle, the 1911, the Bible in my pack, and a dozen other things on my person would have been a death sentence without a second thought, if they had captured me.

They moved along the trail, getting closer until about 15 feet away. I kept still. My lungs started to burn with that coaxing that without air I was going to die. That same reminder your brain tells you when you reach the bottom of the pool and tells you that you can't stay down here enjoying the quiet and peacefulness for very long.

As the three military scouts moved on quietly, the burning sensation slowly turned into a silent spasm within my chest. I could feel I wasn't able to pay attention to much around me as my brain started demanding all attention must be diverted to my lack of air.

At the point where I couldn't last a second longer, my throat started to squeeze in on itself. I shoved my face into the inside of my elbow and gasped for air with a gulp that couldn't stay in. It was thrown out again and replaced with a fresh gasp. I tried to make it as quiet as I could, but it sounded like thunder in my ears.

I gave a panic look in the direction of the trail, to see if I could find the men; but it was so dark inside the shadows of the pine trees. I couldn't see them, nor hear them. Maybe I was safe?

I dared not move for several minutes as I laid with my chest pushed into the dry pine needles of the forest floor. At some point, I wasn't sure how long I had been lying there, I felt myself growing tired and sleeping from hiking through the day and into the evening. I knew I had several hours to go before I was going to lay in hiding through the day. I had to get back on the route again.

It felt like it took a giant wedge to peel me off the forest floor, force myself to get up into a crouched position, and listen and look around for a minute longer. It was instinct just to want to stay still, invisible, and safe. I imagined the feeling of someone terrified of public speaking standing backstage, looking out over a full stadium of people, and knowing it was time to step out and walk to the podium.

I eased up very slowly from my position, shouldered my sniper rifle and took out my .45 cal 1911 to stalk slowly forward to the trail. Several times in that 15 feet to the trail, I had to stop and un-snag the ghillie suit from a pine tree limb. The bad thing about the suit being made of netting, is that by its very nature, netting tended to catch and hold things. The irony of it almost caused me to chuckle aloud.

When I reached the edge of the trail, I slipped down onto one knee, and eased out in the slowest of crawls so that I could look westward along the trail after the three men. They were still well out of my ability to see them. My concern was that with their night vision goggles, if the one in the back looked back towards me, would they be able to see me?

The same sensation of needing to force myself out of the illusion of safety, and into the midst of great danger rushed over me until I had to grit my teeth, pull myself to my feet, and start heading down the trail again away from the men.

After two minutes, I figured I had made it away safe. No one behind me yelled to stop, nor did I encounter a fast-moving projectile ripping through the back of my arms, legs, or the back of my head.

I picked up the pace to try and make up some time, and to put more distance between myself and the three military scouts. As I moved on though, I recalled their conversation on the radio. He called himself Scout Charlie. Where was team Alpha and team Bravo? I hoped that they were sent to different areas to patrol. Hiking east on the path team Charlie walked down, seemed safe. They had just finished searching the area I was going.

The more time that passed, as I put distance between myself and the military scouts, the better. It was right about then that it occurred to me that the apache on the horse that had passed by me was on the same trail the men had come from. The rider would have passed right by the men. There had not been any calls, commands, or gunshots from the men. How had the rider not encountered the three men? I had walked the same path now and there were no alternate routes or places to hide a horse from being seen in that area.

My mind had so much to consider that distance and time seemed to blur together. Right about the time I was thinking I was getting tired; I came to where the land started to slope down again.

I knelt next to a tree and put the sniper rifle against the tree to pull my GPS out a pouch on my chest webbing, to confirm my position. Yep, I was at the part where the land sloped down to a large field with another small man-made pond that the forest service constructed decades past, to collect water for the elk and other animals in the dry times of the year.

A glance at the time in the corner of the GPS told me I wasn't far behind on my schedule. It was 0300 hrs. right now, and it was going to take thirty minutes to get down to the lake to refill my canteen. I spent a few minutes taking the filtered water out of my canteen and refilled my camelback pouch. I prepared the freshly emptied canteen to collect up fresh water with the filtering straw as I had done before.

Prepared now, I snatched up my rifle and moved on along the way again. I was careful going down the hillside in the trees. The Arizona mountains had an abundance of loose rock underfoot and sharp-edged boulders. The mountains had been created by the upheaval of volcanoes hundreds of years before and it was an unforgiving land.

Arizona really wasn't a place that welcomed man into it. Between its scorpions, diamondback rattlesnakes, Gila monsters, black widows, Brown Recluse, mountain lions, bears, 115° summer temps, flash flood monsoons in the winter and just the overall apparent plan that any man coming into this area would statistically be killed before the end of the week.

It wasn't like growing up in Michigan, where with a knife and a jacket, you could walk out your back door into the forest and go weeks, finding your own food and drinkable water, while making your own shelter. Arizona, I was certain, was God's way of showing mankind what Hell was going to be like.

The temperature had been dropping fast, once the sun dropped down below the horizon on the west. It was in the mid 70's in mid-afternoon, but now it was dipping down and heading below 40°F.

The Great Lakes in Michigan, as I was growing up, prevented such a drastic temperature fluctuation as we have here in Arizona. The water in the Lakes absorbed the heat from the sun and as the sun dipped down under the horizon, the Lakes naturally released this heat slowly.

Michigan has over 15,000 inland lakes. It was hard to find a place that you were not within four miles of a lake of some size. Sure, Minnesota bragged that it was the "Land of 10,000 Lakes", pfft. People in Michigan chuckled at it. We never fussed too loud, we figured Minnesota needed something to feel good about, so we let them continue to brag.

Here in Arizona though, dressing in layers, wasn't just a backpacker's way of life. In the spring and fall, the temperatures could fluctuate 40-50° between the day and night temperatures. If I wasn't hiking and carrying so much weight in my pack right now, I would have had to stop and put on a sweater and some gloves. For now, with my heart rate up at a satisfying pace, I was chugging along and feeling just fine. Now, if there was rain, or I started to sweat and got wet, that was a whole different situation, hypothermia would be a real danger.

I managed to make it across the open field to the edge of the pond, kneel and refill my canteen without incident. It was slow going in the dark because I dared not use my flashlight. The light of the moon and the stars was the only help I had, trying not to stumble in ditches or across large rocks along the way.

I capped the canteen with the pond water and tucked it in my pack. Remaining crouched, I listened for noises for a few minutes longer.

An elk bleating far off reminded me that I hadn't heard a plane fly over in several months. There were some upsides to a societal collapse.

I fought back the urge to groan from my sore muscles, as I rose back up to a standing position. Time to get back on my route eastward. There were a few more hours I needed to get put behind me before sunrise.

My GPS told me the terrain ahead was going to be a steep incline as I came up out of the valley for an hour. There was another small pond expected at the top in another open field, but I was doing well on the amount of water I had on me. These small refilling stations relieved a substantial amount of stress in that regard. It was the long hike on the last day that was the greatest concern. It was going to be a full night's hike to get to the power station, a day of hiding, sleeping, and then another full night returning to a water source. It could easily end up being three days with the only water being what I could carry (my camelback and two canteens).

I had to stop for a break halfway up the steep hillside, take off my pack and get a nice long drink. I ate the pack of M&M's I had saved from the MRE earlier. It was only a five-minute rest, but it revived me and put a spring back in my step.

Trying not to stick myself in the eye with a branch from one of the pine trees, or stumble across a protruding rock on the path, kept much of my attention. It was probably helpful that it was a tough hike because it worked to fight against my mind worrying about Jordan, and if she had enough insulin now. Was she caught, for being involved in the underground church group in Flagstaff? Had she been executed for being found with a Bible or noticed praying? Was she alive still, held in one of the many re-education camps as slave labor for the government?

It was so simple to fall into a great depression worrying about these things. The only thing that pulled me back from the black abyss was a constant state of prayer. I wished I could put in some earphones, listen to some worship music as I hiked, but that was impossible while trying to listen to the dangers around me in the forest.

About five minutes farther on, I fell face forward onto the trail with quite a commotion. I wrapped my arms around the sniper rifle as I fell, tried to twist to land on my arm and hip to try to protect the weapon. The rifle was not damaged, but the tradeoff was a searing pain in my shoulder and my hip where I slammed into the jagged rocks of the trail.

My mind raced across a multitude of worries instantly. Was the ruckus I just made heard by someone? Did I dislocate my shoulder? What did I trip over?

I rolled over onto my back, moved my arm and confirmed it was not dislocated or broken, but I had to grit my teeth in pain. There was going to be a massive purple bruise I would have to deal with for a couple weeks. My hip felt the same way and I eased over onto my knees and pushed myself up. This time I was unable to hide the groaning of pain as I got to my feet.

I limped to the side when I tested my hip, but it didn't feel broken. I was going to have to deal with a limp though for a day or two, I was certain.

Looking back behind me, I squinted to see what was on the trial that I face planted over.

It was a large object a foot or two high and it stretched clear across the path. It was not moving. Perhaps a log?

I pulled the small flashlight off my chest harness and flipped it on while cupping the end of it with my other hand. I had got in the habit of doing this to make sure that the red lens was on the end of the light. I did not want to expose my position so easily if someone was looking in my direction.

When the red light spilled out between my fingers, I removed my hand and took a careful look at what was on the trail.

I sucked in a gulp of air in surprise and then dropped to one knee as I switched the light into my left hand and pulled out my 1911 in my right. I was on high alert now; I was in the nucleus of something terrible.

On the path in front of me, was a man dressed in military gear. I scanned the area with the flashlight, another not far off the trail also still and face down. A third man was on the opposite side of the trail, but it didn't look quite right. Something was off about it.

Chapter Twelve (Megan)
Where Are my Neighbors?

October 14

I prayed that either Todd or Jill would come out from around one of the buildings to greet me as they heard me coming down the road, but they never did. I could hear one of their horses inside their barn make a bit of noise, then their chickens clucking about like it was just a normal day in their coop.

My heart started to sink as I feared the worst. It was then, that their German Shepherd burst out of the blackened remains of their home in a fury of rage.

Riley yelped in fear and darted around behind me, yanking on the leash while trying to flee.

I called out to him and called his name, "Butch... Butch, you okay Butch?"

The large dog slid to a stop about halfway out to me, snarled, and bared its teeth at me. I lowered my rifle and pointed the barrel down at the ground.

I could see that Butch had several missing patches of fur where he had been far too close to the fire and paid the price. As he stopped his charge, he started a slow pace back and forth to protect the charred house. I could see he was slightly limping on his right front paw, probably also burned from the fire. He was traumatized to say the least, I could feel my eyes well up with tears as I knew that his humans must be dead inside the house for him to be carrying on like he was.

Riley stopped trying to yank herself off the leash in the opposite direction, and submitted to just sitting back as far away as allowed by the leash.

I pulled slack in the AR-15's strap to slip it around to my side again. I pulled out my canteen, and the small collapsible bowl I used to give Riley water. Stepping back to join Riley, I waited.

Butch watched me intently, as I prepared the water for him. He had met me several times and it was taking him a while not to consider anything and everything around him a threat.

Butch wouldn't approach until Riley and I backed up a considerable distance. It wasn't until we were a significant way back that he hobbled up to the dish of water and lapped it up with his muzzle buried in the water. I think half of the water was splashed all over the sides of his face, nose and around on the ground in his frantic attempt to get the water in as fast as he could.

Riley and I stayed back, and didn't move until he was completely done with the bowl of water. He looked up at the both of us, and carefully sat down next to the bowl. He was still favoring his front right paw and held it slightly off the ground.

I wasn't sure if I should move closer to him or not, until he bent down and pushed at the empty bowl with his nose. He then sat back up and looked at me. He wasn't snarling at me anymore or barking, this was an improvement.

Riley wasn't having anything to do with getting near the German Shepherd, so I unhooked the leash from her chest harness and let her scamper back towards our home. She didn't go very far, but she seemed more at ease knowing she was able to run to safety without the leash keeping her from getting away.

I turned to put my attention back on Butch while holding the canteen in my left hand. I very slowly approached the large dog as I started talking in what I hoped he felt was a reassuring voice, "I'm so sorry Butch. We're going to make sure you are taken care of big-fella."

He appeared to recognize me slowly, his body language loosened, and became less confrontational. As I got a bit more near, his tail twitched a little. It wasn't a full wag, but it was encouraging.

As I got close, I held the canteen out towards him to let him smell the water, that perked him up and brought me into the friend-zone solidly. His tail moved into a full wag now, and he came to his feet, minus a slightly lifted burned paw. Butch moved to put his muzzle down close to the bowl, eager for me to refill it.

As fast as I could pour it into the bowl, he lapped it up and sucked it down until I found the canteen empty. Oh well, maybe I could find some more water around the McVeenson's homestead for myself and Riley. If not, we were only a mile from home.

I recapped the canteen and put it back in its pouch on my left hip, as Butch was finishing up the last of the moisture in the bowl. I didn't reach out to pet him, I just held my hand out from my body and let him come to my hand, sniff at it and then nuzzle it. He then moved his head up under my hand and press up on my hand to push his ears against my hand.

Accepted; nice. I gave him a loving light scratch around his ears, "You're a good boy Butch, good boy." I was very soft and careful; I wasn't sure where he had gotten burned and I didn't want to cause him any pain.

Butch was fast to warm up to me and push up against my leg. He was enormous compared to Riley and his weight against me surprised me a bit.

I looked back up the rugged road to look for Riley and saw she had come back about halfway to me now. She looked agitated, jealous that I was giving attention to Butch.

Butch completely ignored Riley. If he had wanted to be concerned about the small dog, it would have taken just a single gulp to swallow down the little lapdog.

It didn't look like Riley planned on ever warming to the large dog any time soon, she stayed several yards away and wasn't coming any closer.

I retrieved the bowl from the ground and collapsed it, to tuck it away in my pack. I would have to tend to Butch's injured paw, but right now, we had to build our trust before he would let me do something like that.

Butch could still move well when his mind was set on something, but when the adrenaline dropped, his limp became far more visible. The large German Shepherd began to lead me towards the burned down home, stopping, and waiting for me to catch up to him before he went any farther. It was evident that I was going to have to deal with this. It was something I absolutely did not want to have to see and deal with. Why wasn't Jack here? He could deal with much better than I could.

Butch wasn't going to wait for me to get comfortable with all of this, he led me to a charred break in the front wall, to what was once their living room. The second floor of the house on the left side had collapsed down into the ground floor living room and dining room. The couch was half melted and burned, sticking out from under the collapsed upstairs that was resting on it now. The upstairs bathroom had been above that area, the toilet was sideways in the pile but the sink wasn't porcelain and it was melted into a lump of black hard solidified ooze. The hot and cold-water handles sticking out of it was the only way I could tell that it used to be a sink.

The footing could not have been any worse. Each step was placed on something that shifted and moved when I put my weight on it. Some places felt as if they would give way and I would fall into the basement below. Other places shifted and slid like I was putting my foot on ice. It wasn't an even surface either. I took a step over the couch and a wide reach with my next foot across a gap. I put my weight down on some unidentified metal that slid when I stepped on it.

Butch was trying to show me a safe route to follow him towards the stairs to the far right. It may have been a simple route for him to find his way over there, but I only had two legs and my center of gravity was much higher than his.

It wasn't an easy go. I was glad I had on a pair of gloves. At one point when I had to reach out fast to keep my balance, my hand shot across a sharp glass edge. Without the gloves, my hand would have been sliced open like a chicken breast on the cutting board.

I finally reached the base of the stairs, while Butch moved up to the landing. The stairs leveled off, and then turned back the other way around a wall to reach the second floor. I took a few breaths to get my wits about me, and looked out across the smoldering lower floors to get a view on Riley. She was staying outside, too afraid to come into the house. That was best, I was glad she wasn't trying to come in with me.

I was careful to step on the very outside edges of the stairs nearest the walls. I could tell the boards were weak from the fire and standing on it fully very well might find me falling, crashing into the basement below.

At the top of the stairs, the second floor opened into a hallway with doors on the left and the right. It looked somewhat normal, until the point where the second floor just dropped off and it became open air and a straight drop into the living room below.

The first door on the right was the back of the house, the master bedroom. The door was open. Butch sat in the doorway whimpering at me. He got up, sat down, and then got up again. He was anxious, and wanted me to come right away.

Something strong hit my nose right about the time I came up to the open doorway. Was it the burned and curled up melted carpet or spongy padding under the carpet blackened and melted? Was it the painted furniture black and charred? Was it the plastic items in the room or the chemicals and glues in everything in the house that had been burning?

But it smelled sweet in some way, almost like a pineapple infused barbecue sauce. When I stepped into the doorway and looked in, that moment, became the moment when I never again would eat Pineapple.

Todd and Jill were in their bed twisted in a tangle together. The wooden bedframe was burned away, the legs of the bed, the side rails that held up the box springs, and the mattress had also burned up and fallen away. The box springs were burned away but the mattress was only half-way consumed by the flames. The bottom of the mattress had burned heavily and surely had filled the room with thick choking and smothering smoke. The only reason I could figure that the top of the bed did not fully burn was that as their bodies burned their blood and fluids in their bodies boiled out onto the bed around them and put out the fires nearest them.

It was a sickening thing, to try to put logic to what I was seeing. The more I tried to put science to it, the more it made me imagine the details; and that was making it worse.

Both of their mouths were stretched open in agonizing screams, tongues charred black like burned steak. Their eyes were missing, boiled out and burned up. Almost every bit of their hair was gone, skulls, faces, necks and entire bodies a jet-black color. Their clothes and blankets were melted into their arms, legs, and torso. I could not tell where the blanket began, and their body ended. In the fire, they sort of meshed in the heat to become a new combined thing.

Butch whimpered at me as he climbed up on the bed next to them, and anxiously pleaded with me. How could I tell a dog that his best friends, his family, would never again call his name, cuddle with him in bed, or play with him in the yard?

I fell to my knees, again grateful that Jack had gotten me the tactical elbow and knee pads, as my knees crunched into the burned slag of the room. I sucked in a deep breath, was I sobbing? Then I heard myself. I was.

Reaching around to the canteen, I flipped up the cover of the pouch that held my mask and pulled it out. I turned it so that I could tuck my chin into the chin cup of the mask, move it up over my mouth and nose, and then pulled the straps back around my head. I tightened it so that it would stay in place snugly.

The smoke from the house wasn't so strong as to make it hard to breath, but the stench made it difficult to concentrate. The smell made me want to find a way out of the area, to get away.

I'm not sure how long I stayed there kneeling on the floor by the bed. I felt numb, it felt as if I was having a bad dream. I don't remember Butch moving over to me across the bed. It was his licking of my forehead that broke me out of my trance. I reached up without thinking if it was a smart idea or not, and wrapped my arms around his neck and hugged him.

The large German Shepherd didn't pull back away from me. Instead, he nuzzled into my neck and whimpered. I don't know if it is real if a dog and a person can share in something so deep and emotional, at the same level. It appeared as if what

I needed was Butch in this moment, and what he needed was me.

After some time, I loosened my hug on Butch's neck and he moved to get off the bed, to be close to me at my side. It appeared to me, that he was transferring his bond from Todd and Jill to me. I was the only one that could comfort him, care for him, and that was enough, for now. Butch and I were now inseparable.

Butch led the way out of the master bedroom and back out into the hallway as I got up off my knees. I took great care not to glance back for another look at my neighbors, as I adjusted the AR-15 on my hip and joined Butch out in the hall. There was so much going through my mind right then. They had horses, goats, rabbits, chickens, and all the equipment, feed, and the supplies needed to care for them. We'd need to tend to, and move them all to our place to make sure they were properly cared for. If not, they would be picked clean by mountain lions, bears, coyotes, or other people. If we were to be able to take care of them, we were going to need to relocate the barn, and sheds to our property piece by piece so we could reconstruct them again.

Why wasn't Jack here? How could I hope to get my arms wrapped around all this stuff that needed to be done now? Did Todd and Jill have family? How would we find them and inform them?

Butch sat in the hallway and waited for me as I twisted the door handle of the room across the hall and pushed. I had to shoulder the door open, to get into the room beyond. It was the only other room remaining on the second floor of the house, I figured I'd best check it out to make sure I knew everything I was dealing with.

When I shouldered the door into the room, I managed to keep from losing my balance by holding tight onto the door handle with my right hand and then reaching out and grabbing onto the door jamb with my left.

A quick look around, I confirmed no big dangers or threats. It looked to be a simple spare bedroom. It stank like everything of smoke but for some reason it wasn't burned up like the McVeenson's room had been.

I tried not to consider what their last moments may have been like. They did all they could to keep their animals and house safe, but alas had to collapse in exhaustion and get some sleep. During that sleep, is when the fire must have crept in and got too close to the house. Smoke filled the air and overwhelmed them as they slept. Butch must have tried to wake them up. Maybe he wasn't with them and was outside, maybe locked out of the house? I had so many questions, but it felt better just to push them off and try not to consider them yet.

I'm not sure why, but I closed the door behind me and moved along behind Butch as he led the way down the stairs and into the living room below.

The kitchen was to my right as I descended the stairs. It sat along the back wall of the house and under the master bedroom above. The dining room beyond had been smashed flat by the second-floor collapse.

I took a quick look through the kitchen to see if there were any emergencies that needed my attention at that moment. The fire had gone out completely now. What was going to burn, had burned up, and was just smoldering now. Everything that was plastic was limp and twisted and in pools of goo. The counter had its thin layer of cosmetic fake marble curled up, the wood beneath dark and burned.

I figured I'd check the cupboards later and the fridge for stuff that might be saved and brought home. I turned to head back through the chaos of the house to go check on the animals in the barn, but that's when I spotted the pantry door. I twisted the handle and pulled it towards me. Wait, this wasn't a pantry. A set of wooden stairs led down into the basement. I figured they had a basement, but never spent sufficient time in their house to identify how to get down there. The fire had spared the basement, from the looks of it.

I pulled my flashlight from the pouch on the side of my armored vest, flipped it on, and made my way down. Butch sat at the top of the stairs in the kitchen and watched me go into the basement, waiting for me.

The stairs brought me down to a small landing, then it turned to the right under the living room. I didn't even try and turn on the light switch on the wall. Even if there was electricity still working somehow, I didn't want to risk some open wire reigniting the fire in the house.

The basement had a large amount of smoke in it and my flashlight's beam only reached out about five to ten feet at the most in places. There wasn't any air circulation down here, so the wispy smoke was going to take forever to dissipate.

Their basement was wide open, without any inside walls and doors. The basement was one large concrete floor with concrete walls. I started moving to the right to make a large circle, to see what was in the area.

Under the kitchen, Todd had a woodworking bench against the wall with a pegboard filled with all manner of hand tools. Saws, screwdrivers, wrenches, hand drills, several other old hand tools I didn't know the names for sat in their organized places.

I was glad I had the mask over my face now, my eyes were watering in the smoke. I couldn't imagine how I'd be hacking a lung out, if I didn't have the mask on down here.

I continued along the back of the house, to find that the entire backside of the basement was a floor to ceiling 2x4 frame with pine boards making up shelves. The shelves were filled front to back on every shelf with canned goods, jars; jams, canned meat, berries, and dozens of different types of foods preserved in glass jars. There was enough food down here for two years, easy.

On the far side of the basement, away from the stairs, was another long bench. This one was set up with a nice stool in front of it and it had Jill's sewing machine on it. The wall behind the bench was another peg board filled with spools of thread and other sewing supplies for the clothes that Jill always made for her and her husband. Below the bench, the shelves were filled with bolts of various cloth and textiles. I didn't spend much time looking over what was there, Jack was the one that did the sewing in our family and he'd know what was useful.

I made my way back along the last wall, feeling confident with the way things were going and that's when I found myself falling face forward and completely out of control. I flailed out to try and grab something, but my arms and hands didn't manage to find anything before I crashed to the floor with a clatter and a calamitous ruckus.

Butch barked surprisingly loud, as he called out to ensure I was okay.

"I'm okay Butch," I managed to call up to him from the floor. I wasn't sure if I was lying to him yet, but it was something that sort of just came out without thinking.

My hip had a sharp pain in it and I was careful to roll over onto my back and take a couple moments to see if I was bleeding or if I had broken anything in the fall. I didn't want to spend the next several days laying in our neighbor's basement waiting for Jack to get back, and then come find me. Now that, would be a horrific thing to have to live through.

Luckily, after a couple moments I figured I'd make it just fine, having nothing worse than a nasty bruise on my left hip for a week or more.

I needed my flashlight. Where did it go?

I saw a thin glimpse of light across the floor in the smoke and made my way in that direction. Crawling on my hands and knees towards the wall where the flashlight had been flung under a shelf, I stretched my arm out under to try and reach the light. If the flashlight wasn't on, I never would have found it again. The grey beam of light in the smoke was the only reason I had any idea where I needed to go.

As I got near, I could see it more clearly and it was a simple retrieval. Once I had the light, I pivoted around on my knees in a crouched position to shine the light back at whatever had made me trip and fall. The wispy smoke prevented clear sight and made it hard to discern what was over there. I forced myself to my feet with a painful reminder of my new bruise on my hip, moving over to check the situation.

A shape in the beam of light was all I could determine. I neared closer, and then froze in fear. A hand lay on the basement floor. I moved closer, reluctantly to see a black sleeved arm attached to it. A shoulder, and finally the entire body of a man lay there on the basement floor of the McVeenson's home.

I felt sick to my stomach, coming across yet another dead body. At least this one was not burned to a crisp in the fire. It looked more human, and comforting than what I had to witness upstairs.

I forced myself to kneel next to the body and check it closer. It wasn't until then, that I saw the pool of blood under the man. A knife wound? A gunshot? Why was this man dead on the floor?

I had to learn as much as I could to discover what was going on. Without moving him, I couldn't see any injury that would explain all this blood. I reached forward and grabbed at his black hoodie at the shoulder, pulled him towards me to get him to flip over onto his back. I couldn't manage it very well until I grabbed his hip with my other hand by hooking my gloved finger into his belt loop. Then, with both hands I was able to yank him towards me to flop him onto his back.

The cause of the blood was obvious now that he was on his back. A large mass of mangled skin and meat was exposed on his chest, in what appeared to be a shotgun blast at close range.

On the man's face was a black mask with the Antifa emblem on it. They were a common roaming group that terrorized people randomly, with no rhyme nor reason. The group had organized with a basic uniform of black hoodies and cloth face masks with a capital A inside a circle, as their emblem.

We had lucked out, up to this point, with not having to interact with this group of government shock troops. But, with this man's body on the floor before me, it forced me to admit that they were within a mile of our house. It wouldn't be long before we were going to be engaging them.

The government gave waivers to Antifa, so that they could use vehicles, and be armed. They were given immediate government approval to neutralize any threats to the government. This meant, if their roaming group in vehicles stopped at any home and found a Bible, found that they had a gas-powered vehicle or had any infraction against the federal laws, that they could kill anyone on the spot.

Beyond being the death squads for the government, Antifa would take what they wanted from your home. Your food, your water, your daughter, whatever they thought they wanted.

To find one of their members dead here in the basement, set my mind spinning, and on high alert. This wasn't just a visit to go check in on Todd and Jill any longer. This wasn't even discovering our neighbors burned alive in their home. This had just gotten a great deal more complicated.

I checked his body and couldn't find any weapons on him. So, that meant that others of his group were here with him, had stripped him of what they wanted, and left him here dead in the basement before they moved on.

The body was stiff and not flexible. I had no idea how long it took a body to get this way after it died. I didn't know if this was very recent or was a couple days ago. They hadn't come up to our house yet. I didn't know if they would find their way up the mile trail to our place or if we would have dodged their visit for a while longer.

I stood back up, and made my way back to the stairs to get out of the basement, to find Butch waiting for me in the kitchen. Now, I understood why he didn't want to follow me down earlier.

Previously, I had not noticed, but now that I'd walked down the stairs and back up, I saw that on the floor in the kitchen, beneath the ash, there was a generous amount of blood that was smeared. My best guess was that the Antifa guy had been killed up here, body was drugged down into the basement to be left there. It smelled like a cover up to a murder right now to me. Had Todd or Jill killed the guy with their shotgun while defending themselves? Then been killed and put in their bed to make it look like they had died in the house fire?

I worked my way across the living room, out through the broken gap in the front wall with Butch following along behind me, limping on his burned paw.

142

It didn't take very long at all to walk around the house and confirm that the pine needles on the ground near the house were not burned. It was clear that the house was set on fire by the Antifa thugs, and not from the forest fire.

Who would I show this to, or tell? Nobody. There was no justice, or law any longer. There was survival, and protecting yourself and those you loved. Government now, was not a way to protect the innocent and maintain a civil society. It had been replaced with something that ensured chaos, destruction, and the enslavement of anyone not at the highest levels of the organization.

Now, my level of paranoia was at maximum setting. My attention was not just on what was close around me, but farther out a full mile, searching for any movement. I waited behind the wall of the house for five minutes before I moved across the open area to the metal sided barn.

The barn, at one time had been a simple pole barn with a roll up door and a small metal door to one side. As the McVeenson's found themselves having to turn their weekend mountain home into their main residence, they walled in some internal walls and moved a couple horses inside as well as a penned in area for their three goats. Off the rear of the makeshift barn was a chicken coop. It had a yard for them to get out and walk about in the weather when they wanted. For their safety, a walled in and covered roof of chicken wire had been made to keep them from becoming owl, hawk, eagle, coyote, and mountain lion food.

The horses had a sliding door off the right side of the building. This allowed them to get out to run in the fields. Right now, it was closed and probably had been closed before the forest fire came through. The horses were likely traumatized from the fire and anxious from being locked up for so long over the last few days.

It was going to take us weeks to take off the ridge cap from the roof, the sheet metal roofing, the sheet metal siding, disassemble the internal walls, take down the framing of the building, then we had to move it all up to our land and rebuild the entire thing like a big kit.

I tested the door on the front and was happy to find it unlocked. Once inside, I had to turn on my flashlight to get a careful look around.

Both horses thudded against their walls as they bucked and jostled around in their stalls. The barn was smoke free thankfully, so I pulled my mask off and slipped it back into its pouch on my side. I needed to get more light and fresh air into the barn for the animals. I needed to get them more relaxed. I fumbled around with the release levers for the roll up door and then hefted and heaved the door upward until I got it to roll up. Sunlight spilled in and filled up the barn with a gust of fresh cool morning air accompanying it.

Behind me, on the left wall; the rabbits scurried about in their hutches. They hopped about in their cages while trying to find places to hide, the bright light of the day hurting their eyes.

The more I looked around, the more I felt weighed down by how much work it was going to take to move everything a mile up the road to our place.

With the daylight filling the barn now, I had a chance to look around and take a quick inventory from my position.

On the left, I guessed there to be nearly a dozen rabbits in cages, water bottles, a couple bales of straw for bedding, and some sacks of rabbit pellets/feed in large bags over top. Behind the rabbits, a short wall of wood pens was made to hold their three goats.

On the right side of the barn, a tack room filled with harnesses, saddles and hundreds of different things like pitchforks, a wheelbarrow, and all sorts of stuff for the care of the horses.

Beyond the tack room was the sliding door that let the horses get outside. Beyond that gap, between the tack room were two horse stalls made of thick wood planks and heavy iron hinges and latches. I wasn't sure about what names Todd and Jill had been calling them. I was sure one of them was named Hugh. It struck me funny at the time.

At the far other end of the barn was another door that I knew led out to the chicken coop, and the wired in yard. On the left side of the back door were large sacks of oats, grains, and other supplies to feed the animals. On the right side of the back door was a random collection of items used on the farm. There was a horse drawn plow for tilling up the ground for planting. The wall was covered with pitchforks, shovels, mining picks, pulleys, some come-alongs, and dozens of various things needed to run a small farm.

Overhead, the rafters had been planked across the joists to provide a place to store hay and straw for the animals. They had done very well preparing to care for their animals as best they could, the small barn was filled with everything needed.

Would it be easier to dig up our bunker and rebury it here? It may be easier than moving all this a mile up to our property. I felt overwhelmed, this was going to take all winter.

We would need to make temporary fencing and overhead shelter for the horses, goats, and rabbits while we disassembled the barn to reconstruct it. We might even need to put the rabbit hutches inside of our house. I didn't like the sound of that at all. Would the smell ever be able to be removed from the house after that?

For now, I had to do what I could to take care of these animals now. I would have to start moving what I could, but for now, the animals had eaten all the food they had been given and were eager for more.

It took a while to find what I needed to tend to their care. I used a little wagon to take five-gallon buckets out to their hand pump, fill them with water and bring them back to fill the water bottles, troughs, and buckets for the animals. It was hard work.

I found which feed, went to which animals, and tried to guess how much I should give to each group. After a couple hours, I had to take off my jacket and cap while the morning warmed up.

I had to remind myself to stop, peek out, and listen to see if Antifa was returning. I really needed another set of eyes to help. Luckily, Butch appeared to discover this was his new responsibility. He kept close to the open roll up door of the barn, and kept alert on what was going on outside.

I found a large bag of dog food, made sure to give him a proper bowl of food, and some fresh cool water from the well also.

Riley was still jittery around Butch. At one point, when I went to the well, she ran up to me and stayed close. She was never more than a couple feet away, underfoot from that point, wanting me to keep her protected from Butch.

After I managed to get the animals squared away, I did a careful walk around their property to check if there was anything else, I may have missed. That was when I found a small garage back on their property. The forest fire had moved off south of their property and not carried itself up to the garage so it was still well hidden in the pine trees that survived there. I could see the roof of the small garage was covered in solar panels, that was an encouraging sign.

I checked the door of the garage, and found it was locked up tight. I had no idea where the key to the door might be hidden. A short walk back into the barn to get a crowbar, and bring it back, allowed me to then wrench the padlock off the door.

"Ah, sweet," I heard myself say with a smile.

Directly inside the large front door, was an all-terrain vehicle, a Polaris UTV meant to carry two people with a small cargo area in the rear. It had a roll cage over the top, and was a very popular vehicle that most families had up here in the mountains. Now though, they were illegal to have, so it made sense why it was hidden in the little garage.

A quick look around the small space and at the back behind the Polaris vehicle I could see a small two wheeled trailer. It was hooked up to the hitch at the back of the UTV and I found myself smiling bigger now. Still though, the sound of its motor running was a terrible idea. It would be able to be heard for half a mile if anyone was near enough to hear.

I looked around the building for gas cans but couldn't find any. If there wasn't any gas, I'd have to get some from what we had hidden on our property.

Under the workbench, in the small garage though, that's when I spotted the bank of marine batteries that the solar panels were charging. Following the wire from the batteries it led me to the vehicle. Perhaps they were just trying to trickle charge the battery to keep it fresh?

When I pulled the hatch up on the back-cargo area to look at the engine and battery under, that is when I had a nice chuckle. The McVeenson's had removed the gas engine of the vehicle and replaced it with several golf cart batteries, and golf cart motors for powering the rear wheels. They had tied in the drive system so that the front wheels were also powered. It still had 4-wheel drive ability. Ingenious! Technically, it was legal because it was not a gas-combustion engine vehicle anymore. Perfect!

I almost skipped around the small garage in excitement. I was not only going to be able to ferry supplies from here up to our place, but I should be able to do so silently, without drawing attention to myself in the process.

I checked the tires on the trailer and on the vehicle, then unhooked the charging wire to the batteries and got it ready for use. Hopping into the driver's seat, I had to get back out and lift Riley up and put her in the passenger's seat. What a silly little dog.

A turn of the key on the dash, and nothing seemed to happen. A little green LED light came on the dash. So that was a good thing, right?

I moved the shift lever to drive and then gently pushed down on the pedal. Woosh! The vehicle shot forward and I jerked my foot off the pedal. It slowed down and came to a stop again. I'd never driven a golf cart, I had no idea how much torque they had, and how fast they applied power to moving. I guess it made sense. Those electric cars at a stoplight could take off lightning fast.

Extra careful now, I eased gently on the pedal and pulled out of the little garage far enough to get the trailer out so I could get out and return to close the building up.

I saw Butch halfway to the barn. He was always keeping a careful eye out on things, and seemed on edge. He was ready for those Antifa thugs to come back, that I was certain of.

I eased the vehicle up in front of the barn, did my best to back the trailer up into the barn, but after the fifth attempt I just gave up and pulled it up sideways so that the trailer was just outside the door. I don't know how Jack was so amazing at backing up trailers. I guess it took a substantial amount of practice.

This was one of the most exhausting days of my life. For the next several hours, I loaded up the little trailer and the back of the electric vehicle from what I found in the barn. I slowly crawled up the trail to our property and started finding places to start stacking up things. Anything food related to the animals; like the rabbit pellets, I put inside the house in the living room. I figured everything was going to be packed in every corner of the house before this was all over with.

Butch took a long while sniffing at everything around our yard, checking things out. I had to leave the front door of the house open while I carried things in, the large German Shepherd checked out everything he could inside the house as well.

Riley still wouldn't leave my side for fear of the larger dog, but Butch didn't seem to give Riley a second thought. It took until lunch, before Riley would stop shaking in fear when Butch came near.

Sometime around lunch, I had to stop and make some food. The dogs liked the break, and both curled up for some sleep. Butch took the front porch of the house and Riley found a place under the table inside.

The remainder of the day was moving more back to the house with the trailer until the UTV batteries had been drained and almost spent completely. I barely made it back home with a load around 3:00 pm. I had to plug in the UTV to recharge from our own solar system. Luckily, we had a huge bank of batteries way over sized for what we needed, so the rest of the day it would charge from the solar panels, but then it would be drawing power from our batteries to finish charging itself through the night. By morning it would be fully charged for another day of hard work.

I hadn't planned on the batteries running dead when they did, so I had to walk back to the barn on foot to see to the animals' evening meal. I was worried I wasn't going to be able to get the horses back into the barn on my own, so I had to leave them in their stalls. I felt bad, but I'd feel worse if they ran off and someone saw them and killed them.

A couple trips to the hand pump with the five-gallon buckets and the little wagon and I couldn't think of anything more I needed to do. I made sure the chicken feed barrel still had feed in it and that they were also watered. I then locked things up as best I could and trudged on back to our property.

On the way back, Riley finally let Butch come up, and they exchanged careful sniffs of each other. It seemed they had a nice truce set now. Riley wasn't so freaked out after that.

I was going to collapse after a nice hot shower tonight. The temperatures were dropping fast now, and I had to put my jacket and cap back on before I got back to the house.

I felt blessed, lucky really. Jack and I were still alive, and I had managed to make it through the day without encountering any of the Antifa thugs. I had hoped to sleep in the house now that the forest fire had gone and that wasn't a threat any longer. But, with Antifa roaming so close to home, I knew I wouldn't be able to sleep in the house. Not after seeing what they did to Todd and Jill.

I double checked everything, made sure I wasn't being watched, then slipped into the shed with Riley and Butch.

Butch didn't know what to think about the hatch down into the bunker. I had to carry Riley down and leave Butch up top with the hatch left open.

I came back up to pet Butch and comfort him. I figured I would need to leave the bunker hatch open for a while before he got comfortable enough to come down. The idea of getting him down the steep stairs by carrying him was unpleasant. He could probably climb up the steep stairs to get out, but going down the steep inclined steps I figured would be too hard for him to do.

I hung my jacket and cap inside the bunker after turning on the LED lights inside, hung up the AR-15, the belt that held my 9mm holster and knife, then hung my armored vest up as well. It felt amazing to shed all that weight after this exhausting day.

Riley made her way back to the bedroom and hopped up onto the bed. She was fast asleep as I stripped everything off and got into a nice hot shower.

The shower felt so refreshing. Every muscle in my body was just spent and at its very end of endurance. Nothing would be able to wake me up tonight.

I was drying off after the shower with the towel, bending over to dry my legs when I let out a squeal, and jumped forward in shock.

Oh, for heaven's sake!

When I turned around it all made sense. Butch had managed to find his way down the steel stairs into the bunker. When I had my back to him drying off his wet nose found its way... well, no need to mention where.

My squeal had scared him and caused him to dash back into the decontamination room and pace around, frightened that he'd done something terrible wrong.

Well, that put me into a fit of laughter. I had needed something to break the stress of the day and I kept on laughing for a long while after that. I wrapped the towel around myself and went out and pet Butch for a while to let him know everything was okay. I climbed up and pulled the bunker blast hatch closed, turned the inner toggle bars closed to seal myself in solid.

Both Butch and Riley were waiting for me at the bottom of the stairs when I came back down and they both appeared intent on me, not bothering to pay any attention to each other. That was pleasant, they seem to have agreed to consider each other part of the same family now.

I didn't mess around with any cleaning of the bunker or organizing. I didn't even pick up my dirty clothes off the floor.

The dogs and I just trudged on back to the bed and climbed in, turned off the lights and were fast asleep.

Chapter Thirteen (Jack)
All Hail the Power

October 14 evening - October 15 morning

I turned my light off, listened, as I searched around for what could have killed these three military men. I knew they were not the same men I encountered hours earlier. Those men had been going in the opposite direction, to the west. This could be scout group Alpha, or Bravo. Regardless, if they had been killed, and not responded to radio calls and checked in, they probably had GPS locators on them. A rescue team would be arriving at any moment.

I moved to the man that was off the trail that looked strange. When I came upon him, I had to turn to the side and empty the contents of my stomach onto the ground in violent heaving.

The man's torso was on the ground but his stomach had been ripped open and emptied of its intestines and organs. The lower half of his body had been dragged off away from the trail, a smearing of blood as the hips and legs were pulled across the ground.

I wiped my mouth with the back of my arm as I forced myself to look back at the man with my flashlight. The guy appeared to be less than 30 years old as best as I could guess. It was difficult to guess with the shredded flesh that claws had left across his face, neck, and chest.

His helmet had been knocked off his head in the fight for his life and his rifle was likewise a few feet away on the rocky forest floor.

I sucked in a gulp of air and held it to get as quiet as I could. What was? Yes, there it was again. I could hear a helicopter in the distance.

I didn't have time, I had to bolt.

I snatched up the soldier's helmet that had night vision goggles on it. I ran back to the trail to rip the harness off the man laying across the path. The chest harness was a plate carrier with several pouches of ammo and other gear, including a radio. I pulled the earpiece out of the soldier's ear and then took off at a jog to the east on the trail. I used my flashlight for the first 100 yards to keep from tripping, then I pulled out my GPS to check the topography of the area. I moved off the trail, for a deep gorge in the rocky mountain, to hide, and to use it to move farther away.

Five minutes after leaving the men on the trail, I hadn't determined if it was a mountain lion or a bear that the men had encountered. I ran several scenarios through my head about mother bears and their cubs. The mountain lion idea just didn't add up very well. A mountain lion would stalk a single hiker for hours through the mountains without attacking until just the right moment. Even then, it was rare. Attacking three men at the same time just didn't seem logical for a mountain lion.

The sound of the helicopter was strong now, as it came across the tops of the trees, and moved on to where the three downed soldiers were lying on the ground. I didn't hesitate or look back. I eased down some boulders into the narrow gorge, deeper between the walls of rock to the valley floor below. A couple times I slammed my hip into a rock and a shout of profanity almost burst out. Instead I hissed out a "FFFFF for the love of God". The hip wasn't going to heal very well if I continued to abuse it like this.

Once safely at the bottom of the gorge, I slowed back down and used the flashlight to guide myself along the back and forth zigzag between boulders. The GPS told me this would add an hour of hiking out of my planned route, but it was my only option. It let me get away from the well-worn path, the best way to make it difficult for anyone to find me.

An hour later, I figured I had made it about three miles away from the site. I started searching for a place to take shelter and get some rest. Behind schedule on my route, with the drama, and the injuries, I was going to have to call this an end to today's hiking. My attention turned to finding a safe hiding place, before the sun began to come up in the east.

The first overhang in the rock wall I found I decided against. There were rattlesnake tracks in the loose sand inside the tiny cave. The cold nights under 40°F would be putting the snakes into hibernation from now until the warmth of the summer months returned, but the lines in the sand unnerved me. I pushed on to look for a better place.

It was another ten minutes before I found a wide crevice cutting back into the rock wall, large enough for me to crawl back into.

I had to take off my ghillie suit and my pack to fit into the large crack in the mountain wall. Carrying my gear, the armored vest from the military scout, the extra helmet and night vision goggles, I felt like a pack mule. I was completely exhausted.

I went in with just my pistol and my flashlight. I left my gear on the gorge floor and investigated deeper into the wall.

It never did open into a nice area that was spacious and comfortable, but comfort wasn't something I was expecting until I got back home. It was going to have to do. There was no apparent evidence of danger within, so I decided it was as proper as any place to rest through the day.

A couple short trips back to the gear and I brought each item deeper into the crack, placed it where it appeared like it would be the most out of the way and then settled in. I sat on the ground in the gravel and small stones once I had everything inside the little home to get comfortable.

My attention was then turned to the scout's helmet, to investigate the goggles, and to see how they turned on and how they were to be used. They had a mounting slot on them that had a pivoting bracket mounted to the front of the helmet. My own helmet had the same standard bracket, but the scouts helmet had a large block of lead, or heavy weight at the back of the helmet that offset the weight of the goggles. It helped so that the helmet would not constantly be falling forward over your eyes from the weight of the goggles. My helmet had a place to attach the weight and it took some time to pull off the items from the scout's helmet and to reinstall them on own. It gave me the time to examine them closely, and to see how they worked.

The goggles had a screw plate that could be removed with a coin, knife, or screwdriver. Inside was a small cylinder battery to power the goggles.

I was sure I had a few of these batteries back at the bunker. However, once they were gone, they were gone forever. There was no Amazon.com (™) to run to for next day delivery.

After I affixed the goggles and the counterweight to my helmet, I tried it on to feel the weight. It was certainly noticeable, adding the weight of the goggles on the helmet. I wouldn't plan on leaving them attached to the helmet unless it was a night. That weight would be far better placed in my pack during the day. Since I was traveling during the night, it was perfect.

I checked the soldier's plate carrier, and went through the pouches with the dim glow of my red lens flashlight.

The ammo pouches had eight magazines of .308 Winchester which was a fantastic find for my sniper rifle. The magazine did not match my rifle, but the ammo was the same. I could put that ammo in my magazine later. For now; I stuffed the eight magazines into my backpack. Right now, leaving them in their magazines was an easy way of keeping them organized; without having rifle rounds rolling around loosely somewhere in my pack.

From the plate carrier/vest, I pulled his radio off and connected the wire from the earpiece and just listened to the radio as I examined the other items I was removing, and claiming as my own.

In one of the side pouches on the vest, I found a military ID, a couple photos of what seemed to be the man's wife and children, a pack of gum, earplugs, and a pack of playing cards. It brought me back to reality. Even these Federal troops doing the bidding of this tyrannical government had people that they loved, and that loved them back. It wasn't as simple as the old movies made things look. Those who persecuted you justified their actions as being the best for them and their families. Perhaps they followed orders to ensure that their families were kept safe by the government. It wasn't the first time in history, that great atrocities were committed under the excuse that they were just following orders.

I kept the gum, and the playing cards, but returned the man's ID, earplugs, and photos to its pouch.

Scrounging through the rest of the pouches. I found that the plates he had in his vest were a higher rating than what I had myself. Meaning, the Kevlar plates inside his vest that stopped the bullet(s) could stop more powerful and more deadly bullets in the soldier's vest than I had myself. It was a simple choice to pull his plates out of his vest, and replace mine. I put my plates into his old vest. I don't know why; I was just going to leave all this extra stuff here in the gorge anyway. But who knows, perhaps someday, some guy would find this gear here and it may make all the difference for him.

In the last pouch, I found a medical kit. I was fit with some premium things like blood-stop powder, a tourniquet, bandages, and the like. Also, in the pouch were two batteries that matched what was needed for the night vision goggles. Bingo! Awesome!

I wish I had a vehicle of some sort, or more time. The weapons scattered about that bloody scene were top-notch and were almost priceless in the current economy. I had days of hiking and no way to carry all the extra weight or bulk. If I had time, I could have stashed all the gear some place to retrieve later.

I heard a coyote howl in the distance. It was still dark out, and the sun had not started making itself known yet. The coyote howl was then responded to by another, and another. A scattered pack of coyotes calling to each other was an eerie sound, even more so in the dark.

It wasn't the yipping and barking of a pack on the hunt, circling around some animal to overwhelm it and attack. It was a strange call to each other, as if warning each other of an intruder in the area.

At that moment, with that crossing my mind, I frantically began searching the gear again. It took me a full minute to find under the soldiers' helmet, on the inside padding was a blinking red light.

NO! A GPS tracker!

I threw the helmet deeper into the crack between the rocks and rushed to get my pack on, my ghillie suit next, and snatch up my gear. I pushed and scraped the skin off my arm as I lunged out of the narrow rock walls, and out into the gorge again. I Flipped the night vision goggles down into place and then turned the on switch.

The world around me lit up with a green shade of light and allowed me to see shockingly well on the dark valley floor. I didn't have time to send in a product review report to the company now.

I turned to the left and bolted at an outright run to get away from the area.

I had to slow down to get the backpack belt around my waist and connected. At this pace, it was lurching around on my back and made me off balance. The goggles were amazing though. I could go at a full-on sprint in complete darkness without a worry at all, about plunging into an outcrop of rocks.

The sounds of my boots slamming into the ground, the wind past my ears and the growing sound of my heartbeat in my ears masked the sound of the approaching helicopter.

It would have fared better for me, if I had heard it earlier, but as I bolted out of the south end of the valley I turned east again in the thicker trees. It was at that point that I heard the beating blades of the helicopter pulling back into a hover. I slowed to a jog as I looked around. I spotted a thicker group of trees growing closer together and darted over there quick. Sliding like I was coming in to second base in a game, I then pressed against one of the trees in the center of the cluster to watch and listen.

As best as I could tell, it was hovering right over where I had been hiding with the gear. I had hoped throwing it deeper into the rocks would have made it harder for the satellites to lock on and give an accurate location. I was wrong.

I figured the pilot, or helicopter, would have night vision ability, perhaps thermal as well. Still, if I didn't move, it would just be a matter of time before they found me.

Checking my GPS for the topographic layout of the area, I laid out a plan to use the hills and trees to plan a route away from the area. I wanted to keep as much blocking their view of me as possible. Still, if the helicopter went up high and looked straight down, it was going to be difficult to keep hidden.

I memorized the route, then stowed the GPS back away. Remaining knelt on one knee behind the tree, I closed my eyes and prayed. It was a simple prayer, "Heavenly Father, if it be your Will that I come to see you tonight, so be it. Please keep a look out over my wife and daughter until they can join me. If on the other hand, you have more plans for me here... please help me get out of here alive... Amen."

I got to my feet then and turned, looked over the area to double check the terrain and remember my planned route to get away.

I started at a slow jog, directly away, down the hill. The area was thick with trees, and I was trying to use that to get distance while the helicopter was unloading a scout team to check the area. Or, that's what I guessed was happening.

I made it to the bottom of the hill, then turned more south. It was taking me a little out of my way and would make my mission take longer to get to the power plant, but that couldn't be helped now.

Ahead, I could see that the trees started to thin out and a huge open area was ahead. I turned along the edge of the field. Staying close to the edge of the trees though, I was able to cover a great distance using the trees to block the view of me.

I'd been running about five minutes when I heard the hovering helicopter blades change pitch. I chuckled as I thought about it. Pitch, angle of attack, sound, and tone; the English language always made me chuckle.

At the far east side of the field, I turned again, but this time I was going northeast and uphill. This was leg burning hard work now, running uphill with a full pack was no easy matter. I'd made it about a mile away from where I'd thrown the helmet, so that was comforting. If the helicopter stayed moderately low to the horizon I could keep concealed.

I guess some people call it a second wind. I suddenly didn't feel tired at all. My legs stopped burning and my chest stopped heaving. If I had to explain it to someone, I would say it felt as if my pack went from 40 pounds to about three pounds suddenly. I felt like nothing could stop me right then. I felt so amazing that I broke into an all-out sprint, going up a steep hill and darting left and right around trees. Megan would never believe this. I was a full-on Wolverine superhero in action.

Seriously, it was supernatural, and I started chuckling a little as I picked up the pace even faster.

I topped the hill, bounded over the edge, and kept on running like a deer across an open field.

That's when I heard the helicopter. It didn't sound further away, just different in some way.

I slowed to a jog, then stopped at a rise to get a look back from where I came. That's when my stomach sank a bit. The helicopter was climbing straight up to get its best vantage point to search for me. Oh, not good!

"Oh Lord, here we go. I'm either getting ready to see you soon... Which is super awesome. Or you're going to have to help me out here somehow," I found myself openly talking as I turned and sprinted off again.

I shivered then as I ran. I must be coming near a lake or some other body of water because the temperature started dropping. Not your normal desert after the sun goes down type of a drop. Instead, it was a drop in temperature much like you get when you open your front door in the winter and walk out onto the front porch in a t-shirt and bare feet.

I raced onward, night vision goggles leading me along and around obstacles, and this new-found strength and stamina that would make an Olympic medalist jealous.

The helicopter continued to raise up. It would be any moment now when I knew that the terrain would no longer be hiding me. The hill between me and the aircraft, the thinning trees, nothing would be able to hide me from their thermal either.

That's when I felt a snowflake on my face, and then another. Within moments, I had to stop running because I was blind. From the drop in temperature, to complete whiteout conditions it was only 20 seconds. The wind whirled around in a howl that was deafening.

Okay, even growing up in Michigan near the Great Lakes, I never saw the weather change that fast, and dramatically.

Sometimes I can be a bit thick, slow to catch on to a joke or the finer details of what someone is trying to tell me. It was then that I understood God was in control of all of this, and he was answering my prayer.

I wasn't worried any longer, a calm came over me that just doesn't make sense. I started running again, completely blind to where I was going but as I picked up speed and ran faster and faster, I started singing. Probably super stupid, but the faster I ran the louder I started singing to God.

All hail the power of Jesus' name!

Let angels prostrate fall.
Bring forth the royal diadem,
and crown him Lord of all.
Bring forth the royal diadem,
and crown him Lord of all!

I think it had been more than 25 years since I'd sung that song in church or even heard it. But it came to me as simple as my heart beating.

The whiteout blizzard continued to rage on. If it stayed like this for a prolonged time at all, there would be two feet of snow here in the mountains before sunrise.

That song flowed into the next, and I must have covered five hours of hiking in one hour. Most of it, I was utterly blind to where I was running. There were times when I lost my footing completely and fell several feet into open air, only to land, pause and sprint off again like a madman. Another time, I was headlong dashing into the white nothingness and I suddenly was shoved to the right, staggered a bit, and then kept on running.

At some point, the blizzard started to subside and I could start to see the area ahead of me. I slowed to a jog. The temperature didn't get warm by any means, but the bitter cut of the blizzard gave way to the normal late October nighttime temperatures.

I glanced down at my watch as I slowed to a jog, then a comfortable walk, and saw that it was 4:00 am.

I moved over to a large tree to lean against it for a moment.

I could not hear the helicopter at all. It had to be miles from me, or I would at least hear it a bit.

Pulling out my GPS, I checked my position. I then had to double check it with the printout of the route we had planned on the map.

I had to triple check, but every time I did it kept telling me the same thing. I had covered a full night of hiking and half of the next night's distance. I was exactly where my planned route had me going. I was early now, as the first peeking of the early morning sun started to show its arrival on the eastern horizon.

I spent ten minutes finding a proper place to hide during the day. I set up beneath a large tree that had been pushed over in a windstorm. In the shadow of the upturned roots; I burrowed in with my tarp to provide protection from any rain or snow that may come while I was sleeping. I spent another ten minutes collecting branches and pine boughs to conceal the tarp as a natural appearing thicket. I then climbed in under the tarp and got cozy within.

I couldn't sleep for an hour, even after having a meal. I just kept wanting to sing. I was never going to be able to explain what had happened to anyone. Let alone convince them I had not gone mad.

I did finally drift off to sleep, leaning back against the roots of the tree.

Chapter Fourteen (Megan)
The Power of Prayer

October 15

I have no idea what caused me to wake up. The clock said it was 3:00 am. I felt a heavy weight on my chest, like someone giving me CPR. Butch and Riley started barking at something at the foot of the bed, while I turned on the light at the head of the bed. Nothing was at the foot of the bed, but the dogs sure appeared intent on it.

I had an uncontrollable impression that I must immediately start praying for Jack. I did have a similar feeling, before, when the Holy Spirit was telling me something I needed to do.

I flipped the blankets off. The shock of the cold bunker hit me fast, but I didn't care. Sort of wished I'd put some clothes on after the shower. I didn't have time for that now. I knew every second mattered.

Knees on the cold bunker floor, I bent over at my waist onto the sheets of the bed and buried my face in my arms. I pleaded for Jack's safety.

I didn't know what trouble Jack was in, but I was certain he needed me to pray for his protection. So, I did. The pressing nature of it, felt as if everything in my life had brought me to this point before God, for this moment and this purpose. There was no explanation, it just was.

I prayed for his safety, and for some reason I felt the need to pray for speed, to give him strength and swiftness. I prayed like this for some time. I could feel such intensity that sweat was dripping from my face onto the bed. At one point, I felt some relief, calmed by something, it was as if Jack was doing okay now.

Butch and Riley started to whimper as they remained on the bed. I glanced up briefly to see them looking behind me at something. Nothing was there. I'm not sure what they ate yesterday, but whatever it was I needed them to keep from eating it again. They were seriously acting strange tonight.

I closed my eyes again, thanking God for protecting Jack and helping him; thanking him for safety, speed, and strength for the man I loved.

It wasn't a minute later, and that same feeling pushed down on my shoulders again with its weight. Jack needed more help. This was so weird. It was as necessary, as my next breath, and nothing seemed weird other than I'd never done it before. Otherwise, it felt ordinary and essential right now.

I could feel sweat running down my back and neck. It was still barely above 60 degrees down here in the bunker, but this praying felt like I was in the middle of a six-mile run on a treadmill.

"Please Lord, hide Jack and conceal him from the enemy. Help him go undiscovered, so he may continue on with what you want him to accomplish in his life with us," I don't know where it came from, but that seemed the most natural thing I had ever prayed for, in all my life.

The importance of my plea was no less detrimental than it was before. I begged God with everything that I had. I wasn't bargaining with him or promising him things to get what I wanted. This was nothing like that. This was the necessity of voicing aloud in the bunker what I absolutely knew was important to ask for.

I'm not sure how long I was there on my knees praying, but I think that Butch and Riley had laid back down on the bed. I couldn't feel my legs any longer, my neck muscles burned. I still couldn't rid myself of the feeling that I needed to keep doing this.

There was one point, where I felt a surprise come on me, "To the Right!" I screamed out. I have no idea why, and the dogs howled together and carried on like hound dogs at me.

It wasn't long after, a calm came over me that everything was going to be okay. Much like a heavy wet blanket wrapped around my shoulders falling off, the urgency to pray vanished.

It took every ounce of effort I had in me, to push myself up off the bunker floor, fall onto the bed and pass out. Dead asleep; I didn't even have the energy or time to pull the blankets over me before I was out.

****

The clock on the headboard read 9:06 am when I was able to focus on it. Butch and Riley were both licking my face to wake me up. I managed to push them away so I could roll onto my side and get a look at the clock.

A sniff and, "Eww," I needed another shower already. That prayer last night had drenched me in sweat. I was probably going to have to wash the bedding as well. To make it worse, the dogs weren't the cleanest companions to have in our bed either.

"Oh, the farm," I suddenly remembered and moved to get out of bed with haste to get ready. When I tried to stand up, that's when my body reminded me of all the time on my knees last night. I fell on the bunker floor awkwardly. The dogs looked worried, but when I laughed from the cold floor, they hopped down and thought I was playing.

Life was so funny sometimes. I found the towel I had worn to bed the night before and brought it back with me through the bunker to the shower again. Before I got in the shower, I let the dogs out through the airtight bunker door into the decontamination room to do their morning business. I'd have to clean that up later of course, but right now, I had to get warmed up with the shower and get this day started.

I tried to conserve water this time, so I kept my shower quick and to the point. Though I did make it considerably hotter than I normally do. Within a few minutes, I was out, drying off, and then padding my way back to the bedroom with an arm load of dirty clothes I picked up off the floor from the night before.

I'd have to wash my clothes and the bedding later in the day. Right now, I needed to get back down to the McVeenson's and get those animals fed.

I am not normally much of a breakfast person, so grabbing a small bag of dried wild apples was going to be well enough. Fresh clothes on, armored vest, weapons all loaded up and my backpack and I was ready to go.

I was delayed climbing out of the bunker, by having to clean up the dog's messes in the decontamination room. In short order, I was going up the steep stairs, out of the bunker, and into the shed above. Butch appeared efficient at coming up on his own, though he was still favoring his burned paw. I'd try later to get a look at that today, if he let me.

Once up and out of the bunker, I pushed the heavy blast proof bunker door down and latched it in place. Booting up the security camera monitors, I ensured the area outside was clear before exiting.

The front door of the house was still closed. There weren't any visible vehicles in the front yard or up along the driveway. I checked the camera hidden at the end of the driveway out at the rugged road and panned it slowly back and forth each way on the roadway and confirmed that it was all quiet also.

I saw an elk, not far from the solar panels on the back hill behind the house. I figured that was a favorable sign, that the forest would slowly come back from the forest fire.

It appeared clear. I powered down the security monitors to save on battery power, closed the cabinet doors, then opened the shed door. I moved on out with the dogs. Dashing ahead to get outside and into the open. The dogs appeared to get along just fine now, with Riley keeping close to Butch and teasing him while wanting to play. Butch still seemed to find it in his benefit just to ignore the little ankle biter. He gave her a minimal amount of attention, to maintain civility.

I locked up the shed, then went to check the electric Polaris (™) UTV. It indeed had recharged the batteries fully during the evening from the bunker batteries. Now that the sun was up, it was readily recharging the batteries in the shed and the others down under the floor of the bedroom of the bunker. I disconnected the vehicle from the charging cord and tucked it back away and out of view.

I let the dogs keep running around, while I climbed into the vehicle, flipped on its power switch, and gently eased on up the driveway. The dogs kept roaming around, smelling things as I went along slowly up the driveway. When I turned down the road towards the McVeenson's, they slowly moved along with me and kept in view.

I stopped a few times along the way when I came to rises in the road, or corners where I wanted to ensure it was safe to proceed. At these places, I used my binoculars to search around until I was sure it was safe, then moved on again.

I rolled on up into the McVeenson's homestead without any surprising threats. I did see that elk once more along the way in the distance.

The animals in the barn were eager for fresh water. I started the day of bringing them water, feed and then began shuttling things from the farm back to our house.

After an hour of caring for the animals, I was able to shed my jacket and cap while it warmed up into the mid 60's. That's when I shifted my attention to hauling the food items from the basement, up and into the trailer attached to the UTV. I lined the trailer, and the back compartment of the vehicle, with horse blankets to cushion jars of food until it was fully loaded and couldn't hold anymore.

It took over two hours to load it all up for this first load. It probably would have taken half that time if I didn't have to keep stopping and looking around for Antifa every time I came outside with a box of supplies.

It was a slow rolling trudge back up the rough trail to our home. I was cautious not to break the glass jars along the way. The way back was a success, when I rolled up next to the shed and stopped the vehicle, Riley flopped down on the ground as if dead. She was exhausted from all the outdoor activity, the hike to and from the farm. It was a funny sight. The joy of her friendship and companionship brought me a smile.

The first thing I did was plug the vehicle into the cord from the solar panel station to start recharging. It took me another two hours to unload the vehicle and the trailer. I used the same wooden crate I got from the McVeenson's basement to load up the jars, carry into the shed, and down the stairs into the bunker. I stacked them on the storage shelves in the decontamination room. We had a bountiful supply already in place, so it took even more time moving items around to make room for this load from the farm. I figured there would be four more loads to move from the basement of the farm before I got it all emptied out. The woodworking tools, sewing machine and supplies I would put in the house, but all the food I wanted to put down here in the bunker. I was going to have to put most of it inside the main bunker. We'd have to find places for it in the totes under the floor for long term storage.

I took a break for lunch, to feed and water the dogs, before heading back for the next load. My watch told me it was 2:30 pm as I started cleaning up in the kitchen of the house. I tried to pick up the pace to get more accomplished and get back to the project as fast as I could. These next several days and weeks were going to be absolutely exhausting.

I locked up the house, unplugged the vehicle, and started to make my way back to the farm. Riley this time, was having none of the mile-long walk. She made me get out and put her on the passenger's seat. Again, I took great care to stop a few times along the way to scope the horizons with the binoculars.

When I was nearing the farm, I heard a boom in the distance to the West. There were no longer the sounds of planes going overhead or UTVs playing around on the weekends. To hear anything other than an elk call, coyotes, birds, or the sound of the wind in the trees dramatically stood out and grabbed your attention these days. The hair on the back of Butch's neck stood up and a deep growl came from his throat as he moved to the West side of the UTV like he was protecting me. Riley, on the other hand, appeared clueless, as she lay on the passenger's seat and licked at one of her front paws.

I reached behind the seat to pull the map out of my backpack. I checked what could be in that direction. We had taken the pictures that The Silent Majority had tried to erase off the camera data card, and did our best to line up where each picture had been taken. We printed out a couple topographical satellite pictures to keep with us and on them we made some mark, notes to help us know where things were.

To the West, and the general direction of where I thought I heard the explosion, I could only find one home we marked on the map. It was more near the main road. To explain a little about where our home was, there was a paved road five miles away through a National Park. Off that paved road broke off a gravel road. From that gravel road, several gravel roads split off in different directions. Off from one of those secondary gravel roads, was the trail our home branched off from for a mile before it reached our home. So, to get to our home you had to leave an actual highway, travel down a paved road for ten miles, then onto a gravel road for three miles and then down another gravel road for three miles before you got to our rugged trail. Down that rugged trail a mile you would find our home. To say the least, we lived purposefully in a place that was off the beaten path.

The best guess I had for the location of the explosion was a mile west of the McVeenson's home, half-way down the gravel road that branched off another, and came this way. It appeared logical that it may be the Antifa thugs that had killed Todd and Jill. They must have passed that way as they came to Todd and Jill's farm. Surely, they went back the same way to get out of the area. Perhaps the neighbors there cooperated with the terrorists the first time they passed and this time they tried to defend themselves. Maybe Antifa just decided this time to take more than the residents there were willing to give without a fight.

I looked back up from the map to see the start of billowing black smoke coming up on the horizon in that direction. I confirmed on the map, it indeed was the home we had marked on the map, in that direction. It appeared they were destroying another farm. Likely more people were killed by the roaming band of government shock troops.

I didn't know if the thugs were going to come back up this way. The way they dealt with the McVeenson's made me think they didn't have a real reason to move back up this far on the road again. The threat was real, they may. Perhaps they would want to come back and loot the barn for more items. I didn't think they would want to deal with horses, rabbits, goats or even the chickens. They were well-fed and housed by the government. They got whatever they needed, so I doubted they would want to work their way back up this way again to come after what was left. The shotgun that killed the Antifa guy in the basement, I never found I suspected they took that with them. I found no other weapons either, so I think they already took what they wanted from the farm.

I decided this load with the trailer would be my last for the day. I'd load up from the basement, feed, and water the animals, and move the last load back to the house and call it productive for the day. I didn't want to push it into the dark where I'd need to turn on the headlights of the UTV and give away my position.

This time, loading up for the trip, took me three hours. Each time I brought up a load from the basement, I took a considerable amount of time to make sure it was safe to go down again for another load.

By 6:00 pm, I was pushing my luck. I closed the barn after the animals were cared for, and then worked my way back towards our home. If I had delayed any longer, I would have had to turn on the vehicle lights.

When I pulled up next to the shed, and hooked it up for recharging it was well dark out. It took until 8:00 pm before I had the trailer and the vehicle emptied out, and everything down into the bunker below.

It was going to be a late night by the time I heated up enough water to fill the wash tub, hand wash the sheets from the bed, and my clothes from yesterday and those I was wearing today. I stripped down, took a warm shower, and then bundled up with sweatpants, a sweatshirt, and slippers to work on the laundry. One nice perk of being in a bunker 30 feet under the ground was that I was able to crank up some great music from the laptop on the bigger speakers to sing and try to feel like life still had some manner of normalcy while I cleaned.

It was well after 10:00 pm before I had a little snack, poured myself a glass of wine, and sat down on the couch to take out my Bible, read and relax. A half hour later, I found I was too drowsy to get up and head to the bed. I just pulled the blanket off the back of the couch, laid down, calling it a day.

Butch and Riley curled up on the floor in the kitchen area and in short order we ` had all drifted off to sleep for the night.

Chapter Fifteen (Jack)
Canoes, Snakes and Dreams

October 15

I woke up a few times during the day. Here in the shade of the tree roots and tarp; the area kept cool for a long while. By noon, it was getting warm enough that I woke up hot and had to strip off my jacket. I stowed them away in my pack to keep them out of the dirt. It didn't take long before I drifted back off to sleep and returned to dreaming of canoeing down a shaded river in Northern Michigan during my college years.

My best buddy Fred was at the bow of the canoe talking to me about various types of fish and the trees as we moved along in the current. We'd both taken several wildlife, fisheries, and forestry classes at the same University, but for some reason, the only class we ever had at the same time was a forestry class. It was probably a good thing. We had a way of teaming up to find weaknesses in the various systems and processes of the University to exploit them in a humorous battle against the "system".

For example, in that forestry class, we took satellite imaging of various square mile sections of land covered in trees. The class had us examine the trees, lay out maps to categorize the various species of trees, as well as their sizes and health. The end project in the class was to develop a land use plan for the United States Forest Service.

In that class, part of it was to use a clear plastic sheet with several small dots on it. You would place the sheet over your drawn-out plot of land, count how many dots were within each meandering section of trees and then with the scale known from the photograph and elevation of the plane, you had an average area of the trees in question. So, you'd pick that sheet of plastic up and drop it again and count the dots and keep doing that multiple times for every section of trees. The more times you did, it the more accurate your estimate was, of the acreage of that segment of trees.

The other students would get an average of accuracy of about +/- 1-2%. That was normal from class to class and year to year that the professor had become accustomed to.

However, Fred and I would have none of that. There was nothing average about us. We were intent on breaking that mold and going way beyond what had been done in the past.

What we did, brought our average down to 0.0001 error rate. We took that 1-mile square of land that had been drawn out on paper, cut it out of the printed-out sheet of paper. One-mile square is 640 acres. So, we now had a square of paper about 8 inches x 8 inches and we weighed it with a Mettler (™) analytic balance in the chemistry lab down to a .0001 gram. Now that we knew how much 640 acres weighed, we cut the mile square of paper up into the various types of land. A pile of little cut out sections for jack pine 8-10" DBH, a section for open/unused land, a little pile of land for red pine 10-12" DBH, etc. So, we had all these small piles of land and trees that added altogether to 640 acres and we had a known weight. At that point it was easy to just weigh each smaller section and use a percentage, weight of the small pile divided by the weight of the entire mile's weight, and so we knew how many acres each plot portion or type and use of land was.

So, while the rest of the students did what the professor expected, Fred and I found a way outside the system to make our project(s) hundreds of times more accurate than any student in the University had ever managed.

These were the type of things that we did together and why our bond was so strong. We were "outsiders", within a system of sheep and followers. It didn't make us popular, but it made life a lot more bearable than being a nameless cog in a meaningless machine of society.

My dreams have always been a place of refuge for me. It was a world where I had a great deal of control. For example, when I was rather young in Junior High, I saw a movie. I can barely recall. I remember a Japanese man in the movie did something called Kinch. The idea was that he could touch some small item with the tip of his finger and manipulate his skin to expand and then contract into the surface of the item and thus grip it with the tip of his finger and lift it. It was crazy science fiction, mystic type, and my mother and I sort of made an inside joke about it. If I dropped something, she'd say I should have used my Kinch, things like that.

Somehow, and I have no idea how it transitioned, but somewhere I was introduced to telekinesis. The idea was that with your mind you could move something. Back in the 1980's there was a huge fear that spread through all the churches that Satan and his demons were spreading across the world influencing and controlling people. If you did anything wrong, it was probably a demon that needed to be cast out. While there may be some truth behind the fears, I still think that people were taking it to an extreme, seeing a demon behind every corner.

Anyway, to stay focused and on point, being able to move something with your mind was considered a taboo and forbidden thing to contemplate, or talk about in polite company. There were rumors and videos going around of people bending spoons with their minds, and as many videos disproving them as hoaxes.

Well, in my dreams, it started at this young age that I wanted to try to move something in my dream with my mind. For over a year, all I could manage was to move an empty aluminum soda can. As the years went on, I was able to move larger and heavier things, but for some reason could only move them towards me or away from me and never up and down and left and right. I can't explain dreams, your mind can put its own restrictions on itself, even in a place that is only limited by your mind.

As decades passed, my ability advanced to the point where I could pick up a car and throw it. It was just one of the examples of how my dream world was a place that evolved and became a custom world where I could retreat to and gain a great deal of comfort. It was a place where if I didn't like what was happening, I would just wake up and go back to sleep for a reset with a completely new situation.

But here, in this dream, I was in the canoe with Fred lazily drifting down the Manistee River. I could almost smell the cedar trees and the musky smell of mud on the banks of the river. The warm clean spring wind softly moving across my face, refreshed me, and the cool river water felt so real to my fingertips as I rested the paddle across my lap, leaned down a little to reach the surface outside the boat with my fingertips.

Fred dropped back to his preferred quiet status as I picked up the conversation. It was our natural balance; I would jabber on about anything and he would hold off on any comment until there was a pun to be made or an introspective thought that would take the conversation in a more productive or theoretical direction.

I was reaching down in the water at the moment he turned around at the bow of the canoe and saw I wasn't paying attention and properly keeping the canoe steering. He swatted his paddle into the water to splash it back at me to get me wet. The water hit my face and was shockingly cold.

And that's how I woke up today. Some melted snow sluffed off the tree roots onto my face.

I had to chuckle at how the real world had merged logically with what was happening in my dream. The mind continues to amaze me. I had so many examples on how in hindsight my mind had been warning me of something or pointed something out to me that I didn't understand it at the time.

However, now, I was back in the real world and the sun was going down fast. It would be fully dark in an hour and I would be able to get back on my way towards the power plant.

My eyes were open now, but I was purposeful about not moving in the slightest. I just listened and looked around with my eyes, without turning my head. It was a habit I tried to remember when I woke up out in the wild. If a noise had woke me and my mind pulled me out of my dream to keep me safe, I wanted to be sure to keep still and not betray my position. Perhaps this meant I was paranoid. It's not like it's saved my life yet. However, I was still alive, so perhaps it had.

After a few minutes I was sure I was safe to move around, I fished around in my pack for some food and remained tucked away under the tarp and branches for a while longer while I went about my morning duties. I did my best to keep quiet, and stowed my trash bits away into the pack before pulling out my Bible for my devotions. I still had a bit before it got dark, but it felt darker here under the tarp than it was outside, so the reading was a bit difficult. I didn't want to flip on any flashlight or use up the battery on the night vision goggles if I didn't need to. I just strained and squinted until it was too dark to read anymore.

Tucking my Bible back away in my pack, I took a swig of water from the canteen and refilled my camelback (™) bladder. I was quick about getting out, collecting the tarp, stashing it in my pack and then getting on my ghillie suit, I was then on my way again.

Now, I used the night vision goggles on my helmet right from the start. It was going to accelerate the entire trip. They let me move at a fast walk, even in unfavorable terrain.

As I slowly began to pick up my pace, I pulled out my GPS to check my route to burn the terrain into my mind. I wanted to be able to adjust and modify if needed, by knowing the valleys and hills along the way.

I suspected that the military had a few teams out looking for me. I'm not sure if they blamed me for the death of their team or not. They may know that it was a wild animal of some type that killed them, but for sure they knew someone came upon the scene and took some of their equipment. I just didn't know if they would dedicate resources to coming and dealing with me any further.

With the night vision goggles letting me keep a faster pace than we had planned, I counted off the miles and estimated how much further until I reached my planned recon location. I traced out on the GPS my route, due east for a mile then scissoring down a steep hill where the tree line gives way and things become far more open and where cover is hard to find. Traveling at night was so important, using the terrain like gullies and hills to hide me.

Once out in the open, I'd have to head northeast about three miles before I'd moved into some steep hills again. Then northwest up through canyons until I came out of them after about a mile and half. I would have to go across an open plateau for two miles, then drop back down into canyon valleys and hills again. The last two miles was going to be climbing up a rather steep rise to a mesa above, then dashing into place before the sun would rise.

With the route firmly in my mind, I tucked the GPS away in its pouch and then moved into a slow jog for a while. I didn't feel the unshakable power of unlimited endurance and speed like I did last night. I still don't know what that was all about. There was nothing that made sense that would explain it, nothing based on my abilities. Had God reached down and protected me?

Over the next few hours, I dropped back down to a fast walk. When the land was a bit smoother or open, I'd speed back up to a jog again. At one point, the wind swirled around me just enough to bring the smell of my body up to my nose and I gagged. All this travel and exerting myself had really given me that European scent.

I was now down in the flats where the trees had given way. The goggles made all the difference in the world. I could see the roadway I would parallel for a couple miles so stayed off the road about 100 yards as I went along. At one point, I had to dive down and lay on the ground and stay still. Headlights of a vehicle I spotted while it was still miles off. In the goggles, the smallest light was a glaring beam that was impossible to ignore. The vehicle moved from the west and was going east. So, it was leaving Springerville and heading towards the New Mexico border.

After the pickup truck passed by, I got back up, crossed over the road, then moved beyond and started paralleling again.

Several times as I went along, I paused to listen to coyotes, a few times the calls of elk to each other. The elk were far off at the tree lines, but the coyotes were prolific out here in the open flats.

At midnight, I found a ditch to climb down into. It looked like it only had water in it after a rain, the bottom was gravel with a few larger rocks. The sides of the ditch were eroded and jagged like each rain would dig away the walls with the rush of water.

I shed my pack for a small break and pulled out food to recharge. I really missed Megan when things slowed down, and I had time to tune things back from high alert. I had always wanted to find a way where we could have our own business. I wanted some way to spend all day together in a common goal, working side by side. I'm not sure if she felt the same way, I suspected she did not. She had a very independent personality that didn't seem like she really needed me on any level. I was needed to do painting, to fix things and to do projects. But emotionally, I felt like a handyman called in when needed. I could leave at the end of the day and it wouldn't affect her at all. I may be wrong, but that's the way it felt. I knew she loved me, but it was in her own way. Not judging.

But for me, she was my life's blood. She inspired me to be a better man, to pull my mind away from myself, and to focus it on her and on helping others. My natural tendency was to burrow in and protect myself, but her instinct was to give of herself to others.

I stuffed my empty wrappers into the trash sack in my pack, then got up and started back on my route.

Even before the collapse, this area of Arizona was a desolate land with nothing in it. Any source of light in the distance, or sound, was out of place. However, now, when everyone was in hiding and so many people were moved off to the camps and farms, things were even more vacated. A few houses in the distance that I could see, were completely dark. Much of it was because of the blackouts and rolling cuts in electricity, but most everywhere felt abandoned and empty.

To my advantage, this allowed me to travel faster, anything out of the ordinary I could hear or see and adapt.

The miles slipped by, following the valleys, and moving along. Now I was in the canyons, where the plateau above was 100 feet overhead at places. This gave me the ability to travel with nobody able to see me at all. On the other hand, someone could be up on top of the canyon looking down and I wouldn't be able to see them watching. It was a gamble, but the odds were in my favor in the middle of the night.

About 1:00 am, I started climbing up out of the canyon, heading towards the plateau at the top.

At the top, I knew that highway 60 would be moving east and west across my path. I would need to break across that open flat area at a fast pace, to get down into the canyons on the other side. It would be two miles and I'd have to do it at a near run.

It took half an hour to work my way up through the rocks to get to the top. That half hour felt like three hours of hard hiking. When I got to the top, I was spent. I stopped, lay down on the ground, listened and watched to catch my breath and to get some water in me.

After ten minutes, I had still not heard any vehicles or threats. I got back on my route. My legs felt stiff and tight, so it took a fast walk all the way up to the highway before I could make myself break into a jog and cross over the pavement. Down the other side of the ditch, I then start hoofing it as best I could directly northeast, to what I hoped was the safety of the canyons beyond.

I took some comfort in knowing that there were some scraggly bushes on the plateau. It wasn't just open desert highland. There were many six-foot-tall green thorny bushes, about five feet from side to side. The bushes would allow me to conceal myself, but just like the canyons, it also kept me from noticing others.

I came across several gravel roads that seemed to meander across the plateau. I hadn't realized they were when I was examining our maps. I was tempted to use them to make my travel across faster, but the comfort of the bushes concealing me won over the debate. I continued to cross over the various gravel roads, back into the bushes to continue.

It took about ten minutes of this frantic pace before I saw cliff edge in the land ahead.

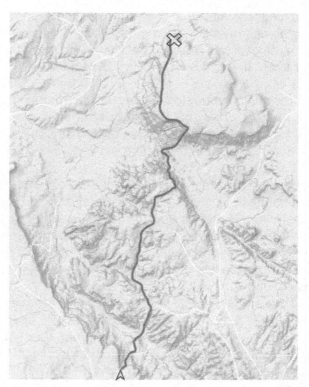

Scurrying up under one of the bushes nearest the canyon edge, I kept in its shadows. If it had been daylight out, I would have used the binoculars to scan the valley below, across the land to the north, and over the last five miles to my goal. The night continued to be a two-edged sword. It concealed me, while it also concealed possible threats out there.

It looked like a gravel road was nearby, went down exactly where I had laid out my plan for descending into the canyon. Perfect! The world looked almost surreal in its green night vision hue. I took a bit of a rest as I sipped on some water, and took out the bag of dried wild apple flakes Megan had packed for me. While snacking, I watched a coyote chase down a rabbit on the canyon floor below. The rabbit was quick and nimble, but the coyote was tenacious and would not give up. Given enough time, it exhausted the rabbit to the point where the furry big eared creature just stopped completely. The coyote just had to walk up to it and snatch it around the neck, and shake it violently to snap its neck. The poor rabbit had done all it could to get away, but finally just collapsed, unable to defend itself at all.

It was a bit sad to watch. It was a scene that played itself repeatedly in the wild, and in countries. No matter how hard you tried to run, hide, and just want to be left alone; sooner or later, a force would come upon you that was so tenacious and vicious that there would be no running or hiding any longer. It would exhaust you until you had no fight left in you, and then you die. RIP United States of America! The Communist Democrats had snapped your neck.

Okay, time was up. Time to get back on my feet and go again.

I decided to use the gravel road that went down the canyon edge. It would make the descent quicker and safer.

Going downhill was always harder for me than going up. My knees felt like I kept jamming my kneecaps up into the muscle. I'd rather feel the burn of my lungs, and the savage thump of my heart in my chest going up a hill, than the knee abusing torture of going down.

I was probably more distracted by watching the loose gravel on the road, than I should have been. I looked up just trying to stay alert to what was in the valley, when I saw the light across the valley.

The gravel road I was on turned sharp to the right and worked down the slope to the bottom of the valley. It then turned back to the left across the bottom of the valley to head up again up to the approaching vehicle coming down the other side.

I crouched down on the roadway and watched as the vehicle's bright lights blinded me. I wouldn't be able to see what it was until it turned at the bottom of the hill. When its' lights shed off in a different direction from me, I should be able to inspect it better.

I was within a handful of miles now from the power plant, so it was critical not to interact with anyone this close. If they saw me, and even if I managed to hide and get away, they would know someone was in the area.

It took a minute for the vehicle to get down the steep slope on the other side and then turn. I had to blink away the bright white spots from my vision to get a proper look on what was going on now. About then, the vehicle was blocked from my view as a hill between us briefly blocked my view. With patience, I waited for it to emerge on the other side of the road. It came into view again, and I saw it was a full-size pickup truck. The color was impossible to tell, everything was a different shade of green in the goggles.

I glanced at my watch, 2:06 am.

The back of the truck looked to be packed with boxes tied down with ropes. I couldn't tell how many people were in the cab from this distance. Back on my feet, I broke from the road and started heading directly down the slope to the north. It looked like I would have the time to get down into a valley a little to the left of my area, and hide in that while the truck came up the road near me.

Sliding down the slope a bit, I tucked down into the valley and lay down still on the ground. I could peer over the edge and watch the truck go by the way I arrived.

It only took a few minutes for the truck to work its way up the gravel road and come into view again. I was pretty sure I wasn't spotted, but I was so happy I wasn't up in the open without any place to hide.

After the truck's taillights faded up the road, then went out of view over the top of the hill. I slowly got up and peered around. I was in the belly of the beast now; I couldn't risk being spotted by anyone.

I had to keep reminding myself of the necessity to push on past the pain. The sore muscles and the desire to be somewhere safe and threatened my resolve. It was too important to get the Ham Radio access, to let my pain win the battle inside my head.

After a couple minutes of listening and looking around I was back at it. I worked my way down to the valley floor, then got back on the gravel road the truck had come down. A sip of water and an increase in my heart rate, I ground my boots into the gravel to hoof it up the slope. The road turned to the right at the top, that's when I broke off and went cross-country again. I could see the steep rise of the mesa just a few miles off now, but there was a plethora of canyon between myself and there yet to traverse.

I was glad it wasn't the heat of the summer now; the rattlesnakes would be loving these areas I was traveling through. Having lived down in the valley, I learned that the rattlesnakes had a window of temperature that they would be active in. If the nights started getting down below 50°F that sync'd with the days having less sunlight. Less hours per day for the snakes to warm up. So, as a rule of thumb, when the temperatures got below 50°F the snakes would hole up and hibernate, and wouldn't come out again until the nights were consistently above that temperature.

It was in the low 40's right now and a few hours before sunrise. Hoofing the pack up and down these canyons was keeping me plenty warm. The last few miles went uneventful, other than a nasty cramp in one leg that made me walk around in circles trying to stretch my calf and get the cramp to leave. I popped a ThermoTab (™) with a generous drink of water to help with the dehydration issue. In fifteen minutes, I was limping along at a steady pace again.

When I breached the top of the mesa, I saw that on the far northeastern edge there were more trees and shrubs than over here on this side. It was closer to the power plant and would offer a better view. Pushing myself, I got into a hobbling sideways jog to cover the distance as fast as I could. I could see the very faint beginning of the sunrise to the east, the far edge was still a quarter mile ahead.

As I neared the trees, they started to get thicker and offer more cover. That's when I could see the power plant to the north about two miles off. It appeared so strange to see so many flood lights and so much activity at the power plant, considering that coal power plants were illegal. The government was running it and producing electricity. It didn't make sense that vast portions of the State were without electricity every other day. Like most things involving the government, it was all smoke and mirrors. Lies hidden behind deceit, deception hidden behind corruption and concealment. Seeing with my eyes, an electrical producing coal power plant in full operation was aggravating. Everyone believed it when they said these places were out of service and decommissioned. With the internet shut down, and only government media allowed to put out information, the government manipulated the people to retain control.

The rolling blackouts, I could see now were part of the illusion. They had a great deal of electricity, they just shut off vast areas and complete States on a schedule to make it look like there was a shortage that needed rationed.

This was why The Silent Majority wanted footage and proof of what was going on here. If they could get this information out, it would do well to undermine the lies of the government. To get that information out would take weeks of handing copies of pictures, and pamphlets in secret. Sharing information that wasn't approved by government propaganda had gone back to 1790's technology. It would also take the same amount of time to spread that information.

I wasn't going to use the tarp and branches this time. I didn't want to create some dark blob that wasn't there the day before. Instead, I found a few of the bushes that were close to each other that created a deep layer of shadows in the middle of them.

I eased myself among the bushes once I took off my backpack. Stuffing the pack up against the base of one of the bushes, I crawled in on my stomach. I took some time pushing jagged rocks, debris, and sharp sticks out to the sides so I would have a comfortable place to lay down and stay throughout the entire day. I would have to get some pictures during the daylight to get the most detail with the camera they gave me. But I would wait until it got dark out again, before I pulled out the drone to get an aerial view. In the sunlight the drone would be too easily spotted.

Now, would be a great time for a little nap.

Chapter Sixteen (Megan)
Will Never Be the Same Again

October 16

October 16th found me waking up to Butch licking my face, nasty, but cute all at the same time. I hoped that the German Shepherd didn't have the nasty habit of eating dog poop like Riley did. Dogs could be so lovable, adorable, and utterly disgusting all simultaneously.

Riley was scampering on the floor beside the larger dog, begging for me to reach down, pet her, and remember that I should still love her more. It was a fun way to wake up.

I worked my way through the bunker to the entrance, opened the gas tight submarine door to scoop the dogs each a bowl of food, and fill up their water.

After washing my face in the bathroom sink, I went about my morning routine, of a cup of coffee, and my Bible at the table for the next half an hour.

The clothes I had worn the day before were still a bit wet and would need to dry the rest of the day, before I could fold them up and put them away. I pulled out a new pair of jeans, shirt, bra and got dressed.

I checked the AR-15, and the 9mm as I prepared to head up to the surface again. Before I pulled on the armored vest and backpack, I paused to close my eyes and to pray. I prayed for Jack's safety through the day. I prayed for Jordan in Flagstaff, that he would give her the strength she needed. For her to be surrounded by people that loved her, and that she would be safe. I forgot to pray for myself, but that's okay. I figured that would be a little selfish anyway.

Armored vest on, weapons loaded up, I picked up Riley in my arm, shut off the LED lights in the bunker, and worked my way up the steep stairs to the surface above. Butch tagged along carefully behind, until we climbed out the hatch in the shed, and he bound out to join us.

Checking the monitors with the outside cameras went smooth, no threats seen and soon we were out of the shed and in our yard by the garden.

I did the standard walk around, to ensure the solar panels were functional, the well, pump, and then last the house. We'd made it another day without Antifa coming to raid what we had.

Riley was pleased when I put her in the vehicle. Unplugging the charging wire from the batteries first, we were off for the McVeenson's farm to get a couple more loads moved back to our house. I knew the horses and the other animals would be excited for my arrival, to get their food and water. They had begun to get accustomed to me, and become more comfortable around us being there.

The smell of charcoal was still in the air from the forest fire. It had dissipated enough that the gas mask wasn't really needed anymore. Maybe by mid-day I'd wish I'd worn it all day, but for now it felt nice to breath without sucking the air through the filter packs.

I stopped a few times during that mile trip down to their farm, stopping to listen, look around with the binoculars for any trouble. It looked as if it might be another productive day without any interruptions. Fantastic!

When we got close to the farm, Butch was quick to approach, and check things out before I got closer. His burned paw appeared to be troubling him less and less now. I couldn't check it and clean it yet. He licked at it when he laid down, so I figured that was going to be better than if I tried to wrap it with some bandage. I'd have to keep an eye on it, to see if any infection started though. We had antibiotics we'd stocked up before the collapse. We would have to figure out the weight of the dog to know how much of the pills to grind up into powder and put in his food, if it came to that.

Butch didn't set off any barks of alarm and was back at the barn waiting for us when we came rolling up to a stop outside the large door.

The animals were eager for their morning meal, and I was quick to start loading up the trailer with things from the barn. I decided to wait on the huge sacks of rabbit pellets, grain for the horses, and the chicken feed. I was going to need Jack's help moving for sure. So, I gathered up things like shovels, racks, pickaxes, buckets, coils of rope, and equipment like that from the barn.

An hour or so after loading the trailer, the goats started making a loud fuss, as the dogs started barking excitedly. It wasn't a warning or a threat, but something they were excited about.

Turns out, one of the goats had decided that today was a perfect time to give birth to twin kids. I had missed the first one coming out. When I came to the pen where the goats were, the mother was licking at the baby, while giving birth to the second one. Insane; animals are hard-core.

The goats didn't mind me getting into the pen with them. I used clean straw to rub on the kids and dry them off. It was cool out in the early morning, so after I got it dried off, I found their heat lamp and hooked that up. I connected it up to their solar battery system when I found their inverter. The heat lamp wasn't DC power, so I had to get the inverter out of the shed where I found the vehicle first. It delayed my progress moving. It meant I was only going to get one load accomplished today. However, that was fine, we now had two more goats to add to our farm family.

It was noon, by the time I had the two new kids comfortable in the pen with their mother. They appeared healthy, and were already nursing from their mother. What a beautiful thing to witness and be a part of. I was by nature a city girl and this was all peculiar to me. Jack was the one raised in the country and wanted to get back to that type of life for all the years we had been together. I can see now, the beauty in this life. I had been so focused on keeping busy and getting all the fun I could out of life with movies, restaurants, music concerts, plays, baseball, hockey games, and travel. None of it was Jack's sort of life, but he soldiered on regardless to care for me and Jordan.

I took a break for lunch, sitting on a bail of straw in the barn. As I ate, I looked around the barn, imagining all the hard work that would take us weeks to accomplish.

Half-way through my sandwich, I heard a boom outside a far distance off. I stuffed the food back in the Ziploc bag and shoved it into my pack. Snatching up the AR-15, I moved to the door of the barn and looked outside.

To the south, about a half-mile away, I could hear a gunfight erupt with several rifles shooting. The pop-pop and ratta-tat of the gunfire was unnerving. They had already killed Todd and Jill. It looked like they had attacked a farm yesterday to the west. Now, they were attacking a farm to the south. Would they be coming to our house tomorrow? I didn't figure it would be a smart idea to let them encircle our house at will and let them attack when it best suited their agenda. It would be best for me to engage them now, when there was a situation already developing. I might be able to come in from the north and help turn the tide of the gunfight.

Right about then, deciding these things, I turned to the side, and heaved my sandwich out onto the ground. The realization that I had just decided to preemptively put myself into a gunfight was terrifying.

I wiped my mouth with the back of my hand, and wiped my hand on my pants with a disgusting snarl. I had to trick the dogs into staying in the barn while I closed the main door of the barn. I couldn't have them trailing along with me on this, barking or giving away my position as I got near, would ruin it all.

I gave them each a loving pet and hug, then gathered up my gear, slipped out the small door, and closed it behind me.

This time, I decided it was a appropriate time to pray for myself. I took in a deep breath and started talking to God aloud as I walked down the slope of their farmyard and into the valley between two hills, "God, please help me keep my neighbors alive. If it be your will, please have these Antifa punks flee and leave the area. Let them decide we are not worth their pillaging and thieving and just leave us alone. Lord, if it be your will, give us victory over these Godless followers of the evil one. Give me wisdom, give me speed and accuracy and let us triumph over these lost children of Satan... Amen."

I used the hills to hide my approach as best I could. I crouched over to keep low with the AR-15 at the ready. Stopping a couple times along the way, I eased up the slope to peek. The first two times was a waste of time, because I was still too far away.

On my last attempt I was much closer. It looked like my neighbors were now in their house. It was a single-story home with a tin roof. I'm not sure what they call them now, but several years ago they were called double-wide, or manufactured homes. It was a home that two trucks would bring in. One half of the house on one truck, the other on the other truck. The house had a nice porch on the front with a porch swing and a nice handrail. Their driveway was gravel up to the road. In the driveway, were two pickup trucks. Antifa for sure, for anyone else having a gas-powered vehicle was a death sentence from the government.

A body was on the porch in front of the door of the house, and there was another body on the ground where the steps led up onto the porch. My guess was that the owner confronted Antifa at the front door and shot the Antifa thug. Unfortunately, Antifa were cowards and they always fought in huge packs. It appeared that the homeowner, my neighbor, had then promptly been shot by several others. My guess was that the remainder of my neighbor's family were inside the house now.

The Antifa thugs, had taken cover behind their trucks, and behind a small shed, so that they could hide behind something and shoot into the house. I counted six of them. Four guys and two women, from the best I could tell, from where

I was at. I was about 50 yards off from the house. They all had their backs to me for the moment. I knew that after my first shots they were going to narrow in on where I was shooting from and then any plans I had made would be thrown out. There was no way for me to predict how anything after that point was going to turn out.

I wished it was dark out, or that the forest fire had not taken away all the trees here for me to hide in. The trench among the hills was my only protection. They had a horse corral farther south I could probably get to but that would offer almost no cover either. There were six horses in the corral but... Wait. I saw a large metal watering trough there. That would probably be my best cover. Any bullets coming at me from them would have to go through the metal of the trough, through the water, and then through the other side of metal before it hit me. That was way better than where I was at right now.

I pulled back, away from the top of the slope, and then moved along the bottom of the trench. After a while, I had to get on my hands and knees. I pulled on my gloves and adjusted my knee pads. It made a surprising amount of noise in the jagged gravel of the trench. I hoped the exchange of gunfire would keep them from hearing me crawling off to the side near the corral.

The last 20 feet, I was going to have to be out in the open. I took a careful look, then leapt forward in a sprint for the corral. In just a few paces, I was at the wooden rails of the corral, foot placed, heaved up and over the top rail, and then I dove down behind the watering trough.

The horses didn't like my aggressive approach at all. They ran around frantically, making all sorts of noise.

I took a few moments to lay on the ground behind the water trough, and to gather my wits again. I wasn't sure if they spotted me in my dash for cover or not.

Crawling on my stomach to the right side of the trough, peered around, down near the ground. A couple of the Antifa people I couldn't see now, but the other four I could, and I had clear shots at them.

I brought my rifle around in front of me, adjusted on the ground to get into a prone position where I could just peek out from the side of the trough and stay laying on the ground. I felt my knee squish into some horse poop, I grimaced a bit, at how nasty that was but didn't look down to look at it.

Flipping on the reticle light on the holographic site, the little red crosshairs lit up to show me where the bullet would be

182

going. This was making me feel sick to my stomach again. Nothing about this was okay.

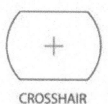

CROSSHAIR

I took in a deep breath a couple times, then closed my eyes just a moment. One last short prayer, then I opened my eyes to move the crosshair down onto the head of the Antifa thug hiding behind the truck.

I eased the tip of my index finger slowly into the trigger guard and rested it super soft on the trigger. Jack had replaced the trigger with a custom trigger that took just the tiniest amount of pressure. He had explained how if you practiced with it enough you could almost shoot with it as fast as a fully automatic M-16. But neither he nor I wanted to waste that amount of ammo, so we never went crazy like that with it.

One last pause, there was no going back after I launched this ship. The pit in my stomach felt heavier than ever before.

The red crosshair centered on the side of the man's head. He ducked down behind the truck to reload his gun and I moved my finger back off the trigger. Phew, that was close. I probably would have missed.

I moved my aim down to reposition the crosshair on his head again, while he was changing out magazines. Fingertip back on the trigger, I gently squeezed.

Crack

The man's head didn't explode or snap back like in the movies. Instead, it tilted away from me like he was trying to crack his neck by craning it to the side. He didn't pull his neck back up after relieving the tension from his neck. Instead, he fell over onto his side onto the ground.

I didn't reposition the gun to aim at him again, I honestly didn't want to see him dead on the ground. I don't think I could have held myself together right then if I did.

The horses didn't freak out any more than they already had been. I just prayed they didn't move on over to me, and stomp me to death.

I wasn't sure if any of the Antifa had seen their friend taken down, or if they'd heard my shot. I didn't think they had. There was so much gunfire going on right now, from inside the house, and from the Antifa thugs, I wasn't surprised when they didn't all look over at me from that shot.

One down; five more to go.

Inside the house, someone screamed out in pain. A horrific howl of sheer terrorizing pain. Oh heaven, another one of the neighbors had been shot.

I moved the rifle to the left, to start taking aim at another of the thugs behind the trucks. This one was around at the front of the truck furthest away from me. He was aiming a longer hunting rifle across the hood and shooting carefully into the house. He was smiling, happy. I think he was the one that just shot my neighbor.

There was an abundance of screaming back and forth. It sounded like a couple more of the neighbors were still in the house and they were cursing at the Antifa guys outside. The thugs outside were declaring what they were going to be doing to them, and their dead bodies when they got a hold of them. It was pure evil.

I settled my crosshair on the man and felt a shiver go down my spine. This was pure torture and I knew this was going to mess me up for a long time. I slowly pulled the trigger back towards me with the tip of my finger.

Crack

The guy moved just as I shot, and I missed the side of his head. The bullet went into the side of his neck, and passed out the other side with a spray of blood. He dropped his gun on the hood of the truck with a clatter and it slid down the hood and fell onto the ground. The man's mouth was open, gaping like a fish as he spit out blood. He held one hand at one side of his neck as he tried to hold himself up with his other hand. A spurting of blood arched out of the other side of his neck with each beat of his heart. It sprayed the front window of the truck in a macabre display of art.

My luck had run its course. One of the women behind the truck moved out of view of me, as she started shouting, "Sniper behind the horse trough!"

This caused the remaining four Antifa thugs to rush for other cover that would make it hard for me to see them and shoot at them.

I remained in the prone position, at the edge of the trough scanning the trucks for a target. That's when one of the women rushed from the truck to try and run around the house to flank me. I had about two seconds before the house would hide her from view. I tried to track her with the crosshair of the

AR-15. The house was going to be in the way, I was running out of... I squeezed the trigger.

Whoops. The shot was low. The 5.56 rounds ripped through her left knee and she tumbled forward out of view. The house was now in the way, as she slid face first into the ground with a shattered knee.

Crack! Thunk Splash!

One of the guys behind the trucks had shot at me. It hit the side of the metal trough and then into the water inside.

I pulled back behind the trough, curled up into a ball with my knees under me so that I could get up into a kneeling position if I had to. I had to stay as low as I could, my chest pushed tight on my legs so that my back would not show above edge of the water trough.

I couldn't see them, and it made panic threaten clear thinking. Were they flanking to my left, my right, or coming directly at me? I couldn't see a thing.

At some point I was going to need to see what was going on.

Crack! Thunk Splash!

I jerked and nearly jumped out in panic, but then flattened myself back down again.

I moved my rifle so that I had the proper grip on it, glanced to make sure the safety was off, then rose with the AR-15 coming to my shoulder.

One of the guys was running to the valley I had been in. The other guy was running straight at me with a pistol in hand. The last woman was back at the truck shooting. The woman at the truck was the one that had shot the water trough twice now.

I hurried, to shoot center of mass, at the guy with the pistol charging me. He was only 30 yards away, and closing fast. His eyes went wide, he brought his pistol up but it was bouncing all over, while he was running, trying to shoot one handed. Also, worse, he was shooting it sideways like some ghetto thug with a single digit IQ.

We both shot at each other at the same moment. I saw the flash from his pistol, and I think I peed myself just a bit.

Behind me, one of the horses screamed out in horrific pain and panic.

My shot was on point, it hit him in the center of his chest. He managed another three paces before he started falling face forward onto the ground. As he fell, he pulled the trigger on the pistol a couple more times. The shots went randomly around. I don't think he managed to hit anything important.

I dropped down behind the trough as fast as I could as I heard the woman's rifle. Crack! Also, another horse behind me let out in terrific pain.

The horses were in full panic now. In a joint effort they smashed through the corral fencing. In a cacophony of noise of breaking wood, they neighed with painful cries of terror as they burst out of the coral and into the open fields beyond.

I moved back a little on my knees so that when I came up again, I wouldn't be in the exact same position. Hopefully the woman with the rifle wouldn't be ready to shoot me as fast.

I knew the man was up and over the hill by now, coming at me through the valley. I also knew where that valley opened and wouldn't give him any more cover. I had to risk my speed versus the woman with the rifle at the truck. This guy was going to be up close and on me soon. Without the trough to protect me from his angle, I was going to be an easy target.

I counted to three, checked my rifle again, then shot up as fast as I could with my rifle already pre-aimed at the valley where the man should be.

The man was there, running at me. He started to raise his rifle. I moved my rifle to my shoulder, but the butt of the rifle caught on a pouch on my vest and caused me to delay.

CRACK! The woman at the truck shot with her rifle.

Something knocked me right off my knee and threw me to the ground behind the water trough. I'm pretty sure it was an invisible giant with a tree sized baseball bat.

My rifle, where did my rifle go?

I suddenly smelled a strong sense of sulfur but I didn't have any time to contemplate the abrupt change of smell in the area.

Someone kicked me in the stomach, then a punch in the side of my face. The world was getting fuzzy and warbly, like after too many wine coolers, but with more bright flashes of light mixed in.

I could smell the stink of a man in my nose with a thick choking sense of sulfur; an evil laugh accompanied his bad breath. I felt him lick the side of my face, and that's when I finally managed to relieve myself of that puke I had felt coming on.

My eyes cleared just well enough at that moment to see him jerk his head to the side. With my vomit all over him, he looked back to me with a look in his eyes that told me that he was going to kill me right now.

I felt him jerk me off the ground and then I felt cold water of the horse trough. I held my breath, as I felt my head hit the bottom of the water trough. My legs were still in the air outside the trough, but he had me bent over backwards at the hips over the trough edge. My head and chest were down into the bottom of the water. He was going to drown me.

Chapter Seventeen (Jack)
Praying for Antifa

October 16

After getting into place I saw that the sun wouldn't be long before it peered up over the eastern horizon. I grabbed vegetation around me, cut off pieces of the bushes with my knife to tuck them and weave them into the ghillie suit. After ten minutes or so, I identical to the bushes if I wasn't moving. I was confident that someone walking past wouldn't think I was anything other than just a bush.

I pulled out the iPhone and turned it on, making sure it was in airplane mode. Checking the alarm, I set it for 3:00 pm. I hoped I could get pictures and even drone video before sunset if I woke up by 3:00 pm.

It didn't take me long to drift off to sleep, I was exhausted. All this traveling cross country, up and over mountains and through canyons really took everything I had to keep going to the end of the day's journey. I didn't even bother to eat a meal before bed, I was so worn out, that sleep sounded more important than stopping the growling in my stomach.

In my first hours of sleep, I was dead to the world. I think a coyote could have come up and started chewing on my leg, and I would not have woken up. I hoped I was not snoring. Those first couple hours of sleep, after a hard day I was impossible to wake up. Once my body determined it had enough to balance out its absolute necessity of needs, it released itself back to me.

I do not know how long it was, but at some point, my dreams returned to me. My dream was one of the most unusual dreams I had ever had. I was looking at the world around me with Megan's eyes. I was driving Todd and Jill's converted off-road vehicle, pulling a trailer, and coming up to the barn they kept their horses and other animals in. Riley was beside me in the passenger seat, sniffing the air and eager to get down out of the vehicle when I stopped.

I did not realize I was seeing everything and experiencing everything through Megan's eyes until I got into the barn. I started feeding the animals, and opened the large roll up door for better lighting. I walked back to the vehicle for a drink of water from my canteen and saw my reflection in the windshield of the UTV. It surprised me at first to see Megan's face coming back at me in the reflection. I also noted that I was not able to do what I wanted in the dream, which was extraordinary for me. I was fully an observer, a passenger in this dream.

I did not grow frustrated with it though, it was comforting to be close to Megan like this. It was a lovely dream. I did not know why she had Todd and Jill's UTV, nor why she was caring for their animals. It did not much matter, it was just a dream and dreams can be strange.

At one point, I heard gunshots begin to ring out and I (Megan) rushed to the roll up door and look out. That is when I saw the McVeenson's house burned down. That explained why she was taking care of the animals. It amazed me how my mind filled in gaps, to make things appear logical in a dream.

That was when the distant gunfire in my dream did not appear to make sense. It was too rhythmic and evenly spaced. A helicopter perhaps?

That is when I felt a stiffness in my body, a sore hip, and I began to ease my way out of the dream and to an awakened state. The dream faded and the things around my body started to take over. My hip lay on the mountain rocks, my muscles ached from the journey through the hills. I now knew for sure, was the sound of an approaching helicopter.

My ghillie suit was pulled up over my head, covering my face while I was sleeping. This blocked my view, so I had to take great pain to move extra slow to move the fabric and vegetation off my face to get an unobstructed look.

A helicopter had arrived from a direction I was not sure of but it was now coming into a hover and preparing to land inside the power plant fence. I eased my hand into a pouch and removed The Silent Majority camera. Bringing it in front of my face, I turned it on to get a couple pictures as the aircraft as it was touching down.

Simultaneously, as it was landing, the large fencing gates were getting pulled back by military personnel, and two city school buses were turning off the road to pull into the power plant. From this distance, with the camera, I could not read the name of the city the school buses were from. They appeared very much your standard high-school yellow bus.

With the camera out, I took a thorough look around the power plant and snapped several pictures as I went. They had some lookout towers, with sandbags stacked up around where the lookout remained. Inside the fencing, there were a few areas that I knew would be important to take pictures of.

One, was a communications tent, where two tall radio towers were erected near it. The entire thing was surrounded by Hesco barrier walls.

Another area of interest, were the several sandbag walls around the power plant catwalks. I could see one or two men in each position where they had a superior position elevated above the ground to see everything inside the power plant property, and well outside the fence to the wide-open fields around the facility.

Last, was the area near where the helicopter landed. Several small white buildings had been lined up in rows, with netting over them for shade. The way they were laid out, and the larger building near the end confirmed by my experience in Iraq, that this was the housing area for the military, and their bathroom and shower structure.

It did not take long before I was sure I was not going to get any more useful pictures with the camera. I tucked it away in its pouch, pulled out the drone, synced it to my iPhone$^{(tm)}$, and set it up in a low hover in front of me. As I watched the iPhone screen, I could see what the HD camera on the drone was sending back to the phone and recording. This allowed me to stay on the ground on my stomach, hidden under the ghillie suit, and to send the drone off to the north to get closer for some better pictures and video.

I moved the drone down, to follow the ground, so that it was not up in the air and so visible. I also knew I needed to keep a significant distance away from the power plant because of the noise of the four little blades that worked in a fury, creating their distinctive whirring sound.

The camera on the drone allowed me to tilt up, and down, and to also zoom in. When I got about half-way to the power plant I zoomed in with the camera, and was able to read that the buses were from Springerville, the nearest town.

At that moment, the video feed was lost from the drone. My screen on the phone showed the software working, but that it lost signal with the drone. At that moment, the CRACK sound of a sniper rifle reached my ears and I looked up quickly.

I was not sure which of the snipers had spotted the drone and shot it out of the sky. This was not an encouraging turn of events. I only had one drone, and I really liked it. Worse, now they knew someone was within range to control a drone. It was not going to be long, before they narrowed down the many places, I could conceal myself, and capture me.

I gulped, as I saw the helicopter crew rushing into the open towards the helicopter. About eight men, running for the unarmored Humvee parked near that area as well.

The helicopter blades started to spin, and pick up speed. The Humvee doors slammed shut and engines started turning on.

A horse snort at that moment sent me into a higher state of alarm. I turned as fast as I could, someone was right behind me.

As I turned onto my side, the sun was blocked out by someone kneeling over me at my side. His face was silhouetted by the sky behind him. I reached as fast as I could to my knife.

The man's hand clamped over my wrist, like a vice-grip. I could not move to get to my knife.

That is when the man leaned forward close to my face. I could see it was the same Apache I saw on horseback the day before. He looked into my eyes, from only a foot away, and I went calm. There was something in his look that was ancient, powerful. I felt as if I was looking at the Grand Canyon for the first time. I just stopped struggling, as I investigated his face with awe.

"Megan needs you now!" he said with an incredible urgency. He grabbed me by the armored vest and jerked me right up off the ground and to my feet.

I reached down, grabbed my rifle, and pack. With his help, I started putting on the pack and shouldering my rifle. I have no idea how to explain my immediate trust in him. I knew I had to do what he was saying without question, and to be fast about it.

His horse was a dark brown horse, with a black mane, and the saddle was rather simple. The horse turned to the side so that I could get up on it easier. As I got my left boot into the stirrup and started to reach for the saddle horn, the Apache grabbed me by the hips and lifted me up onto the saddle. I felt like a small boy getting hefted around by his father. The strength of this man was shocking.

I reached up to grab the reigns, then started to turn to say something. I had no idea what I was supposed to say or ask. There appeared to be no answers as to what was going on, I did not know what I was expected to do.

I could see the helicopter raising up off the ground at the power plant, and the Humvees racing out of the open gate towards me. It would be a long shot, but a skilled sniper could probably hit and kill me from this distance if they got eyes on me.

I opened my mouth, to stammer out a question and that is when the Apache hit the rear flank of the horse. The horse bolted forward.

I almost slid off the back of the saddle. I bounced around with no clue how to ride the horse properly. I had to lean forward, and push my boots into the stirrups to get some stability so I would not fall off. My backpack bounced widely around and made it harder to keep centered on the middle of the horse's back. My sniper rifle kept smacking the back of the head as it bounced. This was not a pleasant experience.

The moment I was moderately convinced I would not be thrown from the horse and I grabbed onto a little confidence that this was going to work, I looked ahead and saw a huge pile of boulders and cactus.

The horse leapt, to jump over the boulders, and that is when a bright flash of white light blinded me. Was I just shot by the sniper? What was going on?

I was not sure if I was dead, or was there really a flash of blinding light that I could recover from? Was there a flash bang that was thrown at us? Is that what a flash bang feels like? No, there was no ringing in my ears and balance disorientation, this was only light.

I blinked to try to get my sight back. I dared not rub my eyes with a hand. I feared I could not let go of the saddle horn and the reigns, for fear of falling off the horse.

The temperature changed abruptly. It felt like moving from a porch of a house to the inside where there was a large temperature change.

As my vision slowly came back, I could hear a shot from a high caliber hunting rifle and then what sounded like an AR-15.

My vision came back as fast as it had vanished. I was no longer on the mesa near the power plant. I had no idea where I was. I saw a double wide home quiet near with a metal roof. There were two pickup trucks parked at angles in the driveway. Two people were near the trucks lying dead on the ground. There was a man on the porch of the house shot dead. In the front yard was a woman bleeding out from a gunshot to her knee that she was trying to tie a tourniquet on to stop its bleeding.

The horse raced towards one of the trucks where a woman was leaning across the hood shooting a hunting rifle towards what looked like a horse corral on the left side of the home.

I saw a man racing from a gully far to the left and into the open. He was sprinting towards the corral of horses.

I was not sure where I was or why I was here until the moment I saw Megan peek up from behind the water trough at the corral. The woman at the truck shot the rifle and I saw Megan get knocked to the ground sideways behind the trough; falling back out of view.

My panic kicked in to protect her. That is when the horse came to a sliding stop near the woman at the truck. She started to turn when she heard my approach and that is when time slowed down. It appeared to anyway. A choking and oppressive smell of sulfur gripped my throat.

I reached for my Bowie knife on my side as I launched off the horse to land upon her. I wanted to bury my blade into her neck or chest. My mind was in a dark place. There appeared no option other than to end this woman's life in the quickest method possible.

It was then that there was a shimmer around the area like a mirage. A wave of light waves spread over the area that changed everything I was seeing. So many peculiar experiences had happened over the last two days that the unexplainable was becoming less shocking.

The woman, that was turning towards me, appeared to be moving in super slow-motion. At this moment I was able to see several men appear around her. Like a Klingon Bird of Prey decloaking. Calling them men would fall short in a proper description though. They stood upright like men, two legs, two arms and a torso, but there were massive discrepancies from men.

The first major difference, was that the men had large black raven like wings coming out of their shoulder blades. They wore ancient medieval metal chest armor over rusty looking chain mail. Over their heads, they wore a black cowl, and their faces were churning mist and smoke. The beings had black swords in scabbards on their belts, and a feeling of dread emitted from them like looking at them pulled you into a feeling of helplessness.

It was then, that I realized that this was not a battle that was going to be won with me fighting and coming to Megan's aid, by playing the part of the hero and protector.

No, this was a spiritual battle, it was going to be the power of God that would win this battle.

I slid off the horse and landed beside the woman. She was still in slow motion, and was looking up at where I had been sitting on top of the horse. Either I was moving at unspeakable speed, or she and everything in the area had been slowed down to a crawl.

The four black winged men around her did not appear slowed like she was. They went for their swords with a ring of steel as their blades were pulled out.

I left my Bowie knife and did not remove any weapons. Instead, I moved up to the woman as fast as I could and I hugged her, and buried my face into her neck, "Heavenly Father, Son and Holy Spirit, I plead with you to free this woman from the angles of darkness that have seduced her mind. Father; please return these demons to the pit of hell where they can do us no harm here. Please free this woman from the enemies grasp."

I had my eyes closed as I was praying, and I did not see what was happening, but I heard a battle with swords around me. I felt the fury of wind from wings whipping the dirt off the ground and into the air. There were howls of deep twisted screams in a gnarly and grunting language.

I opened my eyes with my chin still resting on the woman's shoulder to see, at the corral the Apache that had given me the horse standing at the water trough. The Apache grabbed the man who was holding Megan under water, and flung him through the air. He tumbled like a ragdoll out of the corral and into the field behind. There was no way the man did not break at least one leg and an arm upon landing. The force of the throw was so violent and forceful. The Apache, had enormous white wings like a swan coming out of his back, while he pulled Megan up out of the water and laid her on the ground behind the trough.

The battle of swords near me quieted. I turned my head from the woman's shoulder to see two men with white wings finishing off the last of the black winged demons. The minions of Satan hissed in a screeching gurgle of pain, while the ground split open in a fissure of molten lava. Black swirling smoke with red crackling sulfur wrapped around the demons and pulled them into the ground.

This was well beyond anything I had ever seen in a movie. Had I gone insane? Was this really happening?

The ground sealed back closed, and when I turned to look at what I assumed were the angels near me, they were gone. As was the horse. Completely gone.

I looked back to the corral for the one who had helped Megan, and he was also nowhere to be seen.

That is when I heard a horse on the horizon to the south. I could see on the crest of the hill, the Apache who had helped me sitting on top of his horse. He raised a hand in a wave to me, then turned and slowly moved down over the hill, and out of view down the other side.

The woman I had been hugging and praying for pushed me off from her, "What the hell?"

She still held her rifle, but she was not pointing it at me.

"I am sorry," I tried to put words into some form in explaining things, "I thought you needed some help."

The woman looked down at the rifle in her hands and appeared perplexed as to why she was holding it.

I could hear Megan over in the corral coughing water out of her lungs, while she was hunched over on her knees gasping for air.

The horses from the corral were still spreading out across the fields in a sprint. They were intent on getting away from the Antifa thugs who had shot a couple of them in the gunfight with Megan.

The woman who was shot in the knee had stopped her effort with the Tourniquet, she had slumped over and had bled to death.

The man who had been thrown through the air by the angel was laying quite still on a pile of rocks. The pile he had landed on was where the farmer had been collecting the rocks from the field he was trying to farm. By the angle of the man's neck, I was certain he was, paralyzed; probably dead.

The woman with the rifle started to look around the yard with a puzzled expression. She attempted to ask a question or two but after only a couple words she gave up. She waited a bit longer before trying again. She appeared to not even know where she was, or why she was here.

I deduced; she was not a threat any longer. Of the several people that arrived in the trucks, she was the last of them alive. Those in the house started to yell out to me, "Who is there?! What's going on?"

I stayed behind the truck for cover, I did not know the people that were in the house. I responded as I did not know if they were a threat or not, "I am a neighbor. I heard the gunfight so came to help. Are you okay?"

A woman called from inside the house, "They killed my husband, and I have been shot. My kids are okay."

I yelled back to the house, "I need to go check on my wife at the corral, is that okay? Before I come help you?"

The woman's voice came back out to me, "Yeah, the bleeding has stopped, I will be okay."

The woman at the truck with the rifle finally managed to put her thoughts together well enough to form a real question to me, "Um, where am I?"

I offered with a slight shrug, and what I hoped was a comforting face, "You are in the White Mountains near Springerville." I did not want to say exactly where she was, because she might return to Antifa and share with them what happened here if she got her memory back.

She looked confused still, "White Mountains, where is that?"

Oh dear, she must be really befuddled, "Northeast section of Arizona."

This response to her question just made it worse as she looked around befuddled, "I am going to school at Berkley, why am I in Arizona?" She paused for just a second, "Am I being punked? Did you guys put something in my drink?"

That is when she started to focus on the people on the ground that had been killed. Shot in the head, in the neck, in the knee, the man killed on the porch and the man with his chest ripped open by the shotgun. This was not a punking situation. The color in her face started to fade and turn pale as the horror of what she was in the middle of now started to take on a complete picture. She had arrived in a truck with these people, had a shoot-out with my neighbors in the house and there had been a substantial amount of killing.

The woman dropped the rifle onto the ground and stepped back away from it.

I glanced over and could see Megan in the corral still on her knees, pushing herself up to get to a standing position.

I was not sure what to do about this woman who had been fully under the control of the demons. For now, there were others to tend to. Perhaps the 1980's scare about the demons was not so far off after all.

I left the rifle on the ground where the woman dropped it. It would not have helped to pick it up and take it with me to keep it from her.

There were several guns scattered on the ground from where her other friends had fallen. She could just get another gun if she really wanted one.

I made a quick beeline to Megan; up and over the corral wall to drop to her side, and to wrap my arms around her as we held each other for a long while.

While I hugged her, I could see the man that the Apache Angel had thrown through the air. He certainly was not alive any longer. His neck had been snapped when he landed on the pile of rocks.

Megan was drenched from the watering trough, but I held her tight as water dripped down from her onto the dry and dusty ground at our feet.

After a short time, Megan pulled back from me enough to look at me face to face, "How are you back already?", she questioned with a confused look.

My face I believe, did not show that I had an answer that would make sense.

Megan kept her arms wrapped around my back as I tried to explain to her that; last night, I had come upon a military scout team that had been killed. Her expression showed deep concern as I explained how I had taken some gear and then went to find a place to hide and sleep. I continued in my story about how I moved away so that the helicopter would lose track of me in the terrain and trees.

I tried to comfort her by leaving out some of the fear and panic that I had been in. As the story continued, with my sudden plea to God, my burst of energy, speed and an incoming snowstorm, the look on her face gradually gave way to a wide smile.

I was telling her how I was running as fast as a horse, and was not winded or tired in the least when she interrupted me.

Megan interjected then, "Last night I awakened with the necessity to pray for your safety and for you to be hidden. It did not make sense, until now."

We both just stood there then, speechless. Our eyes glossed up with tears and we both looked up into the sky simultaneously to watch a Red tail hawk gliding far overhead in the blue sky.

When we looked back down at each other, our faces were plastered with the widest grins, and silly expressions. We started laughing as we held onto each other.

I leaned my head forwards towards her, and she to mine. We pressed our foreheads to each other as I started to pray, "Heavenly Father, your wonders amaze us. We humbly follow the path you have for us in this world. Use us Lord, keep our hearts and ears open; always ready to move when you call us."

Megan offered then in the prayer, "This World and our lives here are temporary, we continue to surrender them to you. Please let us be a light for you in this dark world. Lead us to where you wish to work. Use us however you wish Father."

We paused in quiet then, until we opened our eyes and looked to each other.

We were an emotional wreck, with tear-soaked faces. We could not help but softly chuckle to each other from the overwhelming feeling of having been so close to the work God was doing.

I explained that I had made it to the power plant way early and set up my spot to take the pictures. I then waited until sunrise while napping.

I told Megan how a helicopter had woken me up, and let her know about the pictures I took, the drone, and it being shot down, then the chaos that all happened concurrently.

It was then that I slowed down to spell out the most recent events with more care, "An Apache I had seen earlier, was suddenly at my side with a horse. He had snuck up on me where I was hiding and held me tight so that I could not defend myself. He told me that you needed my help and then he yanked me up off the ground and put me on his horse."

Megan was listening to every word, but I could see it was hard for her to put logic and reality into the story as it progressed. It was developing into something like a tale of fiction in her mind as it went on.

I tried to leave out what I thought was not critical to the story, "The horse charged across the mesa and jumped this huge pile of boulders, and then I was blinded with a flash of light. When my eyes adjusted back so that I could see, I was here." I nodded, "Yeah, I was here. I went 37 miles in the blink of an eye, and was here at the front of the house on the horse."

Megan blinked at that, and looked over to the house and the trucks where she was getting shot from. She jerked back from me a bit in fear as she saw the woman who had shot her.

I noticed her reaction, and why, and held her tight to me, "It is okay love. She was possessed by several demons. That is what happened next. Time slowed down and God opened my eyes to the spiritual realm and I saw the demons around her."

Megan looked back to me then, eyebrows squinting down and looking confused.

I explained further, "I jumped off the horse and hugged her tight because she was not moving, like she was in slow motion or I was super-fast. I just started praying over her and begging God to free her from the demons. It was so beyond anything I can put to words. It was instinct, like I had fully given myself to the Holy Spirit and I was on auto-pilot."

Megan glanced back over at the lady by the trucks and then back to me.

I tried to wrap up the story then as fast as I could, "She cannot remember a thing now. She was going to school at Berkeley California and does not remember anything. She had no idea why she had a rifle or why she was even in Arizona." I then added, "I do not think she is an immediate threat at all now."

Megan and I embraced once again, in a tight hug. This time she winced with pain and grunted from it.

We took a step back from each other, and I checked her out as she turned to the side. There was a hole in the side of her armored vest and fresh red blood was oozing down her hip from under the vest.

I took in a deep breath and let it out with a slow sigh, "Okay baby, let's check you out. Come on over to the trough and sit down. Let us get this vest off you so I can look."

We moved her over to the watering trough and pulled her vest off up over her head. I then pulled her shirt up so that I could see what was going on.

Of course, both our hearts were beating fast and we were in full-on business mode and focused on what we were dealing with now.

After I washed away some of the blood with my canteen water, I could see two holes in her side just under the ribs. One was the entrance of the bullet and just a couple inches away was the other hole where the bullet had gone out.

I looked up to her with a big smile, "You are going to be absolutely okay baby. It went in under your ribs and came right back out just a little distance away. I do not think there are any critical organs right there."

I pulled open my medical kit and started opening up the packets I would need to bandage the wound, "I am just going to bandage this up right now. Later I will need to sew up the holes and ensure it is cleaned out." I went on to add a little more information to try to comfort her, "Your ribs protect your lungs and your liver as well. This is below your liver. I think it missed your intestines too. You are just going to end up with two cute little scars on your love handle."

She swatted me on the shoulder hard then, "I do not have love handles anymore!"

We both laughed at her response as I placed the bandage over the wound and taped around the edges to hold it in place.

I started putting the medical things back away while she pulled her shirt back down and put her armored vest back on.

Over at the house, the mother in the house, had come outside to check on what was happening. She and the girl from Berkeley were in a screaming match. The west coast girl was taking cover behind a truck, trying to explain that she did not know what was going on. It was a real mess.

Chapter Eighteen
Diplomatic Relations

October 16

Jack and Megan concluded their catching up with each other, and Megan's medical needs, in exchange for a swift walk from the corral towards the house. They hoped to fend off the impending fight to the death, between the two women there.

The new widow of the home was kneeling beside her deceased husband on the front porch while keeping her shotgun aimed in the direction of the California girl hiding behind the truck.

As Jack came first around the corner of the house and into view, he raised his hands, "Okay, I think everything is going to work out now."

The woman kneeling beside her husband snarled at him, "Work out? They killed my husband! Also, they shot me!"

Megan then came in to view to stand beside Jack as she tried to lead in the conversation now, "The lady hiding behind the truck was part of the Antifa group, yes. They killed your husband and shot you, this is true. Additionally, four of them are now dead. The lady behind the truck shot me also."

Jack looked at Megan with a sideways glance and muttered quietly to her, "You are supposed to be helping right?"

Megan chuckled at her man's comment, but spoke louder so that both of the other women could hear her, "The woman behind the truck is no longer an immediate threat. She has weapons available to her behind the truck and is not holding any of them. She is posing no direct danger right now."

The woman on the porch did not appear fully convinced that she was now safe, "If I lower my gun, she is going to get one of those guns and kill me."

Jack continued to slowly walk, to put himself between the two conflicting women, "Miss Berkley, can you please just come out from around the truck and show her that you mean her no harm now?"

There was a long pause before she complied with the request, and stepped out into view, and started a slow and careful walk towards Jack.

Megan remained off to the side near the corner of the house, being careful not to give up the strategic position until the situation was completely disarmed.

When Miss Berkeley came up more near Jack, the woman on the porch finally relented and lowered her gun. That is when the adrenaline of the fight finally released her, and she collapsed in sobbing grief over her husband's body.

The lady from Berkeley looked horrified and confused, "How did I have anything to do with this?" she asked Jack when she stopped near Jack.

Jack extended a hand to the lady, "First, let us get on a first name basis. I am Jack," he offered.

The woman reluctantly offered her hand to shake his, "I am Tiffany."

Jack nodded to her, and then started to explain things as best he could, loud enough for the woman on the porch to also hear, "Your last memory is of being at college at Berkeley California, correct?"

Tiffany nodded to that, "That is correct. I went to a political rally, and then we went to a party after."

Jack listened closely and then asked, "What was the date, if you can recall please? Month and year if you would."

Tiffany looked uncomfortable at the strange question, "February 2021."

Jack kept a serious expression on his face and tried not to smile, "Tiffany, that was two years ago."

Tiffany shook her head at that, "This is not funny." She sounded upset, angry, and annoyed, that some elaborate prank had gone way past the point of humor.

The woman on the porch was half listening now and looking intrigued at what Jack and Tiffany were saying.

As the conversation developed, Megan moved closer to the front yard and slung her AR-15 over her shoulder, helping to de-escalate the situation and show more trust.

Jack could be seen ruminating on how to proceed with the conversation before he spoke, "Tiffany, I can only tell you what I know, and the things I have seen with my eyes and experienced. What I am going to say though you will probably not believe. I can only offer to your truth, to gain your trust. I cannot alter what happened with a lie and expect that to help."

Tiffany, the woman on the porch, and Megan all turned their attention to Jack at that point. A 16-year-old girl inside the house and a 12-year-old boy came out to stand in the doorway of the home as well.

Jack took in a deep breath, and then looked Tiffany directly in the eyes, "Two years ago while in Berkeley you fell under the spiritual influence and control of several demons."

Tiffany took a step back and looked insulted.

Jack pressed on as he held up a hand, "I am sorry Tiffany, but I am going to explain this all. Where I do not know for sure, I will tell you."

Tiffany did not look convinced.

Jack went on, "It was at that point in Berkeley where you stopped having your memories, that these demons fully controlled you. They preyed on your anger, jealousy and rage as you fully fell into their control." Jack then added, "I do not know what happened in detail between then and now, but at some point, you joined Antifa and have been working with them. You have been robbing, raping, and killing anyone that has stood up against the current Federal government. You have been acting as the right-hand thugs, like the Nazi of Germany, to terrorize the people and subjugate them to the tyrannical government."

Tiffany was trying to listen, but she kept turning sideways and walking a bit away, and then stopping and then moving a bit away again. She was having an incredible hard time taking what Jack was saying seriously.

Jack added in closing, "Most recently, you have been going to the homes in this area taking what you wanted and killing anyone that refused your demands. When you came here to this house, you killed this woman's husband when he stood on his porch and refused to give in to your demands. Your crew of Antifa killed him and shot his wife. You, with my eyes as my witness shot my wife," he said as he motioned to Megan.

Tiffany fumed with anger, "This is stupid! Then why do I not remember any of this?"

Jack could not help but grin a bit now, "Now this will sound even stranger," he warned. He went on, "When I arrived, I saw the demons that were surrounding you. I went to you and prayed for you. I asked God to free you from the demons. That was when he sent angels to fight them, to send them back to Hell. At that moment, that is when your mind was returned to you."

Tiffany laughed openly now, mocking.

The woman on the porch could not help but snicker and snort a bit as well.

The teenage girl in the doorway spoke up, "No, it is true mom," she retorted, "I saw it. I was in my room praying and looking out the window when I saw this man appear out of nowhere on a horse in a flash of light. He jumped off his horse and ran to Tiffany and hugged her. That is when I saw three black winged men with swords start to battle two glowing men of light with wings light swans. I saw it. Honest mom, it was as real as I am standing here right now."

Everyone stopped at that point to listen to the girl in the doorway. There was a nice long silent pause where everyone just kept quiet.

Jack was the first to speak, "I am sorry Tiffany. I know it is extraordinary, unusual, and quite unbelievable. However, you have your mind to yourself once again, and you can choose a different path. You can keep your hatred, your rage, and your jealousies and the demons will return to you and control you again. Alternatively, you can try something new."

Tiffany looked around the yard and she finally looked at the lady in the front yard that had bled to death from the artery blown out of her knee, "Renee?" She recognized the woman.

Though Jack's story was senseless, it was the only story she had right now to explain why she was here and why her college roommate was lying dead on the ground nearby.

Tiffany dropped, to sit on the front lawn and just stare off into the sky. She was unable to take in what was told her, unable to wrap logic around the information. Incapable of forming an acceptable narrative that was understandable.

Jack moved to tend to the woman on the porch's wound. Megan walked closer to the front of the house as well, to keep an eye on the area, and act as the guard over all; to keep things from getting out of control.

Jack helped the woman to a porch bench to sit on as he tended to her leg wound. After exchanging names, Jack and Megan learned that the mother's name was Lyn Glade, the daughter's name was Isabella and the son's name was Paul.

Jack had to have Lyn pull her pants down to expose her thigh to him. To offer her privacy, Jack pulled a towel from his pack to drape over her lap and around her hips. Lyn's wound was not as easy as Megan's had been to treat. The bullet had buried deep into her leg and stopped half-way through after bouncing off her bone.

Jack removed his surgical kit from the medical supplies. He had to go into her leg with long forceps and pull the bullet out.

There was a great deal of screaming, and some powerful curse words erupting over the front yard before it was finished.

Jack was able to sew up the entrance wound with a suture and bandage it properly. He promised Lyn he would come back tomorrow with antibiotics for her to take over the next several days. Also, he said he would come back with bandages for her to change each day.

Tiffany had moved from the ground, to stand near the porch and watch Jack take care of Lyn. At one point, she left with Isabella and Paul, to go get some hot water for cleaning. There was a strong tense feeling between Tiffany and the family, for a legitimate reason.

It became gradually understandable that Tiffany had gone through a traumatic situation. She was not the same person that she had been a half hour before; screaming and shooting at the family with the other Antifa thugs. She appeared to be a completely different person now.

Over the next hour, Jack and Megan presided over a strange sort of intervention. The family was going to be in a terrible amount of trouble, with the man of the house now dead, and the mother dramatically incapacitated because of her leg injury.

Jack and Megan felt like diplomats, trying to broker peace between two middle eastern countries. There was great mistrust between them, but also an essential need for them to find a way to help each other.

Tiffany was lost. She was hundreds of miles from home and needed to find some foundation of reality and purpose in her life again.

It took a full hour to come to an agreement. Tiffany would stay with the family. She would help on the farm with manual labor, with the horses, and anything else that needed done while Lyn was recovering from her wound. The family would house and feed her, bringing her in to their family.

Jack and Megan collected up the guns and equipment off the Antifa that had been killed. They let the family know that they would be back in a few hours to drag the bodies off and bury them.

It appeared that the situation at the house was calm enough now to leave. They had to get back to the other duties they needed to accomplish.

Jack and Megan began the slow walk back towards the McVeenson homestead and continued to catch up with each other. As they moved across the fields and hills back in that direction, Jack started first, "So, what has been going on since I left?"

Megan did her best to fill him in, "The McVeenson's were killed by Antifa. Their house was burned down to cover up their murders. I found one of the Antifa guys killed. I think by Todd, in their basement. I've been taking care of their animals and moving all their canned and other food storage back to our place. They had this converted electrical UTV and a trailer that I've been using to do it. Their dog, we are now also taking care of. Riley and Butch are back in the McVeenson's barn."

Jack glanced over to her frequently as they were walking, nodding, and listening carefully to the flood of information as it was coming along.

Megan continued, "I have been moving the rabbit feed, chicken feed, goat feed and bags of oats and stuff for the horses back to our place as well. I figure we will need to disassemble the barn and put it back together on our property, and move the animals as we can in the process."

Jack nodded to that, "If we do not, the animals are going to die. We can put them to use, so it sounds like a solid plan."

Megan then wrapped up the update, "When I was loading up this morning's load into the trailer, I heard gunshots down at the Glade property and you came upon what was going on there and saw for yourself."

Megan was visibly upset as she glossed over the story. She had to stop walking as her eyes teared up.

Jack stopped as well, moving to her, and hugging her tight. He did not say anything, but just kept his arms wrapped around her as she sobbed.

Megan was distraught, having to kill someone at the Glade house. It was going to take months, if ever, for her to get over the flashes of memory that kept coming into her mind.

Jack and Megan took a bit to sit down and have a small bit, to eat from Jack's pack, to drink some water. Jack tried to distract Megan a little in conversation, "I have what we need now to get the Ham radio information from The Silent Majority. I will need to contact them and get them their pictures and video I took with the drone."

Megan nodded her understanding, and tried to get her mind off what happened at the Glade home, "We are going to need to hide the Antifa trucks so people that come looking for them, so they will not bring down more trouble on this area than there already is."

Jack hummed at that, "Let's take that trailer load you have loaded up already to the house, unload it and then head down and bury the Antifa bodies out at that huge rock pile in the field. We can take the trucks out into the middle of nowhere, hide them, siphon all the gas out of them and take whatever we can use out of them."

Megan agreed to the plan, as they got up, and started walking back to the McVeenson's barn in the distance, "It is going to take months to move everything from the McVeenson's, to our place."

Jack smiled at her comment as they came up to the barn's door, "Well, that should keep us out of trouble, and give us something to keep our minds distracted with through the winter."

Megan opened the barn door, to be greeted by Riley and Butch with much tail wagging and happy scurrying about. Butch was a little apprehensive around Jack for about an hour, before they got comfortable with each other.

Butch was quite protective of Megan and the smell of her blood kept him close at her side the remainder of the day. He refused to leave her side, and moved to put himself between her and anyone who came near her, including Jack.

Jack and Megan did not split up again today. They took the UTV and trailer of supplies up to their home and worked together unloading it. They put the guns from the Antifa people down inside the bunker, then Jack and Megan took a shower together.

It took them about an hour to get cleaned up, for Jack to sew the two bullet wounds in Megan's side closed, and dressing it again with a fresh bandage. Butch barred his teeth, and almost bit Jack during the process, but constant calming by Megan prevented the dog from attacking during the medical procedure. Jack went through his medical cabinet in the bunker, took out the right amount of antibiotics for someone of Lyn's weight (he guessed) and brought the medicine along with him.

The UTV ride back to the Glade's house was slow going, over the rugged road, but they arrived without any further encounter with Antifa.

Lyn, Isabella, Paul, and Tiffany were in the side yard with a pickaxe and a shovel taking turns digging. Lyn's husband was wrapped in a blanket near where they were working, to give him a proper burial.

Megan had to call Butch back to the UTV as they neared, he took off running at the family to attack. The German Shepherd was in high alert since Megan's return to the barn.

Lyn, her daughter, and her son all kept guns at arm's length. They soon had their guns at the ready as the UTV approached. It was Megan calling Butch back to the UTV that calmed the family, recognizing Megan's voice.

Jack and Megan pulled the UTV and trailer up in the front yard, then walked over to the family, noting that Tiffany was not armed. That trust still needed some time to build before they would likely want to see her with a gun again.

Lyn was adamant that she wanted her and her children to dig the grave they were working on. They did not want any outside help. It was something she wanted to do alone, as a family.

Jack and Megan worked hard over the next three hours loading the Antifa bodies into the trailer and taking them out into the field, and covering them with rocks from the large pile.

There were only a couple hours, of sunlight remaining before sunset as Jack drove one of the trucks off across the field. Jack took it about a mile off into a deep gully, hidden by overhanging trees. Megan followed along with the UTV and trailer. They picked the truck clean of anything valuable, to add into the trailer to keep. They removed a government radio, a tall whip antenna, a winch off the front bumper, the vehicle battery and alternator, as well as the belts from the engine. They shared a ride back in the UTV and then returned with the other truck as shadows started to form with the setting sun in the west.

By the time darkness was beginning to really get a grip across the area, the trailer was well loaded down. They did not know where all the stuff came from, but the trucks had a plethora of things that Antifa had been looting from various neighbors as they rampaged through the area. No doubt, some of the neighbors had been killed during the looting, and some of this equipment felt somehow wrong to keep.

Jack surmised, "We can split some of it with the Glade's if you want, but we have no idea who it belonged to or where they are. We may as well take with us anything that is useful."

Much of the gear were things like guns, ammo, knives, a compound bow with hunting arrows, some food, bags of potatoes and bushels of vegetables, as well as some more medical equipment, coffee and other rare items that would fetch a generous price on the recently formed black market.

Before leaving the trucks, Jack insisted on setting them on fire to destroy them. He was certain that the trucks had GPS locators in them and if they did not destroy the trucks the government would be returning for revenge. Finding the GPS devices in the trucks would be extremely difficult in the darkness, and the level of paranoia these days did not allow Jack to assume that finding one GPS did not mean there was not another one hidden somewhere else on the truck.

The trucks readily burned with a brilliant blaze. They had taken care to hide them in a ravine so that the bright light of the fire could not be seen. The darkness of the night also concealed the black rolling smoke churning skyward. The only thing they could not properly hide, was the smell of burning rubber, oil, seats, and carpet that could be smelled for a few miles downwind.

Jack took over driving the UTV when darkness completely came. With his night vision goggles, he was easily able to meander around larger rocks and obstructions on the way back to the Glade's home.

They drove the UTV with the lights off as they approached the home and Megan called out loud several times as they neared. Lyn called back to let them know that they could come into the yard without getting shot at.

By flashlight, Jack and Megan handed over some of the gear from what was in the trucks, to help the family. Megan also handed them a handheld radio and talked to Lyn about what channel to keep the radio on. She explained that she was called Mama Bear on the radio, and Jack was called Hawk One. The two ladies spent a few minutes talking about being careful not sharing too much information on the radio, because people were listening. Also, they set up a plan for how to change channels if they thought they were being listened to in a conversation. They set up a couple code words to use that meant they wanted to meet, they needed help or that they were under duress.

Jack promised to return with Megan tomorrow. They would use the radio to let Lyn know when they were getting close to their home. After tomorrow though, Jack explained that they had a great deal of work to do before winter's grasp fully tightened on the mountains, so they would probably only return once a week, unless called for help on the radio.

Departing was a little awkward because they were leaving Tiffany with the family. There was that feeling that the first night trying to sleep with her in the house was going to be quite difficult. Also, the idea that this would be the first time Lyn and her children were going to be going to bed after their husband and father had died. It was going to be an emotional night for them.

Jack and Megan rolled away from the Glade's home into the night with the UTV lights off. Jack with his night vision goggles down over his eyes, and Megan holding Riley in her lap as they crawled along.

It was getting surprisingly cold, now that the sun had went down. They had overlooked proper jackets upon their return and were now shivering as they pulled up their driveway.

A quick trip into the house to get some warm jackets, hats, and gloves, then Jack and Megan spent an hour unloading the trailer and carrying most everything down into the bunker. Megan showed Jack how she had been charging the UTV. He nodded his approval with how it was done. They could make a more permanent charging station later, but the wire Megan had set up for the job should do just fine.

Husband and Wife brought a light meal up from the bunker, with some dog food, and the family sat on the porch of the small home, as the chill of the mountain gripped the land firmly.

Jack took in a deep breath as he leaned his head back and looked up at the stars from under the edge of the porch roof, "How do you feel about moving back up into the house soon? The threat of the fire is gone, but Antifa is a real threat. I do not know that they will cease to be a threat though." He looked over to Megan as she looked at him, "I know you have a hard time living underground, but you went through something dreadful today. Would you feel safer, for now, staying down in the bunker at night?"

Megan stared off across the tops of the hills, where before the trees would have blocked the view, "Perhaps just a few more days in the bunker. Let's have you get what we need for the Ham Radio and let a couple days pass, to see if things calm down first."

Jack nodded to that as the dogs were finishing up their bowls of food, "Tomorrow, we can get Lyn the bandages she will need over the next several days for changing her dressing. Then bring a load or two back from the McVeenson's, and then the next day I can contact The Silent Majority to arrange to deliver their intel."

Megan considered the idea, "Try to get them on the radio tomorrow to arrange the delivery of the intel. We can spend the day like you said, but I think you should contact them tomorrow to set up the time and place for that exchange."

The two gathered up the dog food bowls, and the family moved on into the shed and down into the bunker for the night.

Chapter Nineteen
Night Terror and Bible Study

October 17

Megan's scream in the darkness startled Jack from a dead sleep, putting him directly into attack mode. He flung the blankets off, as simultaneously his hand went to the .45 cal pistol on the headboard of the bed.

Jack was on his feet, and reaching for the small tactical flashlight, when Megan's scream turned into words, "Put the gun down! No! No!"

Jack lowered his gun, and turned on the light to see that Megan was sitting upright in the bed. Her eyes wide open, staring at the back wall of the bunker, completely asleep, but in a night terror. She was pleading with one of the men at the Glade's farm for him to lower his gun, begging for him not to make her shoot him. Tears streamed out of her eyes, her face was red as her lips trembled with fear, crying at the same time.

Jack hastily put the handgun on the headboard, left the flashlight turned on, but put it beside the gun, as he got onto the bed on his knees beside Megan.

Jack had no idea what the best thing to do was, so he just wrapped his arms around her to hug her and tried to talk calmly and softly to her, "It is okay Megan, it is okay."

It may have been the wrong thing to do.

Jack found himself being twisted, then thrown on his back, unsure what direction was up or down for an instant. When Jack got his bearings, he discovered he was on his back. At that same moment, Megan was straddling his chest with her knees pinning down his arms. Her hands squeezing around his neck, choking him. Not exactly what he had planned.

Jack heaved against her weight, but she shifted like she was riding a horse, her body adjusted to push down to meet each attempt to free his arms. Tears from her face fell on Jack's face, as well as spittle and snot from her crying. It was not one of the best moments in their marriage, for certain.

At some point, Jack passed out.

The alarm clock on the headboard ready 1:25 am when Jack started coughing and gasping for air. Megan had released him, and was at his side crying and sobbing uncontrollably.

It took a complete minute for Jack to get enough air into himself to understand the situation fully. It was not like a light switch where he immediately remembered what had happened.

It took a bit to remember the scream, the yelling, hugging and then her attacking.

Megan now appeared to be out of her dream. She was sitting on the bed with her back against the side wall of the bunker. Her knees were pulled up close to her chest and her arms wrapped around her legs as she cried.

Megan's voice, in an almost imperceptible whisper carried across the room to Jack, "I killed three people.... I killed three people." A pause, "I am a murderer."

Jack may not be the smartest guy in the County, but Jack had learned his lesson properly now about approaching Megan, "Love, Megan," he tried to get her to look up at him and meet his gaze.

It took a few attempts, but Megan did finally look up to meet his eyes, "I killed people Jack."

Jack nodded softly and tried to make his voice sound as far away from dismissive as possible, "Love, if you had not shot, Lyn would be dead. Isabella would have been raped; Paul would probably be dead."

There was a long pause as Jack's words dug in past the horror of the experience and deeper into Megan's mind where logic still held its place within her.

Megan's gaze dropped from Jack's to the bed, and then back up to him. Her lower lip sucked in just a little as she softly chewed on it, thinking about what Jack had just said. She did not say anything, but the crying had stopped, and her breathing was deepening with long slow intakes.

After some time, Megan nodded slowly. Jack moved up beside her on the bed, to lean against the wall with her, and hold her. He pulled the blankets up around them as he let her lay her head on his shoulder.

Jack did not say anything, nor did Megan. They just stayed there silent in the bunker with the two dogs on the floor at the foot of the bed watching them.

*****

Morning was more quiet than normal in the bunker when Jack and Megan awoke to get ready for the day. Megan was still deep in her mind about what she had experienced yesterday, and Jack was deep in thought about how to help her without making anything worse.

Jack tended to feeding the dogs, while Megan claimed the dining table to study her Bible and sip from a fresh cup of coffee. Butch was still a little apprehensive around Jack, but the two were quickly warming towards the other.

To give Megan more time to be alone with God and in prayer, Jack began hand washing their dirty clothes in the washtub at the bunker entrance. It took some vigorous scrubbing to get Megan's blood out of her clothing and to get the stink out of his.

The absent-minded task of washing the clothes allowed Jack's mind to slip back over the last couple days, and to try to find the reason, and understanding of what he had experienced.

Thinking back, the first time Jack remembered the Apache on the horse, was a short while before he encountered the military scouting team.

Knowing what he knew now, about the nature of the Apache, he could see God's hand on the situation. The gentle nudging of him away from the path where he would have been discovered by the military, if he had not moved away from the trail to hide from the Apache.

Later, when Megan had been praying for him, Jack had been hidden in a sudden snowstorm and been given an unexplainable speed and endurance to cover a dozen miles in just about an hour. These events he personally witnessed, and were a part of directly, and still he found them overwhelming to accept as fact.

Then, to remove any doubt that God was specifically and directly putting his hand on the events, Jack recalled the Apache, the horse, the transport over 37 miles, and the opening of his eyes into the Spiritual World.

Jack found himself leaning over the washtub as his back began to ache. He was not washing the clothes any longer, but just holding them in the warm water and staring at the wall of the bunker. Jack heard himself chuckle out loud for zoning out. The things of God were so beyond his ability to understand.

Having so recently witnessed a glimpse of God's work in the world, Jack became so distracted, that it was hard to concentrate on anything. Jack wanted to keep the memory real in his mind, and to keep it from slipping away.

Jack heard Megan and the dogs coming through the bunk room towards him, so he stood up straight to stretch his back and take a break for a moment, offering Megan a wide smile, "Hey there baby, how are you feeling?"

Megan was holding an arm full of clothes and a folded-up towel on her way to the shower. She stopped to lean against the side of one of the bunks to chat quietly with me, "I little better. I had to ask God to forgive me. But the hardest part was accepting his forgiveness." She paused for a moment to think, and when she spoke again, she looked Jack in the eye, "You are the one that has always had a problem with your rage, with an instinct to solve the problem physically. Why am I the one that had to kill someone? You could have put this in a box in your mind and separated it much better than me."

Jack was not sure if that was an insult or a compliment. It was accurate though. Jack had grown up brawling with other boys in school daily. All his life his nature was to be aggressive and to neutralize any threat in as fast and efficient method as possible. In his mind, that method appeared to be a physical destruction of the threat.

Megan though, she was far more thoughtful and considerate. It was not her natural reaction to solve any situation with violence.

For Jack to be the one to have shown up by a miracle with a flash of light, come to the rescue by hugging the enemy and praying for them; it felt like a slap in the face to Megan.

Megan, to have saved the day with prayer and love, would have been a very expected choice. However, for her to have had to kill people and Jack to have been the one that was the pacifist, was just so upside down. It was difficult to accept.

Jack and Megan spent a few minutes sharing with each other how they both felt overwhelmed by yesterday's events. It comforted Megan, when he admitted that it was strange that their roles had been reversed. But the two of them accepted things as they were, and not as they had wished they were after a couple minutes of prayer together.

It was all in God's control, and they agreed to submit themselves to his Will, no matter how uncomfortable or unfair it appeared to them.

Megan lost herself in a nice long hot shower while Jack finished up the clothes, then hung them on a line, with clothes pins that ran down the middle of the bunker.

Jack was having himself a bowl of oatmeal with some brown sugar at the table while reading his Bible, when Megan came back from the shower in her bra but carrying her shirt.

Megan motioned to the medical cabinet, "You want to put a fresh bandage on my bullet holes?"

The two shared a laugh at that while Jack got up to get what was needed.

Jack asked as he made it to the cabinet and opened it up, "You are going to want some pain killers, right?"

Megan weakly laughed, "Oh yes, most certainly."

After tending to Megan's bandage, Jack turned in the CB-Radio to channel 8, the channel he and The Silent Majority agreed would be how he would contact them when he was ready to set up his meeting with them.

Megan worked on cleaning up in the bunker and the housekeeping while Jack tried to make contact.

Jack: Base 1, this is Hawk 1, do you copy?

There was a minute of silence. Jack repeated the call three more times before a voice came back to him over the radio.

Base 1:   We hear you Hawk 1.
Jack: I have the package for delivery.
Base 1:   Meet us at the farm for delivery.
Jack: Tomorrow morning, sunrise.
Base 1:   Agreed, see you then. Base 1 out.
Jack: Hawk 1 out.

Jack and Megan wrapped up their preparations and climbed up and out to the surface by 8:00 am. The way of course was checked with the security cameras. Jack moved out first, to walk the property and ensure it was safe before Megan and the dogs came out.

Megan had given the AR-15 back to Jack. She only carried the 9mm pistol on her leg holster now. She was not sure if she could use the rifle again, even if it meant to save her own life.

Jack left the sniper rifle in the bunker and put his pack in the back of the UTV. His pack was mostly filled with bandages and medical supplies and a little food for their time away from home.

By 8:30 am, Megan pulled the UTV to a slow stop in front of the McVeenson's pole barn. Butch and Riley darted around the property chasing each other and playing while the chickens clucked and rushed into the coop for safety.

Jack and Megan made sure that the pole barn was safe and there was no one hiding inside. With that small level of assured safety, Megan started to feed the animals, while Jack took a walk around the property to check for any threat.

The morning appeared to be offering both an uneventful experience; a grateful reprieve from the previous day.

Jack turned his attention to locking the chickens into their coop. He starting the process of removing the chicken wire from their fenced in yard. It took some care to pull the horseshoe nails out of the posts. He hoped to reuse them when reassembling the fenced yard for the chickens on their own property. Going to the hardware to pick up nails or supplies was an experience long since ended.

After an hour, Megan finished caring for the animals and came out to join Jack with the project. Working together, they carefully rolled up the long lengths of chicken wire, then used some wire to tie the bundles closed so they would not unroll. These went into the UTV trailer for the trip back to the house.

It took a bit, thinking of the best way to remove the tall wooden poles from the ground, that had been holding up the chicken wire yard. It was decided that Megan would drive the UTV very slowly up to each pole and then push on the pole carefully to tip it over, push and loosen it in the ground. The idea was to back/forth a few times, and this would make the pole loose enough to pull up and remove.

It was a great idea, but it did not work exactly as they expected. When they attempted to push the post, the UTV grunted and spun its ties, but could not get enough leverage to tip the post. They adjusted their technique by using one of the come-along pulley devices high on the pole as they could then hook the other end to the UTV a distance off. Winching the pole towards the UTV was successful. It was slow hard work. By 10:30 am they had been able to remove all the posts, and pile them up into the UTV trailer for shipment.

Jack and Megan figured a nice break had been earned, as they breathed heavily in the thin mountain air. So, they decided to collect up the eggs from the coop and take a walk down to the Glades, to bring them the bandages and some eggs. Of the 24 eggs collected, they kept 8 of them and brought the rest with them to give to the Glades.

It was a short walk of only a half mile, so Jack and Megan took the opportunity to hold hands as they went, letting the dogs run ahead.

When still a far distance off, Megan took out her handheld radio and turned it to the channel she had set up with Lyn, and called her to let her know they were coming from the North. Also, it would be very neighborly of them not to shoot. The two ladies shared an uncomfortable laugh at the bad joke and then Jack and Megan finished the remainder of the walk to arrive at the Glade's home.

The entire family, plus Tiffany, were out in the front yard to greet the expected company. Megan exchanged hugs with everyone, including a reluctant and timid Tiffany. Jack though offered head nods and a proper manly handshake with Paul as the dogs roamed the property sniffing and urinating on random objects.

There was a flurry of shared stories as the ladies caught up with each other. Everyone moved into the house, and made their way through the living room towards the dining room and kitchen at the back of the double wide. A large sliding glass door looked out over the back yard, where a large wood deck behind the home held a gas grill and a picnic table. From the kitchen window on the back wall, the horse corral could be seen, and their herd of horses back safely inside the repaired fenced walls.

Jack fished around in his pack on the dining room table until he pulled out the bundle of bandages and medical tape, and laid them on the table, "I think this should be sufficient to change your bandage every day for two weeks. That should be more than enough, I think. The thing is, to keep it clean. But when you are able, it will need to breathe and get fresh air. It's going to itch once it gets to the point where it starts to form a scab, well, you know all this I'm sure."

Lyn accepted the bandages and medical tape with a big smile, and put them on the kitchen counter off to the side and out of the way as they gathered around the dining room table, standing, and talking. She declined the pain medicine when Jack offered it, explaining that she had some already and did not want to take his supplies if she could supply her needs on her own. She had a healthy independent nature.

That was when Megan remembered the eggs and pulled out the little basket they had brought from the farm, "Do you have something I can put these eggs into?" she asked with a big smile.

Isabella nodded happily and scurried into the kitchen to fetch a bowl to transfer the eggs into.

Megan moved into the kitchen with Isabella to transfer the eggs into their bowl and the two began to chat quietly. Isabella began asking quiet questions, if she had a Bible, if she could help her study, to pray and meet with her to talk about God.

Megan knew that she would need to clear all of this with Lyn, and she told Isabella as much. Isabella confirmed that her mother would be fine with it if they were careful not to get caught. She explained that before the world went crazy that she went to church with her grandmother and that the whole family, except dad, would go on the big holidays. It was last summer that she went to a youth camp in Prescott and accepted Christ.

Enough words from the two girls drifted across the room to the others, that it was obvious what the two were talking about. When glances were repeatedly exchanged, a gradual shift in the conversation included Lyn as they made the arrangements for the small Bible Study with Megan and Isabella.

With the details were being ironed out, Jack and Paul wandered out onto the back deck to talk. It was clear that Paul was stepping up as the man of the house. Jack made it clear that he would offer help when he could with things that needed repairing around the house, perhaps give Paul shooting lessons if he wanted. He offered to teach him things like hunting, trapping, and other skills, he may not have had time to learn from his father yet.

The two guys sat at the picnic table for a while talking. Jack for the most part just listened as he let Paul speak. Paul had seen his father get killed yesterday, and buried him in their side yard with the family. As far as Jack knew, his own father was still alive up in Northern Michigan. He found a great empathy for the young boy. Thinking of his father dying one day made him feel lonely already.

So much of his work ethic, loyalty to his wife and family and friends, and the way he treated people was from the foundation he learned from watching his father.

Now, Jack felt a distinct obligation to lead by example for this young man.

The sliding glass door pulled back and the ladies came filing out. Megan brought Jack's backpack and Isabella carried out a try of food for their family, as everyone started to gather around the picnic table and claim spots to sit.

Tiffany remained quiet, unsure of where she fit in and overwhelmed by the two-year hole in her memory.

Megan did not ask first, but just bowed her head and started praying aloud. Everyone else froze in place and stopped talking. Jack and Isabella of course, had already closed their eyes when she started, but the others were caught a little off guard.

Megan offered thanks for the meal, "Heavenly Father, we thank you for this meal. We thank you for the sun, the rain, and your watchful gaze over our crops, for the elk and other animals we are blessed to care for that have given us such a blessed meal today. Lord, we thank you for your protection today and we ask your blessing over this family and for those that love your Son. In Jesus name, Amen."

Jack and Isabella echoed with an Amen and Lyn managed an unpracticed grunt.

There was not an awkward silence or uncomfortable conversation next. Instead, Megan launched in to asking questions about how Lyn and her husband met and stories about where they were originally from. The ladies slipped into a natural flowing conversation during the meal that brought with it smiles, and even a little laughing before the end of the meal arrived.

As they wrapped up the meal, Isabella, who had been referred to several times as Bella now, cleared the table. Lyn explained that she wanted to fill Megan in on what she knew about the neighbors in the area. That is the direction the conversation then took.

Paul offered to teach Jack how to saddle a horse the proper way and how to put on a harness. Jack was eager for the lesson, the two tromped off across the back yard towards the horses at a quick pace, chatting and bonding as they went.

While Jack and Paul spent time at the corral with the horses, Lyn filled Megan in on several neighbors and their situations. A few of the neighbors had been killed by Antifa already. Two of the neighbors had never made it out of the valley and to the nearby homes. So, those homes had been picked over and looted already by Antifa.

Lyn explained that a couple of the neighbors she could not trust because Antifa let them keep most of their things and did not hurt them. She explained who they were and where they lived and surmised that they were informants for Antifa in the area in exchange for being left unmolested by the group.

Megan did not share what she knew of The Silent Majority and the photos taken by them with the notes of the neighbors in the area. Some of the information was confirmed by Lyn, other gaps Lyn filled in with new data. Lyn did not appear to know anything about the farm that Jack had met The Silent Majority at Megan did not share that information with her. Megan still was not sure she fully trusted The Silent Majority and she did not want to risk putting the Glade's in any danger.

Around 2:00 pm, Megan had to call Jack over from the corral and put an end to the horsemanship lessons. They had a great deal more work to accomplish before dark and none of it was getting done while they continued to visit.

The ladies exchanged hugs and smiles, while Jack shook Paul's hand and gave him a solid thud on the shoulder.

Jack and Megan made their way off towards the McVeenson's farm to get back to work. As they moved along, Megan filled Jack in on what Lyn had shared about the neighbors. She shared the arrangement she set up, with permission from Lyn, to meet Bella every morning at the McVeenson farm for Bible Study. The two ladies would verify over the radios each night for the next morning, for the time to meet.

Jack appeared to be in an outstanding mood as he smiled from ear to ear, "I am actually going to learn how to take care of horses properly. Like a real cowboy."

Megan turned a bit to the side and went to punch him in the shoulder, but stopped with a wince. Turning at the hips sent pain through her gunshot wound in her side.

Jack noticed the attempted assault and laughed, "Ha! Serves you right you ruckus wench!"

The look Megan gave Jack then was far worse than any punch could have been, Jack coward back into his submissive husband posture with a meek grin.

Back at the McVeenson's farm, the two worked together to remove the solar panels, batteries, several tools, and other equipment from the UTV shed. They carried it all to the trailer and piled it all carefully, and tied it down for the trip back.

Megan looked to the sky, "I think we have enough time to get this back home, unloaded, and then back to feed the animals and get home before dark."

Jack cinched up the last rope that was keeping the solar panels from tipping over in the trailer, "That sounds like a plan. Can I stay home and start digging holes for the chicken yard posts while you come back alone? Or, you want me to come back with you?"

Megan looked around, apprehensive for a moment and then nodded slowly, "Just keep your radio on channel 22 so I can call you if I need to."

Jack nodded to that and slapped her on the butt, then moved around the UTV to keep it between Megan and himself so she couldn't smack him.

His plan seemed to be well thought out until he climbed into the UTV driver's seat and Megan climbed carefully in on the passenger's side. Whoops. A playful punch met his arm with her laughing. It was worth the pinch of pain in her side, as the two shared in a loud laugh together. They started on their way home, up the trail.

Jack pulled the UTV up near the shed, so that he could plug the cord into its batteries for recharging. It would take them about an hour to unload the trailer and they may as well use that time to recharge the vehicle's batteries as much as possible.

Jack and Megan worked together to lift the solar panels off the trailer first, carry them over and stack them against the back of the house and out of view of the front yard. They covered them with a tarp to hide them a little better, and then carried the marine batteries from the trailer inside the shed, to put them back against the rear wall. Out of the way, they would hook up and use them later to add to their battery storage capacity.

Jack and Megan took several minutes walking around the property deciding the best place to put the chicken yard. The coop was going to be placed adjacent to it, so they had to plan out level ground and where it would be located, while keeping in mind that they had an entire pole barn to be relocated here on the property as well.

It was going to take several full days from sunrise to sunset to get this move completed and everything settled in and normalized.

Megan helped Jack unload the poles and the chicken wire rolls to where they decided it would be built. She then she unplugged the UTV, and was on her way back to the farm. She flipped her radio to channel 22 and called back to Jack as she started to roll the UTV along, "Channel 22"

Jack responded by un-clipping his radio from his chest armor and holding it up in the air over head while nodding to her. He flipped it to the channel she wanted, clipped it back onto his chest armor and pulled his gloves back. It was time to start using the post hole digger, and get to the task at hand.

Riley stayed behind with Jack, while Butch moved on with Megan for the task.

Megan made the trip back to the farm without incident and was quick to get to the evening chores of bringing water from the well to the animals and dishing out the proper type and amount of food to each type of animal in the barn. It took her about an hour to care for them, and the she spent another hour gathering up random tools like shovels, pick axes, a couple fishing poles and a tackle box that was found in a corner. Random other things that were easy to load into the trailer on her own also were collected.

Megan's return home found Jack still heaving the post hole digger into the ground with pounding thrusts into the rock and stones. From a quick glance at his progress, it looked like it has taken him about 30 minutes per post to get them in, upright, and ready to use. It was going to take him another four hours to get the remainder of the posts secured and ready for attaching the chicken wire around as walls. Then over the top as a roof to protect the chickens from the hawks.

Jack leaned the digger up against one of the posts he had managed to finish, then moved to meet Megan and help her unload the supplies from the trailer. She pulled the UTV up near the shed, so that Jack could plug the wire in for recharging the vehicle.

Jack plugged the UTV in, then moved to give Megan a hug, "I was wrong, I should have gone with you. It felt like you were gone three days."

Megan moved to accept the hug but then Jack's stench of sweat and body odor hit her nose and she jerked back and almost lost her lunch on the ground. Her hand moved to cover her mouth and pinch her nose shut as she leaned over and groaned.

Jack frowned with a sigh and then tilted his head down and to the right to sniff at his armpit and he coughed, "Holy!" He started laughing as he jerked his head back away from himself and gasped for air.

Megan walked around to the back of the trailer to start unloading, "What do you think about staying tonight up in the house?"

Jack agreed with the idea with a nod, "Sounds okay to me. We must be visibly living up here on the surface or people are going to start wondering where we disappear to. They may start hiding and watch us vanish into the tool shed for ten hours at a time and figure things out."

Megan appeared relieved that they would not have to stay another night down in the bunker. Though, the risk of danger was higher on the surface, it felt like she was being suffocated underground in the bunker each night.

The husband and wife duo worked together to clear the things out of the trailer, then they retired into the house with the dogs.

Megan insisted that Jack get directly into the shower before he did anything else. He complied and lathered up in the simple shower of the corner bathroom.

While Jack was washing away the stench of his hard work, Megan tended to watering and feed the dogs. She then went upstairs to select some clothes for her to change into after her own shower.

By the time Megan came back down the stairs and into view, Jack was out of the shower and naked in the living room. He was making a fire in the large pot-bellied stove. Jack was trying to get the cold of the day out of the home and to fend off the ever-freezing temperatures of night that had already started to rush in and claim dominance over the small house.

Megan slipped up behind him, shifted her arm load of clothes into her left arm so she could smack him on the butt.

The swat startled Jack and his hand jerked back from lighting the paper inside the stove and he wacked his wrist on the door of the cast iron stove, "Ouch!", he exclaimed in surprise.

Megan was off and away, into the bathroom while laughing along the way, "Got you back!" she proclaimed in triumph as she shut the door behind herself.

Jack rubbed at his wrist, and rubbed at the black soot that had come off the door. He stared at the bathroom door with a wry grin, trying to conceive a fun way to get back at her with some trick that would be interesting.

For now, the cold interior of the house caused him to shiver as goosebumps grew across his arms and legs, and a shiver rippled up his bare back. Distracted from his mischievous revenge, Jack turned back to getting the fire going in the stove.

It took ten minutes to get the fire going well enough so that Jack could close the door and set the dampener for the airflow into the stove.

Both dogs had finished their bowls of food and had found places on the floor near the wood stove to get comfortable and curl up with their noses tucked into their tails for a restful night's sleep.

Jack made sure the front door was locked, the 2x4 was secured across the brackets so that the door could not be kicked in, and then he turned his grinning gaze to the bathroom door.

Still buck-naked, Jack moved to the bathroom door, slowly opened it as quietly as he could, stepped into the steaming hot mist of the small room and closed the door as carefully as he could behind him.

Megan had her back to the shower door with her head in the stream of hot water coming down over her. Her hair was flat against her head and down over her shoulders.

Jack eased the shower door open, but it made a little noise from the latch and the stainless-steel hinge along the side of the door. He was sure she heard the door open and knew he was there, but she did not move.

Jack stepped into the shower and slowly closed the door behind him, then turned to face her and inch himself closer. His hands reached around her sides to her stomach and pressed gently onto her stomach as he nudged up against her from behind. He just held himself to her while he moved to rest his chin on her shoulder.

The hot water from above rained down over both their heads and faces. It streamed down both their bodies and between them where gaps were available for it to find its way to the shower floor.

Jack had to get up early to meet with The Silent Majority to deliver their pictures, video, and information he had about the power plant. He would probably regret not getting much sleep tonight. But what was life without a little regret? At least he would have this time with Megan to daydream about on his walk north to meet them at the farm.

At one point, Butch was scratching and barking at the bathroom door. He was certain that Jack was hurting Megan in some way. Jack and Megan could not help but erupt into laughter as Megan tried to call to the dog over the sound of the shower and through the door that she was okay.

The world may have turned upside down, but in these moments, Jack and Megan took refuge in their love of the other with such reckless abandonment that the world faded away. There was nothing but each other, and the moments they had right now.

Megan stayed in the bathroom to get dried and dressed and to clean up for bed while Jack restocked the stove with wood. They managed to convince Butch that Megan was perfectly okay.

Husband and Wife curled up and nestled together in their bed upstairs, beneath the heavy homemade quilt Jack's mother had made for him many years earlier.

Jack set an alarm to ensure he was up early enough for the trip north to the farm. Within moments, the two drifted off to sleep in a tangle of arms and legs.

Chapter Twenty
Radio Access, Hide the Bible

October 18

Jack and Megan were roused from their sleep shortly before Jack's alarm would have gone off. Butch's deep bark filled the house from downstairs, and Riley's little yapping call was singing along; filling the gaps when Butch was taking a breath for more barking.

Jack gave Megan a kiss on her forehead, then eased out from under the warm blankets, and into the cold air of the house. The fire in the stove had gone out during the night and the bitter mountain early winter temperatures had come to greet them this morning.

The sun had not quite come up in the east yet. A dim shade of light was just beginning to turn the horizon.

Jack stepped down onto the bedroom floor, pulled the curtains back away from the window, and looked out over the top of the front porch. From the second floor, he could see down into the front yard to the cause of the dog's ruckus.

Megan had turned onto her side to watch Jack, pulling the blankets tight around her like a burrito. Just her head poking out the top, "What is it?"

Jack squinted into the dark front yard. It took him a little time before he saw a large dark shadow in the garden. He kept his eyes on the shape as he whispered in the bedroom to Megan, "It is an elk in the garden. It got over the fence, and is eating."

Megan chuckled softly, "I have everything worth anything picked and removed already. If it is eating anything it is potato plants or stalks, nothing that matters now."

Jack made sure to keep his voice down low, "How are we doing on meat? Should I just leave it alone or do we need more elk?"

Megan considered their stock, "Just leave it be. If we start getting low, you can go out hunting."

Jack nodded, moved the curtain back over the window, and then went for his clothes to get dressed for the day, "I am going to get the fire going and take care of the dogs, come on down when you are ready."

Megan moaned and then pulled the blankets up over her head and nuzzled her face deeper into the pillow.

******

After Jack got the house warmed up, and a little breakfast in himself, he let Megan know he was going down into the bunker to get the pictures and video put onto the data chip in the camera. He explained that he was going to get ready and would come back to the house to say goodbye before he left.

The dogs took to the property freely when Jack went below into the bunker. The elk had since wandered off from the house, and remained unmolested by the barking dogs.

Down in the bunker, Jack moved the drone video off his iPhone onto the data chip. He then made copies of everything for himself onto his laptop. He took the time to load up the metadata on the iPhone video so that he could erase his name, GPS coordinates and personal information out of the video file, then slipped the camera into a pouch and gathered his gear for the hike north to the farm.

When Jack emerged from the shed, and closed the door behind him, he found Megan near the UTV with both dogs. She was all dressed and ready for the day, with a knit cap over her head, gloves, and a warm winter jacket over her armored vest. She had on black swat team like pants with leg pouches, and wore a pair of dark hiking boots. Her 9mm was holstered on her right leg, she looked ready for a day of hard work.

Megan unplugged the UTV, then hung the wire on the hook on the she, "I'll keep my radio on until you get back."

Jack nodded to her, "I am going to bring my ham radio with me. I will tune it to the frequency you are using on your radio so you can hear me. I can put out about a 30-mile signal so you will be able to hear me when I am well past what your small radio can talk to me at. So, I can give you updates on anything that you may need to know. Even if you may not be able to talk to me back, okay?"

Megan nodded to that, "Do you want to just get me one of the other Ham radios and set matching channels for me?"

Jack gave a nod to that and smiled, "That would be better, we can just keep on the same frequency and should be able to talk just fine. The little walkie-talkies are handy for talking to the Glade's, but when we are away more than a couple miles, we really should get in the habit of just using the ham radios for you and me."

Megan nodded, "Okay, you can teach me more about how to use them later."

Jack smiled, then went back down into the bunker while Megan was preparing for her ride to the farm.

Once Megan had the ham radio, Jack showed her the channel, frequency, and explained that they would not be using a repeater, so their range would only be about 10 to 30 miles, depending on if one of them were down in a valley and the other was not. Maybe even as low as five miles if both were down in a valley with large hills between them. But he added, they could go as far as 60 miles if both were up some place high like at the very top of hills in the area.

Jack and Megan parted ways after a short kiss. Megan took the UTV and both dogs south towards the McVeenson's, and Jack heading north towards The Silent Majority farm.

******

Jack switched his radio to the frequency that matched the CB-Radio channel when he was about fifteen minutes away from the farm. The early morning trip had gone without any dangerous or life-threatening encounters, and Jack found himself overlooking the fields near the farm and keying up the radio.

Jack:	Base 1, this is Hawk 1.
Base 1:	We copy Hawk 1.
Jack:	I am 15 out, permission to approach from the west.
Base 1:	Roger, approved.

Jack detached the night-vision goggles from his helmet so that the farm did not know he owned them, then tucked them away into his backpack.

Jack's walk across the wide-open field to the farmhouse did not take too long. The ground was relatively even and a direct path straight at the house quickly brought him into the yard.

As Jack neared the house, he flanked left around the side until he came into view of the front yard of the farm. Jack saw the front door open. Tony stepped out onto the porch; rifle held, but pointed towards the ground. Right behind Tony, the woman from the barn porn stepped out with him and closed the door behind herself; she also had a rifle and kept it safely pointed downward.

The woman stayed by the door while Tony walked towards Jack to greet him, offering a hand out to shake, "You sure got there and back fast, how'd you manage that?"

Jack knew that trying to explain a supernatural intervention of God was not going to be an easy pill to swallow, "Part of it was, I was able to get my hands on a horse. So that helped out a great deal."

Tony ah'd softly to that, the answer looked to pacify his curiosity as a sufficiently reasonable explanation to delay his suspicion.

"Well," Tony started after they shook hands, "What did you learn?"

Jack tapped a pouch on his vest that held the camera, "The power plant is in full production. They are bringing in school buses from Springerville filled with slave labor to work the plant. They have a helicopter that scouts the area and responds with a military squad to any threats. I have pictures of several places in the power plant where snipers are set up. There are also a few Humvees that are armored and have turrets on top with mounted M-60's."

Tony listened to the report and then motioned with his hand that he wanted the camera. Jack handed it over as Tony talked, "We will take a look at what you were able to get, and then if it looks adequate, we will have you come in and teach you what you need to know about using the radios."

Jack nodded to the arrangement and remained out in the yard with the woman watching him skeptically from the porch. Jack did his best not to look at her. It felt uncomfortable knowing what she looked like naked and he made sure not to look at her directly. It probably made him look shifty and untrustworthy, but revealing that he had seen the pictures would be an even worse slip on his part.

After 20 minutes or so, Sal opened the front door and called for Jack to come into the house.

Jack passed the woman on the porch, diverted his eyes so as not meet her gaze. He walked in to follow Sal across the living room and into the dining room, where Margaret was sitting at the table. Tony had gone somewhere else inside the house as Jack was arriving, and was not anywhere to be seen.

Jack still had a strange vibe about these people. He did not trust them, and he was sure they did not fully trust him yet as well.

Over the next hour, Sal and Margaret showed Jack how to use a printed-out sheet of paper that had columns of radio frequencies on it. They had a system that used a letter and number code so you could count down the row with the letter and then over to the column with the number and then draw a line on the paper. Then do the same with a second letter and number combo and where the two lines crossed that was the frequency to be used. It was cumbersome but effective. They spent some time explaining some of the basic use of ham radios, to ensure he would know how to use it properly.

Jack surprised them a little by picking up on it fast and then asking if he could transmit digital files though the frequency. They were not sure at first, Jack explained that he had a modem that could convert the radio analog signal to digital, just like an old dial-up modem. They still were uncertain if this was possible, but said that they may be able to get him in touch with something that may know.

Jack smiled at this; he was sure it worked but the person on the other end would have to know what they were doing as well. They must have a modem for converting back to digital on their end as well. A computer document, photo or even a program could be converted into simple 1's and 0's and sent over the radio frequency exactly as had been done in the 1980's with telephones. At the other end the machine screeching sounds would be gathered and converted back into a digital file on the computer. Tada, pictures, videos, voice recordings and documents could be sent across the country on the ham radio network.

Jack knew it would work, he just had to find someone that knew how to manage doing it on the other end as well.

When it appeared that Jack had the procedures and knowledge sufficient to be trusted on their network, Sal took a step back and crossed his arms over his chest, "We can offer more than a radio network if you are interested," he explained.

Jack folded up the paper, and a little booklet they had given him and slipped them into a pouch for safe keeping, "What do you mean?"

Sal was careful in how he worded details, "Networking for skills for one. Say, you needed a dentist, or a doctor, a midwife, an electrician or a plumber, we help each other out and ensure we take care of our own."

Jack considered the information and nodded, "I assume there would be additional tasks or missions to go on for the group, to have access to these resources?"

Sal grinned wryly, "You catch on quick Kirby."

Jack smiled at that, "If possible, I want to pay as I go. I would rather not get into debt using the services before I can pay for them. Perhaps you can imagine something that I can help with that needs done. I can accumulate credit with you first. I think it would be the smart way to go, rather than being on the back side of a deal trying to earn my way back to a zero balance."

Sal nodded at the wisdom of Jack's idea, "I will talk to the others and see what we need that you may best fit. What sort of skills can you bring to the table?"

Jack grinned just a bit, "It has been a while since I worked up a resume."

Margaret chuckled at Jack's comment as she started collecting the things on the table and hiding them away again.

Jack did his best to summarize the things he may be trained in that would be helpful, "I am skilled at plumbing. I can manage with basic electrical wiring. I can hold my own with construction, framing and finished work. I was a city drinking water treatment plant operator and a sewage plant operator as well, so given the proper supplies and equipment I can create safe drinking water, assuming you can find water to treat."

Sal nodded slowly and could be seen trying to remember all what Jack was sharing.

Jack went on, "I am okay with small engine repairs but modern electronics in cars I cannot do. I can do well with solar panels and battery banks installation. I have, I would say about an EMT level of medical skills, mostly trauma related like sutures and treatment for knife and gunshot wounds."

Margaret pulled out a notebook and started writing some things down as Jack continued, trying to catch up.

Sal looked more pleased the longer Jack talked, it appeared like they had found a decent addition to the cause.

Jack tried to think up other things he may be helpful at, "I am okay at hunting to bring in meat. Not so great at fishing mainly because there is no water anywhere and fishing is horrifically boring." Jack continued, "I can do canning, if mason jars, lids and rings can be provided, tomatoes, peppers, onions, corn and anything really. For meat I have a pressure cooker also. We have a garden that supplies us with our needs, but if there is trade available for things we cannot get like sugar or flour off the black market, we can expand our garden a great deal for trade."

Margaret's pen scratched across the pages of the notebook as fast as she could write.

Jack finished up, careful to leave some things off his list that may reveal more about him and Megan than he wanted anyone to know about, "As you know I can do recon. I do not want anything to do with purposeful combat, attacking and killing people. I will defend myself, but I do not intend to become some manner of assassin." He clarified, "I was in the military and I understand the boundaries of what may happen when in a conflict and will act accordingly, to regain the establishment of our Country from these Tyrants. I do not intend to take jobs like, go kill this target, and things like that."

Sal nodded slowly and then crossed his arms over his chest, "But you would be okay with perhaps running a package of intel or supplies overland to somewhere it is needed?"

Jack nodded, "I assume it's not heroin or a bomb to place beside an orphanage or something, then yes."

Sal smiled at Jack's line of thinking and care in making these arrangements, "We may have options available to you then. It sounds like there is a wide range of things you bring to the table that can be helpful."

Sal extended his hand to Jack, "Okay then Kirby, keep your ears open on the radio at the proper time each day. We will call you if we need your help on something.

Jack shook Sal's hand and nodded his agreement, "I will stop using the CB-Radio to contact you then. It's too insecure."

Sal smiled, "Agreed. Only try to get us on the open citizen band frequencies if something has gone wrong with your ham radio."

On the way out of the house, Sal called the woman by name from the porch to him. This allowed Jack to be able to put the name Rachael to her. The yard was empty when Jack came outside. He did not know where Tony had gone and had not seen John at all.

Jack wished he could snoop around and get more information about these people, but for now, bad idea. He turned to the west and started off across the open field the way he came. He would wait until he was well out of visual range of the farmhouse before he turned to the south. Jack got on the ham radio to contact Megan to update her on what had happened.

******

Butch and Riley made it to the pole barn well before Megan rolled up with the UTV and trailer. The chickens were getting terrorized by the sounds of the dogs running around outside their coop as they clucked and cooed frantically.

Megan did a walk around briefly, to check for any dangers, but with Butch being with her she felt more confident that things were in order. If something was out of order and dangerous, Butch would alert on it and cause a ruckus quickly.

Megan took the time to switch the ham radio into a scanning mode so that it was searching back and forth between the frequency Jack would be calling her on and the frequency that Lyn's family would call her on. She could see now, that the ham radio had so many more useful features than the simple walkie-talkies did.

The animals were becoming accustomed to Megan. They were eager for the morning routine of being fed by her. The horses came up to the edges of their stable doors and reached out over the doors with their heads to greet Megan, and seek her attention. They were getting terribly restless, and would need to be taken out and ridden this afternoon or tomorrow. Their agitation at being kept in the pole barn was growing.

Megan tended to feeding the animals as she sung gospel songs. She was singing out of an unconscious joy and on occasion the McDonald's fast-food theme song would come out as well. She was in a happy place again, the guilt of having had killed the three Antifa terrorists had lost its edge with constant prayer and worship of God. She had been able to balance in her mind the events that had happened and her lack of malicious or vengeful intent during the firefight. Yes, it was not a pleasant memory, but she refused to carry the guilt of it into the future with her.

Megan collected up a dozen eggs after feeding the animals and was thinking about heading down to the Glade's to deliver them when her radio spoke with Bella's voice.

Bella:	Mama Bear, this is Bella, you there?
Megan:	Hi there Bella, I am sorry I forgot to call you last night.
Bella:	It's okay, mom says I can come see you now. I'm done with my chores already. You there?
Megan:	I sure am, I have eggs for you to take home with you after also.
Bella:	Cool, cool, see you soon.

Megan carefully carried the eggs in her shirt into the pole barn and put them in a safe place on a workbench near the saddles. She spent some time sweeping the floor until Isabella arrived.

Butch was the first alert with barking, so Megan came outside to call him back to her. Isabella had stopped some distance away, frozen in place as Butch was charging at her. After Megan called the large dog back though, she started to approach again.

Megan and Isabella took a short walk away from the pole barn, up upon a rise of the land, so that they could sit down and look out over several miles and relax. Isabella had brought a small box to bring the eggs back with her and she sat it to the side after Megan laid out a blanket on the ground for them to sit together.

Once seated and content that they had a nice place to chat and share with each other, Megan took an extra Bible she had from her backpack and handed it over to Isabella, "Here you go Bella, you can keep this if you want."

Isabella looked concerned at first as she accepted the gift, "Maybe I should put it in something and hide it here somewhere. If they found this at our house," he offered while not completing the sentence.

Megan smiled at her idea, "That is a fine idea and smart. You can come here any time you want that is okay with your mother and read on your own too."

Isabella appeared delighted with the arrangement and then the two bowed their heads together and prayed to start their Bible study.

Time got a little away from Megan. The two had so much to talk about in getting to know each other. It was Megan's Ham radio that announced itself that broke into their conversation two hours after they had started.

Jack: Mama Bear, this is Hawk 1, do you copy?

Megan pulled the radio out of the pouch on her pack.

Megan: This is Mama Bear, I copy.
Jack: Mission Success, heading home now.
Megan: That's wonderful news, can you come to the farm? I'm visiting with our neighbor and studying right now. I   could use your help after this.
Jack: Absolutely, will be a bit. Less than an hour.
Megan: Okay, see you soon.

Megan tucked the radio back into its pouch as Isabella nudged Megan's leg, "There is someone between us and the McVeenson farm in the gully."

Megan did not turn and look right away. It was obvious that Isabella was being sly about not giving away that the person had been spotted.

Megan closed up her Bible, she nodded and then faked a laugh before whispering, "Keep checking the area out, let me know what you spot. If the person is armed or on a radio, anything you think is important."

Isabella appeared nervous. Today is was illegal to pray and a death sentence to have a Bible. A more dangerous situation was hard to imagine.

Isabella then sighed and rolled her eyes, "It's Paul, he followed me to spy on me."

Megan likewise let out a little held air from her lungs in relief but she still did not look towards the spy, "Well, that's not bad is it? He's curious."

Isabella nodded slowly to that, "I suppose so."

Megan grinned and reached out and put her hand on Isabella's knee, "Don't we want him to seek after God? To be curious?"

Isabella nodded again, "Yeah, true."

Megan kept her voice down low as they talked, "What's his history? Have you talked to him about Jesus already?"

Isabella nodded, "Dad didn't believe at all in God. He said that even if there was a God that he must be cruel to allow such evil in the world and if that was true, he wanted nothing to do with him."

Megan nodded and kept quiet to keep listening.

Isabella added, "And Paul, well Paul wanted to be just like dad." Isabella's eyes began tearing up about her father's death, missing him, and it was hard for her to get through explaining this right now.

Megan leaned forward and hugged Isabella for a while before saying anything at all, "Well, let him follow you if he is interested. We just need to keep an eye out, in case he has warned the law about us and is leading them to us. You are going to need to get a good feel about him around home. If you think he is interested in God, or interested in getting us caught and captured."

Isabella looked to Megan with deep concern and worry in her expression at the responsibility of it all.

Megan nodded with a soft smile, "Now we have something very tangible to pray about. For your brother and for our safety."

Megan then changed the subject, "Okay, now about these angels and demons that you saw. Tell me about that."

Isabella shook her head back and forth slowly, "I'm not sure exactly what happened. I was freaking out because dad had been shot and I thought he was dead on the porch. I saw Paul looking out the back sliding-glass door at something by the corral, so I ran to my bedroom and started looking out the front window around my curtains. I think I prayed that I didn't understand, and I just started crying to God... why... why... why is this happening?"

Megan listened very closely to how Isabella was explaining what happened and stayed quiet, not wanting to interrupt.

Isabella slowed down as she recalled more specifically what exactly happened at that point, "My eyes felt like they teared over, like what I could see went all wavy like when your eyes are crying and you can't see. When I wiped my eyes dry and looked back out, I could see Jack hugging Tiffany. Around them were these three black winged men with these hoody type hats on. The men's faces were swirling smoke."

Isabella shuddered at the memory of it, "That's the same time that these two men of light, in bright white with white swan wings took out bright glowing swords and all of them started to fight. Jack just kept on hugging Tiffany and praying until the ground opened. A black crack in the ground with boiling red and orange lava. Long arms of black smoke grabbed onto the bodies of the winged black men and pulled them into the ground."

Isabella paused then, "That's when Paul screamed and started swearing about a man at the corral flying through the air and into the field. I don't know what that was about though, I haven't asked him about it. I forgot about that part until just now."

Megan reached to Isabella, to hold hands as they sat facing each other cross-legged, "It sounds like God answered your prayer. You begged him to understand why and he opened your eyes to let you see into the Spiritual Realm."

Isabella nodded slowly to what Megan was saying, "But I thought it was just a meta... a... phoric... um."

Megan clarified, "Metaphorical?"

Isabella grinned at that, "Yeah, like angles and demons were just part of a way to tell a story. Not like real angels and demons."

Megan smiled wide at Isabella and the two shared a moment of truth together, "Well, I guess they are factually true, for sure, you saw them."

Isabella laughed at that and then leaned forward and hugged Megan around the shoulders, "This is something nobody will ever believe. Everyone is going to think I am crazy."

Megan hugged her back, "You let God guide you on that one. If he wants you to share what you saw or to keep it quiet. That was something extraordinary he did for you."

Isabella softly sighed, "I should probably be getting back home. I think we went way longer than I was supposed to be gone, and I don't want mom thinking I am sneaking out of my afternoon chores."

Megan and Isabella closed with a quiet prayer and then Isabella handed the Bible back to Megan, "Can you put this in something to keep it dry and hide is somewhere?"

Megan took the Bible back, "I'll do that. I will find a place near the farm and next time we meet I will show you where. Once we know your brother isn't sending people after us."

The two ladies got up, folded the blanket, collected things into Megan's backpack, and then started walking back to the McVeenson's farm.

They took purposeful effort not to look to where they knew Paul was trying to hide himself. They wanted to ensure he did not think he was discovered for two reasons. The first is, if he was a spy, they did not want him to know they knew. Second, if he was curious about God, they did not want to spook him off when he was curious and wanting to learn.

At the farm, Megan helped Isabella get the collected eggs into Isabella's little box to bring home with her. They separated after a short hug and then Isabella started heading home.

Megan found an empty rabbit pellet plastic bag in the pole barn cleaned it out carefully and then wrapped the Bible in it. She slipped it into a burlap bag for hiding. She did not want to hide the Bible in the pole barn because they would be disassembling the barn. She took a bit of a walk around the property to try to find a place that was a little hidden from view, where retrieving it and hiding it back in place would not be out in the open and easily seen.

After ten minutes, Megan discovered an old broken lawnmower that was covered over with weeds and small thorny bushes. She figured it was a safe place to hide the Bible. On hands and knees, Megan lifted the little spring door on the bottom where the grass clippings shoot out and took a careful look under the mower. Down in the valley it would be a great place for a Diamondback rattlesnake to be laid in wait. This time of year, it would be deep in sleep waiting for the heat of spring. High in the mountains here though, there were other creatures that would take great joy in biting her just the same.

The stash looked safe, so Megan hid the Bible under the mower where the spinning blades were rusted in place.

The ham radio under Megan's winter jacket spoke quietly, muffled under the layers of clothing:

Jack: Mama Bear, this is Hawk One, do you copy?

Megan fumbled under her jacket and pulled the small radio out and held it up to her face.

Megan: I copy, go ahead Hawk One.
Jack: I am at the farm.
Megan: I will be right there, will approach from the east soon.
Jack: Roger.

When Megan made it back to the pole barn it was Butch who let her know where Jack was. The hair on the back of the dog back stood up and his throat rolled a deep growl while he stared at the burned down home.

Jack took a step then out into view from behind one of the burned walls where he was trying to stay out of sight until Megan arrived.

Megan reached down and gently patted the top of Butch's head, "Good boy Butch," she said as she went to one knee and wrapped an arm around his neck and nuzzled against the side of his face, "Good boy."

Butch calmed as Jack got closer and he saw who it was, his tail wagged faster as Jack got nearer.

Jack spent a few minutes explaining how the trip went. First, The Silent Majority had a vast range of resources if they were willing to help them with tasks or resources. He went into some detail and explained his concerns about how to be careful with getting into debt to them and to keep some secrets from them until they were more fully trusted.

Megan filled Jack in on Isabella and their Bible study, as well as what she learned about the angels and demons. Also, the concern about Paul.

The both had a great deal to talk about as they worked to fill up the UTV trailer with items from the pole barn. They were getting a significant amount of the items out of the barn now and actual deconstruction would be starting as soon as Jack had the chicken yard read to go. The first to get moved would be the coop. It may be slow going but Jack was considering using poles to lay in front of it, under it, and having the UTV just pull it slowly across the top of the logs as they rolled beneath the small building. It was an ancient technique going back thousands of years, but it could move the entire building without taking it all apart. It may take two days to move

237

it the full distance, but when it arrived at the farmstead it would be ready just to set in place and be ready for immediate use.

As Megan was packing some small items into the trailer her radio spoke out to her with Jack's voice.

Jack: Mama Bear, this is Hawk One, do you copy?

Megan pulled the radio out to respond.

Megan: I do, what's up Love?
Jack: I'm down at the shed we found the UTV at, I need you to bring the trailer down here if you could please.
Megan: Okay, be there soon.

Megan closed the pole-barn, locked it up, and then got the dogs ready for the short ride down to the UTV shed to meet back up with Jack.

Jack was waiting at the shed with a big grin on his face as Megan took a wide turn so that she could pull up to the front of the shed with the trailer sideways. The dogs rushed to meet Jack and pester him for attention and affection as Megan turned off the UTV and came over to see what was going on.

Jack opened the front doors of the shed and made a big production of an electric chainsaw he put on the workbench. He had found it in a plastic tote in the back of the shed, "It has an extra chain and like 200 feet of high-quality extension cord. I can bring a couple of those solar panels back, cut some of the burned pine trees near our house and use the poles like I was talking about for moving the coop."

Megan grinned at Jack's happiness, it was so nice to see him excited and happy about something.

They loaded the new finding into the trailer and then closed the shed.
                              ******

Jack and Megan were able to unload the trailer, get things dispersed and put around in places that made sense at their place. They took a break to make some lunch and just to sit down and rest with each other and to pray with each other on the porch of their home. They prayed that God would watch over them and protect their home. That God would make this land a Holy place for people to feel safe in. They prayed together that God would send them people that were in need and bring people across their paths that they could care for and show the Love of God.

As insane as the world had become, it never felt more alive to be a Christian.

Megan figured she could head back for another load with the dogs, feed the animals, and get back home before dark. Jack planned to stay back and put in some more poles for the chicken wire yard.

The rest of the day went as planned, other than Jack feeling the need to deviate from his pole digging plan. He felt a strong need to walk around their property and just to pray. He continued with their lunchtime prayer, asking God for protection and blessing over their land. He felt his spirits rise and joy swell up in his heart at the excitement of God using him in any way, no matter how small.

An hour before sunset, Jack found himself on a rise looking over a deep gorge. He dropped to his knees in prayer, pleading to be used by God. He submitted fully and prayed that God be in control of his family, he prayed and released his feelings of needing to protect them, and surrendered them to God.

A massive weight felt lifted from deep inside Jack and he just wept with such relief and joy. He did not care who was watching or could hear him crying out to God.

An elk on a far ridge stopped and watched Jack, sniffed the air, and then bowed its head to nuzzle the ground to try to find any shoots of green to eat in the burned land.

Jack could feel the cold of the evening starting to move in over the mountain and forced himself to his feet to work his way back to the house to meet up with Megan.

Back at the house, Jack returned to working on the chicken wire until Megan rolled up with the UTV and the trailer to get unloaded. They plugged in the UTV to get recharged and then unloaded the trailer as darkness began to settle in.

Jack retrieved the laptop from the bunker so that he could work on their first transmission over the Ham radio to be sent to Jordan in Flagstaff. They worked on several drafts while Megan tended to dinner in the kitchen.

The final draft they constructed into a text document that could readily be transmitted once the modem converted it to analog signal.

Tomorrow at dawn would be the first chance they got the opportunity to send out a message, and they were eager to have it ready to go.

They also took care to encrypt the text document so that it would be harder for a stray eavesdropper to be able to read the message. They knew it would probably take weeks for The

Silent Majority to investigate and find her to give her the message. Jack and Megan were certain that she was deep in hiding within the city.

It read as follows:

To: Jordan Crossman
        Music Worship Leader
        Northern Arizona University (NAU)
               Note: Likely in hiding, use caution locating her,
               so as not to disclose her to the authorities.

From: Jack and Megan Crossman

Buckabo,

We trust Christ is holding you strong as he is us here at the cabin. His hand is visible, and he is taking direct action in our lives here. Miraculous things have happened, and we draw closer to him every day.

We pray for your safety while you are in the city. We pray for his blessing on you and to keep you close to his side.

We have insulin here if you need more. We do not know how you are doing in this regard. Can you please get a message back to the person that contacted you with our message and fill us in on what is going on with you?

As always, you are welcome here with us. But we understand that God has called you to work there and if he still wishes you there, we understand.

Create a text document on a USB drive. Encrypt the file and use all lower case and no spaces

** YourMiddleName-YourBirthTown-YourFirstDog-WordOnYourLegTattoo **

We know it may take weeks before they find you and give you this message. Once you reply, they should let you know how to get in touch with us much faster and we can communicate much more often.

In Christs Eternal Love,
Your Loving Parents

Jack hooked up the modem to the laptop and had the Ham radio ready to go for the morning transmission. It was so exciting that they could get a message to Jordan. They just kept smiling at each other as they snuggled on the small couch in front of the wood stove.

With the door barred, the thick curtains pulled across the windows and the dogs asleep at their feet, Jack and Megan drifted off to sleep on the couch nuzzled up, wrapped in each other's arms under a heavy quilt and drifted off to sleep.

Epilogue

Jack and Megan had such high hopes and overwhelming optimism when they woke up the next morning together on the small couch. The morning went along smooth with big smiles and excitement as they prepared breakfast and fed the dogs.

Just before 7:00 am, Jack booted up the laptop and made sure his modem connection was working to and from the Ham radio wired link. Right at 7:00 am the empty frequency on the Ham radio suddenly burst to life with a man's voice.

Radio: Silent Majority Base 134 Active.

A woman's voice spoke up then, "This is Mother Hubbard, transmitting data pack to Chicago in 5, 4, 3, 2, 1." And then the very distinct and memorable sound of a telephone computer modem spread across the frequency for a solid 45 seconds. When the data stopped her voice came back on, "This is Mother Hubbard, clear."

Jack nodded to himself as to how he was supposed to use this format when it was his turn. He was a bit nervous at his first use though and hesitated.

A man's voice came across next, "This is Big Moose, transmitting data pack to Miami in 5, 4, 3, 2, 1." Again, the expected machine language across the radio filled the room until it concluded, and the man signed out after.

Jack keyed up the radio and held the button in with his left hand as he hovered the mouse on his laptop over the file to be transmitted, "This is Hawk One, transmitting data pack to Flagstaff." Jack then clicked on the program and the short letter was sent out to Jordan in less than ten seconds. He moved the mic back to his mouth, "This is Hawk One, clear."

Jack put the radio down on the dining room table and turned to smile wide at Megan. Megan wrapped her arms around his neck as she leaned down to meet him. They were giddy all morning.

Jack figured it would take a few weeks for The Silent Majority to find Jordan safety, and get her the message, then for a message to get back to them. They would have to follow the schedule for the times of day that the radio repeaters would be brought online and listen the entire time for someone to call out a data pack to him and Megan, or anything designated for Springerville. He would probably just play it safe and record everything onto the laptop every day, voice conversations and data packs alike.

Jack and Megan promised to remind each other over the next several days that they were not going to stress at all, or worry in the slightest for at least three weeks.

******

Over the next weeks, Jack and Megan focused heavily on moving everything from the McVeenson's farm. The chicken coop moved as planned and took a full two days of work. The first snowfall of winter fell the day after they had the chicken in place and happily settled.

The Glade's agreed to keep their horses in the corral with the Glade horses while the pole-barn was being taken apart and re-assembled. While Megan and Isabella had their morning Bible studies, Paul gave Jack lessons on how to care for the horses and how to ride properly.

Paul had watched his father as only a young boy could, and Jack had a great deal to learn from the younger boy. Lyn was able to throw in some information where gaps remained, but for the most part, Paul was an extremely valuable teacher for Jack each morning.

Tiffany was working out well at the Glade's home. She had started her life over, to fit in and make herself useful. She was now learning how to cook from Lyn.

Jack and Megan started having the Glade's over to their house every Sunday for a pot-luck meal, to share time with each other, and to keep the bonds strong that were developing between their families.

It was a week before Christmas when the pole-barn was finished being put back together and all the animals were moved in. The snow had been building up over the last several weeks and was 2-3 feet deep in some places. Still, large rocks reached out from under the snow in some locations with the charred black pine trees standing alone eerily in the stark white landscape.

It was two days before Christmas when Jack and Megan got their message back from Jordan.

■■■

To: Jack and Megan Crossman
               Springerville, Arizona

From: Duane Stewart

Mr. & Mrs. Crossman,

First, yes, this is not your daughter Jordan. We had wanted to contact you since last spring but have been unable. We tried until July, but then decided we could not wait any longer. Your daughter Jordan and I got married July 4th. Yes, it was in a church ceremony and yes, I place God above all else in my life and our marriage has been deeply touched by his hand.

I will not ramble on further about myself, there will be time for that later.

Jordan was captured for leading a prayer group. She has been kept in an enlightenment camp since September 13th.

I have been unable to see her, but I am able to get a secret message in to her and a secret message back from her once a week. This is how I was able to figure out the encryption code to send you this letter.

I know there are groups that are working in the shadows against this oppression. I think you must know of them as well, if you were able to arrange contacting to me in this way.

I have been praying constantly for God's Will in this and I know the both of you will as well.

My greatest concern is that Jordan is going to have our baby. I worry about complications due to her diabetes and the lack of quality medical care in the camp. Her due date is the second week of May.

I know of no way for her ever to be released unless she renounces God. We all know that will never happen.

Please pray for God to lead us in what he would have done.

Your Son,

Duane Stewart

Appendix

1. Sanctuary Cities/States currently:
   Rhode Island, Vermont, Washington State, Oregon, Ohio, New Jersey, New York, Nevada (Las Vegas only), Minnesota, Kalamazoo, Michigan, Lansing, Michigan, Massachusetts, Maine, Louisiana, Chicago, IL, Colorado, California Cities (Berkeley, Coachella, Huntington Beach, Los Angeles, San Francisco), South Tucson, AZ
2. Article 5 - US Constitution
   a. Notes: The US Constitution allows for States themselves to make an amendment, bypassing the congress in case the government becomes corrupt. Article 5 sets that if 2/3 of the States can propose an amendment, at which point ¾ of the States vote to accept or decline the amendment.
      1. Pushed by conservatives to reign in the bloated and out of control central government
      2. Want congressional term limits
      3. Want Supreme Court limit on years
      4. Want Repeal of 17th Amendment so that States choose Senators as before and not popular vote.
      5. Want Balanced Budget amendment
      6. Tax Day 1 day before next federal election
      7. Want States to have a 3/5 vote to overturn congress
      8. Wants 2/3 of States to be able to nullify federal law
      9. Wants a requirement for photograph I.D. and US Citizenship only to be able to vote.
   b. This push for the Article 5 Convention of States puts the established bureaucrats in a state of panic. As more States begin to agree to join in the process and to organize along specific amendment ideas, the government/media goes into full panic mode.
3. Sanctuary Cities/States that come next

      a. Entire State of California, Hawaii, Entire State of Illinois, Entire State of Nevada

      b. Current Total: RI, VT, WA, OR, OH, NJ, NY, NV, MN, MA, LA, IL, CO, CA (14 States)

4. Article 5 - US Constitution

      a. Sanctuary States now have the same number of States as conservative Article 5 States and now they join in to get more States in a race to get to 38 States for the ¾ required to pass the amendment(s).

          i. Platform of amendments:

               1. Restrict 1st amendment to cover only specific forms of media. Not citizens as a whole.

               2. Remove the 2nd amendment

               3. 1 Child Limit

               4. Health Care as a Right (Free) including prescriptions

               5. College education as a right (free)

               6. Outlaw coal and nuclear electrical/power plants.

5. We buy land in the mountains

      a. Purchase bunker made in Texas, install, camp/live in mountains on weekends.

          i. Bunker is hidden (entrance) inside the tool shed.

      b. 6 months later get a small 2 story prefab home from Home Depot for $14,000

      c. Install electrical, insulation, wood pellet stove, well, solar panels, etc.

      d. 1 year after purchase, renting out the house (Bunker a secret) through Airbnb to pay the mortgage and make extra money as well.

6. Gun confiscation @ State level

      a. All sanctuary States

      b. Very little push back from citizens in those states. They were accustomed to being subservient to the government. Decades of public-school indoctrination and media influence.

      c. Those that could, moved to other states at this point.

7. Food & Drug Administration

      a. Outlawed use of Herbicides and Pesticides

      b. Catastrophic stock market crash ($17 Billion/year economy completely shut down)
        i. Stock market drops 30% and never recovers from the adjustment.
      c. 233 companies, 12,171 jobs in these businesses.
      d. Overnight 20,000 unemployed families.

8. Food Shortages
      a. Farms shut down because they cannot produce sufficient food to survive (make enough money to pay taxes on their land, etc.).
      b. Further cascading financial meltdown.
        i. Grocery stores looted / out of business.
      c. Government creates Food Centers

9. Riots
      a. Caused by the food shortages
      b. Stores out of food, cities in a panic
      c. In Democrat controlled States murder and deaths soar over food issues. Knives, baseball bats, machetes.
      d. Criminals still have guns.
      e. All families start gardens in their backyards.
      f. Cities/apartments fully dependent on the government for food.

10. Amnesty - The Federal Government gives full Amnesty to all illegal aliens and opens the borders fully with no restrictions.
      a. +20 million new voters (Democrat)
      b. This flips several States to full Democrat control now.
        i. Georgia, Iowa, Kansas, Michigan, Montana, N. Carolina, Pennsylvania, S. Carolina, Texas, W. Virginia, Wisconsin

11. Farm Yield Reduction
      a. Of those farms that remain in business, the growth of weeds and pests reduce the amount of food production by 80%. (20% of current food production).

12. Complete Democrat Control
      a. Now with the following states in full Democrat control a Republican president will never happen again.
      b. RI, VT, WA, OR, OH, NJ, NY, NV, MN, MA, LA, IL, CO, CA, GA, IA, KS, MI, MT, NC, SC, PA, TX, WV, WI (25 States)

      c. The remaining Republican States are Republican In Name Only, they have been adopting the same policies as the Democrats for decades and at this point, they just give up trying to pretend and it is a one-party country at this point.

      d. The political agenda begins to get pushed forward without any resistance at all. Democrats no longer need to push for the Article 5 option to get their amendments, they can now do it freely and without restraint.

           i. 1st Amendment limitations go into effect.

               a. If you want to be on the radio or television, you need a federal permit.

           ii. Only those who support the Democrat agenda are granted a permit.

           iii. This removes all dissenting voices (conservative talk radio).

               b. 2nd Amendment is Repealed

               c. 1 Child per family limit is enforced

                   i. Forced sterilization

                   ii. Forced abortion if somehow discovered you were not sterilized and got pregnant with a 2nd child.

               d. Free Healthcare/Prescriptions

               e. Free College education

               f. Outlaw Coal and Nuclear Power plants

               g. Removed Freedom of Religion

13. Medical / Prescription Drug Shortages

      a. Pharmaceutical companies go out of business as now their products are free and they cannot produce or do research and development for new drugs.

      b. 2/3 doctors and nurses quit or "retire" for they now must work for free

      c. 2-3 day waits @ emergency rooms, many are dying across the country waiting.

      d. Illegal medical facilities (warehouse/basement/delivery type van) open, black market doctors.

14. Riots

      a. Small militias form in secret

          b. Small unit tactical hits on government facilities.

15. My family moves to the mountains full time.

          a. Abandon home in Arizona valley.

16. Earth Preservation Act

          a. Internal combustion engine outlawed.

17. Food Shortages

          With tractors being outlawed now (see item 16 above) farms need approximately 36 draft horses to equal one 500 HP tractor. Now there needs to be about 18 farmers (1 farmer for each 2-horse team) to do the work of 1 tractor before.

               a. There is a massive shortage of manpower to work on the farms.

               b. Federal government began the "American Food Administration"

                    i. Federal government begins to give 40-acre plots of land to farmers. Vast overwhelming number of these getting land are previous illegal immigrants and the influx now of endless immigrants over the open borders to claim free land.

                    ii. This influx of new voters flips Utah, Arizona, Florida, Idaho, Missouri, Nebraska, Wyoming to Democrat control.

                    iii. There is a shortage of draft horses and mules are the most plentiful in use. Still there is a great shortage and it will be years before enough can be created/formed/birthed to supply the manpower needs on the farms.

               c. National Calorie limit: 1000 calories per day

               d. Authorized meal plans (told precisely what you were allowed to eat and how much).

18. Rolling Regional Brownouts

               a. By Region, scheduled shutdown of electricity and is rationed.

               b. Installation on all homes/businesses of smart electrical meters. The meters automatically shut off your power once you have consumed your allotment of power on your allowed electrical usage day.

19. National Curfew
   a. Sunset
   b. Cannot assemble in groups greater than 2.
20. National Police Force / Military (exempt from combustion limit laws)
   a. All local / county / State police now fall under federal control.
   b. Military now patrol U.S. Cities
      i. 2/3 of military go AWOL
21. U.S. Patriotic Bill
   a. Declares all military that went AWOL domestic terrorists
   b. Anyone with a gun is a terrorist
   c. Anyone that transmits on radio without federal permit is a terrorist
   d. Churches are terrorist organizations
   e. Bibles are outlawed
   f. Any current or past NRA (National Rifle Association) members are declared terrorists.
22. Communications Control Act
   a. Internet is shut down
   b. Cell Phone usage is Federal owned/controlled
      i. All calls are monitored/recorded
   c. To offer employment, the government hires 4 million employees to   man the Communications Control Facilities, so a live person is monitoring every phone call.